BRUCE CROWN
HOW DIM THE PROMISED LAND

Library and Archives Canada in Publication Data

A catalogue record for this book is available at *Library and Archives
Canada* at:
395 Wellington St,
Ottawa, ON
K1A 0N4

Library and Archives Canada information:
Crown, Bruce, 1989—
How Dim the Promised Land / Bruce Crown
FICTION / Noir
FICTION / Literary
[Toronto, Ont]: AP Publications, 2015.

Printed in Canada and the United States of America.

ISBNs:
978-0-9918883-4-4 (Print)
978-0-9918883-5-1 (eBook)

"A painter should begin every canvas with a wash of black, because all things in nature are dark except where exposed by the light."
LEONARDO DA VINCI

ACKNOWLEDGEMENTS

Vorrei ringraziare Vania Sparro che mi aiuta a tradurre la mia storia in italiano.

Herzlichen Dank an Julian Lautenbach und Lillian Wilde für ihre Hilfe bei der Übersetzung der deutschen Sätze.

En tak til Martin Christensen for hans vejledning i at oversætte de vanskelige danske sætninger.

For my sister MOHABAT,
Whose hair dances like waves in the wind of silent forest trees after autumn rain.

HOW DIM THE PROMISED LAND;
OR,
The Agony of the Enlightened

PRIMORDIAL

An artist's job is to create something beautiful. What is beautiful is subjective. Some things that are beautiful represent Beauty; there is a difference between the beautiful and Beauty. Ideas can be beautiful; a woman can be beautiful; a moment in time in a life can be beautiful. Beauty is... I don't know what Beauty is but I know what it's not. Beauty isn't swiping right on a screen nor is it the beeping of cashier computers in a store. Beauty isn't clicking of a turnstile and it isn't videos of cuddly animals on a computer screen. Beauty isn't a pedantic and focus-grouped politician telling you what you want to hear nor is it chanting revolutionary slogans and wanting to change things. Beauty is not a film you've been told to like nor is it a piece of garbage hanging in a museum being called creative Beauty. Beauty is none of these things. In fact, people use the term Beauty as almost synonymous with the beautiful and having no passion for either word they destroy it with every breath. They call their designer clothes and their pets and their fleeting lovers beautiful thinking it represents Beauty, and every once in a while, when they come face-to-face with Beauty they can't recognize it.

BC.
August 2014

NIHIL

Colonialism has a new face. No longer a naval armada invading with swords and arms bearing the flag of the queen. Rather, men in expensive suits with pens bearing the Golden Arches, a green mermaid, a slightly eaten apple, or a big G.

During the day, I watch the leafing blades of hazel-green grass the color of my muse's eyes while her sun-colored hair illuminates thoughts of furthering this broken "civilization." But it's mostly during the night, when the sky is the color of her dress I see things as they are; where I realize that to call this "civilization" barbaric is a gross understatement. We've put savagery to shame and a Neanderthal would be insulted if we self identified even with their extinct genus.

* * *

What is it those who wander the planet in agony pursue? Freedom? Peace? Lavish comfort? Financial security to the point of excess? ... *Love?* Whichever it may be, the common element is illusion. These are nothing more than fabricated abstracts designed to distract the mind and body from its *natural* purpose and infallible nature: to pursue the Truth not as a means of linguistic manipulation, votes, or stock prices but as an end in itself.

Why do some of us feel so alive despite being alone and yet some of us feel alone despite the constant presence of others? How can one combat this loneliness? In this battle, who can one turn to? How many times have we seen a couple blistering with love and yet so full of despair? Why and how does this happen? Is there a simple answer? That no one, not one sentient being can ever contemplate escaping the shackles of truth? The truth that surviving life is a physical impossibility? In other words, no matter how many quantifiable things someone performs in the short duration of a fleeting life, no matter how many lives someone touches, or how many lives they *deceivingly* save; everything is a lie compared to the great truth. Everyone dies and one day *everything* in our vast space will cease to be.

This truth is so painful that we turn to illusory abstracts we've fabricated to *delay*. If we are truly free, then we are free of death; if we are comfortable then death won't be painful. Perhaps we can *buy* more *time* if we had enough money. If we are in love death won't be lonely. Would Death spare us if we were in love? Is Love the opposite and more successful arch-nemesis of Death?

How can we explain these motives? Some measure of fear from arguably the only verified truth in the universe?

PART ONE:
ASCENSION

SPRING

I
POST-IMPRESSIONISM

DEATH WOULD BE rapturous. To break free from the oppressive shackles of physicality and float through the cosmos as unsullied Being. Life is a unification of barriers, a barrier of discontentment and torture that humans abide until the moment they become truly free. Death is that freedom. Death is being the negation of the very thing that gives our physicality its falsehood. In the end, our lives are merely accepting death.

Above a narrow hill among the grass idling through the windy rains of the divine sat a river amidst the tree line. Civilization had corrupted the left side of this river with its presence in the shape of lavish country homes for the wealthy should they grow tired from robbing those under them. Laura Erigone Vayne believed with a fierce heart she'd benefit from the clear country air when she convinced her husband to buy one years ago. She had no idea, nothing with an iota resembling the slightest clue that the river where the alleged *pure* water of the land was supposed to glide freely from one end to the other, was cursed with being. Over a quantifiable period of time Laura became a prisoner of her own despair. Within this prison she was shackled by the fear of loneliness. A loneliness from herself and her identity. Despite being relatively successful by society's standards and mildly attractive by the divine's, there was nothing she could do to escape. Never having believed in any sort of religion or having even a semblance of a spiritual experience, she thought her salvation laid only in death. She was an avid believer of freedom and her erroneous assumption was that the price for freedom was death. Though she was probably right, the way she went about it was certainly wrong. She had to have known... somewhere deep down, hidden behind her feigned smiles and weak handshakes, buried beneath her cruel memories and consuming darkness she knew. Eventually she'd have no choice; it *had* to come to this, there was no other way to atone. There was no surreal, invisible, and magical man above the horizon to grant her absolution. She was in the end, lost within herself.

She had the kitchen knife too in case things didn't go her way. Hopefully her husband's pills would be enough. ... And as if they were Smarties, she shoved an entire bottle of his painkillers down her throat and sank into a deep pool of her own tears. They isolated the voices of the sycophantic idiots drowning in the adulation of their own feeble intellects. She knew better than most people how useless they were and their long-term effects wouldn't help her one bit. None of that mattered now anyway.

* * *

"Van Gogh's colors are incredibly expressive yet we consider him a morose painter. Forget that you know anything about what he said to his brother," I pointed to the projector doing a grave injustice to the colors of *The Parsonage Garden at Nuenen with Pond and Figures*, "Contemplate the painting and its colors independently; what do you see? ... Anyone?" I looked into the puzzled faces of my students.

"The bright blue is vibrant, like a patience descending upon the foliage green of the earth, which can represent fertility, life, and beginning," a voice called through the crowd.

I spotted the culprit. The only student who ever talked in my class: Elroy Wolfe.

"Very good, how about the amber at the edge of the tree branches?"

"Perhaps abundance? The coming of autumn."

"Amber can also mean mellow and despondent. Just as blue can represent melancholy or green separation."

"So there's no wrong answer here professor."

"There most certainly is. If you had said this painting was not overwhelmed with the representation of a man exhausted by loneliness and solitude I would've berated you for being an uncomprehending buffoon! ... Notice the way he draws his subjects: almost always without a face, silhouetted, or covered by darkness. He creates distance when he contrasts his dark colors with the light ones towards the sky; the black is oppressive. The people he's drawing are oppressed. By economic or personal struggles perhaps. The deep purple represents an enchanting aloofness. Look at the woman in the right-third quadrant of the painting. Even though the shadow of the ravine is behind her and she is surrounded by white, his use of white borders coldness and isolation since she is alone. The only other lone character is the shadow of the man, and all we see is the shadow of him walking towards her. Go across, the only other use of white in this painting is *this* woman *crossing* the ravine," I pointed to the figure with my hand and my finger cast a shadow on the screen, "Who is practically consumed by the shadow of her partner. And in the distance... a church with a terra cotta roof, representing the earthly warmth perhaps? A welcoming sanctuary in contrast to all other figures in the piece. Notice that it's directly behind the woman in the horizon. This solace of hope... all the figures have their backs or sides turned to it...." A man in an olive green suit with neutral gray stripes had entered and was standing at the top of the lecture hall to the right of the podium. I lost track of my lecture. There was only four minutes left of class anyway.

"That's it for today Mesdames et Messieurs. Do the readings for next week and look at Gauguin's *Van Gogh Painting Sunflowers* and *Self-portrait with Portrait of Bernard (Les Misérables)* from 1888. Notice the yellow," laptop screens closed and papers shuffled into bags; phones were tapped, "Contrasted with the green and the disregard of conventional spacing."

I could always spot those who were in here to fulfill their graduation requirement and those who *chose* this course as a means of satisfying their curiosity. Of the two *classes*, pardon the pun, the former seems to be relentlessly unhappy; they're never satisfied with anything because their freedom has been taken away. The latter seems to be more successful, in the end they can say they *chose* the road to damnation.

I'd barely gotten a third of the loose pieces of paper into my leather holdall when the man in the suit started walking towards me. I assumed he was a military man judging from the base color of his suit, more specifically a sniper or a spotter. He looked methodical. I knew I'd have no choice but to listen to what he had to say. He approached with a pitiful gaze idling in the back of his periwinkle eyes.

"Professor Vayne?" his voice lingered in the air.

"My wife kept her maiden name; my name is Maximus Epochézētō. Everyone calls me Max," I should be nursing a migraine right about now and it was a good thing I wasn't because I'd forgotten my pills at home. I put my laptop in my bag and extended my hand, counting my lucky stars.

"I am Detective Ben Britten," he shook my hand and sighed.

"Coming to learn about the nature of color in the blackened world detective?" I threw some more papers into the bag, including Pieter Bruegel's *The Elder – The Triumph of Death* from 1562 when I realized I'd forgotten to discuss it with the class.

"No professor. Unfortunately I am the bearer of bad news," the wrinkles around his eyes tightened and I got a glimpse of the kind of stern disposition reminiscent of an army-man. "Can we sit down somewhere?"

"What is it?" I gripped my bag tighter; had something happened to Laura?

"Doctor Vayne, I don't know how to tell you this…"

I couldn't think. The white of the arctic in my dark red blood froze me in place.

"… Earlier today paramedics responded to a 911 call from your neighbor to your house."

"No…" I pulled the bag in front of my chest and held it tight.

"I'm sorry. They found your wife unresponsive. They tried to stabilize her and take her to Håbløs General but she'd lost a lot of blood."

"She's gone?"

"Yes. Paramedics reported that she passed away in the ambulance on the way the hospital; I want to …"

Everything else he said glided through the air like sound waves in space. I felt faint and weightless.

"I'm sorry professor. I don't want to make matters worse but even though her death has been ruled a suicide. We need some time to investigate."

"I know. I can't go home until you guys do your job. Will you let me know when I can?"

"Of course."

"I'll be staying at the Amstel in the meantime. ... Please be careful with her stuff. She was very particular."

He began to walk away and I sank back into my chair. He said something I didn't hear and began his long departure to the exit located at the top of the hall.

Through the misty dusk I'd become death; I walked into the hospital the detective had mentioned she was in and found myself in the morgue. I sat on one of the benches in the emergency room and looked at a fixed-point in the wall. There wasn't a single painting in the place, just four walls painted prosaic beige. On my way out a man in a suit and a sling on his broken right arm shoved through me and entered the red-lit streets.

In the hotel lobby I sat in a chair deep in Van Gogh's blue at the thought of Laura and of things that could be, that never were, and of things that were never going to be until everything faded into the distance of the illuminating stars and the color of the night sky.

II
Hostis Humani Generis

"Hit me," he coughed through the cigarette lying limp on his lips. Specks of ash had landed on and ruined his coffee brown Ralph Lauren suit.

"King of Clubs. That brings you to 28," the dealer turned a card over, "That's a bust sir," and he raked the stacks of chips away from the fingers of Kane Ventoni.

Kane played with his gelled and styled dirty blonde hair and scanned the pit. "Poker's more my game anyway," he scoffed and pushed his chair back. The dealer shuffled four more decks of cards and placed them delicately in the automatic shuffler, "The high roller game is at eight o'clock sir. You do however, require an invitation."

Kane pulled out a gold-plated envelope. $150, 000 buy-in. Not a problem for one of the senior partners of *Ventoni, Kalumnia, and Van Couperville* who's also running for office, "Way ahead of you son."

'I'm not your son you prick.' "Excellent sir. Good luck."

"Doll," he signaled one of the servers, "Noch eine Runde. Aber schnell!" he shook his head back and forth to refocus as he caught the gaze of a passing cocktail waitress, "Toots! Who do I have to sue to get a drink around here?" he shoved a $50 down her underwear, "Martini. Easy on the vermouth. With a lime on the side *and* one squeezed in. Chop chop," he tapped her on the back of her thigh and pushed her forward a bit.

"Very well mein Herr," the waitress pretended to enjoy the attention from the ogre with too much money and walked away after exchanging a disparaging look with the dealer.

"Remember! ..." he pressed his fingers together, "One *squeezed* in!" his raunchy chuckle made her shiver.

You should never trust a man who's good at poker. Poker is the only card game on the planet that is not determined by luck but by some remnant of divine ability. The divine ability of deception. Though amateurs will argue that a good or bad hand is contingent on Lady Luck, professionals relish the fact that the element of deception means you can outplay even the best hand with nothing. Most *skilled* poker players would make excellent politicians, bankers, and lawyers, and most who aren't without fail aim to become one of the three.

Kane was an excellent lawyer and an even better poker player. His only weakness was his hubris; he loved the eccentricity of his own legend. He was particularly good at bluffing when he had nothing and rarely played through a hand when he actually held the cards to knock another player out. It was his way of challenging himself. Like clockwork however, he'd never win because about three-quarters of any game he played other higher-tier players would wise up and force him to play through a hand he'd bluffed before the river. He never won anything but it didn't waver his pride because not winning to him didn't equal losing. He was a lawyer... everything was black and white only when he needed it to be. He rarely ran out of money to play with anyway; others' blood pays well, and Kane was paid in the best thing the world has ever discovered: money.

III
THE CHARGE OF THE LIGHT BRIGADE

There's only one thing that makes a good private eye, and until June 8th of his 27th year on this earth, Michelangelo H. Eycsüp knew what it was. It was precisely the moment he laid eyes on her he forgot, or chose to forget. Either way, it was then the entirety of his previously average existence took a fateful turn to transcendence, but the particular moment was in the middle of this labyrinthine tale. So to abide by the most common of human errors, we will view time linearly and begin when everything began... if, in eternity, such feeble abstractions are even possible.

Michelangelo preferred Michel (pronounced Mishel) and this was the only rigid thing encompassing his otherwise perfect manners and noble-like demeanor. He was born in Denmark but no one ever believed it. His hair was as brown as tree bark and his eyes as dark as a woman's heart. After a while when asked where he was from he just replied "Here. Born and raised," here being New York City. He neither cared nor respected material things and as such, material things didn't possess him. He had neither money nor fame and most importantly, he didn't have a woman, at least not until the day he forgot the only rule of private investigation.

He never wanted to be a private eye either, following and taking pictures of cheating spouses or embezzling businessmen from a car filled with rotting fast food was not the glamorous life he'd envisioned for himself but it was something he stumbled upon after returning from his tour in Afghanistan.

The war on terror was nothing like the wars of old; wars he'd read about in history textbooks or historical fiction or just good old American propaganda. No. War isn't what it once was, the unstinting amour western media has for blood, gore, and misery inflicted on others changed everything. We are who we kill in the name of *better* freedom and transnational marketing opportunities. A drop of oil; 200 people. Fair trade. No. *Free* trade.

* * *

Home sweet home. Any home is sweet as long as it's not risking your life for oil profits. 'Anywhere but here,' was his monotonous response to all of his brother marines fighting in Kandahar. *Oorah* old friends. Three tours, two friends dead, one life to give, and not a cent to his name. His captain recommended that he see one of his friends.

"He'll have a job for you Mike."

"Thanks cap," he said while pondering how much he detested being called anything but Michel.

Nonetheless, he found a small measure of tranquility in writing love letters or poems to an ideal of love, to the perfect woman that couldn't exist. Most of his free time he spent painting. The splashing of the colors on a naked canvas calmed him in such a way that he forgot about the world. There was no war, no peace, no air, and no oil; there was nothing but the canvas and the colors perturbing from within.

His studio was a loft with no sense of order. Everything seemed to pile up on the one couch he'd placed in the corner and pieces of paper with rhymes, dictations, cantos, sonnets, and freeform lines covered the floor.

The latest painting hovering in the corner across the armchair on an easel was a profile of a light-haired brunette from his bus ride *home*. She was glossed with Michel's circular brushstrokes in her alabaster yellow skin and cobalt blue irises, the purple-hued sky behind her, and a dark orange leather jacket lingering over her arm.

A few minutes later he sat on the patio of the nearest café in the thundering rain. *Kun Kaffe* was nice enough to keep away the lackluster bred quasi-intellectual hipsters because the place didn't serve soy lattes with extra foam or a caramel double-pump flavored with vanilla skim milk medium roast cappuccino blend. It was an artful place. Coffee. Tea. Espressos. Hot or cold. Those were the options served near the brick fireplace during winter and ice-cold air-conditioning during the summer and Michel appreciated that. For the time being he appreciated the cleansing rain sparking little droplets in his espresso and its water streaming down his face and masking his tears.

He walked back inside after he'd had his espresso with water dripping from his hair and chin, "Thank you," he always spoke with as few words as possible; this limited his communication but he always thought he had nothing of importance to say to others.

"You're soaked!" the perky waitress behind the counter galloped over with a towel.

"It's fine," Michel bowed and shook his head.

"You sure?"

He nodded.

"The news said it's going to be a bad one!"

When are they ever good ones, he thought.

"How much for the espresso Madame?"

She looked at his wet clothes then at him: an arched aristocratic spine and a neck held high. He had a wide and pleasant face without a vestige of external strain. Though some lines had formed on his forehead and his cheekbones seemed hollow, he had the skin and complexion of a man in his twenties. The middle of his face seemed to appear in the distance, held between a strong jaw and a Roman nose. His eyebrows were small but they came up a little towards his nose then pointed up as if he existed in perpetual perplexity.

"Don't worry about it. It's on the house."

He bowed again, "I am obliged to you," and before she could say another word, he'd become one with the rain behind the pattering window of the café.

Michelangelo slowed his pace because he wasn't ready to go home just yet. He liked the rain and felt at ease with it. That is, until the rain called his name,

"Michel? Michel! Hey… Eycsüp!"

He turned around, "Yes."

"It's me!"

He just stared at the man in the designer leather boots, the expensive umbrella keeping out the relentless raindrops, and the Burberry trench coat.

"It's Elroy! Elroy Wolfe. We went to Cambridge together." Elroy Wolfe. A better and richer student than most. His name was a derivative of the French *Leroy*, which means "The King," and he certainly thought he was.

"I remember," of course Michel remembered his name the instant he saw his face. He was hoping Elroy would prefer to stay dry than talk to him.

"How've you been? I heard you were overseas. I thank you for your service man."

Michel nodded. Raindrops soaked his hair and were icing his brain as Elroy kept his stare.

"Whoa!" lightning lit up the horizon for a second, "… It's going to be a bad one. Well listen. I don't want to keep you out here in this weather. I'm close-by. Here's my card," he handed Michel one of his silk-infused business cards. "Give me a call sometime. I'd love to catch up. You can tell me about your trip to Palermo."

Thunder struck the middle of the road to his left.

They shook hands and Michel continued towards his studio. Elroy had remained dry throughout the whole interaction, only a minute set of speckles darkening his tan-colored leather boots.

IV
ACTORI INCUMBIT PROBATIO

"Your honor..." Kane sat on the armrest of the judge's chair and not on the chair, "This is absurd. The people have failed to meet their burden of proof!"

"This is ridiculous your honor. A witness identified the killer seconds after the murder—"

"The killer isn't my client!"

"Respect courtroom etiquette and speak in turn," the judge said from above his eyeglasses.

"The killer worked for your client. It's a well known fact that Don Calvano has been leading the—"

"Well established fact?" Kane chuckled throatily, "If there's evidence the people haven't submitted about my client let them submit it now. There's absolutely no evidence my client is linked to any of these murders; he's not a felon. He doesn't have as much as a parking ticket."

"That's because he pays off or kills everyone in his way," the prosecutor murmured.

"Hey!" the judge groaned, "Watch the crosstalk."

"Your honor Doctor Ventoni is twisting the facts to fit his version of events. The facts are simple. The murderer killed Miss Veritá and was spotted seconds later. Ten minutes later a phone call was placed from a pay phone to a disposable phone linked with Don Calvano's right hand man."

"Your honor I'd like to strike the crown's mention of "Don" every time he mentions my client. Have him refer to my client as *Mister* Calvano."

"You heard him counselor," the judge jotted something on the stationary in front of him and motioned to the prosecutor.

"It's not far-fetched to think that *Misterrrr* Calvano ordered the hit because Miss Veritá was about to testify about the financial irregularities of Acheron Homes."

In the meantime, Kane had slipped comfortably into the chair and was pretending to be snoring on the chair, "I'm sorry your honor. The crown has put me to sleep with such a beautifully poetical fairy tale. Where's this cell phone the call was made to? The call itself originated from the pay phone... how do we even *know* the killer was the one who used the pay phone and not someone else simply calling to talk about the weather or the Knicks?"

"This is absurd your honor. He's making a farce of these proceedings."

The judge took off and threw his glasses on the stationery, "You two are giving me a headache," he rubbed his eyes, "And as absurd as it sounds counselor, Doctor Ventoni is right. Bring the phone records of the cell phone and call Mister Calvano's so-called right hand to the stand and we'll go from there."

"Your honor! The phone was a disposable phone, that's why they use them. So they can't be traced."

"That's tragic," Ventoni could hardly keep out his smile. How much he'd rake in in bonuses that the casinos would then rake in from him. Time is cyclical.

"And the right hand?" the judge asked impatiently.

The prosecutor dropped his shoulders and his gaze idled on his designer lace-ups, "He took an impromptu trip to the Tuscan coastline."

"Your honor I move to dismiss."

"I'm inclined to agree. You went to the grand jury too soon. Your case isn't complete. I'm dismissing without prejudice. Bring more evidence or subpoena a witness and you can re-file down the road. For now, case dismissed."

Ventoni latched his briefcase, "Thank you your honor," and the door closed behind him.

* * *

Minutes later Kane had ventured into the local dive. The storm had wet his suit and he'd forgotten his umbrella but he was untouchable. His case was dismissed. He was about to receive a new bonus and perhaps buy a new car or a new girlfriend.

"Martini," he snapped his fingers at the bartender, "Easy on the vermouth. Lime on the side and another squeezed in."

"Right away sir."

"Danke."

Everyone seemed to be talking about the weather. They were either wet, shivering, complaining or all three. Kane detested the rain but there are things you can't change so he never let it bother him.

"God I hate this city," the thunder cackled over the sound of the bartender as lights flicked on and off and the patrons looked around at the ceiling and outside. "Your martini sir."

Ventoni gave the guy a $20 bill and took his drink, "Say... where are the broads at?"

The bartender sighed and looked around the bar and Ventoni just noticed that *everyone* was actually the bar staff. There was only one other real customer in the corner of the bar. He donned beige dress pants and a plaid sport blazer sitting by himself in the corner of the bar. His face was half-lit in the candlelight from the table and his shoulders slackened under his neck.

"What? The guy's dog die or something?" Kane motioned to the man with his eyebrows.

"No Herr Ventoni," the bartender's stern disposition revealed a man of strict habit and routine. A trustworthy man who'd be loyal to the last breath but Ventoni didn't, no, wouldn't notice such things. As long as he had a lime on the side *and* one squeezed in he wouldn't have noticed even if God himself had served him the drink.

V

FAUVISM

I don't know why but I'd wandered into a bar across the street from the courthouse after I'd received Laura's death certificate. I'd gotten wet from the rain but I only noticed it when I noticed how wet the leather was after I'd gotten up to hang my coat. Ligotti's *Conspiracy of the Human Race* was somehow dry in its jacket pocket though and there was some satisfaction in that I guess.

There also happened to be a happy lawyer at the counter ordering drinks seeming rather pleased with himself. The TV affixed to the ceiling talked about the storm and how it was best to stay indoors and how much rain to expect. It would go on for days. There was some mention of an *accidental* hospital bombing by an American drone strike but it was quick and fleeting and overshadowed by the number of votes cast in favor of the latest contestant on *Too Pretty to Work*.

I took out a Polaroid of her I'd carried in my wallet since my twenties and caressed it. How I'd drained the life out of her. It was creased and beat to hell just like she was before she decided her life was no longer worth living. I kept promising to take her to Paris but never did. I kept saying "Next month Laura. I'm busy." Why did I say that? I was never too busy to take her to Paris. Why didn't I take her to Paris? Why? Why? WHY?

I was yelling at my gin and tonic crumbling the Polaroid even more. I took a couple of my pills and washed it down with the rest of my drink. I'm sixty-two years old; what was I to do now? Where was I to go? Questions. All I had were questions and what bothered me were the waves of truth that no one would have answers.

The wallpaper closed in on me and began to suffocate me like a noose tightening around my neck. The color didn't help. It was red. Blood red. A tint of mahogany and oaky wood spun in circular motions around my shoulders. Taupe stripes around the bar counter illuminated how little the owner cared about his clients. It was clear he wanted the place to appear bourgeois and upper class but only to appear that way. It was obvious he had no idea what he was doing short of glancing at an interior decorating article written by someone dumber than him. I couldn't get past the taupe stripes. They were so banal; the upbringing of someone who never had more than he needed while the deepening-red contrasted the passions of someone who in fact sometimes didn't even have as much as he needed. To pretend to be something or someone one is not is the worst sin of all... to reflect the real illusion of the conscious self. Maybe it was the suffocation of the place, maybe it was the seeming sudden truth of present circumstances. Either way, I was getting nauseous sitting there. Disgust and an overwhelming feeling of failure possessed me. I'd failed her.

I wanted to be the shadow in the spotlight and the light in the darkness. I wanted to breathe something that was real. I wanted to be the brushstrokes on a painting. I wanted to be the contrast and the cohesion of all the elements working together to form a picture and yet at the same time, I wanted to be nothing. I wanted to fade away and mist into nothingness. Why did she leave me? Why did she force this sorrow upon me? It's been raining and thundering non-stop since her death and they say it won't get any better. The weather emulated what I was feeling and what I was sure to feel for the rest of my pathetic existence. I was nothing without her. Why did she leave me alone to dream of her alone under the night sky? Whys were useless. I straightened the Polaroid and put it in my pocket, taking all the cash out of my wallet and placing some under my tumbler. The cards and IDs I threw in the trash before I walked through the door into the raining wind.

"The train station please," I whispered to the cab driver.

"Right away... It's going to be a ba—" he turned up the radio volume to the weather forecast as droplets seemed to be trying to break the windshield.

I was about a third into Ligotti's book and I didn't find him too absurd. His idea that consciousness was a disease. The idea that everything is meaningless and humans from the core deceive themselves in believing in meaning and purpose. To him, the desire to survive is an illusion perpetuated by humanity.

Perhaps this idea wasn't completely off... what remains if we strip emotional connections? What else has meaning? What else has purpose? Are there things that can even remain of ourselves if we can attain enlightenment on such matters? How does the inevitability of death alter this notion? If I weren't emotionally connected to Laura, what would be the purpose of her death? What would be the purpose of her life?

"... He... sir."

How can I find meaning in a world that doesn't illuminate any meaning but rather only demonstrates utter and complete meaninglessness?

"... Sir!"

How many wars have been started for no other reason than the profit of combative governments? What is the meaning in that? To attain little pieces of paper with pictures on them?

"SIR!" the cab driver seemed to be yelling through the screen.

I'd forgotten where I was, "Yes?"

"We're here sir. The train station," he looked puzzled and somewhat apprehensive.

"I'm sorry," and right then I noticed the pattering raindrops on the windows of the car followed by the deafening noise of unfolding my bills as I paid my fare. It was the sound of closing my door, the engine moving away, and the sound of the thunder that foreboded a migraine and I had to take a couple more pills. I only had a few left and should've really searched for a pharmacy to get a refill but I didn't want to miss my train. How amusing. I didn't even know where I was going, what train I was taking or what I was going to do once I got there but I didn't want to miss it. The rain cooled my face as a valet standing under the arch of the train station's doors beckoned me under the awning.

VI
THY DAYS ARE DONE

"Does he always smoke?

"He's a chain-smoker," Elroy tried to wipe the dampness off his dress pants, "He always smoked these long Italian cigars. Not that Italian cigars are any good... he must've found a proclivity for them when he lived there... a lot of people smoke. Well, people like him. What you enjoyed about his smoking wasn't that you never saw his hands free of a cigar but the *way* he smoked them. He held it backwards between his pinky and second-last finger," Elroy demonstrated with his own hand. "When it was idling between those fingers the smoke came up from under his chin and so he always looked like he was coming out of this weird haze," the rain got worse for a second and the sound of it on the windows turned his attention to the sky. "Anyway, it was almost like he wasn't smoking *that* cigar, but the dimming memory of one previously smoked. He liked to watch the circular ember turn the cigar to gray ash. 'It's fitting for timed beings like us,' he said once. Like his reconciled nature, he made something so simple like smoking cigars as abstract and unnatural as he was."

"Tell me about him," Johann Bréanainn Brahms queried.

"Who?" Elroy lost track of the conversation with his friend "... Oh... Michel. Everyone called him *The Surgeon*. He was... well let's say he was an intense man. I mean there are a lot of intense literary or artistic types but he was different. There's the seller: the person who wants their books or paintings to sell so they write or paint whatever will sell even if they don't believe it. The creationist: the guy who doesn't believe tradition or the guys before him had anything to offer. He has a bit of an inferiority complex, always yenning to *invent* a new style of writing or painting movement. Most of them are untalented hacks that live in fear and envy of others. The classic: the conservative, sticks to the rules and has no interest in crossing the line, which is somewhat contradictory in the artistic mind. The genius: the one whose brilliant ideas invent a new style. The beautifier: the one obsessed with aesthetics, everything has to be hedonistic and beautiful," he looked at the dulled overcast through the window in hopes to spot a pinch of sea-blue hiding behind the tyrannous clouds.

"Which was he?" Johann had leaned in with widened eyes.

"Michel was the skeptic. Don't get me wrong he was brilliant, but he never let on what he was thinking and it was for the best. He was quiet but when he started talking all you wanted him to do what was shut up. He said the most vexing things. Like his skepticism didn't allot him the belief in a self but he knew who he was. His idea of the self consisted of there being no idea of the self. I tell you Bee-Squared, I don't think anyone understood him. Actually, now that I'm thinking about it, I don't think anyone could really stand him. No one except Mædeleine."

* * *

Michelangelo emerged through the mist of his cigar on the patio of Caffé di Francesco, where Paseo de Gràcia met Carrer de València. Every restaurant on Gràcia retained a somewhat nostalgic feel of a traditional and quaint European café. If you'd been to one, you'd been to them all, but something had drawn Elroy to Francesco's and it wasn't that it was merely steps from his hotel. Michel not only failed to ascertain why they were at Francesco's but why he'd come at all. These questions bothered him; a man can't and in fact shouldn't arbitrarily select what questions his mind attempts to ask and should instead welcome all questions of abstract overtones.

Before he'd left, Michel actually had trouble getting a taxi in the foreboding drizzle and even when he did, the driver took him for a little ride around town and he ended up on the opposite side of València's one-way street. He was forced to wander back towards the café before Elroy and his friends welcomed him.

"Michel," Elroy stood up first, "This is Johann," he pointed to the man sitting to his left, "Johann, this is Michelangelo."

"Call me Michel," he extended his hand out to shake Johann's hand. Johann didn't stand and gimped Michel's hand with a lackadaisical eye.

"Hey," he wiped his hand on his pants.

"Michel. This is Komtesse Alfhild Baldure," Elroy shifted Michel's gaze to a deific form in the shape of a woman with a flushed face. She straightened her little black dress and stood.

What a beautiful name, Michel's thoughts rooted to the cement of the patio under the now strengthening downpour. He slipped his hand directly under hers with the slightest touch, "Pleasure," almost afraid to embrace her delicate hand for fear of breaking it. The romance was nauseating.

"Alfhild," her features exuded an imprisoned passion as if she weren't permitted to be who she wanted to be, "Elroy says you're an artist," her voice carried to him with a directness he hadn't felt since Mædeleine.

"He's too kind," Michel exerted himself when he tore his gaze away from Alfhild and glanced at Elroy, "I splash paint on a canvas and throw words on a page."

Michel sat across Alfhild while they waited for the waiter, "You're a Norwegian countess? I thought Norway had no official *aristocracy* outside the royal family."

"They don't," her smile pricked all over at his body.

"How many paintings have you sold?" Johann's question attached itself to a batch of thunder in the distance.

"About as many as Van Gogh," if Michel cared for pieces of crumbled paper he wouldn't have become something that allotted him minimal *things*.

"That's really good," Johann burst with excitement as Alfhild and Michel exchanged a glance in the same time Michel shifted his eyes to Elroy.

"Honey, Van Gogh didn't sell a single painting during his lifetime," and Johann exchanged a threatening glare with her as a reprimand for *his* idiocy.

Michel stared through the umbrella placed above them towards the sky and tried to *feel* the raindrops through it. Johann's designer suit and monogrammed scarf answered the question for him. Of course a woman like Alfhild would need a lot of money over a little brain to give any man her attention. Money *is* everything. A good woman will cost you, and for the second time in his life, Michel wanted to be rich. He wanted to paint something that would sell rather than something that would feel. He wanted to do what he said he does to people who ask, to simply 'splash paint on a canvas' with no thought other than pieces of paper.

"What can I get you guys?" the waiter appeared in a white tailcoat.

"I'll have the... this one here," Elroy pointed to something on his menu.

"The Fino? Exquisite choice sir."

"I'll have a bottle of Cava. Bring me whatever you think is good."

"Very good sir."

Johann completely ignored the waiter after that, "We were..." he motioned to Alfhild and himself, "At El Xampanyet yesterday afternoon and it was a riot," and he used this opportunity to sit closer to Alfhild.

"And you sir?" the waiter jotted something down in his notebook and looked at Michel.

Michel hadn't even opened his menu, "Ladies first," he looked at Alfhild, and Johann's face turned as red as pomegranate seeds.

"Thank you," Alfhild shifted her gaze away from Michel's intense irises and studied the menu again, "May I have the *vi blanc* here?" she pointed to something from the wine list.

"*Ampolla?*" the waiter asked.

"No, a glass is fine for now."

"Excellent choice Madame. Also, we have special on, how you say? *Tapas de carn...* beef tapas if you order bottle," the waiter's English hid beneath his obvious Catalan roots.

"No, a glass is okay for now."

"No problem," the waiter nodded and averted Alfhild's cobalt eyes with an ease that invoked Michel's jealousy.

"Gràcies," she was nowhere near fluent in the language but every word she spoke made Michel want to hear more.

"You sir?"

Michel's meshed fingers rested on the menu, "Espresso, and a warm cup of milk."

"MILK?" Elroy chuckled slowly as Johann's contemptuous look pierced Michel and landed on the puddle across the street. "Wait," Elroy grabbed the waiter's forearm, "Bring him a pacifier too! ... MILK! ... WARM MILK!!"

"Sir?" the waiter stopped.

"Nothing, nothing. Go on."

The waiter merged with the ambiance of the restaurant.

"Have you been here before?" Alfhild inquired and before he could answer, "Because this place is known for its coffee."

"No. It's what I always order," and silence reigned over the sound of Elroy and Johann's whispering.

A bunch of people walked on the sidewalk in front of them on the other side of the patio chanting and singing songs. One of them was carrying a red and blue striped flag with an oddly divided coat-of-arms on it. As time progressed, people walking and chanting and singing increased. Michel watched each one closely and Alfhild and Johann watched him with a peaked curiosity.

The waiter returned with a tray of their drinks, "Here we go," and started placing the drinks on the table just as a crowd of people marching up the street screamed something in unison that ended in "SAA! SAA! SAA!" and basked in the water falling from the sky with an envying tranquility.

"The people walking. What's going on?" Michel idled his cigar on his fingers.

The waiter placed his espresso in front of him with the little spoon and a piece of dark chocolate, "Sir?"

"The people," he pointed at the passing crowd with his cigarillo, "Què està passant?" and motioned with the fingers balancing the cigar.

"Ahh, people *walking*," the waiter seemed to want to point to a building hidden behind other buildings, "És el Derbi Barceloní. Barcelona and Espanyol. Big match. Camp Nou. Like coliseum. Battle," and he pointed to the buildings again.

"Battle? Like War? What's the word... *Guerra*?" Michel unfolded a napkin in front of him and set it on his lap.

"Si. Fútbol. Guerra. How you say in America? Saucker? El futbol aquí és molt important," and he set down Johann's bottle of Cava.

"Gràcies," Michel and the waiter exchanged nods.

"Anything else?"

"No," Elroy waved him away.

"Gràcies," Michel repeated to erode Elroy's wave.

"You speak Catalan?" Alfhild turned to Michel, who was so consumed by the people marching in the rain he didn't really hear her.

"MICHEL!" Elroy snapped.

"Yes," Michel turned back to Elroy, having to look past Alfhild for a second that lasted for an eternity.

Elroy pointed at Alfhild.

"Yes."

"You speak Catalan?" she repeated.

"Yes," Michel moved his hand out from under the umbrella and little droplets of rain landed on his forearm.

"Michel got back from the war a few years ago and has been traveling Europe since. You settled down in Italy six or seven months ago right?"

"Yes."

"Italy?" Alfhild's eyes widened and sharpened on the part of Michel's hand sprinkled with rain.

"Yes."

"Do you speak Italian?" she put her palm under her chin.

"*Un po*... a little."

"Wait," Johann giggled, "You're a dude named Michelangelo who lived in Italy?" he cackled like a schoolboy.

"Yes," Michel took a sip of warm milk.

"You don't mix them?" Alfhild glanced at the espresso while twirling her index finger.

"Never."

More people wearing different uniforms than the others who'd passed frolicked by them and cheered.

"Soccer... pffft," Johann interrupted, already swimming deep in two or three glasses of Cava, "What a stupid sport."

"They call it fútbol here sweetie," Alfhild turned to Johann.

He stared at her and shrugged his shoulders, "Whatever. Rugby's the only sport *I* respect," he adjusted the knot of his scarf.

Alfhild turned back to Michel still staring at the chanting people and watched the cigar smoke from under his chin take the shape of his face.

"Unity," was the only word he whispered to himself as a piece of the remnant ash left on his cigar dropped down to the puddle at his feet.

"Unity? There's no completeness in sports. They're all dumb," Johann chirped. Alfhild elbowed him in the ribs lightly, "OWW!

WHAT?" he rubbed his chest, "It's incomplete. How can a sport complete anything? It's a circle," he curved his eyebrow to emphasize his contempt.

"Time... is a multi-dimensional circle of insensible matter." Michel's slow turn carried an eerie chill over the thundering sky. "Only perceivable through human consciousness as linear," the chanting of the passing crowds and the nonstop rain seemed to fall silent but for Michel's dominant timbre. "It's because we're so primitive we can only process time forward. *To-be* rather than Was-Is-Will Be all at once. Even when we're remembering something time moves forward *as* we're reminiscing. If you ingress another, more complex consciousness, one that can perceive time multi-dimensionally, you'll find that all the mass, volume, and matter of the universe functions much like an elliptical, or like you pointed out," he took a drag of his cigar, "A circle. The big bang, crunch, expansion, reversion. Everything's incomplete."

"How do you know all that?" Johann slanted his eyebrow and turned the Cava in his glass.

Michel was supposed to acquire a PhD in Supermassive Black Holes and the anti-gravity or *dark energy* that makes stars drift from each other, but that was before the war. *Where* things occur is just as important as *when* they occur, and as such, space and time are forever doomed to dance together among the stars. There was no need to mention any of this to Johann, who was looking to crush anything anyone else said and would probably mistake *supermassive black holes* for that song by Muse.

"Look up Gödel's incompleteness theorem," Michel said after putting down his cigar in the ashtray.

"What are you, a painter or a physicist?" Johann slapped Elroy's shoulder lightly while chuckling towards Michel.

"I wonder if it is possible," Michel drew another cigar from his inside jacket pocket and lit it with a strike-anywhere match, "To be both at once," and he pointed the tip of the cigar to his own face and watched the thin orange line burn everything away.

"Whoa," seemed to suddenly escape from Elroy's lips.

"That's a trivial abstraction. Abstracts aren't real. They're trivial, they take up," Johann sipped his Cava and looked *through* Michel rather than at him, "So they waste *time* that could be better spent thinking or doing other things."

All philosophies that deal in abstractions are fated for incompleteness. They're limited by the analyses of the perceiver and since human minds are limited in their perception and analysis, nearly nothing of value can ever be truly complete.

Michel tuned him out and his words no longer registered on Michel's cyclical mind. Johann spoke with the faintest of British accents, like a man who was naturally of the isles but spent too much time in the States. The stretching and quickening of words only found in the transatlantic riffled through whenever he spoke more than six words, which seemed to Michel to be too often.... He seemed to be nothing more than a man running from himself in a circle, a descendent of a murdering, thieving nobleman who says one thing but believes the opposite.

The tuck of Michel's cigar had burned back while idling on his fingers and the long trail of ash on its head cast his face in a shadow of smoke. Alfhild followed his eyes across the street where two bars in close-proximity cut off the street with a dark alley between them. The rain had abated and a vicious overcast surrounded the alley in deathly black.

"What are you looking at?" she asked over the cawing of a raven who'd replaced the gentle sound of mizzle on the Catalonian tiles.

Michel took a breath and searched for the bird before glancing at the *countess* and guiding her glittering pupils across the street where a waiter soaked with the divine's tears was clearing out the garbage in the alleyway. He looked up at their awning and looked towards the alley again; the waiter had disappeared in its darkness, "I wonder what the darkness thinks. How does it decide whom to condemn to loneliness? How does it justify those it curses to love? To decide whom to imprison in the night with nothing but the eventual promise of dark matter. Nothingness," he took a puff of his cigar as Elroy and Johann looked at each other perplexed. "How does it force some to follow it through this nothingness blinded by it, and how does it ignore those that crave the darkness? Some stars dim and some shine, some hearts are as perilous as black holes and some are luminous with hope. *Where* and *when* does this distinction occur?" he snapped himself back to reality and saw everyone just staring at him but he didn't really compose himself until his eyes caught sight of Alfhild's designer heels and clutch beside his glass of milk. No matter how close two objects are, a black hole swallows them through infinite distances.

* * *

"Don't you remember?" Elroy shook his head in disbelief, "You were *there* that day! The day you met him."

"Oh yeah! I don't really think he knew what he was talking about. Pffft. I know physics too but you don't see me blabbing about it any chance I get," Johann licked his fingertips and started wiping some dirt from his leather lace-ups.

"Yeah Bee-Squared, I'm sure you're a professor of cosmology and temporality."

"I'm serious!"

"I believe you. ... Nice scarf by the way."

"It's not a scarf you tasteless amateur; it's an ascot."

"... Hellooooo there," Elroy waved to two women sitting close to them and Johann blew them a kiss.

"How was the orchestra?" he beckoned them over.

"I wanted to kill myself after thirty seconds."

"I hear the Flying Dutchmen lost too," he looked away from the women to Johann.

"Yeah. What a bunch of scumbags."

"Not a good week for you! *Come on. Come on. Come to papa. They'll be here in a second,*" he whispered.

Finally one of them giggled and they came over.

"Hi boys, would you like to buy us drinks?" the one walking in front asked with seduction pouring through her skin.

Johann looked at Elroy, "But things are looking up," and snapped his fingers at a passing waiter, "Three bottles of Cava."

VII

CUBISM

I rummaged through all my pockets but couldn't find my ID. In my haste I'd made an obviously detrimental decision. I only hope I won't need it.

The train stopped in Barcelona for a few hours before it was supposed to depart to Málaga. Perhaps I'd make my way towards Casablanca and see some of Morocco. I decided it was the perfect time to go into the city and see the Picasso Museum. It's not that hard to get around in Barcelona; they have a more than satisfactory subway system if you're attentive enough not to be pickpocketed and more than enough wonderfully priced and hospitable cab drivers. I took the train in and decided to take a cab back to the station.

I was lucky on the train because it was some sort of big fútbol match between two Catalan rivals, and I suddenly missed watching Ajax put Feyenoord in their place. Everyone was cheering and getting along and waiting for *Les Corts*, where I assumed the stop for the stadium was located. The stripe-wearing *culés* sang their team's song with passion paralleling the red on their jersey and yet at the same time with a cold, elegant, and calm electricity indicative of complementary blue stripes. They didn't think they were *representing* a team of any sort but rather they embodied the team as one. One of them grabbed my shoulder and started singing what I presumed was their official anthem and I hummed along and blurted out the words that I knew were being repeated. It stirred something in me. For that brief train ride, I forgot about Laura's disdain for life. It wasn't until the train had cleared out of all the fans hyped with the anticipation of victory and the announcement of Liceu Station that I was snapped back into the gloom of a now everyday existence without my beloved. The vibrant colors of Picasso (as long as I stay away from his Blue-Period works) coupled with his devoted expression of Jacqueline were sure to calm me.

* * *

I walked down *Montcada* and entered the museum where a grave silence hovered in the air. A few people had entered with me but quickly moved through the three front rooms to get to Picasso's *Cubism* area. I sat in the middle of the first room with off-white, barely blue painted walls and looked at the classically themed paintings from afar.

One painting in particular, "Retrat del pare de l'artista," *Portrait of the Artist's Father*, with an ivory birch wooden frame caught my eye. It was a classic portrait of a darkening brown background and Picasso's father as the subject with a long beard and mustache carrying a melancholic look. The expressionist grey stroke on his collar illustrated the sleek and modern movement of Picasso's thought and there wasn't much else I could think of regarding Picasso that hasn't already been thought. Still, the glowing coffee brown background leaned towards a rich dark gold that aired an intuition and a divinity for the opulence attributed to Picasso. The ivory-birch colored wooden frame added to the classical theme, invoking the objectivity asked of all scientists but with a comforting and soft delicacy that provoked paternal feelings of subtle support.

I stood at that painting for so long a small crowd gathered around me in fear that I was seeing something they weren't and they began discussing the painting and offering ideas on what they thought Picasso had intended and what they thought drew me to the painting. It was time to move on.

An employee in a slim-fit charcoal gray suit with a ginger tie asked an Oriental girl in a tan raincoat to delete the photo she'd taken, pointing to the many signs in each room of a camera with an X through it. She giggled and nodded.

Sculptures dominated the next room, and the Oriental's broken "Excuse me," at one of the other patrons drew the guard over again and he caught her trying to take a photo of a vase with a green eye on it.

I stopped in front of one of the portraits of Jacqueline: *With Flowers*, with a cool blue background to her left, light-pink flowers, and a red background to her right forced a reverie of Laura and I required a moment to collect myself. I hazed towards the corner and walked outside into the outer area, balancing myself on the brick balcony just outside the gallery.

The only wish a true lover has is to be the first one to die because he knows he could not bear to function without his beloved, and it seemed that this one wish I'd had ever since I met Laura wasn't granted. Why did you leave me Laura?

I had trouble breathing and had to sit on the edge of the balcony.

I'm restless without you. I think of nothing else but holding you in my hands once again. Now I can only do this in my mind in a crossing of my present and your past and this is just not good enough. How can I ever enjoy an impressionist sunset again? How could I ever contemplate the regal-hued purple emanating through the moonlight? Why couldn't you see through the pains of the world and ache for the plight of my lonely sorrow? I'm as crazy about you as I was when I saw you carefully analyzing *Boomwortels* from 1890 in the Van Gogh Museum, and I'm even crazier than I was then and not in the way that either of us would want. I'm unconscious to everything around me like I am nothing more than a systematic machine going through the motions of a being with aberrant consciousness. What sort of wine would relegate these thoughts to the subconscious? Even thinking of wine reminds me of you nursing a bottle of chardonnay while listening to Mozart. Why did you leave? Now I can only dream of holding you in my arms. How impatient I am until the moment of nothingness because of this sadness. I detest the naked truth and see it for the ugly skeleton it is.

How could it be that in a world of such vibrant colors and landscapes, a world of passion and grace; there'd be this pain disguised as love to sneak inside you like a spider and crawl under your skin for years as it grows until it tears out of your heart with purpose, a purpose of death disguised as happiness? What discipline must I search to acquire answers to these questions?

VIII
DE DIE IN DIEM

The penthouse suite of an unnamed hotel squeaked open. Kane wandered in with his tie loosened and a mist of cigarette smoke and coughing greeted him.

"Welcome. Take a seat," the guy who'd opened the door guided him to a big circular table in the middle of the room.

"Eight players. 40 thousand buy-in. Texas rules. Drinks and food are on the house. Would you like to get acquainted or begin now?"

Silence reigned before Kane growled, "I came to play poker, not make friends with gambling addicts."

The man across Kane's left shoulder preened his baby blue Lacoste polo and glared through him. Basic intimidation tactic; poker's all mind games. It's never about the hand.

Kane smirked at him and leered past him to the window being wet by the rain.

"High card for dealer," a friend of the doorman stood over them handing out cards. A man in jeans and a plain-white t-shirt with a fedora and pilot sunglasses won the dealer button with the Queen of Clubs. Kane had to start out as the big blind.

The ring game had begun. The first couple of hands are just players feeling each other out and hence mean nothing. The only thing won and lost is the knowledge of the perceivable weaknesses of your opponents. These are the most important hands; Kane was a defense attorney so he had a natural inclination towards duplicity.

The cutoff for the first hand was a woman to the right of the Timberlake lookalike and she tried to buy the hand after the river with a big raise but Kane wasn't having any of it.

"Ich nehm's," he laughed and called her raise with the board at two fours, a nine, a three, and a king. There was no way she had anything more than a two-pair. At best she was holding a three-of-a-kind, which was a cheap buy for Kane to learn her maneuvers this early in the game.

"What language is that?" another player asked as he folded his hand.

"Svine they are; Ameri*cants*," he muttered, "German," Kane took a drag of the cigarette he'd lit and breathed through the smoke.

"HA! Damn Krauts!" baby blue was trying to get under Kane's skin.

"Better a damned Kraut than an ignorant American," and just like that, Kane had turned the tables to his benefit.

"Take it easy guys," one of the guys in charge of the game called over as he laid down on the sofa.

"Showdown," the dealer said.

"Read it and weep hotshot," the woman smooched over to Kane, flipping over the Seven of Hearts and the Seven of Diamonds.

Two-pair was what she'd raised with, matching the second Four of Diamonds on the turn.

Kane chuckled and slid his two cards to Timberlake: the Nine of Clubs and the Three of Spades, "It's not a woman's game."

"Pot to the gentlemen in the green tie."

"It's a curse really," Kane doused his cigarette in the ashtray.

"You sure talk a lot," baby blue looked at him with his oak brown eyes.

Kane was getting under his skin and he knew he was a couple of hands away from knocking this sucker out, "I have *Fingerspitzengefühl*. I can get out of any sticky situation with my instinct. All the books, art, literature, and power can't buy you that! ... Wait. Do you Americans even have art or literature?"

* * *

Cards shuffled the hours away. Baby blue was up eighty grand but then went down 14 and had to quit. After 9 hours of playing time and three packs of cigarettes, Kane had the dealer chip for the last time.

Everyone less Timberlake had been eliminated between Kane and the woman from the first hand.

Kane made a large bet at the pre-flop and forced Timberlake and the woman to call him.

His hole cards were the Eight of Spades and the Three of Spades.

The flop contained the Seven of Spades, the Ace of Hearts, and the Six of Diamonds.

Timberlake checked but the woman raised 2000.

"Zweitausend...?" Kane chuckled, "I guess that means you're out Timberlake," and he called her bluff; he was sure she was bluffing, she had to be holding an Ace at worst and an Ace or Seven or Six at best. If he could get the flush on the turn everything would be aces and he would take home five hundred grand.

The fourth street card was the Ace of Spades.

Kane had to reevaluate. He needed a spade on the river to make his flush but the presence of the second ace meant that Pumpkin-Spice Latte could potentially be nursing a three-of-a-kind. He would have to scrape it. Championship rings aren't won by miles.

She tapped the table.

"Check?" Kane was sure she had nothing otherwise she'd raise. It was difficult for him to fathom that he was being baited and coaxed into staying into the hand so he could later be destroyed. Men who play others often fail to see when they're the ones being played.

Kane raised 10, 000.

The smile on her face meant she was ready to call.

"Call," she immediately blurted out and then composed herself, "Schönen Abend noch Sweet Prince," her German was atrocious but it got the message across.

The river card was the Five of Spades and Kane couldn't hold his ear-to-ear grin, going all-in as soon as he could. He had to borrow 120 grand from the house to call her bet.

"Showdown," someone idling in the back room walked over. Someone was about to get knocked out.

"Whatch'ya got Pumpkin Spice?" Kane preened the lapel of his suit.

She said nothing but actions speak louder than words; she slid her cards towards Kane and he slammed his fingertips on them.

Cigarette smoke seemed to come out of his nose and ears as he turned over the Ace of Clubs and the Seven of Diamonds.

He knew he was beaten before the room had seen both hands. He sat in silence frozen to the chair and shrunk himself down.

...

...

"HEY!" someone finally screamed, "Your cards Suit!"

"Suits they are," he tried to play it off and threw his cards face up on the table.

Awe reigned in the room for a moment, well not the classical kind but the kind of hell-ridden modern awe that takes thousands of people to stand in line for something they don't really need.

"And my full boat quietly murmurs along your river hotshot," the woman's voice glittered with excitement.

"Ahh well, you win some and you lose more... good game gentlemen... and lady," and he stood up to walk away.

Someone stood in front of him at the door.

"You owe us 90 grand bigshot, plus 50 from last month," the bulging triceps of the man in front of him was not something Kane would look forward to seeing ever again.

"You know I'm good for it."

"I know you owe us 90 big ones at three points. I want the first payment in 2 weeks. That's..." he looked up and moved his fingers to count it out.

"$3300. That's thirty-three hundred big ones."

"You got it! Here..." he took off his watch, a stainless steel and gold sports watch, "This is an '89 Rolex Datejust TT Jubilee. It's worth at least $4200." Kane tried to open the door but the guy just looked down at him.

"This'll do for now," ... he put it on his wrist, "You better get the rest! Two weeks! Don't make me come looking for you."

"Look for me? Don't be absurd!" and Kane in a moment of anger tried to rustle open the door and it patted against the man's back.

They stood in silence for a few seconds before the goombah stepped to the side. Kane squeezed through the door with no intention of ever paying them a single dime. He wasn't afraid of them nor did he have any confidence in their ability to find him once he'd left town like he'd planned.

IX
TWO IN THE CAMPAGNA

"That's just how he was," Elroy slurped his orange juice.

"Your eggs sir," the waiter put down his plate.

"Hey! Get back here," he called the waiter back, "I said over-easy. Does this look over-easy to you?"

"Over... easy sir?"

"Over-easy," he slid the plate back towards the waiter, "It's not rocket science."

"Yes sir," and he walked away.

"You'd think they could at least make eggs. Damn idiots. That's why he's working as a BUSBOY I guess," Johann scoffed.

"Yeah... anyway, where were we?"

"Michel."

"Right. It's always Michel. You don't really like him...."

"So how'd he become an insurance appraiser?"

"Fumbled into it I think. He liked to think he was a P.I.; Bogart or McQueen investigating painting prices and assigning values to people's objects was as glorifying as solving a murder conspiracy to him," Elroy shook the ice in his cup towards the waiter and pointed to it.

"Why?" Johann picked some lint from his pants.

"Why do you think?" he scoffed.

"I don't know, why?"

Elroy smiled, "Ignorance is bliss my friend. Drink your beer."

* * *

Michel wanted to go back to the southern hills of Italy to paint. He wanted to be in sight of the Duomo. He wanted to breathe in the air and smell the blossoms but he knew this wasn't practical. In fact, he had to think about finding a real job or depicting zoo-like scenes in what passes for art these days. In other words, art that sells. He wasn't ready to sell his soul... not yet. He had to find a job and his Italian wasn't good enough nor the people he'd pissed off there forgiving enough for him to move to Italy.

His latest painting was *Warfare*. An unnamed man with an uncanny resemblance to Johann wiped his shoes with his fingers while his scarf was caught in a gust of wind. Wrinkled and bloody hands reached up from beneath the subject's lace-ups. Though the scene depicted small gray raindrops around the canvas, the man's vision remained unhindered across the canvas to a waiter, drenched in his own blood dumping garbage into a dumpster and a stray dog sniffing the bag he was holding.

A single painting aged him years, he didn't eat and slept even less than usual. He was a flab of skin after every stroke on the canvas, working from dawn to dusk. How was he to maintain social relationships, community obligations, or satisfy a woman? If the passions of his soul demanded every morning, noon, and night to actualize these potential expressions?

He exhausted himself to the point where he needed a walk. He found himself traversing Portal de l'Ángel Ave. at the intersection of Carrer de Montsió. It was there he entered 4Gats. Picasso hung out there along with Gaudí and Lluís Millet so it seemed like a place with gusto. He walked by the grand reproduction of *Ramón Casas and Pere Romeu on a Tandem* by Ramón Casas (the original exhibited in the Museu Nacional d'Art de Catalunya atop Montjuïc hill) and sat in the main room.

"Benvingut senyor," the waiter was dressed impeccably and his professional attitude made it clear why notable people had wandered into this place.

"Com estàs?" Michel followed him as they walked towards a table.

"Bé. Gràcies, i tu?" the waiter seated Michel in a comfortable booth in the corner.

"Bé," Michel didn't need to look at the menu, "Espresso, *ristretto*. ... Oh and a warm glass of milk please," was what he ordered, "Gràcies."

"De res."

Even when he wasn't painting he painted in his mind, planning the brushstrokes in his head for when he got back. He sat in the dining room and fiddled with the off-white, creamy tablecloth. He mixed the colors in his head and thought about how best to convey the contrast of light through the sky on the canvas and for a moment, his mind rested when he saw a couple at the table perpendicular to his. They were in their mid-to-late twenties chuckling and giggling like young people in love. It bothered him. He hated seeing people happy together. He didn't believe happiness was possible; it was an illusion human consciousness played upon its subjects. The only way he knew to subside these bothersome moments was to sketch the scene at hand. He extracted a little 3.5 x 5 inch Strathmore sketchbook he kept with him at all times and began sketching the man spoon-feeding his *Pastisset de Yuzu Japonés amb Salsa de Vainilla* (Japanese Yuzu cake with vanilla sauce) to his amour, leaving strands of her red hair open so he could color it at his leisure.

He feverishly adjusted the lines where the chair met her supple back. He was so immersed in detailing the woman's pursed crimson lips that he didn't notice his espresso had arrived.

Suddenly he felt someone standing over him, a distant perfume overwhelmed his nostrils and he looked up with an intense glare at the person watching.

Many wars had been fought and many innocents had died since he last saw her. Her athletic hips and flat stomach honored that particular space in the universe with her presence and none of that even came close to her eyes: crystals dissolving in the boiling liquid of her pupils. She donned a long maroon dress with a wool vest tied around her elegant neck.

He felt paralyzed and couldn't summon the power to close his sketchbook.

"Michel."

Why did he feel such elation from the simple pronunciation of a word he heard on a regular basis?

"Contessina Baldure," he stood, and for only a second, his left hand twitched.

"You don't have to call me countess Michelangelo."

He hadn't heard his full name pronounced in so long he'd started to forget who he was but he didn't want it to be a woman to remind him. It wouldn't end well. Nothing ends well.

"Call me Michel," he walked around and pulled back her chair, "Please, join me."

"Thank you," she sat down, "I like Michelangelo better. Reminds me of the renaissance, and you seem like a Renaissance Man yourself. N'est pas?" and the man feeding his girlfriend dessert glanced at Alfhild once... twice... thrice as she sat down.

Michel nodded, "Who am I to deny simple freedoms..." to a perfect woman. He left the last part out but thought it. No matter how much he hated Johann he wasn't the type of man to ruin the sanctity of a relationship. How ridiculous that sounded in modern society. How absurd to respect something that wasn't a piece of paper printed by the Federal Reserve.

Her slender body moved with graceful deliciousness, every slight jerk as chiseled as a precise brushstroke on a canvas. She sat, talked, walked, and laughed like an extinct being made specifically for the pleasure of others' consciousness. You couldn't stop looking at her radiance, listening to her sensuous voice, smelling her blossoming perfume, and if you were blessed by the divine to touch her, you could bet you'd be touching a piece of the '*Love that moves the universe and all other stars.*'

"Freedom... you think too much!"

"It's always good to stay away from illusionary abstracts," he sketched her shape in his mind and found a conscious unity in her presence.

"Illusionary? You're doing it again!" though a paradox in all aspects of science, her motion occupied the same space and her voice slowed time.

"Doing what?"

"You know what," she rolled her eyes as the waiter came over for her order, "Have you eaten?"

"I don't eat when I'm painting but do not let me keep you. Please eat."

"Are you sure?"

"Always," from her alabaster neck and shoulders down to her scorching body Michel thought of Botticelli's pursuit to paint the perfect woman. She even bared a slight resemblance to the sad innocence of Simonetta Vespucci.

The waiter stood with a handkerchief on his forearm like something out of a classical novel.

"I'll have this," she pointed to something on the menu as Michel stared at its artful cover, "The seafood tomato with special sauce, and an espresso afterwards."

"Sí, Tomaquet farcit de 'salpicón' de marisc i salsa especiada? Espresso after. Excellent Mademoiselle," and he took the menu away.

"I'm staying at the Majestic. I heard about this place. Apparently famous people ate here," she looked around with indifference.

"Picasso designed the menu," Michel guided her gaze to the menu on the table beside them.

"Elroy said you were a soldier in the war," she took it and examined it. Her long blonde hair captivated his senses and carried the cool Catalan rain even while examining a piece of art on a menu.

"Yes."

"I want more than a one word answer Michelangelo," she tossed the menu back.

It was the way she said his name that persuaded him; her melodic voice that carried through the space and landed on his ears. "We were led by Col. Koolema. A man of small stature. Nothing special, but he commanded great respect from us."

"What was it like? I remember when they attacked. Your president wouldn't stand for it."

Michel scoffed, "It's easy to stand for things with sixty-seven hundred bodyguards behind a nuclear-proof bunker ordering others to bleed behind enemy lines."

The indifference in her eyes dissipated when she looked up and down at Michel's hands resting on the table.

"We were an army of conscripts Contessina, blue-collar workers, artists, electricians, writers, mathematicians, philosophers. Funny how no one rich and powerful was ever *conscripted* to fight for the ideals they believe in more fiercely than those below them. Nearly none of us had ever seen a weapon."

"And you?"

"I wasn't conscripted. I wanted to join even though I was a student. Still, this…" he tapped his temple, "Was my weapon."

"Was?"

"Death and destruction follow us—"

"They wanted you to be a machine."

"Yes."

"You can't feel sorry about yourself; you did what you had to. You survived."

"Somehow I don't find that comforting. The cost…" children die so the *free* market can thrive on the spilled blood of the innocent. Where do the souls of the children go? Cradled and cooed by the *invisible hand?*

The waiter arrived with the food and set it down in front of Alfhild, "Bon profit!"

Alfhild thanked the waiter in English. There was something about her face through the candlelight that didn't unsettle Michel's psyche.

"Moltes gràcies," Michel nodded to the waiter.

"De res," the waiter walked away.

She cut a small piece of the tomato and dipped it in the sauce.

"So why'd you join the war?"

* * *

One of Michel's earlier mistakes had been attending some event for his alma mater. He regretted his RSVP seconds before he entered the banquet hall. These idiots hadn't said, done, or thought anything of value since their cancerous existence began on our scorched earth. In a world that prices things right down to a man's soul, most of them were worth less than a bottom-feeding porker who wouldn't know food from crap.

The most popular of these pagliacci was an overgrown douchebag from some forsaken Southeastern European country who had more height than depth. Captain of this and star of that but ask him to string more than seven words together and he struggled like a politician explaining away the booze and escorts seen coming out of his hotel room. He over-enunciated everything and thought it made him sound intelligent; his stock responses to whatever others may have said *to* him or simply *around* him were never more than a trio of childish words stretched for effect. He'd deepen his voice and say "Oh Naaaaawww son," or "Hooww greatttt," and the school's personal favorite: "Awwee-somme dooode," and so on. Destroyer of words and beauty he was and would still be.

This walking lobotomy was nothing compared to the pretentious asshat from somewhere in West Asia. He thought he had the world's biggest dick and the universe's greatest intellect, and being the manliest of men... his eyebrows were always plucked into a thin curve and you could always count on him misusing ostentatious words so the bimbos with too much makeup and not enough closed-thigh discipline would boost his ego bigger than his little pecker.

Alas, in the distance beside the punch bowl stood the nostalgically coveted cheerleader who was now an intern or waitress, if one can even spot the difference. Her head took up more air than brain but she wasn't the worst. The worst of these people were a duo of guys who were pseudo-artists. Losers whose parents bought them expensive cars and professional cameras so they thought they were natural born photographers and artists of the modern age. They could've been useful citizens to society but what did they do with their influence and opportunities? They waited in lines and trees for hours, outside doors for days, and squandered years of their life by giving legitimacy to the great Follywood propaganda machines by trying to snap a useless picture of an irrelevant man/woman others have deemed a celebrity... these were the creative expressionists of Michel's generation. Stein had used "you're a lost generation," a few generations early.

Make no mistake; these people were the bottom feeders, the worst clan of men, and the least beneficial to society. But who was he kidding? He was right there with them... walking and sipping gin without a care in the world, knowing from the bottom of his soul that it was beautiful to be alive... yeah right. A part of him, the part of him he hid deep within himself and out of the predatory sights of others, knew he only showed up in hopes of catching a glimpse of Mædeleine, and when she showed... it wasn't disappointing... not in the slightest.

Her golden curls bounced left and right and she seemed to float off the ground in her black dress. She was the only person who looked better than she had in years past. Every eye in the place was on her from the moment she entered, the women out of envy and fear, and the men out of lust and braggadocio.

The memory comes to him in incomplete fragments; he doesn't remember how he found her outside gazing up at the starry night. The moon was in its dark phase and the city lights had been dimmed to conserve energy so the purple in the sky contrasted the glowing white lights of aged albeit dead stars. He does remember lighting a cigarillo and the sound of the igniting match caught her attention.

"It's beautiful isn't it?" she continued looking up.

He didn't take his eyes off her, "Yes."

"We never really take the time anymore; our eyes are always in a little screen in our palm, always looking *down*. We never just... take a look at that."

He can never remember the conversation in its entirety: chancing upon her mesmerized by the night sky, the sound of his cigar match being lit, and, "Michel, my feelings do not go past friendship," somewhere down the line are the only pieces he's retained. The words— friendship especially—echo in his brain like a desperate howl from the bottom of a canyon. There is no search and rescue for the recesses of the mind. It was his love that'd said this to him. He'd realized then he loved her. He didn't love her insofar as he hated her; he hated her confidence in her rejection. Most of all, he hated his cruelty and callousness after,

"... Don't call me Michel then," his broken voice hollered from the root of the abyss. He was angry and he didn't know why. Why was he angry? Who was he angry with? With her for rejecting him? With himself for being rejected? For not being good enough? Anger is the poison we drink willingly.

* * *

"Michel? ... Michelangelo. You okay?"

"Huh?" he shook his head back, occupying a finite space inside 4Gats and the present moment in time. "I dozed off."

"Are you all right?"

"Yes. What were we talking about?"

"Why you went to war," she cut another piece of the tomato and waited for his answer before it was blessed from the touch of her lips.

"I was search and rescue," he looked around to orient himself.

"I didn't ask *what;* I asked *why?*" she chewed a small piece of tomato.

"Honestly? I was in love—"

"AWWWW!" she blushed.

"Yes."

"Sorry, I didn't mean to interrupt. Go on."

"She didn't feel the same... how do I put this? I wasn't rich enough for her. A man isn't worth loving if he doesn't have any money. Women need money."

"That's not true!" she pretended to be outraged at the mere suggestion that women want for things.

"After that I had to get away." Michel ignored her, "It was only after I'd gotten there I realized I hadn't gone far enough."

"You were overseas," she laughed, "Where *should* you have gone?"

"I... should've been submerged beneath a frozen lake in the final circle of Hell."

"What?" she put her fork on her plate.

"...That would've been the farthest place in the universe from her," he wiped his mouth with a napkin and sipped his espresso, "You know in Florence they say *nella guerra d'amore vince chi fugge.*"

"What's it mean?"

"Vernacular translation would be something like: When combating love, he who flees is victorious."

"So you fled from her?" she raised her eyebrows in surprise.

"Yes. I fled from her incessant fleeing."

"You're funny," she leaned back, "Great sense of humor."

* * *

"Don't let the artist act fool you," Elroy shoved an egg in his mouth, "He's more calculative than a computer."

"What do you mean?" Johann tapped his fingernails on the table.

"He's incredibly patient; he'd always peel a peach in one go, in *one* big roll, even if it took him an hour. He was the same way with women. If he was interested in a woman, Mædeleine for example, he could wait years and years for the perfect opportunity to strike."

"What a pansy, if I don't get some every night... I'm gone."

"Then why you don't dump her?"

"Leave the Norwegian princess?" he put his hand on Elroy's forehead, "You feelin' all right? What are you, an idiot?"

"Right..." and Elroy finished his eggs, "Waiter! Check."

X
POST-MODERNISM

The large yellow and red prints hanging along every grey-bricked wall of matadors drew my eye to the luminous bookshelf filled with drinks. Their faces standing tall like Hemingway described in *The Sun Also Rises*. Their yellow suits complementing the red capes resting on their shoulders. That's where I want to sit. I want to face the matadors.

"Benvingut a *Cachitos* signore," a man in a white tailcoat tuxedo greeted me.

"Bonsoir. Do you speak English?"

"A little… for one?" he walked over to a side table near the bar and grabbed a menu, "English. Please follow me."

"I'd like to sit across those bullfighters," and I pointed to the prints.

"Yes of course," and he guided me to a table under the prints. I sat in the center where I could bask and take in all the details of the four faces above me.

To my left a lip gave way to a set of stairs that led to a more romantic dining area where tables were situated in front of a little greenhouse of small green trees, creamy flowers, and red plants.

I'd been staring at the prints for a good ten minutes when I realized I hadn't even glanced at the menu yet. Each of the categories on the menu had a different background of light-yellow or light-pink hue. They had tapas, traditional Spanish appetizers; seafood; a tasting menu of varying sorts; Montaditos served on crusty bread; mini Spanish sandwiches served with different kinds of meat; and daily market dishes.

Wanting something different and refreshing, I really only checked under the daily market section. Three dishes caught my eye: the zucchini tagliatelle with cuttlefish and prawns, grilled monkfish with vegetables, and the grilled quid served with a potato. While I was deciding the waiter came over to get my drink order and I ordered a glass of *Moët and Chandon rosé* for 14€.

While I waited for him to come back and get my food order, still having to decide between the three dishes, I suddenly missed going to the Bagel & Beans with Laura when we were young on Van Baerlestraat every morning, with their colorful coat-buttons painted on their mugs, or our first date at Italaans Restaurant on Paleisstraat with their cozy décor and pizza oven right beside you. The tables were so small our feet touched when I sat down after her and I didn't want to stop touching her legs but slowly retracted mine away, and until she moved her leg forward and rested it against mine once more I wasn't sure if she even liked me as much I liked her.

I still remember the exact moment I knew I was going to marry her. We'd spent the day together, hanging out with coffees on the grass field behind the Van Gogh Museum. She'd just moved to Amsterdam so she wanted to walk around and discover things. That's how she was: adventurous, lovely, brave.... We walked to the *Taschen* bookstore on Pieter Cornelisz Hooftstraat and looked through their extra-large print books together, and when the page of the Sistine Chapel ceiling from *Complete Works of Michelangelo* unfolded onto her lap and she started talking about the spacing of the colors and how they contrasted for emphasis I had a suspicion she'd been thinking about it.

The next day we entered the Rize Gallery on P.C. Hooftstraat past the Louis Vuitton to look at the *art*. There was a metal sculpture right as we entered, a cold, ugly bull hammered with no real precision or emotion. The charcoal gray spray-painted over it was dull, conformist, and detached both the artist himself and the viewer from the *art*. It suppressed what it really could've been, a powerful explosion of life portraying *Toro*! It cost 56, 000€. She burst out laughing, hitting me in the ribs and pointing at the price tag to the point where one of the patrons shushed her. I knew right then she was the one I wanted to spend the rest of my life with, to live with and to die with.

There were moments where I thought she was having an affair. I thought she was seeing someone but I was always wrong. Men always have to worry "...Sir..." when they have an attractive wife. It's the price that comes with getting what you want, and every single "...Sir..." man pays it gladly.

"Sir," the waiter stood bent over me with one of his hands behind him, "Have you made your selection?"

I snapped out of my reverie and glanced at the menu again, "Sì. Give me something from the Daily Market list."

"Very well sir," he disappeared into the red aura behind the bar and I took back to staring at the matador prints.

I nursed my rosé and looked at the plants behind the glass. Their green sat well with me. They were like a forest deep in the urban jungle of someone's thoughts or ideas actualized through a little greenhouse *inside* of the restaurant.

I must've dozed off because the waiter came towards me with a plate on his hand and it'd only been a few minutes.

"I brought you the zucchini tagliatelle with cuttlefish and prawns sir. It was the freshest dish and it is a restaurant favorite."

"Thank you. It's perfect."

"Anything else?"

"No..." and as he started walking away, "Wait. May I get another glass of rosé please?"

"Of course sir. I'll bring it right away."

XI
Non Compos Mentis

"You're not gonna believe it!" Kane chomped down his rib eye and made loud chewing noises.

They don't teach manners at law school. In fact, they erode any kind of manner the student was brought up with, replacing it with the justification "I'm a lawyer." Anyone who's ever been in an argument with a self-proclaimed shining example of justice knows that when the chips are down the only thing these thugs with a license to practice law can say is 'Watch how you talk to me. I'm a lawyer.'

"I'm late. Do you have the butter for this week?" the man standing over Kane's table observed his face closely.

"Are you kidding? Komm! Setz dich! Iss! ... Another rib eye!" he yelled into the back of the restaurant.

"No. I have to get back."

"You guys are no fun," Kane threw a long manila envelope on the table and it shook the unused knives.

"I don't have to count it do I?"

"Do what you have to," and Kane slurped his wine.

"Next week then."

"Nächste Woche... yes... next week." Kane gritted his teeth and knocked a piece of steak out of his teeth with his tongue. "I'm selling my car. You might as well come with me afterwards so I can just give you the cashier's cheque."

"No. Cash only. You know how it is."

Kane looked at the 'Zutritt Verboten. Electronic Shock' sign near the corner of the restaurant where the kitchen met with the computers that handled all the orders. "Fine. Get out of here then. Let me enjoy my steak in peace. *Auf Wiedersehen*," he waved the man away.

The man nodded and walked towards the exit. He shoved the envelope into his Tommy Hilfiger sport coat matched with Adidas runners.... Kane watched him leave before he threw his fork onto the plate and signaled the waitress over.

"How is everything?" she smiled and her rosy cheeks plumped up.

"Ich bin fertig. Danke."

The waitress looked at Kane's plate about a quarter-full, "Was everything okay sir?"

"Es war hervorragend. Die Rechnung, bitte."

"Very well sir. I'll be right back with your bill. Do you need the debit machine?"

"Yep."

Kane looked up and saw Wesley Van Couperville, one of his other two partners at the firm.

"Wes!"

Wesley was a pudgy man of about sixty-five and was a die-hard conservative from head-to-toe. He always wore dark grey suits with black shoes. He even wore those Ted Bundy prescription glasses like the murderer of values and truth he was.

"Kane... how are you?"

"I am well..." just then the waitress came over and Kane turned to her, "Keep the bill going doll, I'll be staying and we'll be enjoying some...?"

"Food and drinks toots."

"Two martinis for now."

The rosiness disappeared from the lady's face but she nodded to get another menu. Wesley took a handkerchief and napkin from the table beside them and sat down across Kane.

"How is everything Wes? How's Otto?"

"Working on some new canvas I don't know. He draws a line and people pay 20 large for it. What a racket! We should've been artists," the waitress came back with their drinks and placed the menu on the table.

"Thank God for these idiot hipsters and quasi-modern artists!" and they chinked glasses.

"What's new with you Kane?"

"Absolutely nothing at all," and when Wes opened his menu Kane pointed to the Steaks section, "Get the rib eye; it's..." he licked his fingers, "... Excellent."

"Sounds good."

"Want to hear something weird Wes?"

"Always."

"You remember Mædeleine?"

"That tight piece of ass you trotted around here numerous times? Yeah she rings a bell," he tapped his belly.

Kane roared with laughter, "She said 'I'm in love with you,' and cried, and said 'I can't live without you,' she was the best piece I ever had."

"I haven't seen her for a while."

"Yes it was right before I turned 43, she was 22. You have no idea how tasty she was, then the slut tried to manipulate me into marrying her. I'm so not down with that! I left her," he sipped his martini.

"Where is she now?"

"Who cares?"

Wesley chuckled and they chinked glasses again, "You took her to Barbados and Aruba too! What else did she want? Women are so limiting."

"I know! What else do they want," their waitress walked by then and Kane stopped her, "Two rib eyes toots. Medium well-done."

The waitress' fake smile revealed only a defeated "Right away sirs."

"... Yeah I don't know what more she could've possibly wanted."

"Wasn't there another one a little older you saw for a while?"

"Yeah... I haven't heard from her in a couple of weeks."

"That's a good thing."

"Oh yeah."

"... You always did like them crazy."

Kane laughed again, "No man is an island."

"That doesn't relate but I see your point."

XII
FAST RODE THE KNIGHT

A fly buzzed and hovered over the long peach peel hanging on the side of the trashcan inside Michel's studio. He hadn't slept for 35 hours and had spent the night staring out the window at the lights beneath his feet. He saw a couple stumble out of the bar, kiss, and walk north. He'd forgotten how many cigars he'd smoked and if it weren't for the butts in the ashtray on his windowsill he'd have told Alfhild he hadn't had a smoke all night. The fly buzzed towards him and Michel tried to swat it against the wall; his hand glided over one of his rhymes taped to the wall and it guided his glance to a bunch of verses beneath his feet. The fly circled around his hair and made a beeline to the window and escaped into the dawning sunlight. Birds had been chirping since 0530; songs that usually informed him it was time to get out of bed. He had a hot shower and read Coleridge's *Defection: An Ode* that he'd taped beside his bathroom mirror as he shaved from the steam and turned his radio to Modern Classical AM. Arvo Pärt's Nekrolog Op. 5 performed by the Stockholm Philharmonic Orchestra played as Michel watched a tree get caught in the wind and the springtime breeze found its way into his studio and chilled his freshly shaven chin. He followed the horizon upwards and saw Mount Tibidabo lost among the trees idling under the church and park, both built for people's amusement. He went through his sketchbook and tried to improve on his study of Alfhild's eyes, rubbing her irises where her eyelashes met with her eyelid. The fly found its way back in and buzzed around Michel's face again before he successfully swatted it towards a copy of Oscar Wilde's *A Lament*. He lit a cigarillo and walked over to the window as he sketched the blossoming tree outside. In truth he hated painting—the radio played a variation of Vivaldi's Winter—he thought it was a representation of the physical realm, of the space and of linear time. Since he thought the physical realm could never yield an accurate depiction of an abstract it was a false image. Painting was then an inferior image that sought to imitate an already incomplete representation of the abstract world. This was also why he rarely included himself in his studies or sketches or painting or did self-portraits. He did not, as he read Plotinus had once said, "Want to perpetuate an image of an image." The tree came out nicely through his mending of the charcoal with the off-white of the paper and the eraser that illuminated the puritan white of his repressed beliefs. Michel flipped back a few pages to his sketch of Alfhild and Johann popped into his mind; something about Johann unsettled him and it wasn't just that he was a *bro* who'd bang anything with or without a pulse. No, there was a darkness embedded behind his glibness and until Michel could figure out *what* it was that unsettled him, he wouldn't trust him. The ferocity in Alfhild's eyes in the sketch was captured with a poignant stillness that Michel thought captured her essence, imprisoned by her class and stature like a rare jaguar in a cage at the zoo.

"This is Modern Classical AM with Albert and Ernest and you just listened to Strauss's *Blue Danube* by the Berlin Philharmonic. Some breaking news this morning, there was a murder last night. That's our 32nd this year."

* * *

"What on God's land am I walking into here?" Britten looked at the grit of this scuzzy hotel room darkened with a shade of neon red and white reflecting from the adjacent building, "Alicia?"

"In here detective!" a woman's voice called from the last room at the end of the hall.

Britten traversed the creaky burgundy carpet until he stood in the white fluorescent light staring at Alicia going over the body of a presumably tortured young woman for evidence.

"Welcome to the Slender Thighs," Alicia's chocolate irises looked red in the light.

"Someone who stays here seems not to have any choice in the matter," he crouched down to the victim tied to the chair and tilted his neck to investigate her face, "She was gagged and restrained."

"Prostitute?"

"No. She's too well kept," he followed the length of her jeans to her hip: Armani Jeans. "And any escort who can afford Armani wouldn't bring her clients to this place," he looked around the room.

"... What's going on here boss?" Alicia moved towards the restraints on her wrists.

"I don't know... everything in here is untouched... was there sexual trauma?"

"No... other than these superficial cuts on her arms and torso, the torture, she wasn't raped."

"What killed her?"

Alicia guided the detective's gaze to her thigh, where he followed a clean cut on her femoral artery and the sticky blood that flowed through the chair and onto the cheap red carpet. He looked closer and noticed the carpet seeping with blood under his long rain boots. "There's a lot of blood," he stood up and around to examine her hands.

"She was restrained," Alicia said as a camera flash whizzed behind her.

Britten tilted his neck towards her hands, "He was looking for something. Where's her wallet? Where did she live?"

"We don't know. First respondent officers thought it was a robbery because they couldn't find her wallet or ID."

"No. This had purpose. They were after something very specific to merit this torture," he looked at her face again. "My guess is they found whatever they were looking for she gave it to them; no one can withstand torture for long."

"How do you know it wasn't just a sicko? A psycho? I trust you Ben but what makes you think this had purpose?" Alicia combed the victim's hair onto an evidence bag.

"You watch too much Dexter; the percentage of psychos is under 10%. Besides it won't change our investigation. It's better to assume they were after something and look for *it* and the killer, rather than narrow the search to a serial before we even know her name. Either way, I don't think this was the last we've seen of this guy," it'd started raining and the sound of falling rain on pavement rattled around his brain for an idea on how to pursue this and what to do with the guy once he'd caught him.

"Close that window would you?"

"Sure," Alicia stood up and with her back to the neon lights, her face and eyes dark with ferocity, and she was every bit forced to be ferocious as a result of her profession. Click. Latch.

Ben turned to a uniform cop rubbing his stomach with his mouth buried in his elbow, "You all right?"

"Yes sir," his voice wavered a little.

"Don't look if you don't want to but I need you to issue a bulletin. The whole ten yards. The tell-women-not-to-travel-alone-at-night bulletin; it's on the board at the office. I'll bet my badge this is not the first," he always called it the *office*, never the *precinct*; he thought that would segregate *this* precinct from *that* precinct but everyone loved to hate each other anyway.

He hated the badge, detested it with every iota of his being. The badge either meant people automatically loved you or they hated you based on pre-conceived notions of past experiences with corrupt public servants. Power *must* corrupt, everyone thought, and either way he was a nobody. He wasn't anything other than a freshly polished piece of copper.

* * *

"That's upsetting," the radio continued, "Yes Albert, a young woman was slain during the night and we're only telling you this because police have issued a bulletin that women should not travel alone at night and if they do to have a friend accompany them to their cars." "That was morbid," the second voice chimed in again, "Now back to Classical AM. Time to soothe you back into your day with some Yo-Yo Ma. Here he is with Bach's Cello Suite No. 1."

Michel erased and chalked shapes frantically as he tried to capture a pickpocket's eyes scanning the street for a suitable target.

He hadn't noticed his door creak open and the footsteps behind him sneaking up towards his left shoulder.

"Nōlī turbāre circulōs meōs!" he whispered behind him. I guess he *had* heard the intruder.

"What?" Alfhild's poetical voice inquired.

"Do not... disturb the circles," Michel put the cigarillo on his lip and brought her attention to the pieces of paper underneath her black Flat Almond-Toe Knee Prada boots.

"Oh," she looked down and saw her boots wetting the papers beneath them, "Sorry. What is it?" she looked closer at the *Study of Spaces/Shapes* with its new wetness forming a second circumference around the circles... "I don't understand... they're just... circles."

"Yes."

She stood in front of him damp from the drizzle and Michel looked behind him and only then noticed it had been drizzling the whole time. The pickpocket bumped into a man with an elaborately unkempt neckbeard in a slim-fit Zegna and with a precise calmness turned the corner and disappeared down an alley to the west.

He looked back and caught her gaze and held it for as long as he could. Fortunately for him, Alfhild couldn't abide by his intensity and had made her way to his fridge, "Have you had breakfast?" she opened the fridge.

"No."

She saw an empty fruit net and bottles of carbonated San Pellegrino water, "Well unless you want San Pell sparking water I can't help," she shrugged her shoulders.

He doused his cigarillo in the ashtray beside him, "There's a café downstairs."

"Okay."

He disappeared into a room that doubled as a walk-in closet and she heard him shuffling for clothes, "How'd you know where I live?" he called into the main room.

Alfhild shuffled the pieces of papers and read the poetry; she looked at the paintings facing the wall and ran her hands over the green of his tree lines and the baby-blues of eyes. Her fingertips caught on the oil specks on the canvas. "I asked Elroy; I wanted to talk to you."

"Elroy.... About what?" his voice was somewhat muffled by the door.

"He swears by your knowledge of art. *'A walking encyclopedia of art.'* He has a lot of faith in you," she moved to a different part of the wall and flipped and turned over the canvas and they were all portraits of women, some naked, some clothed in designer dresses and some casually dressed. One of them, of an urban professional in a light-grey suit, a white dress shirt, and a gold chain around her neck stood out to her. She carried, by his brushstrokes and exact smearing, a sort of spiritual and divine aura around her fair hair. As if she were a modern maiden.

"I would imagine, Contessina, that you of all people should know of studio etiquette," he startled her from the side.

"MICHELANGELO! You scared the..." she looked around and then at him in his black corduroys and unbranded polo, "I beg your pardon?"

"It's rude to look and extract paintings that are facing the wall in a studio or museum," he took the painting from her hand and counted from the wall outwards multiple times before he put the painting in its rightful place.

"Maybe I should ask you to do my portrait," she blushed.

"What'd you want to talk to me about?" he extended his hand to guide her out.

She took a step back, "I need your help."

"I doubt that."

"Are you always like this or are you just not a morning person?"

He walked over and turned Strauss's *Don Quixote* down and then off.

In the silence he lit a cigarillo and the smoke filled the air.

"How many of those have you had since last night?"

"Always one too few."

"IneedyoutocometoNewYorkwithmetoday," she wanted to get the sentence out so fast that she seemed afraid he'd hear it.

"Why?" Michel had vowed to never return to the rotting apple, the cesspool of greed and corruption famous for its lavish lifestyle and modern slavery.

"Don't you trust me?" her coy smile complemented her elegant posture.

"I wanted to visit the Picasso museum today," he was making excuses.

"You'll go when we get back; it'll still be there when we get back, shouldn't be more than a day or so."

"I'm not going anywhere until I know the purpose; the most valuable thing I have in this universe is my time and I have to know where this time is being allotted," he was slowly running out of excuses. He was fated to agree. It takes a definitive nobility to say no to a pretty woman, a nobility not bound by the sanctimonious posturing and seething of false classic antiquity into the modern world. No, it took a divine nobility, and underneath his impressive posture, his darting eyes in elusive moments to capture a quick sketch or a beautiful scene, he knew he was as much a nobleman than the elite were in deserving their wealth.

"I need your help," the more frustrated Alfhild got the more collected and frightening; she spoke with fewer words and her delicate voice seemed to make way to a darkness underneath the delicacy.

He became obsessed with the distinction between value and price à la *The Picture of Dorian Gray*. What was his value and what would be his price? In other words, how much would she need *him*, Michel, specifically, versus any other dispensable shmuck a pretty dame like this could pull off the street.

"It's about art; I need to come look at some reproductions I'd like to acquire for my family's collection."

"No," he repeated.

"What do you mean *no*? I'd trust any price you'd tell me. I don't want to get conned. Just come with me."

"Nature is temporal and finite, what does it matter how much you pay for a *reproduction*? Which is an image of an image of an image." The Neo-Platonist in him slithered around the edges of his brain.

"What? ... I know you won't do it for the money," she took a step closer to him, "You'll do it out of a sense of righteousness because you *'detest liars and thieves with ties.'* I'm just trying to buy a piece of art that'll be immortal!"

"Immortality.... We learn a lot of what we take for granted by our nature, what we perceive as immortal and necessary. In fact we are temporal and finite. The solitude of the soul is irreducible in this cosmic dimension. No human life can exceed the self that's contained in its social standing. We are solitary and alone in death. And here we are, standing as one while you worry about saving a few bucks here or there and getting ripped off for a piece of canvas."

"Why would you say that?" she winced for a moment and her hand shook.

He saw it and looked back up at her, "Fine. I'll do it."

"Just like that? Why?" she walked past him towards the window and looked through the tree at the horizon.

"Why do you think?" he reached for his mini sketchbook and sketched her silhouette in front of his window with the looming sky pressing him to the window. He used an eraser to create shining dots for where the stars would be if it were nighttime and a white line around her head like a halo.

All truths are painful and the most basic truths are also learned with pain. Humanity's lavish idleness and idolization of comfort prevents it from learning any basic truth unless it's forced. Only after genocidal wars, depressions and recessions, political power struggles and coup d'états have demarcated how fragile humanity really is through a presumption of its potential demise will people take note of basic truths. Still, most basic truths will forever be out of our reach, truths like: "Things have no reason; things occur that are meaningless," will never be elucidated in educational systems or spewed by any influential social figures. "Everything happens for a reason; keep your head up champ. Things will get better; be persistent," will still be household mantras and still believed by even the most intelligent of humans. Michel abided these hypocrisies. He abided everything, absolutely everything, and he'd yet to figure out *why*. No woman's hand should ever shake. The entirety of his intensity and dense intellection would now be directed at getting Alfhild the best possible deal for whatever painting she pleased.

"Thank you Michelangelo," her smile; how could he portray this smile in the sketch of her silhouette that had been of her back?

He closed the sketchbook; "*Hild, silhouetted by the light*" was the title he gave it.

"We can go to the café now," she walked by him towards the door just as he put the sketchbook in his back pocket.

Why did she have to say it like that? Why did she have to say "We can go to the café *now*" As if they wouldn't have gone if he hadn't agreed to help... no, agreed to *work for her*. How did it even happen this way? He seemed to blink and it was over. It was becoming increasingly clear to him that Alfhild was accustomed to getting whatever she desired at any moment in time, linear or not, and this made her a quantum miracle.

* * *

He held the door open for her at *Kun Kaffe* just as a blonde woman who looked familiar quickly walked out and turned away from them. She seemed to avoid everyone's gaze as if she were being followed or in fear of being recognized.

"After you," Michel pointed to Alfhild but she was having a hard time letting the mystery blonde go.

"Some people are so rude!" she walked inside.

He crushed a half-smoked cigarillo with his leather brogues and followed her.

"Ørnen," the East Asian waitress he'd met before he saw Elroy called towards him.

His brows furrowed, "Pardon?" as Alfhild looked at her then at him.

"You're Danish right? I looked it up! ... Your nose, it's aquiline."

Alfhild smiled the way the rich do, to the side and not really as if it's a mere formality.

Clouds had formed and merged through the sky and the blue-hue of the sky and the warm sunlight hid behind the gray cumulonimbi that were sure to bring down the spitfire of Poseidon himself.

"Two espressos please," he put up his index and middle finger.

Alfhild turned to catch his profile and started chuckling, "She's right," and she turned to the barista, "You're right! I can't believe I didn't see it!"

"The way the rain drops were rippling and sliding down your nose reminded me of an eagle's beak when you came in the other day."

Michel looked outside and just then saw a mosquito land on the window and quickly fly away.

"What's your name?" she asked and when Michel didn't answer because he was looking outside waiting for the fly to land on the window again, "For the coffee."

"MICHELANGELO!" Alfhild tapped him on the shoulder.

"I apologize. I was preoccupied with Kafka's *Metamorphosis.*"

"That's okay, Michelangelo it is, and you?"

"Alfhild."

"That's a pretty name," the barista smiled while she continued grinding the beans, "My name's Tiffany Hanji. I'm Japanese."

"Japan," Michel turned his gaze to the barista's Eastern face for the first time, "Is beautiful," he painted her figure and face in his mind. How delicate her face was, how sensuous her movements, she'd certainly grown up in Japan; her movements didn't possess the coarseness of the West or the abruptness of Central Europe.

"Yes, I moved here to study. I go to the University of Barcelona."

"That's fantastic, what do you study?"

"Drama," she backed away to get the saucers in shyness, ashamed of what society had deemed valueless.

"That's wonderful. Watch Marlon Brando movies," Michel walked around the counter to grab a napkin.

"Thanks, and I will," she smiled as she put the espresso cups on the counter and Alfhild took them to a table.

A man wearing skinny *Band of Outsiders* jeans and a *Vans* denim jacket walked in holding the newest Damsung Cosmos and ogled Alfhild before he walked over the counter and ordered a "flat-white espresso with a little milk." He must've not known that flat-whites contain a little milk, like ordering a triple-double but asking to hold the sugar. Hipsters...

Michel sat across Alfhild and watched her weave her hair into a single braid, "You come here often?"

"It's close enough to be convenient and—"

"... Big Bad... Swag?" Tiffany called onto the waiting customers.

"That's me," the outsider peered through his unbranded circular sunglasses and went to retrieve his flat-white. He dropped two pennies into the tip glass while he juggled his phone and his drink and ogled Alfhild again before he walked out.

Michel had dozed off doting on the next generation of useless sloths warming up to take over society and Alfhild's phone conversation with her chauffeur had been relegated to the back of his mind as she told him to come around.

He walked over to the counter as thunder struck in the distance and startled Tiffany, "I'm going away for a couple of days."

"No more standing in the rain with your coffee? ... I'll miss you," she was only being friendly, nothing more.

"I'll be back soon," he looked her in the eye and she looked away; this made him feel bad about himself because he forgot how abnormal it was to hold someone's gaze without blinking, "You remind me of a colleague when I was studying Black Holes. She was a researcher from the University of Tokyo."

"Yes, we all look alike..."

"No! I don't mean it like that at all," he didn't understand that she was joking, "The way you gaze onto forms and spaces... reminds me of her."

She blushed, "Your girlfriend's leaving..." she guided his gaze towards Alfhild walking towards the door.

"She's not my girlfriend," he nodded and followed Alfhild out.

A chauffeur held the backseat door of a Volvo XC90 for Alfhild while Michel made a note of its diplomatic plates. It'd started raining, and Michel and Alfhild sat in silence as her driver made sharp turns to ditch the useless paparazzi hell-bent on fabricating facts and blurring public perceptions to fill their own bank accounts. Pop music played out of the Bowers and Wilkins speakers. Some 16-year-old boy sung about the difficulties of life outside of the mansion and what it feels like to be in love. Michel listened for the sizzling sound of raindrops on the moon-roof and put his head against the window. The Volvo clicked its hazard lights on outside Hotel Majestic while a bellhop loaded two suitcases into the back and tapped on the car. The chauffeur flicked the brim of his hat towards the bellhop as they drove off.

He saw *Piscolabis*, the tapas restaurant seating a tourist while the driver took the second right on Rambla de Catalunya onto Carrer d'Aragó. Michel felt nauseous as he watched a child no older than eleven who looked like a vagrant ask a pseudo-hipster walking out of a *Bicardi Fabra Olga* (a lingerie/boudoir store) for change as the driver turned away onto Carrer de Villarroel.

Michel hadn't slept for so long the vibrating headaches and the halfway hallucinations had started. He was dozing in and out and in a moment of lucidity saw a silver Citroën C4 Cactus cut off Alfhild's driver but the driver kept his cool and let the person pass without any sign of irritation. How patient and accommodating the working class seemed, he thought as he dozed off feeling the cold of the windshield on his forehead on Av. Autovia Castelldefels. His elbow had been resting on the window control and his face was being pattered with the rain but before he knew it Alfhild's touch was nudging him to consciousness in the quantum realm he felt least comfortable in.

"You were sleeping; I didn't want to wake you," she talked into the car standing under an umbrella held by her driver.

He looked around and found himself slightly in the distance of El-Prat Airport, "Where are we?"

"On the runway," Alfhild motioned to some people to load the baggage onto the luggage cart and move into the distance.

Michel had found himself in Gestair's runway at Barcelona airport. His eyes darted towards the chauffeur's wet suit and got out of the car. Another person approached him and an umbrella popped open,

"No," he shook his head.

"You'll get wet!" Alfhild nodded to the man and he held the umbrella over him again.

"Everyone gets wet when it rains," some more than others it seemed.

Alfhild watched raindrops stream down his nose like Tiffany had said. His shoulders propped up and squared when he saw the Dassault Falcon 7X parked a few steps away. A staff member stood with her hands crossed in front of her as Alfhild and Michel ascended the 6 steps onto the jet.

The interior of the plane housed luxury white leather armchairs each with their own beautiful walnut-finished desk, a couch in the back for idling or snoozing, and a bathroom vanity that made Michel's studio look like the South Bronx. Michel sat beside Alfhild and watched her browse the net on the newest uPad as the attendant made final checks.

Captain Govad Attar walked in behind them wearing his white pilot's uniform matched with a navy hat and blazer and headed into the cockpit.

Michel fumbled in the chair and tried to make himself comfortable but couldn't. He thought about the people waiting on standby in some airport terminal lounge *hoping* that someone would fall ill so they could see their families.

"You all right?" the white glare from the uPad screen lit up Alfhild's face.

"Yes," Michel turned to the window and felt for a cigarillo in his pocket.

He snuck a peak at Alfhild, who'd looked up from the device and was looking out the window away from him. The small luminous orange of the sunset snuck in through the window and lit up most of her profile. The light bounced off her crossed knee and his intestines turned into a wavering knot.

The captain looked back from the cockpit, "Everyone ready to roll?"

Alfhild nodded.

"I'll bring espressos or tea once we're at cruising altitude," the flight attendant disappeared behind them. The stairs went up and the plane's engine roared to a start.

Michel looked out the window at the empty runway and then in the distance on the opposite side of the sunset towards El Prat Airport. How would he fly regular again? How would he abide by the idling through the lines, the passport checks, and the gates overcrowded with zombies waiting to be called only to abandon any dignity they once had so they could fit their overweight carry-ons above someone else's seat?

He sketched the horizon under the clouds and the darkening sky.

To Carthage he went, where cauldrons of unholy souls would bubble up and boil around him.

XIII
NEO-DADA

By the time I went through El Prat security, the line behind me had snaked around enough times to make a traveler dizzier than they already were. Every carry-on placed against the black tire rolled through the x-ray and beeped, and the ones owned by West-Asian minorities were double checked and triple checked. Ahmed, an American whom I was conversing with while waiting in line was immediately taken aside for a random security check and was instructed to take off his green Converse shoes. A travel-sized baby shampoo he'd bought for his little girl back in New York was confiscated even though it still bore the Johnson and Johnson seal. My white-gold wedding band made the machine go insane when I walked through the last checkpoint but once the woman used the handheld place detector all around my body she waved me through. I walked over to my gate and sat down on one of the scuffed chairs that'd been used so much the faux-leather was thinning.

I had a layover in Amsterdam's Schiphol airport but I chose not to go into the city because I didn't want anything to do with it; it was the place that gave me everything and then with one swift wave took it all away. The place I met the divine light of my soul but also the place I heard about her demise. I couldn't look at it the same way ever again. Every ounce of red or yellow or brown brick reminded me of her touch, every passing color on a painting or billboard made me want to see her, and every ambient noise made me covet the sound of her voice. I not only wanted nothing to do with the city whatsoever, I was beginning to wonder if I would *ever* return, if I in actuality, in fact loathed it. I was also afraid that if I left the airport I'd forget all that and be seduced to stay and idle in the comfort of my apartment and sink back into the soulless routine of my life without Laura.

With the thought of this disorder and the lacking routine of my life came a moment of panic and I called in to check my messages. I had two voicemails: one from the detective handling Laura's case, which I skipped, and one from the head of my department, Prof. Berten, telling me to take as much time as I need and not to worry about my job. As soon as I listened to Berten's voice I execrated the city again and berated myself for wanting to associate with what I labeled a life-now-undeserved-through-perception. I wish I'd tuned my acuity onto what I had videlicet Laura instead of squandering it on analyzing hundred-year-old paintings and spewing it at punk kids too rich to make any positive difference in the world.

An announcement cautioning travelers not to leave their baggage unattended emitted from the airport speakers. I looked up at one of the TVs that showed news headlines, the weather, and important airport updates. I still had 20 minutes before they opened up the gate but I wasn't hungry and wasn't in the mood to walk through an airport I knew like the back of my hand. I watched the news ticker and read the headlines as they came and went: *U.S. employing espionage tools in ally countries*, came as no surprise to me at all but *Egypt uses American missiles in airstrikes against Libya* knocked me back when I considered that both Egypt and Libya were currently allies of the United States.

A flight attendant walked over to the gate computer and as soon as she'd started typing a crowd of people stood off to rush into the tunnel in fear that the plane would take off without them.

"Hello ladies and gentlemen, flight 875E to John F. Kennedy Airport in New York City will begin boarding in approximately fifteen minutes. May we please get those over the age of 65 and people travelling with small children to line up first," she ignored the vicious mob trying to push their way past the gate. "We will also board travelers seated in rows 6-20. Thank you for your patience."

A woman holding a stroller with one hand and her baby in the other tried to squeeze through the line but people had trouble moving to the side. I looked down at my boarding pass. Seat 18A. I pigeon walked towards the gate attendant, using my left elbow to plow through the baboons that couldn't wait their turn. A gelatinous man whose facial features somewhat resembled a pig didn't budge one inch for the woman with the baby; he licked his fingers clean of some fried snack he held and chewed it on the right side of his mouth. He kept his carry-on tucked between his knees. Greed will undo humanity and if greed doesn't gluttony surely will.

The woman and I eventually overcame the maze of idling chimpanzees and walked through the tunnel to the plane and sat down. She was in seat 35J. Her baby sniffled and became agitated as she progressed down the aisle towards her seat.

I put my briefcase on my lap and opened a notebook Laura carried everywhere. It was a travel journal but because I rarely took her anywhere it was just filled with her thoughts. It was all I had of her now. I kept the photo of her on the inside flap and started reading the entries.

"Why does the poetry of the Bible haunt me? I cannot comprehend its artistic prose and yet it's so inconsistent. I know it has been edited many times and it is easy for people to misuse religion to further their goals but in some parts it's ridiculous." I rubbed my fingers over her writing; a man knocked my arm and continued down the aisle.

"How could there be so much on the health of the soul and how to manage and take care of your soul, how not to corrupt your soul and be prepared in your assimilation to God but then nothing on its origin past simple creation at the figurative hand of God Himself? On this note, why would he

condemn the soul to immortality? I thought He loved us... does he not? To be condemned to immortality would be the vilest thing I can think of, especially of something as intangible as the soul. Is time not what gives life its beauty? If the soul were immortal there would be no point in living, doing something today would be the same as doing something tomorrow, and even more, it would be the same as never doing it but at the same time meaning you're always doing it. I don't understand it. How could the Bible suddenly acquire this meaninglessness? Did those who wrote it, translated it, edited it, or did whatever to it not read it over for comprehension and consistency? Do they not understand the words they've written? I wish I could ask Max what he thinks but he'd only ask why I was reading the Bible anyway—"

It's true, that is exactly what I would've sa— "Excuse me," a man in beige neutral Alexander McQueen slim-fit chinos and a Berluti navy wool, linen and silk-blend blazer looked down at me, "I'm in 18C. By the window there."

"Oh," I stood up and backed away from the seat so he could wedge through to his seat.

He sat down, "Thanks. I can't believe they were sold out of first-class seats. Damn it! My feet don't even fit here!" he brushed some dirt off his Gucci loafers. "Waiter!" he looked towards the flight attendant.

I started reading this morning's *De Telegraaf* I'd picked up at the airport, "They're not waiters," I waited until he shifted his gaze towards me, "Besides, they won't serve you until we're in the air," I watched him go pale in my peripheral. I flipped the page: *U.S.A. president faces extreme opposition as he tries to decrease interest rates on the lower middle classes.* I don't know why he even tried, slaving the poor is how countries legitimize themselves.

A flight attendant walked through the aisle after the rush of passenger settled down.

"Excuse me," the designer poster-boy flagged her down and her hazel eyes looked around and stopped in his direction, "I'm parched. I'd like a drink with ice."

"I'm sorry sir. I can't serve you right now. You'll have to wait until we're in the air."

She glanced at his blazer and continued down the aisle, closing the overhead compartments that were still open and probably thinking that money doesn't buy manners.

"Told you," I folded the paper under the Sports section and smiled in his direction.

"This is fuckin' bullshit. I missed my friend's private plane and have to fly commercial... never again I'll tell you that much."

"Some of us don't have a choice," I laughed.

"That shouldn't be my problem," he raised an eyebrow.

"My name is Max, what's pulling you to New York?"

"Johann." He reached out to shake my hand, "I'm going to see my fiancé."

"Does she live in New York?"

"I… uhhh," his eyes glanced towards the empty seat in between us, "… Haven't proposed yet. I don't know when and how to do it."

I thought about my proposal to Laura at the Van Gogh Museum beside Gaugin's *Breton Girl Spinning* with the harmony of its turquoise background meshing with the lighter-greens, reddish-brown of the subject's dress and her short dark-blue blouse cardigan. "It'll come to you. Don't force it."

He unwrapped a wire and took a pair of *Bose QuietComfort* headphones out of a case, "No. She doesn't live in New York. She's there now with one of our other mutual friends to attend an art auction in Manhattan."

I folded the Sports page on top of itself again after glancing at "*UEFA will not discipline Feyenoord over riots.*" "You're going to be in Manhattan? That's a change of pace from Spain. Madrid? Or somewhere else?"

"Barcelona but I'm coming from Málaga. It was too hectic. I'm not a big fan of fútbol and there's been too many important matches during my visit."

"Spain's the wrong place to be if you're not into fútbol," I chuckled.

The captain came over the P.A. system and demanded everyone's attention to the two flight attendants standing at the front of the cabin. Johann cursed in Dutch as they began the tedious safety procedures. Johann put on his headphones and booted up his uPhone. I could hear the house remix beats and hip-hop verses from my seat. I prayed for mercy for his generation.

I opened up the paper to the International section: "*Arrest in West London Bombing.*" The suspect was in fact a British man protesting the spread of Islam and decided to bomb a mosque in the name of *freedom*. I turned back to Sports; the Eredivisie standings had PSV one point above Ajax in first place, with Feyenoord just two points behind Ajax. It'd come down to the wire. The Arts section interested me for a bit before the plane started taxiing in preparation for takeoff. I put the paper in the pocket of the seat in front of me.

* * *

A wailing baby somewhere behind me woke me. Johann's eyes flickered and he yawned while mumbling in Dutch.

"Never flying coach again," he muttered to himself.

We were at cruising altitude and the snack cart was coming down the aisle from the front of the cabin. A man in his forties clutched his crucifix prayer beads and whispered prayers to himself in Latin.

I tapped Johann on the shoulder, "Now if he were of Islamic faith, everyone here would lose their heads."

He took his headphones off, "That's true."

"That's why art is art. It's supposed to be unbiased," I tapped on the Arts section of the *De Telegraaf* on my lap.

"Are you an artist?" he tapped *stop* on his uPhone and wrapped the headphones up.

"No. I'm an art professor at the University of Amsterdam."

"You've studied art? That seems useless…"

"Ladies and gentlemen may I have your attention please?" the captain announced over the P.A. "We're moving in the direction of the wind and should be arriving early."

The cabin crew got to our seats and the flight attendant handed Johann and I bags of pretzels. "What would you like to drink?"

"I'll have a ginger ale please."

"And you sir?" she looked at Johann.

"Sparkling water. *With* ice! Wait… no…. Tequila. On the rocks."

She handed us the drinks. I relayed Johann's over and she moved further up the cabin.

"What were you saying?" I asked.

"Art… it's useless. *Especially* an art degree. Even art*s* degrees are useless. How do you get a PhD in art? Pfffftt," he snorted.

"That's pushing it," I sipped my Schweppes.

"Think about it, what use has art been to the world? What use are museums? Like cemeteries of brush strokes that don't allude to anything."

"What does your fiancé think about this?"

"She loves art, adores it," he scowled.

Just like that I understood his distaste; it was a way to get back at his soon-to-be-wife, to brandish purposeful uncouthness in an attempt to make her seem less important and less desired.

"…I mean… tell me. If Picasso didn't exist, if Van Gogh never painted, if the Met or Louvre didn't exist, what difference would that make to the world… really?"

"It's a form of expression. Like the music you listen to or movies you see."

He shrugged his shoulders, "Meh… whatever. At least the seat between us is empty," he put his scarf down on it.

Why was he saying all this?

"You'll fit right in at a Manhattan art auction then!" I laughed.

He barked something in Dutch again and clasped his thigh with both arms, "My leg. It's asleep. How do people come and go?" like a little child, all he did was moan and complain and whine about how things weren't going his way. "What was that?"

"Why are you going to an auction then? An art auction I mean."

"I'm going for... I don't know why. For moral support for Alfhild—that's my fiancé—I guess. She's buying some pieces for her family in Norway." A light bulb flickered among the crickets in his head, "I have an idea Maxy, you should come with me?"

"To the auction? No way," I reached into my pocket and caressed Laura's journal.

"You sure? It'll be fine."

I pulled the journal out and looked at the floral designs she'd drawn on the covers, "Okay. It sounds fun."

"Perfect. It will be a ball. You'll love it," he winked through me.

I looked behind me and saw a dark-haired beauty eyeing him. I opened *De Telegraaf* to the Finance section again and read some articles about the rise of Foolgle and fall of some provider that wanted to limit the freedom of the Internet. Johann threw his blazer onto the seat and got up, "Watch out Maxy." He hobbled in between my knees into the aisle. I watched him walk up to the restroom at the end of the cabin and turned my head back down to the paper.

I started filling out the crossword; a toddler running up the cabin knocked my knee and my paper and pen fell to the ground. I followed the shoes to my left and noticed the ebony-haired woman was missing from her seat. *Pioneer of Totale Football. Six letters.* I filled *Cryuff.*

"Let me through Maxi," Johann stood over me.

I stepped out and he snapped his foot back into his loafer and sat down.

"You buttoned your shirt wrong," I looked up for a second at his now mangled hair.

"Oh...," he re-buttoned his shirt and giggled.

It took a couple of seconds but I saw the woman walking back to her seat after pretending not to look over at Johann. I pity his *fiancé.* I pity the lustful and the greedy, the lost in excess, and the ungracious.

"I'm going to sleep now. ... Wake me when we land," I put the paper in the seat pocket and closed my eyes.

... Laura. O Laura... Why have you forsaken me?

XIV
VITA NUOVA

Michel saw New York City approaching in the distance through the window. They were about to land in the rotting apple, the place famous for assigning a physical value to a fallen human soul.

"Did you know..." he put his fingertips on the window and the cold surged through his hand, "...That after 9/11, the families of the victims who died in the attacks received different payouts from the government?"

Alfhild turned to him from across the aisle and yawned, "What?"

He looked over at her blinking eyes. "I didn't know you were asleep. I apologize. Never mind. It's not important."

Her now rested eyes glowed with the ferocity of a sea, "No. Tell me."

"The government assigned a Master of the Fund—fund of relief—for victims' families in exchange for not suing the airlines for the lack of oversight in pre-Orwellian airport surveillance. Anyway, this *Master* and sage, Steinberg or Lieberg I think his name was; a real greaseball in a suit. He decided some lives were worth more than others."

"I don't believe that."

"Believe what you want," he looked out the window again, the green dot in the distance slowly transforming to the Statue of Liberty, "The janitors and custodians got between 250-300 grand but the bankers, or the 'high earners' as Lieberg called them, got between 6 or 7 *million*."

"Those figures are inflated. They have to be," he could slowly see the hope drain from her eyes; the country meant to stand for freedom and equality sinking to the depths of the totalitarian states it banishes from the international community as soon as they have too much oil.

"Look it up later if you want. The figures are solid. What bothers me isn't even that; the world is unfair, it always has been and always will be."

"What bothers you then?"

"The government decreed two requirements. One was to take into account pain and suffering. Two was to evaluate the economic circumstance of the victims."

"Then it makes sense. A janitor makes less per year than a banker."

"But that disregards one. By this logic we're only accounting for two. He'll live to be X years old and work this much per year, here's the sum. What about the pain and suffering? The janitor's family suffers less and has less pain than the banker making a million per year?"

"You know too much for your own good Michel. I mean it," she didn't. Even though he didn't say much she loved to hear his voice carry through the air.

65

"…Placing moral value on lives he said," Michel mumbled to himself and looked at his cigarillos on the table in front of him.

"What was that?"

"He said later 'I'm not placing a moral value on life.' How could he say that? Isn't that exactly what he's doing? Isn't that what he was *hired* to do? We're only as worthy as our bank accounts.

Modern capitalism is grand, eroding and eventually owning the souls of man at the expense of dollar signs, legal trickery, and conniving tax-evasion tricks by powerful corporations," of course this meant Alfhild was worth far more than Michel. She was, but not because of her bank account and he understood this.

The Falcon turned away from Manhattan and headed towards New Jersey.

"Aren't we landing in JFK?"

"God no!" she laughed, "That place is horrid! We're landing in Teterboro Airport in Jersey."

"Bergen County?" he asked.

"I don't know what that is but it's close to Manhattan. 18 kilometers or so I think."

"Should be a 40 minute drive."

"More like 20," she was being hopeful. No way they could make a kilometer a minute.

"I doubt that."

"Let's bet on it. Johann and I play games like this all the time."

"I'm not a betting man," he didn't want to know what she'd have to bet to satisfy a creature of Johann's lust.

"Come on! Are you a natural enemy of fun or did it take practice?"

"Experience…" he whispered, "Fine. What do you bet?"

"My class ring," she held up her right hand, her glistening University of Oslo graduation ring.

"I'm not taking that when I win."

"Yes you will."

He sighed, "Against?"

"That notebook you carry around."

He felt for his sketchbook in his left jacket pocket laying beside him.

"That's the one!"

"Forget it."

"If you know you're going to win it's a sure thing. Technically, it's only a formality."

"The rich make their living on *technically* (not illegal). I can't, I won't, bet this," his sketches were like a writer's notebooks, a soldier's weapon, or a lawyer's amorality. They were a part of him, the latest one especially but then he watched the rain form sharp lines outside and some of them splattered on the window. The notebook was a *thing*, a physical thing. Everything exists on the same plane. There is no was, no now, and no would be. There is no Michel and there is a Michel; the notebook is none of these things. "Fine. You've got a bet."

She took off her ring and put it on the empty table in between them. Michel tossed the notebook beside it. Alfhild reached for it. "Uh uh uh," he wagged his finger, "Not unless you win."

"Terms?" she asked.

"You said 20. I'll even give you a 10-minute margin. If we get there in under half an hour you win. If we get there between 30:01 and 40 minutes then I win. Hmm..." he turned his shoulders towards her, "I'll be a gentleman, if it takes longer than 40 minutes you win too."

"So you only win if we get there between 30 to 40 minutes?" she had a hard time believing it after he made such a fuss about not betting the notebook but he wanted her to win. He wanted her to see the verses he'd written. Most of all, he wanted her to see the sketches and studies he'd done of her.

"Time starts the moment the car starts moving. Oh... and no telling the driver what route to take. No shortcuts. We let the navigation decide."

"That's a bet!" she smirked.

"Good," he turned back to the window and watched the lines of water appear and disappear in rhythm.

XV

RENAISSANCE SUCCESS IS COUNTED SWEETEST

"Ladies and gentlemen we've arrived at John F. Kennedy International Airport. The weather is rainy and thunders are expected to light up the sky later tonight. It's 13 degrees and the local time is 1:37 P.M.. Thank you for flying with us today; we hope you've had a pleasant flight and enjoy all the wonderful things New York City has to offer. Please wait until the plane has come to a complete stop and exit in an orderly fashion. Thank you again... flight crew..." and the rest of the message was garbled.

As soon as he clicked off the intercom some people stood up. A flight attendant asked them sit back down and wait until the plane had stopped. Finally it did and a stampede of hyenas ran towards the door. It was still closed and so they'd successfully cut off others from getting out of their seats and retrieving their luggage from the overhead compartments. The 747 pulled into a terminal and the tunnel extended out and connected itself to the door from the outside. Johann kept his headphones on and sat still until the doors unlatched and people started exiting. Then he scribbled something down on a piece of paper and handed it to me, "I expect to see you there Maxi!"

Canvas Gallery inside Kaashibys. 6 p.m., Located in between Madison and Fifth on East 74th St. In the building beside Caravaggio restaurant.

"Is this the auction?"

"Yeah! They have some paintings and stuff you can look at. You don't have to buy anything."

"I don't intend to."

"Max you're my kinda guy. If they hassle you at the front tell them you're Johann Brahms's guest."

"Thank you Johann. I'll see you there."

We got up after people had cleared the aisle and got our luggage. I thanked the flight attendants and entered the airport. It was a nightmare to get my luggage; people crowded around the tire and I had a difficult time standing for an extended period of time without my walking stick. After forty minutes luggage bags started coming through and people lunged for them like balls in Hungry Hungry Hippos. I saw the girl hand Johann a piece of paper in the distance and they both walked towards Passport Control. Ahmed was stopped by two plainclothes TSA agents for a *random search of his bags and person*. I saw my modest coffee-colored bag running along the tire and I tried to grab it but missed. I chased it along the tire until a Japanese man snatched it up in the blink of an eye and handed it to me.

"Thanks," I took it from him.

He bowed.

It took another hour to go through Passport Control but I finally hailed a cab and asked him to take me a decent hotel.

The driver recommended Manhattan NYC, a branch of the Affinia on 7ᵗʰ Street. The people were like a colony of ants. So many of them moving in the same direction so closely to one another, cars seemed trapped in endless mazes of one-way streets and construction sites left unsupervised in the rain.

"We've had reports of flooding in some parts of Brooklyn..." the radio reported.

"Turn that up my friend," I asked the driver.

"Sure thing boss," his hand turned the knob clockwise.

"That's local news Jimmy! We've also heard that there's a huge rainstorm in Germany and the Netherlands..." one of the two chuckled, *"It's a global storm folks."*

"Thanks. You can turn it back down if you want."

"World's swirling down the drain."

"We're already pretty much at the bottom," I reached into my shoulder bag and took out Heidegger's *the Origin of the Work of Art.*

"You mind if I ask you what you're reading?" he asked me through the glass.

"Not at all," I turned the book cover towards the glass, "Heidegger."

"He's far too dense. Maybe it's better in German."

"It's not. ... You've read it?"

"Yes," he opened the glove box and shuffled through some of the papers as we exited the highway towards East 35ᵗʰ Street.

An Oxford World Classic of *Faust: Part One* pattered against the glass and weaved with the sound of raindrops on the yellow metal of the cab. "I like Goethe."

"That's not any less abstract than Heidegger."

"No," he chuckled, "But at least it's in rhyme," he turned left onto Lexington Ave and then immediately right into East 31ˢᵗ Street.

"Are you formally educated or are you an autodidact?" I was curious what kind of society would allow such a man to drive a cab rather than doing something far more worthwhile with his time.

The car slowed and I saw the hotel sign on the left, "I had a classical education. The rest I learned myself—we're here."

The fare read $45 flat rate because I came from JFK and travelled into Manhattan. He got out and unloaded my bags. I handed him $200. This was not a man who should have to struggle.

"This is too much."

"If anything it's too little my friend. Keep it," it was as if I'd given him the world; his face lit up and he looked up at me almost in shame that he *needed* it and *had* to take it.

He reached into his pocket and gave me a card, "This is my cell phone number. Give me a call anytime and I can come take you wherever you want. My name's Nicholas."

"Patron saint of students..." I had to laugh.

"And repentant thieves," he handed me my bag.

"Then you should pick up fares on Wall Street," I smiled.

"It won't work. They aren't repentant..." rain was caught on his eyelashes and streamed down his cheek.

"That's unfortunate. Thank you for a wonderful drive and conversation Nicholas. I'll call you later today. I need to get here by six," I handed him Johann's card.

He covered the card from the rain, "Hmm. East 74th. Yes of course—"

"Max."

"Of course Max. I can be here to pick you up at 5:15. We might get there early but better than getting there late."

"That's perfect. See you here at 5:15 then."

He nodded and got back into the car, waving out of the window while the rain claimed his forearms as its own.

I waved back and when he disappeared from view made my way to the lobby.

The room wasn't as spacious as I would've hoped but in a population this dense any place than can fit a queen-sized bed is fitted for a king. I figured I'd relax before Nick got here and enjoy a snack at that *Caravaggio* restaurant Johann wrote down on the card. It's down the street from the gallery and the name of the place intrigued me.

I walked down to the lobby and bought the day's *New York Times* and read it on one of the couches. The Arts section had a famous guest cellist with the philharmonic this season. *Chloé Lysettensen will be performing at Lincoln Center late spring. A stoic and beautiful cellist only twenty-seven years of age, she blends Arvo Pärt with her own compositions that have been echoing ethereal sounds all over Europe. She will also be performing various Bach Suites with the philharmonic.* There was a website and phone number for tickets. I'd never heard of her but it sounded like something Laura would've loved.

* * *

It was still raining when Nick got to my hotel as promised but we arrived quite early. He offered to pick me back up once the auction was over but I told him it wouldn't be hard to find a cab on Madison. I walked into Caravaggio and had to wait a couple of minutes to be seated. The décor was wonderful. Donald Baechler paintings of people's faces with bright-red lips in different positions covered the entirety of the back wall. A mural of a big blue flower was painted on some of the faces in the corner.

My waiter was a somewhat young gentleman in his late-twenties to early-thirties and refilled my water twice and brought me a gin and tonic while I made my selection. It was 5:52.

"I'll have the 'Ossobuco di Vitello con Risotto Milanese;' the veal ossobuco with saffron risotto please."

"That's a house favorite sir. Excellent choice," he took my menu and walked away.

I looked around and saw a modern sculpture by Frank Stella; the gin and tonic took hold and I dozed off. There was a tranquil ambiance to the place even though most of the patrons looked to be among the city's elite. It was quiet; the lighting was a perfect complement to the small art collection and the food... well I hadn't tasted the food yet but I was paying $55 for a veal Ossobuco so I expected it to be good.

Johann was a troubled character. How was he supposed to get married and support his fiancé if he didn't respect her? That is a relationship doomed from the beginning and I treaded back and forth on the thought, whether or not to tell his fiancé that he's no good but I didn't want to get involved. What do you do when you know two people don't belong together? Life isn't long enough to love *two* people.

The waiter arrived with my veal shanks, "Your Ossobuco sir."

"Thank you... I love the artwork by the way. Modern and sleek and yet classical at the same time."

"The owners sir, the Bruno brothers, believe both the body and soul must be nurtured. They believe in the soul's training through art, the wisdom of their ancestors from Salerno in Southern Italy."

"That is beautiful. Please extend my compliments."

"Will do sir. We recently acquired four original Henri Matisse stencil lithographs that hang in the private dining room. Perhaps you'd like to see them after your meal?"

"If there is time I would love to."

"Very well sir," his posture was firm while he walked away.

The veal shanks were delicious, steamed in the aroma of white wine and tasty Italian vegetables. Not only was it worth its price in food, the experience itself, the art and the conversation with my waiter Murphy made me feel as if I wasn't paying enough. Manhattan before dusk was magic. It was 6:25. I rushed my last two bites and couldn't enjoy its taste. I put $100 in an envelope and caught Murphy walking by, "Here Murphy, I'll come look at the Matisse lithographs some other time. I have to get to the auction next door."

"Not a problem sir," he looked inside the envelope, "Give me a moment and I'll bring your change."

"That's for you and the chef my friend," I had trouble getting up from the table until I grabbed my walking stick from beside the table leg. Father Time was catching up with me and I was in no shape to outrun him.

"This is too much sir…"

"Call me Max."

"Max I can't take this."

"Nonsense. I had a gin and tonic too. I'll be back to look at the Matisse pieces. I've got to get next door," 6:29.

"You're going next door? To Kaashibys? Don't buy anything Max. They'll take you to the cleaners."

"Don't worry my friend. I'm meeting acquaintances and checking out the gallery," I walked towards the door and he followed me.

"Bye Max."

"I love the color and the lighting… pass that on to the decorator or the owner or whoever is responsible for it."

"You look like an artist Max. You talk like one too."

"I wish Murphy. I'm an art professor. Much worse."

"Do come back. I'd love to talk with you about the Matisse stuff… I don't want to keep you right now."

6:33, "I certainly will."

I hobbled towards the door as the maître d' bid me *ciao*. The restaurant was across the Whitney Museum of Art. I planned to head there the next time I ate there and converse with Murphy about the Matisse pieces.

No one guarded the entrance of Kaashibys. A man in a grey Brooks Brothers suit guided me to *Canvas*.

"The auction starts at seven sir. Would you like a number?"

"No," I was relieved that Johann had given me an earlier time; I wasn't late. I looked at the smiling shirt collars and the backs of people's head in hopes I'd recognize the one I'd seen twice before.

I saw a young man in a white Givenchy sweatshirt with black floral patterns on it turn to the redhead beside him and ask if "he could be trusted." The hidden squeak of his voice to make his tenor sound deeper than it actually was moved me towards him.

"Johann?"

He turned and looked at me up and down, "Nah gramps," it wasn't him.

"MAXI!" a whisper shouted from the opposite side of the room. I glanced over and saw Johann waving. "Over here Maxi!"

I walked around so I wouldn't have to walk through people's knees and approached him.

They had the four seats closest to the aisle; mine was presumably saved beside a wiry gentleman sitting beside a young blonde woman whose hands rested on her crossed lap. Johann's black Brioni suede-color wool polo long sleeve rubbed against my forearm and its softness was something to be desired.

"This is Alfhild," he pointed to the blonde and she stood up and straightened her Bottega Veneta crepe dress.

"Pleasure," her slender hand slipped into mine with ease and her cobalt-blue eyes seemed to puncture my body to the bare soul. Her eyes reminded me of Laura and I felt myself getting nauseous.

"We met on the plane babe!" Johann tried to whisper.

"Aren't you glad that you flew commercial then?" she joked. It took twenty seconds but now I *knew* he didn't deserve her. The man standing to Alfhild's left stood like a sculpture. His eyes fixed on a point on her forearm. His broad shoulders connected to a slim but strong chest that connected to a narrow waist and deer legs.

Johann rolled his eyes, "Don't even… get me started."

The other man had now fixed his gaze on Johann and for all his charm Johann purposefully averted his eyes. I looked up into them for one second and I understood why.

"Max."

"It's nice to meet you Max."

"Alfhild. That's a rather unique name."

"It's *weird*," Johann chirped from behind me.

Her faint smile accepted and tolerated him. She was reserved enough to be a baroque painting. With easy elegance she turned to the man standing beside her… and that is how I met

"Michelangelo Eycsüp," it was *his* voice Johann had been trying to emulate, and his handshake was as sure as his voice.

"Max."

"It's a pleasure."

"The pleasure, I'm sure, is all mine," it was getting progressively more difficult to repress the angst in my eyes.

"Michel is an artist," Alfhild stepped back towards her seat.

"And Max is an art *professor*," Johann chuckled and sat down.

"We must have quite a bit to talk about then," Max nodded to me.

"Yes."

I wondered what kind of a personality I'd have to be to meet a stranger twice my senior on a plane and just invite them to where I'm going. How do these people understand these social conventions so well? How do they interact with each other with such ease? How do I learn them?

A man in a Burberry slim-fit cotton suit stepped up to the podium and introduced himself as Martin Lourell, auctioneer and bid caller.

"Wolfe stayed in Málaga by the way. We were at this event at the CAC Museum of Modern Art and he heard there was a museum of wine and couldn't resist."

"*You?* ... Went to a museum willingly?" Alfhild didn't believe a word of it.

Silence reigned for a few minutes until it was too much to bear.

"I thought *that* was you," Max leaned behind Alfhild and I to get Johann's attention, and pointed his amber eyelashes to the man sitting next to a redheaded hipster on the opposite side of the room.

"Who?" Johann leaned forward.

"That guy, with the floral shirt. Beside the redhead."

"*Him?*" Johann covertly pointed with his pinky.

"Yes."

"Maxi, that's the Winking Bull."

"What's a Winking Bull?"

"Let's switch seats Max," I stood up to help him get closer to Johann.

"I need to sit beside Michel," Alfhild switched with him again. Everyone was happy except Johann. This made *me* happy momentarily but when the second passed I realized how petty and childish we men were in the presence of beguiling women.

I peered my ear to listen to Johann's anecdote about the Bull.

"That's a peculiar name for an art dealer," Alfhild whispered in my ear and handed me paddle number 9 from under Max's seat.

"The Winking Bull is vicious. He used to be a boxer. Golden Gloves," and he mocked a one-two combination in his fancy polo. "He was favorite to be the middleweight but wouldn't take a dive and then his dad died so he just retired."

"What's a boxer doing here?" Max asked.

"He came into a truckload of money from his father's inheritance and his wife suggested he invest in art so now he's the biggest art dealer on this side of the Mississippi."

"There was an article in the *Times* that debunked art as a viable investment."

"Try telling *him* that. ... Besides, anything rich people do that pays off is evidence of their brilliant business acumen, anything he does that fails was his accountant and adviser's fault."

He was trying to make it seem as if he were not one of them.

"So his nickname comes from back in his days when he was a boxer?" Max asked again.

"In a way. He always buys up the pieces quickly. I used to never call him the Bull, but once I was walking, well no, I was being driven in front of this bar in Brooklyn and I saw him take out two guys who were hassling his now-wife, then-mistress. 'Blink and you'll miss it.' Same thing with the paintings."

"If he buys up all the paintings quickly, doesn't that mean he also overpays for them?"

"The wealthy never overpay for anything, they simply make an overzealous investment," I said and Alfhild chuckled.

"Don't make me any *overzealous investments* Michel," she touched my forearm.

"You won't pay a penny over what an item is worth."

"Hello everyone," Martin started. "We are ready for lot number 22C: a beautiful oil painting of a sunset by Alexander Graudet. The starting bid will be $750."

"I don't like sunset or sunrise landscapes," Alfhild tapped the paddle in my hand.

It took me a second to process what she said. I was watching everyone else but her in the room trying to get a read on the bidders and the hired hands like me. Who was listening to whom, who was his own master, so on and so forth. "Three four."

"What?"

"We have 1200 here, do we have 1300? 1300 on the phone," Martin pointed to one of the Asian ladies nodding and/or shaking her hand on the left side of the room.

There were proxy and phone bidders too, "We could've done this over the phone?"

"I want to see what I'm buying Michel."

"I agree. I meant to better understand our competition and our enemy."

"Don't take it so seriously. So what if we don't get the ones we want," she was so reserved I had trouble understanding the actual words that came out of her mouth and had to look for the slightest disturbance of her body language to get a read.

By the time I turned back to Martin the bid was at 3200.

"3200 going once... twice,"

Paddle number 3 went up.

"3400 here. 3400. Do we have 3500?" I looked around the room. A man wanted to bet but his wife held his bicep.

The hammer came down. "Sold. $3400 to the gentleman here," he pointed to the Winking Bull.

"Three... four?" Alfhild slapped my shoulder.

"It almost seems like I know what I'm talking about," a rare joke but I really *was* impressed with myself. I couldn't believe people paid this much money to own a canvas with paint thrown all over it.

"Yeah... *almost*," Johann cackled.

Max looked at me and nodded. I shrugged my shoulders and returned his nod.

Time passed, a collection of three prints and a reproduction by some unknown post-modern artist sold for $5500 and $3900 respectively.

A beautiful reproduction of Degas was displayed through the LCD screen behind Martin. Alfhild tapped me on the shoulder.

"Anything over six is robbery *Hild*."

"Okay."

"Up next is lot 3612D, a reproduction of Degas's *Two Dancers at Rest*. An expert oil painter used Degas's own methods to mix the colors that produced this piece. I'd like to stress that this is not an original Degas. Bidding starts at $4500."

As soon as he finished talking the Bull's paddle shot up. Let's play.

I nodded to Martin.

"4600. 4600. 4600. 4700. 4700. 48. We have 48 to the gentleman in the back," he pointed to me. The Bull looked back and our eyes briefly met before his paddle went up again.

"$4900. 4900. Any more sir?" Martin asked me.

I nodded.

"$5000. 5000."

"$5100. 5100 over here to my right."

"$57-hundred," I said towards Martin.

"$5700 to the man sitting in the back there. 5700. 5700. Going once... once... twice..."

Alfhild clutched my bicep.

"10 grand," the Bull blurted out. There was an odd satisfaction in knowing he overpaid for this. I'd have any piece I wanted after this.

"We have to let this one go Hild, but after this you'll have any painting you want. You're not attached to this particular painting are you?"

"No. I just like the yellow."

"Yes. The yellow looks almost like the original. The paint mixing was very precise," Max chimed in.

"I like the blue lines," Johann was feeling left out.

"$10, 000. 10 thousand. Sir?" he looked at me.

"No."

The hammer came down, "Sold again, to the gentleman to my right for ten thousand dollars." He took a sip of water from the glass beside him on the podium, "Ladies and gentlemen, we've now been at it for an hour, let's take a short break and return in 25 minutes."

I needed to destroy my lungs and breathe in polluted air. I put the paddle on my chair and weaved my way to the back of the place. A set of patio doors framed with glossy beige ornaments opened to a small gardenesque area. There were no birds singing, no wind caught in the leaves of the trees. There was perpetual honking and an endless stream of sirens in the background of the city. The lights of the Empire State Building shined though the landscape.

I'd just lit my cigarillo and began to sketch Alfhild's figure in my mind, fiddling with her ring on my left middle finger when I heard the snorting of a bull behind me, "I can't stand people who smoke," he stepped towards me. The cigar smoke filled the air and meshed with the slight drizzle just over the deck, the wood we were standing on darkened on the edges by the water.

I shook my head in disdain, "I can't stand people who disturb me while I'm smoking."

"Put it out," he demanded.

There would be no appeasing his demand, least of all appeasing a buffoon with too much money in his hands and not enough time in his head.

"Hey! I'm talking to you hotshot. Walking in here..." he moved closer and I took my fingers off my cigarillo and laid it dormant on my lips, "Thinking you run the joint. Passing judgment on others on who's an idiot and who's getting robbed," he must've heard me talk about the value of the Degas reproduction.

"Would it not be cool irony... if we fought over impressionist art? Is that the proper use of *irony*, of the word *ironic*?" I looked at him and he was flaring like a cartoon character bent on falling after he's gone over the edge, "Perhaps you wouldn't know."

"Get out of here jerkoff. I don't want to see you in there when we go back. Got it Nine?"

"I'm going to finish this smoke and then go inside and buy some useless reproductions. Maybe somewhere in between there I'll make you really feel like a Three. Don't push your space or your time will disappear to the brink of nothingness."

"What the hell are you saying? I'll tell you what hotshot. I'll give you the first punch. Go ahead. Jab. Haymaker. Hook. Whatever you want," he put his hands down and puffed his chest like a gorilla.

I looked at him carefully and knew he was overconfident; Ali was one of a kind, to be able to talk smack and back it up comes only so often that 99% of the time it's a bluff. With this guy, it was all stories, he thinks he's faster than he actually is because everyone's always talking about how fast he is. He probably doesn't even train as much as he did when he was contesting the Golden Gloves because now he thinks he's just naturally fast and doesn't need to train. I puffed the cigar on my lip and looked him dead in the eye.

People were starting to settle down and taking their seats inside. I looked through my peripheral to make sure Alfhild couldn't see me but I secretly wanted her to, to be able to say *Can Johann do this for you?*

"So are you gonna hit me or—"

He must've blinked because the story Johann told turned out to be a myth. My fist connected so squarely and perfectly that he hobbled back and all 6'4 of him fumbled over the beige ornamental railing of the deck and onto the AstroTurf garden grass. His howling resembled more a wet puppy than a resolute bull. I wasn't ready to head in just yet, not until my cigar had burned the knot in my heart away.

I stared him down as he fumbled back to his feet and walked all the way around while holding his face. I walked in once everyone had settled down in their seats a couple of minutes later and saw the so-called Bull nursing his face with his wife's handkerchief.

"What the hell happened?" Alfhild asked as soon as I'd sat down.

"I was a better matador than he gave me credit for."

She smiled incredulously. People whispered as Martin stepped up to the podium and everyone seemed to be glancing my way in turns. I took the paddle from *Hild* and thought about writing a verse about her later. The rain harshened and thunder boomed through the windows. The *shh* sound of raindrops landing on gravel could be heard in silences and was pleasant to those listening to absent sounds of nature in the concrete jungle.

"Next up is a beautiful reproduction of '*Sunset, Deer, and River,*' by Albert Bierstadt. Circa 1868."

The yellow of the sun immediately jumped out as near identical to the actual painting. Alfhild squeezed my forearm and my paddle went up in reflex. I beat out a sentimental old man taking his cues from his wife and purchased the painting for $450 less than it was actually worth.

Nothing interested us until the last lot. '*By the River of Tuonela, study for the Jusélius Mausoleum frescos,*' by Akseli Gallen-Kallela. Circa 1903. I had to beat out the Bull and paid $100 more than the reproduction was worth, but with the 450 we saved on the Bierstadt, we were still 350 up.

* * *

I was in the gallery after the auction had ended, waiting for Alfhild to work out the logistics of my purchases on her behalf. Johann and Max were a little way down the hall looking at modern sculptures on display.

"What date is it today?" Alfhild asked in the other room.

"May 19th Madame," a voice returned.

"Thanks."

I stopped in front of Kandinsky's *'The Singer,'* on loan from the Guggenheim; thunder clapped outside and the lights flickered. A man entered, "The storm seems to be affecting our electricity. Please bear with us."

The contrast called to me. The brushstrokes were meticulous and the color, what would *I* know about the color? I hovered into the painting and sat at the piano. Outside, rain flooded the alley, a woman covered her hair and a kid sprinted by her towards shelter. A deli owner down at the end of the street swept the front of his entrance. It was a cleansing rain.

"You have that look in your eye," Alfhild's voice was as divine as the rain.

I came out of the painting, "What look?" I thought I heard a pop just as thunder shook the ground and lighting lit up the black sky.

"I don't know. What were you looking at?"

I pointed to the woman in the painting, "Who do you think she is?"

She looked at the description, "Hmmm, the singer? It says so right here."

I left her words lingering with the sound of rain knocking on the window. Max was inspecting a half-finished vase and looked at it with scorn.

"Maybe it's his muse."

"Maybe," I answered.

"You're an artist," she turned away from the canvas towards me, "Do *you* have a muse?"

"No. That would be a feeble abstraction."

"Don't artists need one? To inspire themselves I mean."

"Did you know Kierkegaard was engaged once?" I changed the subject.

"Who?"

"The existentialist. He was a Dane too. He was engaged to a woman named Regina Olsen."

"Nice switch. Why are we talking about some Danish existentialist?"

"You don't understand. He was *engaged*," I moved closer to the painting, "Do you know what that means to an existentialist? It means he not only reconciled the nature of his *own* self, but he united it with *another* self external to his own."

"How'd he do that?" she moved beside me and watched me stare into the eyes of the singer.

"He didn't. They broke off the engagement because marriage and social obligations are illusions in aberrant consciousness. We abide by them to give meaning to meaninglessness, to—" and when I looked back she was gone... shaking her head at a copper bowl on the opposite side of the room.

"I should get going," Max said to Johann as I approached.

"Why?" Johann looked up from his Cosmos 6 tablet.

"I want to go to Lincoln Center. A famous cellist is playing tonight. ... Chloé Lyst... Lystt... Damn it my memory's not what it used to be. She was in the paper."

Alfhild walked over from the bowls, "Lysettensen?"

"Yes that's it!"

"I went to school with her. We'd love to go too. Michelangelo!" she called over to me.

"Yes?" I walked up to them. Johann mirrored my posture.

"Would you care to join us at Lincoln Center tonight? Chloé Lysettensen will be accompanied by the New York philharmonic."

"I'd love to."

Lights flickered again, Max said, "I don't have a ticket."

"Don't be ridiculous," Alfhild reached into her purse and out came her American Express Black Edition. She flipped it and dialed the number on the back. One phone call from her uPhone and we had front row mezzanine seats.

We heard a couple of people whispering in the other room and I eyed Max staring at the wall trying to listen to their conversation. A man wearing a white headset came up to us, "I'm sorry I don't want to disturb you but the gallery will be closing early tonight due to the electrical fuses shorting; the storm's affected us more than we'd like."

"Pffft," Johann snorted, "We were leaving anyway."

Alfhild made another call to her driver; after we'd dropped Max off at his hotel, Manhattan NYC, we got into the Plaza and I went up to my room.

I watched the rain douse the lights of Times Square in the distance and the changing colors of the Empire State building.

Someone knocked on my door while I was shaving.

"Yes?"

It was a bellhop with a suit cover, "This is to be delivered to you sir," he rolled the cart into the room and hung the cover in the empty closet.

"I didn't order anything."

"No sir. This is with compliments of Madame Baldure," he reached on the carpet panel of the cart and put a shoebox under the tuxedo.

Wind knocked on the window outside. I put some money in his hand and continued shaving. For some reason she'd angered me. I couldn't fathom the hubris. How could she assume I didn't have my own tux? This thought was followed by the idea that even if I did have my own tux, it somehow couldn't have been up to her standards. I cut myself with the razor. With a blood drop idling on my chin and rain fighting to crack my window I opened my sketchbook and outlined her figure in the clouds, above the rain and basking in the luminosity of the sun. She had no time or patience for mere mortals, for men full of flaws and empty pockets.

A waiter in a tailcoat tried to outrun the rain on Madison and nearly slipped on the stairs heading down into the subway.

My phone beeped. "Hello?"

"Michelangelo. Are you ready?"

"Just about. Thanks for the tux."

"You're most welcome. Meet in the lobby or the bar whenever you're ready. Johann and I are heading down there now."

"See you soon."

I walked to the closet. A black Brioni Waldorf wool-jacquard tuxedo and a Gucci white cotton shirt came out of the cover. I laid them on the bed and opened the shoebox. Church's. A brand-new pair of New York leather brogues sat in dust bags accompanied by a black Lanvin silk bow-tie and a Kingsman silk pocket square.

The tuxedo and shirt were tailored. The shoes fit as if she'd had a mold of my feet. How did she know my measurements? How was this even possible? I looked at myself in the mirror and agonized over the lack of my material success. Could they be right, the wealthy? Could material comfort be worth the price of everything that mustn't be valued? I felt dirty. It was rare for someone to wear a fancy suit and not have bought it with blood money.

Alfhild and Johann were seated in the center of the bar.

"Whoa. You're looking handsome," Alfhild sipped on her gin.

"You don't look too bad there hotshot. I heard what happened at the gallery. With the Bull that is."

"News travels quick."

"This is Manhattan baby!"

"You want to get a drink?"

"Espresso please," I whispered to a passing waiter.

"Do you drink anything other than espressos?" Alfhild played with the brim of her tumbler.

"Sometimes... water," a waiter pulled out my chair and I sat down.

She roared with laugher. I looked at Johann and peered through his empty eyes. Dragon slayer and knight he was, a regular rescuer of damsels... it was his job to look after her and make sure she didn't get drunk, didn't go past her limit just as much as it's her job to take care of him the same way. Somehow no relationship is ever equal. The lover always seems to lose out to the beloved. Even the thought of someone, *anyone*, let alone Hild, loving Johann nearly made me puke.

"By the way babe, Max called while you were in the shower. He said he'll meet us there so we don't have to pick him up."

"Okay, so we have lots of time!" she swayed a bit.

I tapped Johann's arm in vain hopes of getting him to circle around so she'd have a shoulder to lean on. His eyes fixed on Alfhild's ring on my finger.

"Why are *you* wearing *her* ring?" he growled.

She giggled, "Damn the green lights on Madison Ave. Three minutes. Three damn minutes and it would've been mine."

"Three minutes. Two minutes. No minutes. There is no such thing as time," I looked into her eyes heavy and curtained by the gin.

"What? Madison? What would've been yours?" Johann moved closer to me and his foot under the chair cut off my calf.

"I bet him my ring how long it'd take us to get into town from the airport and he won."

"You bet *him*," Johann talked as if I wasn't there and I wasn't. I was there and I wasn't. I was nowhere and everywhere at the same time. Space is not physicality. "I thought that was *our* thing!"

A waiter passed us and Johann grabbed his forearm, "Green tea!"

What an appropriate color.

"I'll have an espresso as well, but with sugar," Hild's manicured nails flashed in the candlelight.

"Have some tea babe!"

"I don't like tea. I want an espresso."

I did not like where this was going to end up.

* * *

"How was Málaga?" a uniform officer asked Britten as he brushed by, "I heard Alicia was there too," and he raised an eyebrow and winked at Britten.

Britten had read a story in the *Times* about some thug who'd killed a nineteen-year-old over a PlayStation and then drove away. Even though that wasn't his case he wasn't in the mood for small talk.

"The locals didn't want us there, but an American dead anywhere is more important than anyone dead anywhere else."

A cop conversed with an employee in a suit while Britten approached Alicia facing away from him.

"Afternoon Alicia," he walked around her towards the body with a gunshot wound in the temple and a .32 grappled in his hand.

"I miss Spain," she frowned.

"So do I…. Tell me about Kaashibys."

"It's an auction house. They have their own little gallery near the main auction room..."

"Yeah I saw it when I walked by. Witnesses?"

"No, the employees said there was a group in the gallery and a woman finalizing the purchase of some pieces from the auction today. The storm masked the sound of the gunshot. When," she flipped through a notebook, "The dealer's assistant walked in with his supper he noticed the victim just like this. They told everyone to leave and called us."

"Who was here?"

"... There's a list," she flipped through her notes, "Estate of Alfhild Baldure plus three."

"Who were the pluses?"

"They don't know. But one of the guys was apparently a real outlier. He made the bets for her, and... give me a second," she went back and forth with her notes as Britten looked around, "Martin Lourell, the auctioneer, said he made some smart bids and hardly overpaid their reserve price."

"What does that mean?"

"Well these kind of things are controlled. Everyone knows each other, this guy marches in a with a group and *doesn't* overpay? Art doesn't work like that... I think. He just said the guy didn't sit well with him but I have a feeling he's not telling me everything."

"Arrange him to see me after I'm done here."

"Okay," she beckoned a uniform officer over and walked towards her.

"The victim's name?"

"Ahti Laukkanen."

"Whatever happened to the Bills and Johns and Rustys? ..." he whispered, "What did he do? His position and his specialty I mean."

"He was an avid art collector. His boss said he dealt mostly with ocean pieces and landscapes from 1800s American art. He'd just lost an appraisal worth... 9 million. Dollars that is."

"Okay."

She whispered something to the uniform officer and the officer nodded and walked away.

"We're thinking of ruling it as a suicide, it's pretty obvious isn't it? He lost a bunch of money."

"The only obvious thing is death."

"Be serious," she closed her notebook.

"The angle's weird," he moved towards the wound and tried to look into it, the eyes of the victim staring at the door behind Britten.

"What angle?"

"The wound," he turned and faced the direction of the victim and looked through his eyes. "What, did he take the gun with his left hand…" he looked at the gun then at the pen on the right side of the desk, "Hmmmm."

"What?"

"… Did he take the gun and point it not *at* his own temple, which would be a sure way to kill yourself based on what you see in movies or read in books, but he points it *towards* his temple," he moved closer to the wound again. "There's also minimal stippling; the gun couldn't have been pressed against his temple or just away from it," the detective moved with purpose while Alice watched him. He was like someone else as he weaved through the papers and evidence to distinguish what was important, "Plus there's the whole pen issue."

"What pen issue?"

"You can only commit suicide once."

"… Okay."

"If you can only do a thing once, wouldn't you want to try your best to succeed?"

"Maybe, depends what it is."

"You've chosen to end your life. I'd think that'd be one of the things."

"Fine, I'll bite."

"His stronger hand is his right hand. Why would *he*, an *art dealer* with little to no experience in firearms I assume from the *angle* which he shot *himself*, use his weaker hand to commit suicide?"

"Maybe he was ambidextrous. That's good logic," Alicia moved towards him.

"No. …" he pointed to items with his stare, "The phone is on the left side; he took messages down with his right. His…" he sniffed a tumbler on the table, "Whiskey is on the right side. His notepad is in the right drawer. Only his cell phone and notes he'd already written and ergo was probably reading were on his left. If he were ambidextrous there'd be more balanced items on both sides."

"Okay, so he used his left hand."

Britten touched the victim's right index finger, "May I?"

Alicia nodded.

"What's this little cut here?" he pointed to the finger. "It looks fresh."

"Maybe with the letter opener or a paper cut?" Alicia picked up the letter opener in the shape of an artist's palette knife.

"No. It looks more like a graze," he imagined Laukkanen putting his hands in front of a shadow "Stop," he probably yelled, and the assailant was smart enough to wait for thunder to strike before he fired.

The bullet grazed his finger and opened a gaping wound on the side of his temple.

The quiet in the room was contagious and the crime scene investigators in the background ceased their trampling and ambient chatter. "Look," Britten mimicked the position and held the gun at the necessary angle for the wound to occur, "Who holds the gun like *this*?"

"You're right. It doesn't make sense."

"So it's a murder then?" a uniform officer standing in the doorway asked.

"It's looking that way."

"YES!!!" he shook his fists towards the sky in excitement.

Britten glared through his badge and pierced his heart.

Another officer handed him a bill but the first officer shook his head *no*.

Britten was walking towards the door when the headlight of a passing car lit up the room for a second and he stopped abruptly. "I feel like we're missing something."

"Here we go..." someone whispered from the doorway, "Watch this."

Save for the sound of his breathing nothing could be heard. "The Tranquil Detective," Alice whispered. His eyes shot open and if it weren't for the flicker of a lamppost outside Britten would've missed it.

"The color of the wood was paler here when the light hit it," he bent down and tilted his neck near the drawer.

"The color of the wood?" Alice moved closer to him.

The Crime Scene Assistance Team, CSAT, crammed in the doorway like schoolboys peering into the girls' shower at summer camp so they could watch Britten work.

He tapped the sharp edge of his badge and flicked it, "Why was the reflection different?" he laid under the table on his back and the CSAT gabbing of Britten's unorthodox methods loudened. He ripped off a piece of tape from under the table and examined it for a second. "Why's it so hidden? ... What's going on here?" he handed the card to Alice, "Let's try and find this guy," his white latex glove snapped off, CSAT clapped.

"You're a celebrity around here," Alice turned the card over.

"I couldn't find a book in a library without you guys."

Her cheeks turned rosy.

He noticed and said, "I want to know why this guy's card was hidden," to alleviate the tension.

Alice averted Britten's ravenous eyes and looked at the business card that was taped under the desk, "Kane... Ventoni. Barrister and Solicitor. There's a different phone number written on here."

"The card was tripled pressed; luxurious."

"He's a lawyer. His life is built on posturing and excess."

Britten chuckled, "That's some serious animosity."

"I've never met a lawyer I've liked," Alice rubbed her fingertips over the card through her glove, "I'll check it for fingerprints as well."

"Thank you."

He walked out and CSAT stood in the doorway and he shook each one of their hands before he made it to the gallery. The same female uniform officer Alicia had been talking to pointed a man in a suit towards Britten and he stopped walking.

"Hello Inspector Britten," the man was tall with an elongated face and a nose tilted to the left and eyes that were so small Britten could hardly see his irises, "I am Martin Lourell."

"Detective," Britten corrected him and shook his hand, "There was something you wanted to tell me?"

"I need your absolute discretion detective. We can't have these stories getting out into the news..."

"Kids are killing themselves over PlayStations and uPhones. No one is going to report the death of an art dealer."

"Please. I must beg you not to release this information to the press."

"I'm investigating the death of your colleague Mr. Lourell, you don't have to worry about me yelling 'Extra, extra' at Times Square."

"Thank you," Martin was relieved.

"My partner said you had some information for me."

Martin pulled Ben to the side and spoke in half-whispers so they wouldn't be overheard.

"First I want it known that I have nothing but respect for Madame Baldure, who herself is a countess, and her family is the last remnant of true artistry perhaps. She is very elegant and lives as if she lives in a romantic painting...."

"Save the disclaimer Martin, please. What did she do?"

"Oh no. It was nothing that she did. There was a man with her, well there were three men with her. One of them I recognize as her boyfriend, he is quite loud and at times obnoxious. The other must've been a family friend or art expert; he was aged but very well mannered and seemed deeply comprehensive of the pieces and their histories. I spoke with him briefly after the auction and before he headed into the gallery. He was pleasant."

After all the disclaimers and fillers, Britten's patience wore thin, "And the last man?"

"He was very odd. His eyes darted left and right as if he didn't believe what he was seeing. I didn't want to look into his direction. I don't want to press charges."

"You can't press charges because some art collector stared at you Martin."

"Oh no. There was an incident in the garden."

"What happened?" Britten's curiosity overruled his impatience.

"Another gentleman, Jack Ardett, was involved with him in... let's say it was an altercation."

"You mean a fight? *Here?* At an art auction? The world has really... I'm sorry I don't mean to interrupt. What happened?" he suppressed his condescension that was sure to follow laughing.

"The other gentleman, the man in Countess Baldure's party, with shoulders like a quarterback and a waist like an underwear model, stepped outside in the rain during the break for a smoke. My security alerted me because we all thought it was odd. I mean it was raining cats and dogs..."

"Wait a minute. Jack *Ardett? The* Jack Ardett? It can't be. What'd they call him?"

"Yes. He used to be a boxer before the unfortunate accident that claimed his parents' life..."

"El Toro? The Blinker? Something like that."

"The Winking Bull detective."

"The Winking Bull! Thank you! It was on the tip of my tongue. My dad and I used to watch his fights. He was good. ... Anyway, what happened?"

"Mister Ardett stepped outside after this other gentleman. I don't know why and I don't know if they knew each other because there seemed to be some animosity. My security guard...," Martin turned towards a man sitting on a chair near the door, "Told me about the possible situation not because of the altercation but to tell the gentleman to come inside for safety reasons."

"Go on," Britten was now taking notes.

"Before I could make my way over there the gentleman had lit up one of those long thin cigars like from the old Sergio Leone films."

"The kind Clint Eastwood smokes in *the Good, the Bad, and the Ugly.*"

"Yes. Mister Ardett was motioning and trying to get closer to the man. I don't know what they were talking about but before security could make their way over he'd punched Mister Ardett in the face and Mister Ardett had fallen over the railing and into the garden. The gentleman stayed out there and finished his cigar and then came back inside."

"Wait wait wait. Go back. He knocked Ardett down?"

"Yes sir."

"You're telling me he knocked down the Golden Gloves champion with *one* punch?"

"Yes."

"The Winking Bull?"

"Yes sir. I am not fabricating this."

"I apologize. I believe you. Go on."

"Security consulted with me and we spoke with Mister Ardett. He wanted to let it go and not inform the police. And since he was part of Countess Baldure's party, he was betting with her paddle you see, we saw it best not to act. I spoke with Countess Baldure after the auction when she was paying for the pieces she'd purchased and she assured me he must've thought he was in danger."

"What was his name?"

"I'm afraid I don't know. But he is with Countess Baldure and in her contact form she filled out the Plaza Hotel as her address."

"They're together? I thought you said she had a boyfriend."

"No detective, they're not together. Please do not misunderstand. I meant that he was part of her party and was staying at the same hotel as her."

"Who knows if that means anything nowadays anyway...? Thank you for your help Mister Lourell."

"You're welcome detective. Countess Baldure is a swell lady. Please exercise discretion."

Do these suits know any other words? "Of course, one more thing. Can you describe the guy?"

Lourell gave Britten the best description of Michel he could and vowed that he could identity the man again if he saw him.

"What'd he say?" Alicia caught Britten on his way out.

"There's a lead. We're going to the Plaza Hotel."

"Fancy! Let's have a drink after."

"This isn't Spain Alicia. We're on the clock."

"Even after we've clocked out?"

Britten found her interesting, "Fine. We'll have some beers when we're off the clock at the Plaza."

XVI
MASTER OF MUSIC

We had the best seats in the house, seats 106-109 in row AA. You can't really experience music unless you're front row center of the mezzanine. The suit itched my nape and the leather tightened and then loosened around my feet. With a mere swipe of her Black American Express, she'd bought my soul. At what price do we surrender the very things that make us human?

The audience clapped when a beautiful ebony colored man in a Prada tuxedo sat at the piano and began tuning it by playing the first few notes of various Bach Concertos. I could hear the rain outside and it sounded like the roof would cave in to a flood any minute.

Lights lit up the orchestra and the audience clapped again. The lights focused on an empty chair in the center of the stage and after a few seconds a blonde hovering in a light pink dress sat down and took the cello beside her. The stage light reflected off her lips, a shade of red as if dampened by a vintage wine while at the same time pale as if she'd just kissed a ghost.

She tuned her cello. The color of the maple wood looked like a 1700s Stradivarius with a herringbone purfling with an apex at the bottom that looked like it was added later. It looked like it was crafted as a violin cello and had been lengthened at some point.

"What kind of cello is that? Do you know?" I whispered to Alfhild while the cellist positioned herself on her chair.

"The cello?"

"Yes."

"Are you joking?"

"No."

"... I think she said it's a Stradivarius," she leaned towards me.

"What year?"

"She told me once. I think it's a 1709. The Boccherini... Romberg I think. Don't quote me. It was recut and lengthened around 1790 or 1789 probably because there was a debate about what the ideal size of a cello should be. She used to talk about it all the time."

"It's a violin-cello?"

"I think so..." she turned to me, "How do you know so much about cellos?"

"Art is my quarter."

"I thought you were a painter."

"All art is the same isn't it? A Stradivarius. The night sky. The Sculpture of *David*. Vivaldi's *Four Seasons*. Everything exists at once."

The conductor's hand twitched and Arvo Pärt's second movement of *Tabula Rasa*: *Silentium*, started to play with an arpeggiated D minor

89

second inversion chord from the piano as the cellist's bow moved left and right in drifting waves like the calm before a storm on a ship aboard the sea. Different sets of instruments, first violins and second violins, then violas began in different rhythmic speeds. The cellist's position gradually replaced the solo violins. She moved at the slowest rhythmic speeds and began a downward descent of a D minor four-octave scale once she reached the span.

Johann yawned lackadaisically and looked around before he pulled out his tablet. He turned the brightness down and started looking at muted comedy clips, suppressing his laughter each time the video changed.

"Come on Johann. Turn that off," Max nudged him.

I closed my eyes and floated to the roof. City lights flickered like diamonds on black silk. The stars danced behind the storm clouds waiting for their fifteen minutes of fame in this dead city. Under the clouds I saw her, this cellist of magnificent proportions with her hair parted to one side. I have to paint this figure. I have to *know* every orifice of this form. She rose further above me and every movement of the bow sent her higher until I could no longer keep up. I idled under the raindrops as she parted the clouds and transcended the sky to the stillness of life outside earth.

My eyes opened by themselves and my ears listened to the applause. Seconds later the clouds parted again and in the light she glided into herself, standing and bowing with bloodshot and teary eyes. The pianist's athletic frame walked up behind her and tapped her on the shoulder. The stage and my heart both darkened when they left, then the lights went off and chatter immediately started among the audience. The house lights turned on and people got up to leave.

"There's a reception at her hotel in an hour; I have an invite if you'd care to join," I think it was Alfhild's voice talking.

How could someone play as if it was airy magic in each breath? How could they be so beautiful? Are people like this human? I was in shock and awe. Awed in the classical sense… that of a divine belief or a miracle stirring deep within the lamenting of my soul, and shocked that such a being had been allowed to enter this world and live in it. As long as she was here, heaven wasn't perfect. I could believe such things now. Now… then, when. A clock started ticking. Time… existed, and my life ticked away meaning every second I wasn't in her presence.

"…"

"MICHELANGELO!" Alfhild squeezed my hand.

"Yes," the blood rushed from my heart to my brain.

"You really do live in another realm don't you?"

"What was that you said about a hotel?" for a second I had trouble breathing.

"There's a reception at her hotel in an hour. I was thinking of dropping in and extending my compliments. I assume you'll be joining."

"Yes of course," my face betrayed no emotion but I could not believe my luck; I would actually get to *meet* this bender of space and time? ... This master of the physical bordering on becoming an abstract?

She was staying at the Four Seasons. In the car I felt inadequate and thought about what I should say when I met... "What's her name Hild?"

"Chloé."

Thinking about meeting Chloé, I kept fiddling with my bow tie until I caved and asked Hild "How's my bow tie?"

She crossed her hands and said in a low-tone, "You... care... how... your bow tie looks?" then as if a realization flashed across her face, "You're smitten!"

I said nothing and the sound of thunder filled the silence, the roof of the car sang in verses while the clouds cried.

I felt like the first time I saw Mædeleine. Nothing mattered. There'd been no life before that moment and no death to follow. There was mere existence. Was this what poets write about when they speak of love? It couldn't be; love must be timeless. It must be abstract and immaterial. How easy and absurd if it were not and people could just fall in love. To not be in love one moment but be completely altered and turned into a different person. To have different movements, thoughts, and feelings in one second. It didn't make sense physically, immaterially, unless love *was* timeless. How else would this transition occur so abruptly and without any warning? Like a sudden death followed by instant rebirth. How could something ingrained in timed physicality, the self of a person perceiving the self of another from the outside, be weaved with an eternal eloquence so unjustly sudden?

I hadn't noticed that we'd turned into East 57th Street. The G63 AMG blocked off the traffic behind us; we stepped out of the glorified matchbox and we made our way to the Function Room of the Four Seasons. I felt for my sketchbook and found myself calmed when I touched it through my inside jacket pocket as if I expected it to be gone.

Inside, I couldn't find Chloé.

* * *

"Past a certain point a man shouldn't be alone. He starts thinking, especially if he's smart; the intelligent have it the worst. They become destructive to everyone around them. They destroy themselves and their routines and then nothing gets done."

"You seem to admire him Wolfe," Johann slurped his martini.

"That day at the Four Seasons, remember? I'd just flown in. You sent me a text to meet you guys there and I got there late."

"Yeah… and you walked up to Wes and I discussing equity returns and investing in art I think…"

"He made you look like a fool too but we'll get to that. Remember when he was in her proximity? You and Alfhild tried to get his attention but it seemed like he was in a trance. Nothing moved him."

"So what? He was nervous talking to a pretty girl. He's not dominant like us," Johann nodded.

Elroy scoffed, "You asked *me* Johann, this is exactly what I'm talking about. It's not about him being this or being that. Don't confuse being *nervous* with something extraordinary and then accepting the moment as extraordinary. These are two different things."

"Give me a break Wolfe, this is unlike you."

"That's why we called him *the Surgeon*, why do you think you and Alfhild couldn't get his attention? He wasn't ignoring you. He lasers in on things and can remain calm even in the most turbulent situations. It has nothing to do with him being a field surgeon in the war, it's because of this resolute calm, of his ability to focus in on something and then make the proper adjustments to achieve it. Like a surgeon who in a span of minutes has to put someone back together and the slightest error can mean death."

* * *

"Wolfe's coming."

"What?" Hild asked Johann while he tried to catch the attention of a waiter holding a tray of drinks.

"He just texted me. He just got in. I told him to meet us here."

"Okay," she scanned the crowd and tapped my arm in the direction of blonde strands under the ballroom lights maneuvering through the people.

All my life I'd been a mere observer. This was the sacrifice the life of an artist demands. I observed life but I never lived. No one really lives. Not even artists. We cultivate masks of identity that shelter from those that wear literal masks of identity i.e. online profiles riddled with inconsistencies and a classlessness hedged by wealth where public and private lives are compartmentalized. Artists hide their identities in the brushstrokes of their paintings, the verses in their cantos, and the sentences in their novels. The true face of an artist is never on his face and this is what he prefers. Others misunderstand this displaced melancholy with an absence of melancholy. They think that all artists, especially the geniuses of creation, are happy go-lucky people who idle through life by splashing ink on canvases and fiddling words on pages. But there is not and has never been a single happy genius in all the realms of the universe. No space occupied anywhere nor time whence that a genius was jubilant to be face to face with a universal truth or a personification of an abstract.

I'd watched others converse, exchange gifts, connect with each other in kindness and cruelty, and even fall in love. The best I could do was sketch the scene or depict it on a canvas but that wasn't living. Living isn't simply breathing. There has to be a glance somewhere, some feat of recognition from someone else, and in this recognition by another can the self truly exist; the lonely are lonely because they are disconnected even from themselves. They don't live. They *can't* live. They're already dead. They're living, breathing, observers that died the instant they were born. I no longer wanted to be one of them.

Chatter filled the room. The idiots lamented about the playoff hopes of the Knicks or the Rangers while the intelligent damned their friends and the weather. It was only the quasi-intellectuals who had anything worthwhile to say: the stock prices of the day and bank prime rates.

"Latet anguis in herba."

"What was that?" Hild waved to Chloé in the distance.

"It's Latin. *A snake lurks in the grass.*"

"Did you say it?"

"No. It's Virgil. Book III of the Eclogues."

"Who's the snake?"

"I think here Contessina, it would be wiser to point out which people are *not* snakes in order to save time…"

"Can you really *save* time?"

I looked at her, "I need a smoke," and left to smoke a cigar. For all I know I'd been wrong about her. She could've been a snake too. Royal people or descendants of royalty only care about their subjects if they have something to say about the benefits of being subjugated. Royalty only cares about those under them if they see a benefit in the slave labour or soldiering of their people. They'll only acknowledge the importance of the average citizen if they need something purchased to make themselves richer or if they need blood spilled in honor of the country they're running in their own name.

On my way to the patio doors I heard Johann babbling with a Wall St. banker who didn't know what to do with all the money he'd weaseled out of the wrinkled palms of laborers; so he collected artistic reproductions as a hobby. Johann's ecstatic disposition during the encounter irked me while I tried not to listen to their conversation.

He was the most conventional born-into-riches schoolboy. Charming and comedic when it was profitable to his image but unbearable, bigoted, and elitist when the necessity of charm burned out.

Born-into-riches schoolboys are rarely charming by nature. They are these things pursuant to cold calculation as though such qualities originate out of a need to impress and arrive on command. When circumstance requires the need to be funny or unique or boring or optimistic, an instant mask is cultivated out of the fantastical whim of their soullessness. This fantasy, unbelievable and paranoid when externally viewed, erects out of a Kantian dogma of accepted and trivialized interactions meant to increase prestige or wealth. The natural born-into-riches schoolboy is a philistine of pseudo-intellection and quasi-intelligence, housing a quaint library in his manor but never having cracked the spine of a single book. In short, their true faces are insufferable and dull. He revolted me. I think only morons and women fascinated by wealth and affluence were attracted to these disgusting beings on two legs. Even a half-intelligent man or woman will immediately notice and refuse to put up with such blind adulations of preconceived dogmas or feigned optimism, charisma, and idol-worship of money as God. Unfortunately, intelligence, even half of it, was benign in the realm of postmodern society. The born-into-riches reigned supreme over the hoping-to-be-born-into-riches-one-day and the rich-posterior-but-pretending-to-have-been-born-into-it.

"He's trying to be an artist," Johann pointed to me as I walked by and tried to get me to stop.

I had no interest in listening to them talk about the benevolence of the invisible hand, "I must depart for a cigar," and continued towards the patio.

Johann exchanged a glance with the banker and said, "What'd I tell you?"

And the banker responded, "He sure is as rude as an artist," and it seemed like he actually respected me despite my classless dismissal.

Elroy walked through the lobby near me and I thought what it'd take for me to smoke this damn cigar.

"Eycsüp," he waved towards me.

"Hello Wolfe. How was your flight?"

"Dreadful. Commercial flying really is horrid."

"Yes… it is," I thought about how Hild had corrupted me. Now that I'd ridden in her private jet, driven right up to the runway, and not had my luggage weighed nor my underwear checked; how could I fly commercial again? To go through everything that seemed so useless in comparison; it was a step backwards and if time existed, it only seemed to move forward.

"Are you leaving?" he fixed his pocket square and brushed the rain off his Lanvin leopard jacquard blazer.

"No."

He looked at the door, "It's still raining."

"Yes. I am going out for a smoke."

"You left Alfhild alone?" his tone harshened.

"Do you take me for a savage? Johann is with her."

"From a tiger's gaze to a jackal's touch…" he muttered to himself, "Where are they?"

"Johann was speaking to some banker near one of the paintings on the wall. Alfhild is probably speaking to Chloé."

"The musician? They haven't talked in a while," he started to walk then stopped, "What do you think of her?"

"Of who… Chloé?"

"Yeah…"

"Haven't met her yet."

"You'd like her. Smoke your cigar and join us."

"I intend to," I saw Max chatting with an older lady about the colors in Gauguin's *Van Gogh Painting Sunflowers* and made my way outside.

I lit my cigar and thought about Mædeleine. I've been unlucky in love, and I wondered when I started to believe in luck and in love to attribute such qualities to myself. I always sought the loneliest and most complicated women. Was it a quixotic fumbling in some vain hope of rescuing them? Feminists would have a field day if they knew that's what I thought of love. Mædeleine was the first lady who trained me to take morality out of the equation. Murder, charity, justice; everything was relative. Her father was abusive and the rage he'd exuded over Mædeleine and her mom was petty compared to the fate he suffered at the hands of my sharpened chisel. Catalans in Barcelona think there's a balance in such things: luck, fate, and fútbol wins they thought were the result of divine will. If I had permitted myself these simple beliefs despite the influence of physics and metaphysics I could've been happier. Would happiness abide by this balance too? And were the scales finally turning in my favor? Time… would tell once I was able to perceive it at a precise moment on the quantum plane.

"Here he comes now," Hild pointed to me and Chloé's braided blonde hair with a purple lily twined between the second and third braid twirled in my direction, "He's an artist too!"

"You're too kind Hild. I splash paint on a canvas."

"Pleasure," Chloé was ravishing in every sense of the word, I slipped my hand in hers, "I appreciate your modesty," and she pecked me on the cheek. Her lips were warm against the cold of the storm and her body was tender against my war scars but it was her soul beneath the veil of her pupils that mesmerized me. Could things be this simple? Fall in love with a dame. Meet her. Kiss her. Have her. Everything will be all right. ... I knew better.

"The pleasure is mine," I caught Elroy watching me in my peripheral but he pretended to be indulging Wes and Johann in some profound discussion about the English Premier League.

My eyes squinted in reflex when I looked back at her. There was an aura that surrounded her but it seemed like I was the only one that saw it.

* * *

"DAMN IT," Britten was heard screaming down the hallway before he burst through the glass doors of the pit. "WHO LEAKED THIS?" he held up a copy of *the Times Local Crime* section with enraged cheeks. "Whoever it was. I will find you and I consume your badge at my will," his deep voice resonating past the rain behind the windows.

Alicia got up from her desk and took the paper from his hands, "What is it Ben?"

He looked at all the officers in The Pit of the precinct who averted his eyes with fierce shame, "SOME jackoff with a big mouth told the *Times* we were looking for Ventoni. He's probably gone now! POOF! You think a lawyer would think twice about running like a coward?" he shoved papers off the table in front of him and they swayed and floated before falling to the floor.

"Wait Ben! Calm down," Alicia flipped through the pages, "... Continued on C17," she mumbled, flipping past a spread portrait of Ventoni from his law school alma mater, "It wasn't us. LOOK! Read it!" she threw the paper at him.

He clawed at the paper and mumbled words to himself as he flipped through the article, "FRAUD? THE FRAUD UNIT? ARE YOU JOKING ME?" he threw the paper on the ground and stormed out.

Alicia picked up the paper and another officer came to read it.

Kane Ventoni, well-respected attorney with offices in Manhattan, Amsterdam, and Florence has been disbarred from his practice for embezzling client funds to pay his gambling debts. The Fraud Unit asks anyone with information of his whereabouts or anyone who has done business dealings with Ventoni or his firm: Ventoni, Kalumnia, and Van Couperville. He had planned to campaign for mayor in the coming election... he has failed to appear for his disbarment hearing and his family and friends are left wondering where he's currently staying...

"So much for cooperation between departments," the officer said to Alicia.

"Could've gone both ways; we didn't tell them he was a person of interest either. ... I wonder where he is now..."

The officer traced the word *gambling debts* with her index finger, "Probably in hiding. Illegal gambling houses are run by some unsavory characters."

* * *

I laid my clothes down on the bed and walked to the window for a smoke. The city idled beneath my feet. The rain soothed my skin through my ribbed tank top and the smoke was pleasant on my lungs. I thought about Chloé and imagined her behind the clouds among the stars dancing in the music she'd composed. The memory of her floating above herself at the concert with misty eyes was forever engraved in my memory bank.

Is it possible to be in love with two different women at the same time? Perhaps a better question is whether it's possible to even love one person in time and then answer whether this is singular.

What does it mean to be in love? Is "I'm in love" derived out of a fear of loneliness? A fear of sitting alone at meals or having to look at a beautiful moon or a brazen sun without the presence of someone else? If not then how is it different from friendship? Is someone like Chloé lonely despite having her cello by her side? Is Alfhild lonely despite having the physical comfort of that brute Johann? The issue, as always, is time. If love is timed it means it is mortal like my body and it will come into being at an arbitrary moment I inject meaning to and fade when I no longer perceive its meaning whether by force or by accident.

I had a sudden craving for black Sicilian figs.

"Hello Mister Eycsüp, how may I help you?" the voice through the phone asked.

"Do you guys have Sicilian figs... black figs I mean."

"This is Manhattan sir. If you want black figs we can certainly get black figs for you."

Suddenly I forgot why I ever left but the sound of a wailing siren and a muted TV ad for the Marines flashing the words "Freedom" and "Justice" reminded me, "That would be excellent. Thank you."

"No problem sir. Is there anything else?"

"No thank you. ... Oh by the way, if I'm not here or I don't hear you, you can tell the person just to come in and put the figs in the fridge."

"I'll make a note here. Please do not hesitate to let us know if you need anything else."

"I certainly will. Thanks again."

"Good evening Mister Eycsüp."

I hastened back to the balcony in case the *non-smoking* detector went off, and this time with my sketchbook. Immediately an image of Alfhild through the rainfall in the foreground of the night sky flustered me and the cigarillo idled on my lips; I rushed to get the sketch down on the paper. There was a lack of planning and organization in the sketch and it seemed like my hand was moving on its own. The sound of shushing rain deafened me and I thought I heard the door. I watched it vibrate through the screen doors. I walked along the bed and listened...

Knock knock knock.

"Michelangelo?" a familiar voice plagued with agony called through the door.

For the first time in the longest time I could remember, fear tied my stomach into a knot.

"Hild?" I opened the door.

She rushed in and leaned against the door while raindrops lit up her cheeks.

The smoke detector beeped for a second and I flicked my cigar out the window, "What's wrong?" I slowly reached and turned her cheek to the left. A strand of her hair escaped and hovered over my fingers.

"Nothing... I'm fine," she trembled for a second and caressed the foot of the bed with the tip of her index finger before making her way to the terrace. "I interrupted your smoke, I apologize."

"Are you all right?"

The door unlocked from the outside and it startled her. "I ordered some figs. You can relax."

A man of about forty-five came in, "Hello sir."

"Hello," both Hild and I said.

"Where would you like the figs?"

"The fridge please."

"Very well sir," he put the figs in the fridge and left; in my haste to be alone with Hild I forgot to tip him.

"What's wrong?" I walked towards her.

"Nothing. I wanted to see you," she fumbled some of the stationery notecards on the nightstand, flipping through quick sketches of the skyline. It was quiet for a second, so quiet that the rain struggled to muffle the steps of an ant walking under the carpet.

I took the cards from her and tossed them back on the nightstand. Instead I held her hand and looked into her eyes. A drop surfed one of the waves of her sunny hair and drowned the ant under the carpet. Her eyes seemed to penetrate the despair of my soul. "What's wrong Hild?" I asked again.

The hidden moon snuck out from behind the clouds for a moment and lit up her eyes, which misted like the fog hazing over Staten Island.

I was the stupidest man to have never seen any Disney flicks about a princess in need of rescue by a struggling artist. "What happened after the club?" I thought about how it was best to evade the police, how I'd stalk, torture, and finally kill him. But that wasn't me. I'd turn myself in and I'd serve my time, get out, and start my life all over again in the timeless circle of human existence.

The Marines ad played on the TV behind her and the word "FREEDOM" flashed across the screen again.

"Let me get some ice," I moved my thumb slowly up her chin.

"You don't sleep?" her eyes glanced towards the clock.

"Breaking News! Andrea was the latest to be voted off "Too Pretty to Work" last night! Boy what a ride it's been. Record-breaking 97 million votes wanted to see her go! Don't forget to tune in next week to see who's Too Pretty to Work! ... That was the latest in Breaking News! And —" I turned the T.V. off.

Now and then I could hear the dying wind swirling the tops of trees soon to be torn down for more post-modern lofts and the thunder... the thunder was nothing compared to my fury at the sight of Alfhild in this pain.

My thoughts blanketed over themselves and only wanted to know one thing: what had happened to her.

"... I don't know why I came," she wrestled free from my hand and walked towards the door, "I'm sorry."

"Hild..."

She turned as she opened the door.

"Call me anytime if you want to talk. Anytime; I don't sleep."

I followed her footsteps through the door until I couldn't hear her movements anymore and walked outside to the terrace and lit a cigar. The moon plunged behind the darkening clouds and hung across the sky like ripples in a still ocean. Stars tangoed with each other until the clouds extinguished their light. I sketched a study for my next painting: Alfhild standing under a pale reflection of the moonlight beneath an indigo sky on top of virgin snow. To her right and left enigmatic rocks rolled across the canvas and a fog twirling like sea serpents crawled towards her as to strike fear into those intent on seducing and tarnishing her naïveté. Her body was slender and her face and hair were perfect, or so my painting would show. But her heart, her heart was the subject of the piece, bruised from the greed of the serpents around her. It was in her heart where I chose to invoke the most color: wine and ruby red mixed with azure blue and iris purple. I titled it *Timelessness interrupted by the Linearity of Human Perception.* I knew it was wrong to think like this, one event is meaningless upon the coning sphere of timelessness. Even all events that have ever or will ever take place, whether sequentially, subsequently, or linearly placed near each other were meaningless. ... But there was something about the moment, the meaningless moment of the agony in her eyes frozen in still time that I wanted to immortalize.

It wasn't a quick study, and before I noticed the time I noticed the sun rising in the horizon behind the porpoise-grey clouds. She'd shamed the sun with her suffering and I wanted nothing more than to see her smile.

The phone beeped, "Yes?"

"Michelangelo," Alfhild's voice was calmer than before, "Johann, Elroy, and I are going to breakfast now. Would you like to join us?"

"Yes," I had some unfinished business with Johann.

"See you there in ten minutes; it's on one of the lower floors I think, not on the lobby floor. Check the sign on the elevator."

"I'll find it."

"Okay. … Listen… about last night, could you not mention it to anyone?"

"I wouldn't dream of it."

"Thank you Michelangelo."

"You don't have to thank me. I'll see you soon."

I hung up and stepped under a cold shower. I listened to the sound of the water, watched it drip down through my body and circle around the tiles before the pipe gulped it like a child lost in a desert. Monsters swallowed me whole: anger and hate. I looked at the sky, a dulling grey with the scalding sun behind it, forsaken even by the faithful. Honor burned by dying stars turned the sky to ash and the world filled with nothing but anguish for the just, the brave, and the deserved. It takes a beautiful woman, both inside and out, to teach us the world is more beautiful than any man can bear… and this beauty is second only to the woman. The moment I thought this I thought, *which woman are you talking about?*

The music in the elevator was interrupted by the breaking news of two radio hosts who let me know once again, how important it was for everyone to know Andrea was voted off some trashy show that should've taken place in Silicon Stream, or SS for short because it was torturous to have to listen to people talk about it all day.

I walked into the breakfast lounge and saw Elroy and Hild sitting and talking. Elroy nodded at me and Hild stood. I saw a napkin on the table in front of an empty seat and some unfinished eggs. Johann was probably in the little girl's room.

"Morning. I still have to wash my hands. I'll be back in a moment."

"Michelangelo… don't do—" Hild called towards me.

Johann was washing his face in the sink and some guy was in the far stall. I didn't care. I walked up behind him and shoved his face under the water.

He struggled, "HEY!!! What the shit?!!?" but it was futile. I kept the water running over his eyes, ruining his new silk Brunello Cucinelli yellow button-down.

"Hurt her again, and I will erase your physical space from this world... and after a while even memories of your existence will fade. Time will forget you."

He tried laughing but I pushed his face higher. The water ran into his mouth and he choked and gargled some soap. He lifted his knee so he had a clear shot at my balls if things got out of hand... just like the gentleman he was pretending to be. I didn't even realize it but I was choking him and afraid I might kill him, I let up a little. "Michel? What the hell are you on about?" he pushed me back and I let him, his suit, hair, and face wet and pale from fear.

I walked by and washed my hands of him for quite a bit because when I walked back to our table he'd gone up to "Change his clothes," Hild informed me.

"Idiot spilled water all over himself. Looked like he'd taken a shower," Elroy chuckled.

A man with an uneven haircut and a tailored Calvin Klein suit approached me and extended his hand, "Are you Michelangelo Eycsüp?"

I showed him my hands, "I apologize; I've just washed my hands. Yes. Call me Michel."

"My name is Detective Ben Britten. We've been searching for you sir."

"Searching for me?" there was no doubt in my mind that the Bull had pressed charges and I had to answer for it; I wished I'd have inflicted more pain on Johann.

"Have you been to *Kaashibys* recently?"

Here we go, "Detective, if is this about the incident with the Bull there's no need to tap dance around the situation. I can't stand passive aggression!"

Hild's glorious eyes darted back and forth in anxiety; a light drizzle with boring clouds hanging below the skyscrapers oppressed the morning air.

"A bull? Huh? ...What?" his vexed face made me withdraw but he knew more than he let on.

"I apologize. What would you like to inquire about?"

He looked around at Elroy and Hild, "Perhaps we should speak in private."

"Is it that serious?"

"Yes."

I might not have been as smart as Mensa thought but I knew this was more serious than embarrassing a never-was.

We walked around the bar behind the elevators where the detective rubbed his temples with his palm and then focused his irises on me, "There was a murder around the same time you were at *Kaashibys*. Just behind the *Canvas* gallery." Billy Joel's *New York State of Mind* played through the rain and I saw Johann walk from the elevator to our table around the corner.

"A murder?" I loathed this city. If it wasn't one thing it was the same thing. I couldn't stand it; I wanted to be in sight of the Cathedral or touch the light-blue and azure marble stones of Gaudí's house. "That sounds serious. And you think I had something to do with it?"

"I don't know what to think Mister…,"

"Please. Call me Michel."

"I don't know what to think Michel. Where were you last night?"

"I was here all night detective. I worked through the night and before that I caught the *Arvo Pärt* rendition at Lincoln Center."

"May I ask what you do?"

"I'm an artist."

He looked around, the architecture of the Plaza Hotel and his eyes zoomed back into mine, "Post… modern art?"

I held in my laughter, "No. I try to intertwine impressionist colors with classical idealism."

He laughed as he took out a little reporter's notebook from his inner jacket pocket and flipped through its pages.

"But not to create confusion. I was there on behalf of a friend, placing bids on varying artworks. We made a few purchases."

"The young lady back at the breakfast table?"

"Yes," I answered with great care in dread that Hild would be dragged into this metropolitan mess.

"Can anyone vouch for your whereabouts last night?"

I nearly blurted Hild's name but kept myself composed, "Unfortunately no—" and it dawned on me, "Yes actually detective. I ordered black figs. The hotel employee brought it up to my room. You may check with them."

"I will," he said the words but I don't know he meant them. I don't think the murder was last night otherwise he wouldn't have asked me about the day I was there but rather the *last* time I was there. "Thank you for your time," he continued and put the notebook back in his pocket.

"Anytime detective. I will be staying here in the meantime if you need my help with anything…" I looked at him up and down. A grand figure of justice he was; bags under his eyes from the lack of sleep and marks on his dress pants from long, tedious stakeouts. He solved cases with grit and determination. "I do a mean portrait," I don't know why I offered to do his portrait but the words slid out like velvet silk resting on Chloé's skin.

"Are you trying to bribe me Michel?"

We chuckled.

"I wouldn't dream of it... do you mind me asking who was murdered?"

"An art dealer. I can't give you his name you see. It's against procedure."

"I understand." I glanced back towards Johann, who had just ordered a drink in spite of Hild's numerous protests. I wondered how I got into this. How I went from being an artist in serene Barcelona to a murder suspect in the world's loneliest city. I missed the Catalan sky. I missed the music festivals, the Picasso museums, and the short yet enlightening chats I'd have with the girl who worked at the café down the street from my place, Tiffany. But most of all, I missed not knowing Hild and Chloé. "It was nice talking to you detective."

He nodded and started to walk away but then he jerked back, "Michel?"

"Yes detective?"

"May I ask you a question?"

"Sure," I was curious.

"How fast was he *really*? Are you just quicker or is he all hype?"

"Detective?"

"The so-called Bull, I saw him fight back in the day. Blink... and you would've missed his jab."

I hesitated; was this a trap?

"Hypothetically?"

He snickered and rolled his eyes, "Yes."

"He's not hype."

"That's what I figured. Thanks Michel," he took out his notebook again and walked towards the lobby.

Wait. Wait. What just happened? Did I just make myself a suspect?

"You changed your jacket," I said to Johann as I approached and he flinched back when he saw me.

"It's... uhh... colder than I thought."

The waiter brought Johann's drink and I thought I noticed his hand shake when he reached for it. Hild looked through me, attempting in vain to ascertain what I'd done to Johann to merit this behavior. I hated being this weak. You're weak when you have no money. You're weaker when a woman's involved.

Elroy got up, "Let's go."

"I just got my drink!" Johann whined.

"I don't care. I'm not waiting for you to finish that. … It's 10 A.M. dude. … We'll get drinks at the Four Seasons in the afternoon."

"I'm going to have to pass on that," I stood up and shook Elroy's hand.

"You won't join us?" Hild made no effort to hide her disappointment.

I had to get away from her. I wanted to push past them all and run but I knew I couldn't, "No. I want to catch up on some work."

"Leave him alone guys!" Johann made a desperate attempt to drown his face in his drink so the $12 charged to his room wouldn't go to waste… Time and space forbade anything left unconsumed in this city.

My latest study was truly bothering me. I had no canvases here to work and I wanted to get the study down on the cloth before the injected feeling was lost on me. I knew a place in Brooklyn that could provide me with the best canvases in the country if a condo developer hadn't bought it out and demolished it by now. I wanted to see Chloé. My physicality limited me, *time* limited me from doing all these but I knew I had to try to get *one* thing done. I nodded to Hild and made my way to the lobby.

I asked the concierge, Jonathan, to order me a taxi for Brooklyn. While I waited in the lobby for the cab, the T.V. lit up with a news story about an earthquake in the Himalayas and the rising death toll. A man walking with his son glanced at the T.V. and shook his head. At least someone seemed to care.

"Damn it!" he said to his son.

"What is it dad?"

"Chelsea won. We're out of the FA Cup final."

As soon as the words FA Cup left his mouth I became consumed by despair and a sense of vertigo.

The front page of the *Times* had something about the Supreme Court ruling mass surveillance illegal while the ticker on the T.V., when it found time to stop talking about the Giants and their Super Bowl odds, the *Too Pretty to Work* contestants, Brad Pitt's adventures in the restroom of a Follywood café, and the newest uWatch, reported that the House of Representatives are now in overwhelming support of the Freedom Act—oh the delicious irony—which amends Section 215 of the Patriot Act to end mass collection of metadata from domestic citizens but leaves in place sweeping surveillance protocols for international communications. Knowing the kind of prick lawyers that held office nowadays, it was a safe bet calls originating overseas in regard to domestic citizens meant that information about those citizens would still be retained.

Words flickered across screens. Silent depression loomed in the air. Profits stayed the same. Time passed. Nothing changed.

I unglued my eyelashes from the T.V.'s hypnotizing glare and sank into thought. What did it mean to be lonely? To be a jigsaw piece that was lost in the big picture? What did it mean to be a misfit? Was it simply a one of many that didn't *fit* into the status quo? What did I have to do differently not to feel this pain? Could I simply shut my eyes; stop reading; deafen myself; practice apathy while taking in the news? Could I walk into bars and lose myself in the sweet indelible arms of easy women and forego this pain? ... I don't want to know anything anymore; why did it have to be me?

Then I was plagued by a thought of divinity. What if in my haste to eliminate the idea of a sort of Godlike being as the first cause of the universe (rather than the birth of space and time), I had inadvertently thrown out a truth, and in some grand wrath, this first cause was exacting a very personal, very real vengeance on one of his creations... one of sorrow and pain. In this unsettling thought my mind dwelled and circled around. Was this why I felt so alone even now, surrounded by intelligent new friends and idiotic old enemies with new faces?

I felt imprisoned by my own *intellectual* babble trying desperately to confront a material world of objects in space. Objects that are by their very nature unknowable: had I become the post-modern man? A virus of existence spreading his disease through any ecosystem he encounters, consumed by the advanced technology unfathomable by his predecessors? Facing these objects of this world with no relation or intimacy—save for the fastest Wi-Fi—beyond the knowledge of which button must be pressed in order to control the device's workings? This is far grimmer than it sounds since the post-modern man will then actively seek to press the buttons of his fellow men in order to gain *their* workings, be it emotional, social, financial, etc., all to attain some edge through which he can manipulate and further himself in his ecosystem viz. society, until the moment all the resources of that ecosystem have been pillaged, and he can move onto the next one. Technology disassociates, and if it disassociates us from one another then we will be—

"Sir?" the concierge had been calling me.

"Yes?"

"Your taxi sir. It's here."

"Much obliged Jonathan."

Jonathan held an umbrella over my head as I got into the Lincoln Town Car. A chill exhausted the part of my arms that had held Johann.

I gave the driver a general cross street in Brooklyn because I wanted to walk for a bit and see the old neighborhood. On the ride I thought about loneliness again. Was Hild lonely? Was Chloé? Hell even Elroy didn't have anyone... but were they all *happy* with their existence? At least on the outside?

The sun tried to shine through the clouds but its light was dimmed even in us; high noon approached. I looked outside through the tinted windows at the people promenading down Madison. Couples held hands, bankers squeezed through crowds of window shoppers late for their daily thieving but all of them, even the poor, seemed content with existence, some even seemed happy. Nearly everyone's outer shell was delicate and gracious that at the end of it all, on the border of nonexistence, each and everyone was happy to be alive. Everyone carried their heads with a radiance past the space they occupied and glided through time like flamenco dancers in a studio as big as the planet. Everyone wore masks that hid their sorrow (either that or they were sincerely happy) or wore armor that lightened the burden on their shoulders. Worst of all, I could not detect ever a flicker of thought; brains mired behind viral images and videos of people making even greater fools of themselves than they already were. And as the greatest fool of them all, I walked among them, never having learned to don the mask of happiness.

"The loneliest place in the world," I looked towards a man running with his coat over his head.

"What's that sir?" the driver stretched back towards me.

"This city. It's the loneliest city in the world."

"I don't think so sir. The population is... what's the word? ... Packed! There's people everywhere," he chuckled.

"People are consumed by the ferocity of greed in their everyday lives that they *know* they can't trust anyone. So even in anger, in sorrow, or in masked glee they breeze into each other just to feel like their existence has a measure of beauty to it."

"There were too many ten dollar words in that sentence sir. I don't follow."

Silence the rest of the way.

The rain harshened by the time I crossed the bridge to Brooklyn. It was the sort of downpour that forced everyone inside. I stood under the water for a few moments in hope my soul would be cleansed but then worried the phone Hild had given me would break from water damage. I turned into streets and alleys without any real purpose before the flicker of a sign above a bar immobilized me. Two women tried to outrun the rain as they skedaddled into the bar while arguing over the best contestant of *"Too Pretty to Work."* The lights flickered again; the electricity wavered. Street lamps turned off and the music of the wind spiraled onto the windows of the places offering refuge.

People were hollow woodblocks stepping silently through alleyways. Their shadows appeared only under the neon lights of skimpy dives and underground brothels that lit up their shallow minds. A silent desperation loomed through the air. People walked by one another and brushed past each other but I still believed it was the loneliest place on earth. I observed and saw no soul speaking to another and the toxic air smelled like death. That smell of aluminum and steel. There was never any sunshine because its rays were blocked by some bank's head office in ignorance of the space they occupied; it's not the sky their buildings scape, but the third ring of the seventh circle of Hell. It rained hardest in cities like this, the smog, the conmen, the corrupt, and the dead walking, but no matter how hard it tried, it couldn't purify the city's soul. Everyone was programmed to ignore the mortal echoes of their timed life with the drowning sounds of clicking turnstiles and beeps and swipes and taps of their untimed devices.

I walked back and looked through the window of the bar the two women escaped to and saw a yearning for something wet to erode the apathy in their bones. They saw their reflections not in mirrors but the faces of other lonely souls like them. There is no hope in these cities, only a calm certainty that you are venturing through Hell.

I heard the harmonic cutting of the saws as I approached the back door of the factory. It was too uniform and too consistent but the sound of the rain did well to mask the moment. The keys were still hidden in the same place. Everything *appeared* the same but that was where uniformity ended. I noticed a new station on the factory floor past the cotton that then gets stretched around the wood to form the canvas, past the paint cans and varnish that accompany the canvas, and I saw, to my horror, machines *painting* on virgin canvases. Van Gogh. Da Vinci. Da Vinci. Renoir. Van Gogh. Every piece looked the same, I watched them roll off the tire until eventually, after about fifty that had gone through in that order, the paint robots rotated and began drawing a different combination of paintings: Cézanne. Raphael. Monet. Rembrandt... fifty canvases destroyed and soiled by machines. Cold. Ugly. I felt nauseous and retched near a trashcan as a mumbling voice grew nearer.

"HEY!" the voice screamed, "I'm calling the cops! You're not supposed to be in — Michel?" it took a moment but the man recognized me after his scrutinizing eye had gone over me like a military general. "I really *do* have to move the hide-a-key."

I turned in horror and saw the face of my confidant at close quarters and was relieved and disappointed all at once. "How could you sell out like this?" despite my best efforts, these were the words I said to him after fifteen years.

"Empty canvases don't pay the bills. Still lost in the clouds when you're not prattling around in your own brain there? Artists can't afford to paint anymore," how much pain was in his voice as he said these words, "But the rich want prints of poor artists' paintings."

"How do you have electricity?"

"Generator out back Michel. That's how much we're making. So many orders to fill—"

"Of the exact same paintings you mean..."

"Yes. ... So many orders to fill that I can afford to keep multiple generators going and still make tenfold later," a pause. "You haven't changed one bit!"

"Neither have you. I've never seen someone come out as a winner in a fight against Father Time."

"You have your tools of the trade; I have mine."

I smiled. Looking closer, it seemed to me that time moved still around him. He'd hardly aged three days and it'd been fifteen years... fifteen years. That's a long time.

His name was revered in the neighborhood. Easily the greatest influence on the youth, and we were all lost. His hair was still straight and in a buzz cut and he had doe-brown eyes that were always energized. A conversational quirk was that he perpetually squared his shoulders such that mid-way through any dialogue with him, his chest was extended bigger and taller than you despite being only 5'7. His tongue, especially when it came to hoodlums, goombas, or thugs that attempted to exercise tyranny over us in our youth, was mightier than a banker's pen and a greaseball's revolver. He would bleed their souls dry with laconic idioms coupled with a fearless resolve, and if he wanted, if a student or able-bodied employee was worthy of this master's attention, those same words could elevate you to the highest realm of aesthetic absolutes. I was speechless in his presence and only waited to drink in the wisdom of my beloved teacher. Unfortunately this had always created a misunderstanding between us. He always thought I was arrogant and condescending.

"You murder the beauty in those pieces when you reprint them!"

"Then find me original beauty to print!"

I nodded, "I'm looking."

"Still looking? You could spend your life looking for Beauty, and it wouldn't be a wasted life."

"Just now, I'm working on—" my foot cramped and surged and buzzed... it was the cell phone. It was ringing and vibrating.

I was going to let it ring but then Aatos said, "Get it. No one calls anymore, everyone texts."

I took the phone out and tapped the *answer* button, "Text?" I whispered to Aatos.

He shrugged his shoulders.

"Yes?"

"Where are you Michelangelo?" why did sorrow dissipate with the mere hearing of her saying my name?

"Hello Chloé."

"Where are you?" she repeated. No small talk. No unnecessary words or babble.

"Brooklyn."

"Where? I want to see you. Give me the exact address!"

"No. Don't come out here right now. There's a storm out, plus it's not safe."

Aatos shook his head in fierce disapproval, mouthing *that's no way to address a lady*, I think.

"A storm? Oh no! I'll melt…" she rasberried, "I'm a big girl Michelangelo. I don't need you to worry about me."

I relented.

"I'll be there soon. Streets will be clear because everyone is afraid of melting."

The phone was barely off my ear when Aatos's fist came faster than the lightning towards my abdomen. I barely blocked it in time.

"Good! You still got the speed. I always taught you two things. One. Never keep a lady waiting. And two: if a lady wishes to see you, you drop everything and see her."

"You simplify things that are by their nature complex."

"And you complicate things that are by their nature simple."

"Things are complicated by themselves, they don't need my help."

We talked about old times and times to come. I told him about my travels in Europe and the war. I told him everything. I told him about bumping into Elroy and working for Hild but left out the part where I thought her and her friend Chloé were breathing sculptures of beauty.

Aatos's phone beeped and he swiped left and right, showing me the screen to reveal a camera system both inside and outside the company, "The motion detectors picked her up."

"A brave new world huh?"

"You know I liked you better when you rarely talked," he was joking.

"I liked you better when you rarely listened."

"Touché. …" he chuckled. "I'll go let her in."

A few minutes later both of them emerged. Chloé's hair was damp and her skin gleamed with raindrops.

"Oh yeah… we used to make canvases here, blank ones. We had to hide the good ones from Michel though, he would draw on them," Aatos said and Chloé laughed. "Then he told me painting is a distraction on the mirth of existence and switched from Art History and Form to Sub-Atomic Physics and M Theory in Curved Space-time. … Broke my heart," he put his palm on his heart.

I'd lit up a cigar in the meantime and let out some smoke, "Hearts are meant to be broken."

Chloé scoffed and turned away.

"I still have it you know... in the back," Aatos turned to me.

"Have what?" Chloé inquired.

I listened to the rain landing on the tin roof and tried to float away.

"Come with me," Aatos beckoned us both towards a room in the back. He reached into his pocket and took out a single key and unlocked a wooden door that opened to a garage workshop. Sawdust kicked up in the room behind us as the door to the garage closed.

Tools surrounded the garage, everything from mini screwdrivers to a welding torch and the kind of paint I used to paint my oils.

A *Dowco Guardian EZ Zip* cover hid a motorcycle in exactly the center of the place.

"It can't be."

"It is," Aatos walked over to the cover and the sounds of his shoes tapping over the garage floor echoed; the rain had stopped, or I couldn't hear it anymore.

"What is it?" Chloé's voice echoed.

"It's.... It's a bike... *the* bike."

"This my dear," Aatos unzipped the cover and revealed the machine, "Is a 1954 Harley FL Panhead. Restored as it was meant to be."

I walked over and touched the fuel tank, the custom-painted purple stinging my hand with a cold rushing through my veins, eventually it warmed my hand as I gripped the handlebars. Everything, from the pistons to the cylinder base, even the wristpin buttons were as silver as an Olympic medal, polished as if it just came from the factory.

"I told you to get rid of it didn't I?" the moment passed and I snapped out of it.

Chloé put her hand on the other handlebar and gripped the clutch, "Smooth. This is a '54?"

"Yes..." Aatos walked behind us to a long cabinet at the back of the garage, "I used to have Michel fix up bikes for some of the people in the neighborhood back in the day to keep him out of trouble. One day this ... *guy* came in with this Sportster. It was all beaten up. Destroyed. I told him to take it to the junkyard. Michel stopped me. He said it kept him busy. Over the years we kept getting parts from other bikes or buying them when we could."

"And now it's complete?" Chloé walked behind me around the bike.

Aatos took a box out of the cabinet and set it down on the workbench. He threw an open face helmet with a thin maroon stripe at me and I caught it, hearing some keys rattle around inside.

"You know what else I still have that you told me to get rid of?" Aatos dug deeper through the box.

I lit a RyJ by Romeo y Julieta I'd smuggled in through the private jet and watched Chloé. The dark purple of the bike reflecting the night through the skylight and the moonlight through parted clouds accentuating her eyes.

"Where is— YES! Found it!" and out he came towards me with a mid-length Balmain maroon leather jacket.

"Whoa! Now *that's* cool!" Chloé walked over, the light shifting the complexion reflecting on her face.

"No. I'm not wearing that."

"It's a jacket Michel, nothing more. Remember that." Aatos handed it to me.

With nearly shaking hands I caressed it, touching each section of the coat in turns before I'd finally examined it in its entirety. Slowly I put it on, red like spilled blood.

"Take it for a spin. ... I have... a second... YES!" he handed Chloé a helmet and a thick biker jacket. "I threw out the gloves though...."

"Why didn't you finish it?" Chloé asked while she tied up her hair in preparation of the helmet.

"I couldn't find a few pieces."

"Like?"

"The carburetor choke level was a problem. The gear shifter rod for that year was nowhere to be found, but the biggest problem was the rear brake rod adjusting clevis, the sizing had to be perfect," I turned to Aatos, "How'd you find the parts?"

"Every time I had some money left over I'd buy a Harley from that era and take it apart. Scrapped three or four before this baby was born again."

"A phoenix," I followed the golden stripe painted over the dark purple on the fuel tank.

"Hop on!" Aatos told Chloé.

The jacket brought back old memories I'd repressed but now, now, I had Chloé. Things would be different. I dared to hope. When characters in a tragedy dare, that's when things start going sideways. The hope then, was a faith in not living in a tragedy.

Aatos opened the double garage door and cleared a path through the factory floor outside. I waited for him to return.

"Have you ridden a bike before?"

"No," she replied, "But I trust you."

Why did she have to say that? "That's a lot of pressure... hold on. She's got a bit of a kick!" She rested her head on my back and waited.

Aatos emerged through double doors and nodded, "You're clear!"

I pulled the choke and turned on the gas, hit the ignition switch and waited for the light on the fuel tank to turn green. I tugged on the throttle a bit and cranked the ignition pedal... like Chloé's cello she came alive. Vibrating both of us through the air.

"Hold on Clo," I yelled behind me and she tightened her grip around my waist.

I nodded to Aatos as I rode by and entered the despondent streets of this monstrous city once again. We glided through the alleys and streets with the wind on our faces... the rain had subsided so the air was cool and damp like the morning dew resting on flowers. Eventually we went through some streets and ended up near the bottom of the Brooklyn Bridge, where the ground reminded me of Barcelona.

"I have to get back to Spain."

"What's there?" she got off the bike.

Sirens screamed in the distance. This city was a monster not to be conquered with a big sword and a simple *will* to fight, "It's what's not there that lures me away," I lit a cigarillo and turned off the engine.

She leaned against the bike behind me, "What did you do Michelangelo... before you became an artist?"

An artist... what a word, "They said I was a soldier. You do your bit. You serve. You protect freedoms overseas, which is really just fancy jibber-jabber for protecting corporate interests in third-world nations. You kill. You *rescue* those you don't kill. Then you come back here and people tap away on their fancy gadgets and buy watches that do everything but tell time."

She scoffed, "These are fabrications of a propaganda machine. Readers of misinformed articles on the net and useless tidbits of information like *How to make your life more productive in ten easy steps. Click now to find out!* This is freedom to the masses. To post that article and be able to read it is freedom, not to say anything of substance or do anything worth doing... *that's* freedom Michelangelo," she took the cigar from my lip and walked over to the edge of the East River. "Soldiers are martyrs for freedom only in the eyes of sentimental women... readers of entertainment news, VibeFeed, and even DailyElitist, useless information dealers passing off a secret knowledge only known to important members of a cabal: do this to be successful, think like this and women will love you. The ooze of green blood: envy and sodomy of the mind. Imprisoned intellects deluding to freedom. Sentimentality that costs not a thing but one soul. That's what people want. It makes me sick... like this city."

I hit the kickstand and walked over to her, "Your... sentiments lie with nocturnes and serenades don't they?"

"No. Sentiments are a waste of our existence."

I lit another RyJ. "Yet we think we're the greatest civilization in human history."

"We are... I don't disagree; the summation of human knowledge rests in my pocket. In no other time could I hit a button on a device that if I take back in time with me would be burned at the stake for witchcraft and read the lyrics of *Don Giovanni*. In no other time could I type someone's name into a search bar and have their entire life story in front of me to read. In no other time could I send a message to be received instantly to someone in... Spain."

"There's no room for improvement?" I asked. *Pride,* is Archimedes' lever.

"There's infinite room for improvement. We're flawed, dirty beings, no more intelligent than the animals we test our cosmetics on. We think because we know what's produced when you mix one thing with another makes us superior to everything else."

I loved listening to her voice; her body was to my eyes what her voice was to my ears and her playing was to my heart.

Sunset matched the bike, a supernova unseen by the eyes of the damned. In the place above the fog, an eternal resting place of time swam through the deep trenches of a soul in search for itself.

"Wait here for a second. I'll be right back," I felt sick, nauseated, turning corners to lose sight of Chloé in between brownstones and alleys. The skyscrapers in the distance towered over me like monsters in the night. They grew sharp triangular teeth and sought to consume me. They chomped closer; I felt claustrophobic and in vain tried to get away. I weaved in between two of them down another alley to hide in plain sight when I felt sick again and threw up all over a brown-bricked wall. The vomit took various forms and shapes and it looked like I could turn it into a paintin—NO! I will never become a post-modern artist.

Clouds stood in front of the moon by the time I found my bearings and got back to Chloé. She was looking out at the city in the horizon of the East River still smoking the cigar she'd taken off my lip.

"Let's head back."

She jumped back, "You startled me."

"I didn't mean to. ... Let's head back. It's getting dark."

She directed my eyes to the skyline, "The lights, they gleam bright."

I cranked the ignition pedal after I went through the starting procedure again, trying not to listen but not being able to resist the temptation of her voice, "It's not the gleaming of the lights themselves as much as it's the spatial awareness of the light's presence by another."

She got on behind me and held my waist, "I'm not even going to pretend like I understood that."

I started moving.

"Wait wait wait. Stop."

"You okay?"

She threw the RyJ into a trashcan I was about to pass, "… Yes. Of course I am, not all women need rescuing you partisan," and latched the chinstrap.

We found Aatos nailing pieces of wood to the back of a beautiful linen canvas with a smooth and intricate weave. Chloé got off the bike and I took it back to the garage and put everything back the way it was, even the copy of *Art as Experience* by John Dewey back on top of the pile but I kept the jacket. I polished every piece and turned the gas and choke off before putting the cover back on the Harley.

Walking back, I heard the end of Aatos and Chloé's conversation.

"Yes, sometimes for larger paintings artists request rougher texture so the brushstrokes stand out more, but Michel holds and uses his brush delicately… like flowing water down a stream that eventually reaches an ocean."

"Stop talking me up," I reached into my pocket but felt no cigars, "Damn…."

"I made this for you by hand so you can do a portrait of Chloé here."

She looked at me with those eyes that women make when they want a man to do something for them.

"No. I don't want it Aatos," I reached for a cigar again.

"You're taking it, and you're doing her portrait," he puffed up his chest and moved towards me, "It's a crime of the soul not to paint magnificence."

"She's already painted," I blurted out, raising my voice, "Perfectly."

She laughed.

"You are. I'm not going to pretend I don't find you beautiful. Everyone finds you beautiful no doubt."

He wrapped the canvas in a sheet and then a big leather portfolio.

I walked through the front and slowed to a halt when I saw pieces of cut wood laid flat on top of one another, pieces that weren't for canvases.

"Oh those? You believe it? We have to make wood for post modern furniture stores to keep the lights on… at least business booms when we sell to these stores."

Not all the wood was used to create beautiful new canvases that artists would then use. No… they were used to make small couches that fat asses could sit on and heave as their favorite character got voted off the latest episode of *"Too Pretty to Work."*

"We should get going," I turned to Chloé.

"Sure. I have a concert tonight," the moonlight pierced the skylight and reflected off her lips. "Would you like to join the reception after like last time?"

"I'd like to come to the concert if possible."

"It's sold out…" she snickered, "I doubt I can get you a seat."

"Yeah Michel, she's more important than you give her credit for," Aatos chimed in.

They laughed.

"Very funny," I reached for an RyJ and finally, Aatos handed me a cigar he kept in the humidor on his desk behind him, "Here! You're driving me nuts looking for one."

"That *is* a beautiful Harley Aatos," Chloé nodded, "I love the color especially. Dark purple like the night sky after a bit of rain."

Aatos squared his shoulders, "It's funny you say that; I was trying to capture the color of the sky before dawn because Michel is always chasing the sunrise but he's going too fast for it to catch up, so he changes time zones and is always slightly ahead of the day."

"So he mistakenly lives in the gloom of the night thinking that's all there is?" Chloé gasped knowingly and turned towards me.

"I'm standing right here!" I lit the match near other pieces of wood that would soon be … couches for the lovers of nothing and the ignorant of everything.

Aatos handed me the leather portfolio, "This is for her portrait," he wrinkled his forehead, "And *only* her portrait. You must convey her inner beauty, the soul of the musician with beauty on the outside."

She blushed.

I took it grudgingly but he was right.

On the way back to my hotel she asked me what kind of paintings I bought for Alfhild and what kind of paintings I drew. There was a certain hostility in her voice whenever she spoke of Hild and I didn't know how to respond. I gave vague answers out of terror that I would say the wrong thing and upset her in some way. She asked me if I was fluent in Danish and was elated when I said yes. She chattered phrases with a native fluidity and then asked, "I want to revisit our earlier discussion about civilization. You don't believe in progress then?"

"Progress is freedom of destruction. If we're able to destroy all that the previous generations made *normal* in their greed or bigotry or whatever else… only then are we free. But look at the world. Governments perpetuate their power as slave owners to their labour force by backing corporations, and corporations are puppets to the excessive avarice and gluttony practiced by their leaders. In a way, they comprehend the world in ways we never will, but it's not progress and secularization unless we can tear it down on a whim."

"So freedom is possible?" she followed up.

"Freedom in the sense I just described, societal freedom is possible to a certain point but it's limited. Freedom is impossible outside of this because you're imprisoned by spatial finitude and temporality."

"Ugh," she sighed, "You're always so serious!"

"Yes."

"Art is the only serious thing in the world but artists are the only people who mustn't be serious," she smiled.

"Hmm..."

"It's Oscar Wilde."

"What's it mean?" curiosity bested me.

"It means you are in a unique position not to have be so serious... so don't be!" it sounded like a command, an order when the words left her lips.

"That's interesting... I need to stop for cigarillos if you know a place nearby," I reached into my back pocket, "And matches."

"They won't have Cubans though."

"No. ... " My words trailed off. The car stopped on Madison between East 54th and East 53rd street.

"There's a Davidoff around the corner right at 53rd... I'll wait in the car."

The smell of garbage and sound of sirens and people soliciting their CDs was deafened by the high-society chuckle and quasi-political analysis when I walked into an atrium-like lobby and saw fancy leather chairs smelling of people's various cigars. The selection in the humidor was borderline excessive. Every mid-range to the most luxurious brand catalogued and organized by informed personnel.

The manager personally introduced himself while he shook my hand and offered a tour of the humidor. I felt slightly out of place in my *artiste* style clothing: an off-brand leather jacket and black J. Crew chinos damp from the rain. Everyone else seemed to be in tailored $4,500 suits and polished $900 Italian shoes. It was a regular hangout for the power earners of this metropolitan wasteland.

I bought a box of Davidoff Long Panatellas. I had them once, they're milder and the smoke is prolonged compared to the Partagas clubs. It's blended with tobacco from Indonesia, Brazil, and the Caribbean. The binder leaf is from Javan and the wrapper is from Sumatra. A box of 25 was $73.75 that I was soon to be exhaling through my lungs.

The clock on the wall read 6:38. It wasn't even 7:00 and yet the clouds blanketed the sky in grey darkness to give it the real oppressive feel this city deserves.

"It's not even 7:00 yet. Why is it so dark here all the time?" I shuffled into the backseat of her S65 AMG.

"We pretty much watched the sunset Michelangelo," she wrinkled her eyebrows, "It wasn't dark at noon... or one... or two..."

A hipster wearing beige khaki shorts, pink long-john socks and custom spray-painted Converse All-Stars matching the colors of his beanie, and holding a six-pack from a brewery I'd never heard of walked by the car and rolled his eyes at Chloé's Benz. His eyes, green like tree leaves in summertime, were hidden behind Ray-Bans and I felt like laughing hysterically. Laughing until I cried like Garrick.

"It was dark all day. It never *felt* like day."

"Maybe it's a mental thing."

I ignored her, "When's your concert?"

"9:30. Drop you off at the Plaza?"

"That would be obliged."

Chloé hummed various Bach Partitas on the way to my hotel. I wanted to ask whether this was a particular ritual because she had a show or something else but I didn't want to interrupt; I liked listening to it.

Traffic was murder, more so than usual in Manhattan and the radio reported it was because someone had been killed near the gates of Central Park.

My phone buzzed.

"Are you going to get that?"

"No."

"What if it's important?"

"Nothing is more important than the air," I looked ahead and saw the gridlock leading to the Plaza. "Clo, let me get out here. You guys are going the other way; it's quicker to walk."

"It's raining!"

"Rain is the real depiction of poetry in nature. Let it caress you with its touch; let it beat you on the brain with its drops; let it sing to you with its pattering voice. Let its pools in the concrete jungle reflect your soul, and let it wet the roots of dying trees so that one day we may all be free," I hadn't been inspired to write a poem for a while, not until that very moment.

"That's beautiful."

"Don't get me started on Beauty," I got out of the car and stood under an awning in front of a store that had an ad for "Chloé Lysettensen's *mastery of harmony and marvelous portrayal of elation for the ears.*" A picture of her playing overlaid onto an off-black background where the yellow stands of her hair were edited to circle her face and head like a halo.

"Pazzesco!" I whispered to myself.

117

"What was that?" she asked behind a wily smile.

Crazy, "This is—*That's* crazy. It's you!" I guided her gaze to the ad.

"I loathe that ad. Makes me look like an angel in the darkness."

Her window whirred up, "I'll have the canvas delivered to you later tonight or tomorrow."

"That's fine," I overtook the car almost immediately since they were stuck in traffic and still had to find a place to pull a U-turn.

I lit the first Davidoff thinking about how to best portray her in the portrait. The universe, with all the matter at its mercy had sculpted perfection in her creation. How nauseating. If this were true, how would I improve perfection? Wouldn't it be hubris to even think I could? And if it wasn't true, which it probably wasn't—no one is perfect—why was I so consumed by the idea of her personifying the Love that guided Dante or the form of Plato's Love?

In this flawed logic, don't I have *to* love to paint her *as* Love, and then wouldn't it be easy to love *her* to portray her in the best light? Are not all masterpieces the design and product of intense passion? The more I thought about this the more I hated her. I hated wanting to know everything about her: from her earliest childhood memories to her most recent fantasies to her abandoned dreams and her thoughts on art and music and politics and sports. "You hate her!" I repeated to myself so I could eventually start believing it. I didn't want to paint her. Painting was reproducing images and if we are all images of our true selves, the real Beauty transcending our souls, I'd be perpetuating an image of an image that wanders further from her true self.

The idea suffocated me. It was a lose-lose either way and I'd lost enough for one life.

People imprison themselves. Kafka said something like that once; I didn't really understand the gloss of his words but I do now. People build empty monasteries they never leave and then build a window barely smaller than themselves and watch the breeze weave in between trees. Most make themselves the warden of the dungeons and torture chambers they build. Some build prisons of flowers and sunshine and burn themselves with the light. They frolic and pander in fields and are among the happiest of souls. Some build prisons containing both, curious to the somber allegories of suffering, the fright of new unfamiliar ideas, and the gracious light of old habits. They torture themselves not knowing they can build doors made of light and they never tear down their walls of ideas, and thoughts that combat conventionalism are sent to the torture chambers to be broken. Love is a road between two prisons of the same kind... sufferers are afraid of burning themselves with the light and the happy do not believe in the redemptive qualities of agony.

Thus happy people eventually suffer and sufferers enjoy this pain and become happy, each now living in a prison no longer their own. Real people, the creators and pursuers of Beauty, live in the pure white space and contemplate *reality* past the corruption of images at the behest of finite minds, be it their own or someone else's. The true sign of genius, the distinguishing factor between members of the third class from others is their ability to detach themselves from their own influence. They have no walls of ideas or chambers of habit demanding loyalty until death; they're free to think as they wish and act as they think. I thought myself a sufferer and Chloé a genius. I would plague her with agony. My portrait would be a symbol of pain to the purity of her hands emitting Schubert from a piece of wood and some strings.

I walked past a wet coral rose garden and entered the Plaza.

XVII
Fumus Boni Iuris

How does an author suddenly leave a character off "meanwhile" and portray the life of another aforementioned? In films or T.V., there's an establishing shot, the camera pans over a city, mood is captured based on the lighting or time of day or by weather; dancing shadows of trees under the sunlight or a foreboding mist under a street lamp in the dead of night... setting is thus established and we find the character doing what must be portrayed. How does the writer convey this? Does he simply write out "Sirens nudged Ventoni awake in a five-star dump in Hoboken? He woke on neither side of the bed but rather, on the floor under it after a night of boozing and banging."

Are there specific literary devices and allegories in place to analyze and illustrate the totems in place so the reader has an easier time understanding the scene?

When illustrating a scene after having left a character alone for some time, a secondary build-up is needed to fill the gap in time.

He'd mixed the cocaine recommended by the unsavory receptionist behind the barred counter with Jack Daniels and had blacked-out on the mushy carpet. How the mighty had fallen. Car horns worsened his headache as he walked over to shut the window.

"Great..." they were already shut.

A buzzing came from somewhere outside his hangover; he put both his palms over his ears and followed its muffled vibrations. An ashtray fell and the residue of cocaine from the night before smeared on his forearm. He reached for his black Dolce and Gabbana trousers undone at his knees and had trouble locating his brown Ralph Lauren belt. His wallet dropped and flipped open to a picture. When he looked over the room to pinpoint the origin of the buzzing, his escort rose from under the blanket and coughed and heaved. He gulped what was left of the JD from the bottle and retched in the toilet.

It would be simpler to portray this in film or a picture book, simpler to *show* the half-naked prostitute in a flashback kidnapped at a young age and injected with cocaine and heroin to incept a drug addiction that would require tricking to survive rather than write it and waste words. It would be easier to show Kane's wrinkled face to the potential glow of the woman in his bed had she not been an addict and a thief.

The buzzing grew louder.

When is it a good time to introduce a character's backstory once the initial introduction has passed? Do readers really need to hear more about someone once they've heard him talk in a restaurant to his friends and seen him work? Do they need to hear about a person's childhood?

Yes?

As a child Kane concocted the most elaborate and complex lies; it was something of a hobby until it became his vocation. He was not a traditional thief, stealing bread not to starve or paper to write verses was too "small-time" for him. He never murdered a neighbor's pet nor was he disciplined for anything abnormal in school. His parents were not abusive other than inattention common to his generation. This inattention meant that the more people noticed his disease the more he reveled in his ability to fool them. Still, there was no reason for any of his stories and no complex weavings leading to finality nor was there any necessity. He kept no diary or journal of his deceptions and he never told anyone of his affliction; he lied like crickets during summer nights: uselessly, annoyingly, and worst of all, purposelessly. He was an expert by the time he hit twelve. Laying among the farm fields of his family, he'd whistle and dream under the sun's light and the trees' shade about how much he could lie without ever coming close to the truth.

He was a major underachiever in school and was always among the bottom-third in a class of less than ten people. His papers on the classics were written with intent to conflate "Ignorant country hicks who only know *of* Walden and listen to bluegrass." The psyche of Hamlet used evidence and lines from Macbeth, and Robert Cohn was the founding father of the Buendía family.

"Hallo… this is," he cleared his throat and tasted Jack Daniels and blood, "Nicht gut. …" he cleared his throat again, "Ventoni," the buzzing phone had sent quivers up his arm.

"Kane! Where are you?"

Ventoni laughed, "I… uh, don't really know," and mouthed *Dankeschön* to the escort who was getting dressed to leave.

"Wherever you are you better find yourself back at the offices ASAP! You hear me Kane?"

"Jesus Wes, not so loud, What's the matter?" he looked around for his belt for a second time.

"There's people here Kane, they're from the Ministry of Security and Justice. They're going through our files; they took our computers Kane! Our clients' files. Do you HEAR ME?"

Kane was searching under the bed with the phone on the ground beside him, "I hear you Wes, calm down. We didn't do anything so everything is aces."

"*We* didn't do anything? So I shouldn't mention to them the big Bosnians with thick accents that were in here yesterday looking for you?"

"They're clients Wes. Calm down, let them take everything," Kane didn't keep anything incriminating at the office anyway. All his clients' files were safely stored away at the Amsterdam branch of the Deutsche Bank under the name Herman Rilke.

"YOU CAN'T TAKE THAT!" Wes screamed to somewhere over the line, "What could you really want with my dead mother's brooch, it's hanging on the wall for Christ sake!"

"Wes?"

"Kane, if you're involved and you think I'm going to cover for you, you're going to be disappointed... who's that? Oh great, one second Kane..."

Kane whistled *Bunt sind schon die Wälder*.

"Interpol is here Kane, and the FBI. The FBI Kane, they flew in. They handed me a subpoena for... a disbarment hearing? DAMN IT KANE! You have to appear in New York next week, wait..." he turned his attention away from the phone, "That's not enough time! He needs adequate time to prepare a defense! What? Out of your hands? I want names, badge numbers, and receipts for everything you're touching! ... Kane?"

"Ja."

"You're—"

"Wanted in New York. I heard you. ... I always wanted to visit Wall Street. They say it's paradise."

As Kane and Wes spoke, the escort had calmly taken her money from Kane's Bottega Veneta wallet and made her way out with his belt in her purse.

"They suspect you of disregarding the interests of our clients, engaging in fraud through embezzlement of trust funds dictated by clients that impeded the administration of justice. Don't even think about not showing up. You'll be tried in absentia. ... Now we're all under investigation because the funds are held in trust by the firm. ..."

"It's nothing to worry about Wes. I'm telling you. They're trying to scare you."

"Hold up, one of them is coming towards me."

"Is that him?" a third voice over Wes's line inquired.

"Yes."

"Mr. Ventoni?" the phone switched hands.

"*Doctor* ... Ventoni."

"Lawyers are doctors now? Give me a break. I'm on loan to the FBI; we need to speak with you regarding your whereabouts on certain dates and your... associations. Where are you?"

"Mister Loaner, I can barely remember where I was last night," and he looked around the room, *where is that damn belt?* "You want to know where I was... when exactly?"

"Not when. *Where*," the voice answered, and instantly, Kane sobered up, looking around and out the window at the red bricks with gray cement connecting them all the same to the building next door.

"Where was I, not when, but if then, Mister Loaner?"

"The Slender Thighs Hotel. Have you ever been there before?"

"WHAT? YOU'RE NOT TAKING THAT!" Kane heard Wes yell amongst the ambient clatter in the background.

"Not that I can recall."

"Ever been to New York?"

"I'm licensed to practice law in New York; of course I've been there."

"Do you attend many art auctions and galleries when you're in town?" wind howled through the phone and shook the window.

"No."

"Hmm... I'll catch up with you in New York *Doctor* Ventoni, after your disbarment hearing. I look forward to meeting you. Would you like Mister Van Couperville back on?"

"Nein. Auf Wiedersehen Mister Loaner."

"I look forward to our meeting *Mister* Ventoni."

XVIII
THE RIME OF THE ANCIENT MARINER

Hild had paid me a commission for my services at the auction. I have to admit I jumped when I saw the figures. She said it was because the commission is based on how much the pieces are *insured* for and not how much they're *worth* but even then, most of the pieces were reproductions and not originals. How they were insured for so much was beyond me. One of Johann's friends was the insurance adjuster so in a way that explained things.

The cheque was forwarded to me from Minitar Corp. The concierge found me the address. "Just take care sir, that Cortland Street turns into Maiden Lane. Stay on Maiden and turn on William and you'll see Pine Street after Liberty Street and Cedar Street."

"Cortland turns into Maiden. Stay on that street. Turn on William. Pass Liberty. Pass Cedar. Turn left on Pine. Got it. It's not rocket science. Thank you."

"My pleasure sir."

The place was a block away from Wall Street… figures. I walked to 5ᵗʰ Ave/59 St station in the rain, which was pleasant because the Davidoff burned evenly and tasted as coarse as I preferred it. The smoke swirled and danced around the rain.

Trains whizzed by, some were too full to enter, some cars were empty but everyone avoided them either due to gang members acting like hotshots for bankers or homeless people sleeping.

The one I finally entered had a beautiful piece of graffiti art on one of its doors, a man in a suit vomiting uPhones onto his lap and skeletal hands reaching to take them. I stood holding the pole and saw silhouettes of people in adjacent cars looking down as far as my eye could see. I choked on the distance. A couple sitting near me laughed and giggled and made jokes to each other; I hankered their flushed faces. I had trouble breathing. My lungs squeezed themselves. I looked at an empty seat under me and down towards the other cars again, in the distance, the great distance. I had trouble breathing again and tried to muse on Hild and Chloé and the representative images of their forms, and how best to portray them individually or together but the laughter of the couple sent me into a frenzy. I watched a man with widened eyes reading a *Post* headline about the Spanish arresting four people in allegation and ties to terrorist recruitment, spreading libel and propaganda about the West's mission in their country, and living anti-consumptive lives. How useless humanity has become and how meaningless our so-called civilized institutions. I search for Beauty in vain while others search for greed and money with great success.

When I finally got out at Cortland Station and walked by a snaking line outside Dunkin' Donuts, the rain slowed down to a drizzle and the sun tried to peer through the clouds and hit the face of another couple walking and holding hands in front of me. They avoided the sunlight and frolicked into the shade. I looked to where the sun struggled to shine: the lightened gray of the cement over a small puddle and tried to laugh. Nothing came. How we cry when we laugh and cry when we're alone. In a way, we're always crying because in every way, we're all alone.

The couple sat on a bench and she put her head on his shoulder. How quickly time sent me through a wormhole. To remember exactly what it felt like, how much smoother my skin felt when I was with her, how clear was every thought, how purposeful was every action, and how each of those things, including time, have become inverted and meaningless now. When you're in love your universe is another entity. The problem is posterior; when the entity leaves, your universe leaves with her.

The street had finally turned to Maiden Lane and I saw William St. I spotted Pine on my left and saw a man looking at me through the reflection on a storefront window. Do people choose to be lonely? Is it a deliberate choice made with the express purpose of being alone or of living in solitude? Is that why some artists paint pictures of people with long outstretched arms holding someone far away? Because there's always an infinite space between two people? Or could it be something that naturally happens to some people regardless of their wanting it? That's rather tenebrous isn't it? For how could someone feel lonely when they're with others while some are never alone, even when they're by themselves? Loneliness then, must be something more, and what more is there, than loneliness itself? This city is an abomination.

I turned left onto Pine and looked at a newsstand that had a picture of a young man on the front page of the *Daily*. I peered closer: "Saudi Arabian court sentences 23-year-old student to death for renouncing and questioning authenticity of the Islamic faith."

Minitar rented out their offices from the Dark Château, their parent company and co-subsidiary. The rain started up again as I walked by the *Museum of American Finance* housing masterpieces of embezzlement and fraud and the history of the U.S. currency sponsored by the Federal Reserve. The Federal Reserve is an organization and not a government entity despite what people think. It's a bank founded by congress and being a bank, their margins, business goals and interests, and corporate culture is no different than the corrupt overseas banks we invade under guise of democracy and freedom. I read somewhere that for every dollar the Federal Reserve releases to their printers that sends the money to a bank that then releases it to you, a dollar bill that costs them

4.9 cents to produce, they're owed $1.10, that's an immediate 10% debt to them. Once we start talking millions, billions, and trillions of dollars of released funds to defense contractors, insurance creditors bailouts, etc.... those figures start adding up nicely for the fat white men in slim-fit designer suits.

I peered inside the brown-painted wooden doors and saw a panel for a newly released book: *The MoF presents a gorgeously illustrated book featuring the family trees of the 50 largest banks of the United States.* For $50, readers of *History of American Banks* would learn how 50 of the largest financial corporations in the States came to dominate the banking system, teaching the laymen that banking is not as simple as it seems, and these brilliant minds had to evolve with the times in order to create a more stable, progressive society. The logo of the museum actually used the dollar sign in its name. The green posters sitting against every first floor window was a bolded letterpress: MU$EUM, with the dollar sign slightly ruling over the other letters.

Continuing on and cackling like an idiot, I saw the New York branch of the Deutsche Bank at 60 Wall Street across another Dunkin' Donuts. It was a huge building with blue-stained glass windows towering over the city with its penthouse ringing St. Peter's doorbell. I craned my neck to see the top. An avid comparison between the average man and this building would be the opening sequence of *A New Hope*, where the little plane runs away from the camera only for the leviathan Battle Cruiser of the Empire to consume the shot with its sheer volume. *No Hope* is how I felt.

Ongoing construction across the street in the narrow alley inadvertently helped the homeless by providing them with unfinished wooden awnings the workers had left behind in lieu of the rain.

I looked for the Dark Château when a man in dress pants and a designer umbrella pushed me aside and walked into the bank.

I asked for directions from one of the homeless guys and found where I was supposed to go. Italian loafers squeaked against the marble floor of the lobby. Minitar was listed as suites 3610-3613 on the information panel.

The elevator attendant whistled *Moonlight Sonata* on the way up to the 36th floor and the T.V. spat stock prices using arrows pointing in incomprehensible directions. Because if everyone understood how stocks, banks, and corporations worked, they'd revolt and topple these fancy skyscrapers and take back their savings and tax dollars.

The elevator doors opened to hovering souls and spilled blood and the aroma of Hell masked only by a feigned tranquility by a singular ringing phone in the distance. I knocked on suit 3612 belonging to *Mia*

Søvner, Minitar. It was her phone that'd been ringing but it didn't sound like there was anyone ther—

"Hello?" another woman with short red-hair, a tall, thin figure, no more than 30 stuck her head out suite 3611.

"I'm looking for Minitar's offices."

"You found us. That's my assistant Mia's office. She's not in right now but I can help you."

I walked towards her and she opened the door and invited me in.

Kara Næss, Head of Appraisals, Minitar.

There were two half-drunken goblets on her desk when she waved towards one of the maroon leather chairs facing her desk, "Please. How can I help you?"

I had no plan. A surefire way to lose, "I purchased some paintings at an auction on behalf of Countess Baldure and your firm—"

"Oh yes of course. Madame Baldure! You're the famous Michelangelo! I've heard a lot about you."

"I haven't had the pleasure," I touched and pushed the used goblet aside.

"Where are my manners? Would you like something to drink?"

"No I'm okay," the lights on her phone blinked.

"… Those paintings you're talking about," she typed on a keyboard and looked at one of the three screens in front of her, "Were delivered to an address sent to us by Madame Baldure herself. We *had* the paintings under secure lock and key in our vault and our appraiser was careful not to damage anything."

Did they think these were originals? "I was just wondering where the figures came from, of their worth and not of their value based on your evaluations."

"It's all very technical, I could ask you the same question when you were bidding on them. How did *you* know how much to bid… how much each painting was worth?"

She deflected my question, "Instinct I guess."

"Was your commission not satisfactory? We're certainly open to renegotiation."

Did an insurance company just offer me money? No matter how much I was willing to let this go before, now I was curious beyond reason. Art insurers who deal in billions of currency and the office of the appraiser or adjuster or whatever title they give themselves was as naked as a newborn. Not one piece of classical or fairly modern piece of art in the whole place. There was only a post-modern piece sitting inside a gold frame behind her head of a textured pinstriped suit and a button, which I looked at longer than it merited of my time.

"We're a private corporation you see... *we* pick our clients, you can't just walk in here and ask us to take you on."

"I wouldn't dream of it. May I ask who recommended Madame Baldure to you?"

"Johann!" she blurted out, and then realizing her blunder, typed something and the middle screen reflected a spreadsheet from her eyeglasses, "*Mister* Brahms. Are you acquainted?"

I shifted my gaze directly at her for the first time, "Yes I've had the pleasure," some could convey her as attractive but I could see nothing coaxing behind the face with her mouth agape and big turquoise eyes that looked as if they've never appreciated anything worthwhile.

"I won't take up anymore of your time," I stood up; I had the information I needed... for now.

She twirled her manicured fingers in her hair and shook my hand, "Give my best to Joha—Mister Brahms."

"I will. ... It was a pleasure Kara."

The self-satisfied smoke of my Davidoff followed me back to the hotel; I could finally choose.

* * *

Lethargy came over me when I walked into the Plaza. Though I now had the choice, I still couldn't convey the idea as I wanted on the canvas and I didn't much want to. Hild called after me in the lobby but I ignored her and went up to my room.

30 seconds after I'd entered my room and took a fig from the fridge: "Michelangelo. Didn't you hear me calling?"

"No," I put the fig down and opened the door.

"Where have you been? I've been calling you all day."

I glanced at the hotel phone flashing red and my cell phone at the edge of the bed, "I was at Minitar," it was with a cold stare and dry tone that these words entered her ears.

Thunder struck in the distance and sirens wailed across the city.

"Where?"

"Minitar Hild. Minitar, they've appraised your paintings. They think they're originals. At least I think."

"No, I have them registered as reproductions Michelangelo. A Monet is priceless; you think we can just buy up original impressionist pieces?"

"The numbers just don't make sense."

"They're a trusted firm Michelangelo. Johann recommended them."

The mere mention of his name sent a blind rage into my arms. I nearly grabbed her and shook her, "WHAT ARE YOU DOING WITH HIM?" and with this thought I sank into a reverie.

Why does Hild prefer him to others... not exactly me since I am intolerable but to others, to *anyone* else. Someone who's more partial to *her* needs and at least attempts to support her love for the arts, film, or *anything* other than "sex with thin broads," those are his actual words. Do women prefer insignificant and deceptive men because they remind them of a part of themselves? Do they remind them of the malice part of human souls that the refined and the sensitive and the spiritual fight to suppress?

"Michelangelo?" she waved her hand in front of my eye, "Trust me."

Trust me. What a phrase. Is it a phrase or an idiom? I was never a wordsmith and I was too far along in life to even attempt to tackle a problem as complicated as words. Do writers struggle as much with words as a painter does with his paint and his brush?

"Okay," it is impossible *not* to trust a beautiful woman. Even macho noir anti-heroes who talk about staying out of trouble and *doin' nothin' for nobody* always get sucked into intricate snares set for them by beautiful women... I would not be an exception.

She took a step into the bathroom, "They didn't change your towels."

I looked at her in confusion.

"Well they made your bed but didn't change your towels; let me call," she moved towards the phone, "And get some new ones sent up."

"I had the *do not disturb* on Hild. No one came in here."

"But..." she sat on the bed and touched the sheet, "Where'd you sleep?"

"I didn't."

"Again? Michelangelo, how many hours is that?"

"More than enough."

She saw the canvas facing the wall and walked towards it, "Did you paint anything?"

I sank into the chair and thought about the concept of art as a thing. What is a painting insofar as it is art, something that represents something else? What gives art its *art-ness*? How accurately is the idea illustrated? How transcendental the allegory? What makes an artist an artist versus an imitator of scenes or people? I didn't know.

The view of buildings past Central Park made me dizzy and I put my hands over my eyes to calm myself.

"Are you all right?" she asked.

"Yes."

"You loathe this city don't you?"

"I never thought I'd be back..."

"And me..." she continued, "Because I brought you back."

I looked up at her when lightning lit up the room and her eyes saw through the aching plight of my desires.

"Where would you rather be Michelangelo?"

"Anywhere but here," I looked out into the sea of sirens and buildings covering the sky in black vertical rectangles extending as far as the eye could see.

She looked up and down at me through her nose as if she were offended.

"Hild," I sighed, "I don't mean *you*. Don't pretend to be offended... Don't be offended I mean. I'm talking about humanity."

"Pardon me?" she moved towards the window and looked where I was looking, at an Elmo in Central Park soliciting tips from a girl's parents after harassing them for a picture.

"Where do I go? I just realized. I'm homesick... but I don't... I've never had a home."

"The Catalan air seemed to suit you."

"A mask. Barcelona is a city that hinges its hopes on whether a fútbol team will beat another fútbol team and that will somehow end a long-standing political feud and put more food on their tables? Did you know, my elegant countess, that each of these teams are worth over $3 billion?"

"No but that's one city. It's not like that everywhere! New York has people of all kinds!" a siren moved away from us.

How refreshing to hear the ruling class' opinion on the state of the world, "New York City is a city that hinges its hopes that one day bankers will grow a conscience and tear down these skyscrapers so people can see the sky. Or Paris Hild, you're going to talk about Paris next I bet. The haven for artists at one point but now a paradise for gypsies and thieves and people who frolic from one designer boutique to the next so they can take pictures of themselves shopping and upload them on the Internet? ... Everything we do and say and think is monitored and analyzed by government surveillance under guise of security. Security from what? From ourselves? From those different than us? ... I don't hope because I fear disappointment. With the world as it is, disappointment *always* follows," I lost control of my words; the bending words used with brevity and concise elucidation. For a few minutes, I lost control over what I said and how I said it. That was what she was doing to me. That was what I liked about her; the repressed freedom in herself manifested in freeing others.

She walked in front of me and blocked my view of the purple sky shooting airplane lights across its vast space like a barely touched canvas, "That's what separates you from the oppressed and the voiceless. At some point every artist goes through what you're going through," she pointed to my sketchbook on top of the minibar, "You wouldn't be an artist if you didn't."

What did she know about what defines an artist? "I've never sold a painting; I've never published a poem. What is the distinction between an artist and a painter and a poet? ... I'm no artist," I walked by her and touched the window, drawing the outline of one of the buildings darkened by the clouds.

She reached over and held my chin in her palm, "An artist is not how many paintings he's sold or how many poems he's written. What distinguishes an artist from someone else is, I think, *perspective*. To express thoughts with cohesion and simplicity," a countess was defining an artist for me. This was where I'd landed.

Our eyes were fixed on each other and I could feel her breaths, soft as air and as full as her wallet. How much I wanted to kiss her, to tap our lips together for less than a second, "Thank you," I mouthed.

She smiled and leaned in. Our foreheads touched.

I closed my eyes and when I opened them, she was standing in the doorway behind me.

I am baffled by the ironies of time.

"We're having dinner after the reception. Chloé will be joining us."

Those four words at the end. The words you just read, those words slithered inside my body and warped my mind into a twisted frenzy of inquiry. Is it possible to love two people at the same time? Is it possible to love at all? My nightstand buzzed. I wonder if... Elroy *did* say I could ask it questions.

"Hey phone!" I looked at it for a button and pressed it. Nothing, like a porcupine trying to perform heart surgery with a hammer I tapped the button. Nothing. The black screen mirrored the remaining specks of my soul. I kept my finger on it as I threw it back towards the bed, midair I heard the soulless voice: "How may I help you Mister Eysoup?"

The pronunciation... "Is it possible to love two people at once?"

"Checking my sources," the voice returned just as it landed where Hild had been sitting on the bed, and then after a few seconds, "May I recommend AshleyMadison.com?" followed by a list of affair websites and forums filled with people in search of a cure for the disease that I too now ailed from.

"No No No! That's wrong! Okay next question," I held the button again, "Is it possible for a man to love at all?" which the robot interpreted as "A man who gives love to all!" and returned with a *Puffington Times* article about an affluent attorney who gave his riches to a charity he'd founded.

"You're no help at all!" and there, yelling into a phone I saw the blueprint of our destruction. Not because of who, or *what* I was engaging with, but how close we threaded the line between the beautiful and the ugly. I finally understood the difference between children thirsting for a drop of water, and the diamond-engraved plaque on the door of Nestlé's marketing executive.

"That is uncalled for Michelangelo."

"Off."

"There is hardly a need to be so crass!"

"Be quiet."

"Treat me with respect Michelangelo!"

And with that, a computer demanding respect from me, fuming and flaring like a cartoon character, I threw the phone across the room towards the minibar.

XIX
DREAM DEFERRED

It was still early so I went for a walk in search of inspiration for my portrait. Walking down Madison I stopped in front of a bar when I saw Johann caressing a woman's chin. I wanted to hang him upside down and bleed him after cutting off his fingers to stop him from ever touching a woman ever again. I've never been a faithful man but I wanted, no, *yearned* to the bottom of everything I've believed in for there to be a Hell and for him to burn in its deepest and hottest fires. Later that night he would walk in and kiss Hild and her face would flush with admiration.

I couldn't comprehend her loving him. Any love. Mostly I was confounded by the love humans feel for one another. Does this make me insane? Am I not of our kind? More complex and believable as a sentient being because I can react to many things that does not affect others? I do not know. I have no experience of this idea of love; even my adulation of Chloé and Hild must stem from a foolish sentiment of how I ought to feel when confronted by a manifestation of Beauty; tricks of self-delusion and deception in an attempt to perpetuate our virus of a species.

* * *

I got to the reception before Chloé had even finished her performance. I left earlier because I knew it'd be impossible to get a cab during the rain but Hild had hired a car for me; as soon as I left the hotel I had a ride. How much simpler life is with money. Wish I'd have known that before I took the subway to Minitar.

The car stopped in front of SixtyFive, a lounge atop 30 Rockefeller Plaza. There was an outdoor terrace that we couldn't use because of the weather and a panoramic view of the Manhattan skyline being drenched by purifying rain in vain. It was contemporary all around; not a single art piece in the entire place, only leather couches filled by empty heads and empty tables under drunken hands. The ambiance of the place was the laugh of the rich in ascending or descending tones in different harmonies and counts. It's not so much a laugh as it is a "hmmmm" mixed with a "hehehe" in short exhaling bursts. That was the soundtrack of the place. I was the only person there for Chloé's reception thus far; everyone else seemed to be regular customers, happily paying $50 for 300ml of Yuki No Bosha Nigori Junmai Ginjo sake, $60 for a shot of Johnny Walker Blue Label, and $105 for a shot of Don Julio Real.

What's the difference between paying $50 for a sip of sake and a family in Detroit starving to death? Car companies not being able to meet their quarterly profit margins?

The bartender and I shared a chat about the latest aerial drone strikes in Pakistan. "This close. We were *this* close," and his thumb and index finger nearly touched when he showed me, "To getting the terrorist bastard."

"And did you?"

"No. Intel was bad they said," he was a vet; that was about all we had in common.

"So what did we blow up instead?"

A corporate honcho in an expensive suit and a patronizing smile interrupted me and ordered a *Vesper*, which was Bootlegger Vodka, Spring 44 Gin, and vermouth; probably trying its best to resemble the drink from that old James Bond book. And anyone who wears a suit and walks into a cocktail lounge thinks they're James Bond. Corporate thieves in suits are no exception insofar as terrorists in suits that destabilize poorer countries to reap their natural benefits are an exception to the U.N.'s Declaration of Human Rights. What a joke.

He tipped the bartender 84 cents on that $22 drink. Not even a dollar bill.

"Want me to grab you something?" he asked after he was done with the secret agent.

"Non grazie," slipped out because I was thinking about the Tuscan sun.

"What? Was that German?"

"Italian."

"Just as bad. My pa fought them both in the war. Mussolini was one tough mother...."

Somehow speaking in Italian brought up nostalgic memories of his father and Mussolini. I knocked on the counter and turned towards the live entertainment; a man tuning his guitar to the chords of Townes Van Zandt's *Waiting Around to Die* waited for the reception party or more people.

"Eycsüp!"

I turned and saw Elroy walking towards me.

"What are you drinking?" he asked.

"Water, I don't know if they have espressos here."

The bartender heard me, "Espresso? Coming right up sir!"

"Of course they have espressos here Michel. It's five bills for a 2002 Pol Roger Winston Churchill," and with a wave of his hand, he flagged down the other bartender, "2002 Perrier-Jouët. Start a tab," and handed her his Platinum American Express, "It's champagne, apparently Chloé killed it tonight. I wasn't there but man people were talking about her like... like... I don't even know a musician as good as her."

"She's one of a kind," I regretted the words as soon as they left my mouth. Why were words getting away from me like this?

"Look at you! All flustered!"

"Your espresso sir," the bartender put the cup and saucer in front of me.

Saved by the bell, "Thanks."

"Stop it," Wolfe tapped my shoulder.

I stared into the dark brown espresso cup and swam in its helix, "What?"

"Brooding over possibilities. You can't love an idea Eycsüp."

"I don't know what you're talking about," I looked up and through him out the window.

"Can you touch an idea Eycsüp? Can your idea touch you? Can it feel your presence? Does it light up a room when it enters your mind? Does it understand everything that comes out of your mouth?" the bartender poured him a glass of his champagne.

"An idea can't betray me."

"Ideas betray us all the time! How does—"

"I love this city! God I love this city. You want pizza? A block away. Sandwich? A block away. Dessert? A block away. A broad? A block away. You're never more than a block away from anything!" Johann had entered and was hollering at us from across the room.

"How I wish he was less than a block away from death so Hild could be free of him."

"What?" Wolfe leaned in.

"Nothing."

"Elroy! How's tricks?" he laughed beside himself and slapped Wolfe on the back.

"Brahms," Wolfe nodded and sipped his drink.

"And the artist! How wonderful! Everyone is here!"

I extended my hand but he wanted to fist bump like he'd flown in from Baltimore, "I just scratched my balls," he laughed again.

I grabbed his fist and shook it. He irked me to my core wherever he went, always boasting about his swagger in the vicinity of Hild or some other woman, always full of coarse and uncouth jokes which usually aroused the unrefined laughter of his ignorant, round, and stupid-mouthed associates. His style was foolish, a ruddy complexion and whitened teeth that others must've endured because he was always laughing loudly at one of his own stories. He wore the most obscene colors: a pink suit or a purple striped shirt with greenish pants... I drove myself to the point of insanity trying to fathom why Hild never embarrassed, ridiculed, and kicked him to the curb. He took advantage of her any chance he got and I couldn't understand what charm, if any, she saw in him. When others (mostly his friends) called him especially talented or smart or this or that, I never understood what they were talking about. He was like all the others and by that I mean *exceptionally* average. I did not see him distinguished from any other modern citizen. I never caught a glimpse of him doing anything valiant, intelligent, or whatever else they thought he was. Presumably he had told everyone how classy and refined he could be and everyone seemed to listen whenever he opened his mouth. I never believed one word of it. He is a gasconade; the mere idea of him as a charming gentleman was absurd.

"Kara says hi," my eyes watched him carefully.

Wolfe's head shot up and he waited for Johann's response.

He scratched the back of his head, "I'd heard you were at Mini—wait... *who?*"

"You heard me."

"I... uhh... don't know who you're talking... check out this app. It's wonderful! I boot it up," he turned his phone towards us where pictures of women popped up along a map, "And I click on any girl I like, and I hit the thumbs up or thumbs down button right? ... And if the girl does the same thing... like we both hit thumbs up... we match up! Then we message each other! Man... this thing gets you *laid* like you won't believe!"

"How fascinating," would the world be better if people like him were extinct? If there were a button I could push to end the miserable existence of these people... would the world be a better place? Or would it open up a gaping hole to be filled by something worse? Would it be a better place without any one of us?

"You're telling me! Whoever thought of this idea is a genius! A GENIUS!"

I shot a glance at Wolfe, who in shame averted my eyes.

"You should sign up for this Michael. Otherwise people think you're a fruit... what with the drawings and all."

"It's Mishel."

"Blondes, brunettes, redheads, they're all women aren't they? What's the difference?"

"Do you really exist Johann?" I asked, "Are you just a figment of my imagination?" I reached out and touched his shoulder, "A caricature of everything I loathe and everything leading society to its doom?"

"Lay off the Armani bruh," he wiped his jacket where I'd touched it.

"Still at war huh?" Wolfe called over to me.

I gulped my espresso and walked towards the exit for a smoke, "War's over friend. *Everyone* lost."

People came and went under the raining night sky. An off-duty officer asked me for a light and was surprised when I used a match and not a lighter. We had a meaningless conversation about the rain and her job and some of the popular spots around the area. I could tell she was lonely. Her eyes carried a chilling angst lit up by the ember of her *Pall Mall*.

I don't think anyone knows what it's like to be completely alone. Even lonely people aren't alone in the complete sense; they have themselves. Being completely alone means you don't even have yourself. You float through experiences as if they never happened. You string words together but see no meaning in them. You hear things but you don't listen. There is no time. There is no space. There is only the abyss of human existence and you idle at the bottom while those around you float up to the top with each other.

"Are you from here?"

"Yes but I've been away."

"For how long?"

"Not long enough."

"A lot's changed."

"Not enough."

"A lot of zoning permits were filed, there were some renovations… come on. The city looks better you have to admit."

"You're right."

"No. Don't just agree. Tell me what you really think."

Again, the words were at my mercy. "That is what I think." I was back to my old self.

"It's everyone's dream to live here. Actors want to retire on Broadway; artists want their studio here, lawyers want to work on Wall Street. We have everything."

"Hey!" someone yelled across the street and then a bottle smashed against the wall.

"Excuse me," she looked towards the sound.

I thought about what Johann would say to her, loathing the city but lying to her because she seemed desperately beddable.

"I thought you were off duty," I inhaled some of the Davidoff and the burn made me think of my blank canvas.

"There is no such thing in this city," she sighed, "Thank you for the light," she only slightly tapped my fingertip, and then disappeared towards the alley where the commotion had occurred.

"You're welcome," she was too far to hear me.

I looked up at the ivory towers above us all. Nowhere else equals the feral design of this city. Tall skyscrapers that act as gorges hollowing out between flat cement dancing into narrow alleyways like bottomless pits. Building walls rusted the color of blood. Sometimes when you look down the horizon from afar the city looks wider than it is, like a thin field of magical lights gleaming with the hopes of children and idealists; a light on at midnight in one of the penthouses or the changing hues of the

Empire State Building. Most of the time though, the city is covered with a layer of honking cars and greed, sirens and the war cry of solicitors, all full of brambles and impenetrable conscience; garbage, steaming manholes, and heat waves twirling smog and pollution through your lungs like mirages as you walk breathlessly through a boiling desert.

Someone walking past me did a double take and walked back, "Hey... You're the guy... JAKE!" he called his friend over, both wearing the same slim-fit tailored tuxedo, "You're the guy who knocked out the Bull!"

"I'm sorry. You have the wrong guy."

"Nah nah nah," Jake said, "The way you're holding the cigar, that's exactly how that guy held it! ... What's your name? Raphael? Bernardo? Leonardo?"

I looked at my hand holding the cigarillo but didn't see anything special about it. "Excuse me but I'm wanted inside," I hated myself for it but I threw out the rest of the Davidoff.

"Yeah yeah yeah. We'll see you in there. There better be hot biddies in there!" they high-fived each other.

Upstairs, I saw Wolfe with his head buried in his phone, "The Euro is down again."

"And tomorrow it'll be back up. Why do you play these games Wolfe?"

"You have to don't you? Otherwise you don't exist and there's nothing. No truth. No knowledge. No beauty."

"No... beauty?" the thought horrified me.

"Now couldn't you just paint this scene?" his eyes fixed on the doors.

And like the kind of timing you see in a Hollywood blockbuster, Hild and Chloé walked in.

Their bodies were delicate and slender, weaving through the air like silk ribbons. Their skin as white as hot milk and their eyelashes curled in front of their emerald and blue irises like gems among summer trees. They were walking paintings, as still as a masterpiece and as passionate as a poem. The more time I spent looking at them the more and more the ribbon tightened around my neck, and their bodies, pale as they were, were colored like a Van Gogh red, passion-red, blood-red inklings that dripped along on the very marrow of my soul.

"De er smukke."

"Yeah.... Whatever you just said Eycsüp. What*ever* you just said."

There was not a single person in the entire place, other than Johann, whose eyes were not fixed on Hild and Chloé walking towards us at the bar.

They filled the space between us with such ease I felt time slow but speed up at the same time. I couldn't enjoy the anticipation and savor the moment of them walking up to us because it happened too quickly.

The canvas. The portrait. Portraits, it was right there in front of me.

Was this happiness? How do you describe it? A fluttering and spiraling leaf breaking free from a branch in solitude? A leaf dropping and weaving through the air? Its mirrored reflection from above as it lands silently and deliberately on the water and forms small ripples outwards? No. That would be euphoria; a *euphoric* moment could be described in that sense, like when I first heard Chloé play.

What is happiness then?

Time. Moments. This moment. Now gone. Gone forever. Only its memory remains, and from that, the memory of its memory.

"Hi Michelangelo! Sorry I couldn't get you a ticket!" were Chloé's first words to me, with her white dress in perfect cohesion to her yellow hair.

I stood, "I'm sorry to have missed it. Wolfe said you were wonderful tonight. I wish I had flowers to give you."

"That would be cliché."

"ALF!" Johann yelled and stumbled towards us and snickered while he did so, "How were the songs?"

"They are not songs Johann," Hild's head sunk into her chest just above her bosom, contrasting her milky skin with the black dress she was wearing when I saw her in my room just a few hours ago.

It's okay, Chloé seemed to shrug to Hild.

"You like that Michael?" he elbowed me in the ribs, "You call her Hild, I call her Alf!" he cackled and wiped a fake tear from his eye. I wanted to make him cry. How? Simple. Take his money. Take his possessions and he would beg me to give them back. He would beg me with tears like a dog and there'd be nothing he wouldn't give, not even... I dare not tarnish her name in such a manner.

"Wolfe!" I snapped my fingers in front of him and he snapped out of the trance Clo and Hild had put him in. At that moment, I had the title of my portrait: Clohild.

"Sorry!" he shook his head, "Another bottle of this please," he asked the bartender, "And two... three?" he pointed at me and I shook my head, "Two glasses for the ladies."

"You put him in a trance," I pointed to Wolfe to divert their attention away from my own awe.

"PLEASE!" Hild smiled, "The only woman I've ever seen put *the Wolf* into a trance was at a brothel in Amsterdam."

I chuckled.

"Did you just... smile?" Chloé's eyes widened.

"No."

"Yes you did!" Hild pointed to my mouth.

"I did no such thing. It was a mild grin."

"That's wordplay. It was a smile," Chloé laughed.

The bartender brought the glasses and the bottle, "Now it's a *real* celebration," Hild said and they clinked glasses.

I saw Max in the crowd, mingling and talking to people his own age about Chloé's performance and some of the Impressionist paintings at the Met.

"I'm going to say hi to Max."

"Who?" Johann asked.

"Maximus," what a name he'd been given. From the Latin *maximus* meaning "the greatest."

He turned with grace, "Ahh," he shook my mind, "The master of the high renaissance! ... Excuse me for a moment," he told his compatriots and then walked with me to the side, "How is everything?" and shook my hand again.

"I am well. I must say I was slightly eavesdropping and heard you talking about the Impressionist paintings on display at the Met... how were they?"

"Of a different realm."

"I believe that."

"Often I find myself wondering," his eyes misted, "Whether all the bright and bold colors were passionately embraced by their canvases because nearly all of them suffered great tragedies; whether financial, emotional, physiological, or mental."

"There's an old adage about suffering and character isn't there?"

"There's an old adage about old adages."

I chuckled.

"MAX!" someone else called.

"Go ahead," I said, "They want you."

"Even the *arteests* of this city know so little about art that they have to stand in line to be educated."

"We should stand in line anyway," I nodded and made my way back to the gang, where Johann was just finishing a story about having gotten into a skirmish with four men regarding their abuse of a woman on the subway. The audacity... I wonder if he has ever even ridden on the train in his life because I'd only seen him ride in Hild's family limos.

To be fair I could see a mild cut on his face but it looked more like the nail wound from a woman he'd tried to kiss who pushed his chin away. I couldn't confirm it; the idea of him as an ogre and an abuser made better sense to me than those green pants acting chivalrous.

"And there's bruises all around my back and chest," he went on....

"Can I ask you something Michelangelo?" Chloé tapped my forearm.

I walked away from Johann and we made our way towards the other end of the bar, "Of course."

"Why don't you pursue painting full time?"

"What do you mean?"

She'd never even seen my work.

"Johann said you were at the Minitar offices. You're running around for Hild's paintings; paintings already drawn and copied and copied and copied."

"News travels fast," I mumbled to myself.

"You should quit," her eyes consumed my universe. What chance did I have, a mere man, against such a gaze?

"I couldn't live if I painted Clo; the masses don't like *art*. They like lines on blank canvases or copies of old masterpieces that are now just pieces of weaved cotton. They want actors that pretend like they care about Africa and the slave trade and corruption and charities. People who adopt children from Cambodia and make sure their publicists are there to promote and take photos of the adoption, never mentioning how many members of that class they've rendered homeless by the demolition of their homes for their studios and 40 bedroom mansions. We never hear about their investment portfolios, filed away inside bank vaults, being the reason parents from third-world nations agree to have their children adopted for a chance at a better life."

"That is so... wrong," she shuddered, "You're threading the needle between simply being misinformed, and a sophism through manipulative lying."

"No love," I cradled my hands behind my back, "There's no manipulation. People love art but hate artists. They love Follywood because they know actors and actresses are full of shit; they're filthy creatures that lie with every breath they take for money. They love to look at art by dead people at museums and discuss it using big words they don't understand amongst themselves but insult and mock artists because they have a deep knowledge of artists' purities. Artists are particular. They're weird by the standards of normality and the public. At the very least, they *have* to be different. They're bound to have a different perspective on reality, a friend told me that. Well... *good* artists have to have a different perspective. ... And the public hates that. Why do you think artists become famous the second they die?" words fled from me in fright and I was trapped in the Twilight Zone of space and time.

"Because of what their art *could've* been when they were alive if they'd kept working. A sense of tragedy brings people together doesn't it?"

"You're right about the tragedy thing but not the rest. People loathe the different and the intelligent and the honest and the courageous because those people bare parts of themselves that the public could never have. ... Actors erect complex masks to hide themselves behind their marketing strategies and publicists, their masks make them identify with the lower-classes: I'm just another guy like you. I have kids, here's pictures of them; I have a mortgage, here's a picture of my quaint house; I have an unsatisfied wife or husband, here's a picture. They'll coo about it on that pigeon site with a CosmicLoots coffee cup."

"But doesn't that make them like the rest of us? What separates these subsets other than money?"

"People will *think* that what separates them from the masked faux-arteest is money, that's the difference. It's a clever manipulation. I need a smoke. ... Let's walk," we made our way back downstairs in silence. I was glad she didn't press harder because this was not what I wanted to talk about.

The second I lit my cigarillo, she said, "Go on, you said it's a clever manipulation."

"Let's talk about something else," a car honked at a jaywalking pedestrian who walked past us and into the building.

"No, I want to hear more."

"Okay. Where were we?"

"The separation of the lower-classes only thinking what separates them is the money and how it's clever."

"It's the values Clo, the honesty, and courage that lives within those that pursue their dreams. A successful actor is praised for never giving up his dreams to become someone else for a living but to dream to be an unmasked artist is a mortal sin in a consumerist society. Artists don't consume; they create things that can't be consumed with riches. You consume art by seeing, by listening, by feeling, never by buying."

"What about me Michelangelo? I never play my own compositions for a crowd. Variations yes, but never my own work. I have to play the notes Chopin or Schubert or Bach wrote. At best I am an excellent imitator. That's the mask *I* wear."

"You don't think you're an artist?" I wanted to cry. How society had waned her confidence to the point where perhaps one of the only remaining artists of our generation would think she is "At best, an excellent imitator."

"Well. No. I don't. But I wouldn't be even by your definition anyway."

"No Clo. I am not a member of the ruling public, I'm presuming they don't *let* you play your own pieces because analytics have shown that Chopin or Bach or whoever would sell more tickets, so they tell you to play those pieces right?"

"As cynical as it seems, yes."

"Of course... people don't want to hear your pieces, and I don't mean that because they aren't good, I'm sure they're beautiful, innovative, even transcendental. But people want to hear the dead guys because they can't stand change. Someone comes to listen to your interpretation of a Chopin Nocturne, he has *some* idea of what it should sound like if he's heard a Nocturne before. The change required of him, of his ideas of music, his beliefs, and his identity is minimal at most, and he comments or critiques your ability to convey passion or sadness or to effectively hit the notes... or whatever else he deems worthy of a skilled musician. And it's that, it's the label: "musician," because he fails to recognize that as an "art." What makes art a thing, what is it that gives it its essence? He thinks this to be the noblest and purest intellectual pursuit.... Now, if you ask that same person to listen to Chloé's composition of say... I don't know, "The Floating Clouds above the Summer Mist," a completely original piece, only a movement that requires avant-garde art or music will be accommodating. Keep in mind that these people are not members of the ruling class either. And even then, the members of the avant-garde, their support is not out of a passion for originality but rather," I took a quick puff of the Davidoff and she reached for it and took a puff, "Out of a need to be different and a rebellion of the older stuff because they've been emulated for so long that the style is tedious, boring, and still nothing compared to the original."

"So the avant-garde are really puritans wearing masks?" She took another puff and blew it towards me.

"Some of them. NO MORE BACH. I'm sick of Mozart! I'll take anything else. These are their mantras. It's not out of a gratitude of your gift to the world in your sublime execution of pieces written and performed by you... people conflate intelligence with difference, so they'll do anything and say anything so *others* will call them different."

"Ideas, like history, fabricated by the powerful, must go through a certain evolution. I used to think natural musical genius was art. Now when I think about it, natural musical genius doesn't exist," her fingers shook when she took the last puff, consumed by my words. *There is no hope*, she read in my furrowed eyebrows of anger and intense but dead eyes.

"I'm... sorry. Play me one of your pieces sometime. I'd love to hear it," I checked my words carefully. Words more powerful than atom bombs and more cutting than AK-47s.

People are fragile and words, not bullets will break them, and once they break every part of them spills out. Their soul, spirit, identity, ugliness, and their beauty. It's all there, right in front of you if you know where to look. Most people see the ugly and I didn't want to become that. I thought I looked for beauty but then wondered why I often say such ugly things.

"I didn't mean to upset you. You're amazing. And tonight was... *is* a celebration," I'm poisonous, the nerve I had to say these things to her rivaled Johann's shamelessness. "It's as if... how do I describe this... it's like I'm a middle jigsaw piece trying to fight my way to the corner so I can escape. But I'm a middle piece; I won't fit in the corner. So what do I do?"

She laughed, "I know how you feel," she put the cigarillo back in my hand and kept her fingers touching mine.

"No. You can't. You're the picture I think I'm building."

She moved closer but her face was distant, her eyes looked inside me and not at me.

"Miss Lysettensen!" a woman walked up and cradled Chloé's hand, "It was... *you*, were wonderful," and the man standing behind her nodded.

"Thank you," Chloé bowed her head, "I'll join you in a moment."

"That would be ecstatic!" the woman giggled and walked inside hand in hand with her date.

"Excuse me," she walked back inside.

I tasted vanilla on the cigarillo and smoked the rest in great haste trying to savor the taste of her lips.

When I walked back inside, Johann was talking about a watch he'd seen at an auction.

"Trust me, it won't be a waste of money like other auctions," he was telling Hild, "It's a Cartier. 18 carat gold with 126 diamonds at 1.83 carats. The crown has a sapphire cabochon, and the band is a beautiful purple snake-leather texture. It's a Roman numeral face, guided by a deep blue winding mechanism. The case of it all has a convex curve; there's a guilloché dial and its hands are sword-shaped. You can either get polished or satin finished links on the bracelet. It makes you float through these events," the way he talked about this watch, about something that tells us what time it is in the most rudimentary sense, the words he used, the descriptions he gave.... I'd never heard him talk about a *person* with the same intensity or the same vigor.

"Now I want to see what it looks like," Wolfe put down his drink and tapped on his Orion Nanoyear tablet.

"It's the Ballon Bleu de Cartier. It's..." he looked at a piece of paper he had in his pocket, "Here, reference WE900851."

"The white and black of the screen flashed across Wolfe's green eyes, "Got it," and he pointed the screen towards Hild and I.

"Yep! That's it!" Johann signaled for another drink and sniffled, "I have to take a piss," and strutted towards the restroom.

I looked at the screen. 47 grand for a watch, perplexity boiled my veins, it cost more than the average household income of the most civilized country on the planet. "We live in an age when unnecessary things are our only necessities," and I looked towards Chloé talking with some patrons near us.

"What?" Hild was reading the description of the watch and pinching the screen.

"It's Oscar Wilde.... Excuse me," I thought I saw someone familiar in the crowd.

"Yeah! See Alf! Even Oscar Wilde agrees I should have this watch," Johann's voice was drowned by the ambient babble of the crowd as I pushed the people trying to see the familiar face.

The music stopped and the storm popped specks of water on the window.

"Shell..."

I was trying to reach the corner.

"R... goi—"

"Excuse me," I tapped the woman on the arm.

"Yes?" she turned around and it wasn't whom I thought it was.

The music came into focus, "Where are you going Michel?" Chloé wiggled two of my fingers, "Oh... Hello again. Michelangelo, this is Countess Van Schoonenburg; Countess, this is Michelangelo Eycsüp."

I was surrounded by countesses, "It's a pleasure," I slipped my palm under her hand.

"Nice to meet you. Are you the artist?"

How does everyone know who I am? That's all it took to be known in this city, know someone influential and toss money at copies of something once rejected, then accepted, then analyzed, then reprinted.

"No. I'm a paint-thrower."

"Don't be so modest," Chloé scoffed.

"Honey! Sweetheart," a voice called, "Come! I want you to say hi to Othmar Poricus of the IMF."

"Excuse me."

"No.... Please," I turned towards Chloé and guided the countess towards the voice with my hand.

"Thank you."

Chloé snickered.

"What's so funny?"

"Poricus. What a name."

"Yes."

"Sounds funny."

"It's Latin."

"ALF!" Johann called into the crowd and laughed into my arms in drunken stupor. "Isn't that hilarious? ALF! I thought of it today."

"Have you always called her that?" I wanted to cut his tongue out and glue it to the top-right corner of a canvas with blood dripping down towards the center where the tongue-less starved held their mouths open hoping for a drop that just missed them. And the snakeskin of that Cartier wrapped around all the hands.

"You call her Hild. I call her Alf. Together she's Alfhild!"

Exceptionally average. Even his name, Johann, was the German form of John, the most average name I'd ever heard. His parents probably approve of him because he swims so well in the ignorant sea of society.

"No Yo," I took a deep breath, "You call her Alf because you're a small man and you want to make *her* feel small. Like how you make a waiter feel when you order a bottle of the most expensive Cava and snap your fingers at the menu. Isn't that also why she wears flat loafers or rain boots and you never take off those ridiculously heeled dress brogues? So you can stand at her eyeline and feel uselessly equal? Because deep down, you know you're inadequate and you don't deserve her. So you have to work to keep her self-conscious and insecure. It's a great con Hunn."

He pulled up his drink in front of his chest.

"... I call her Hild because she's the personification of battle, a sweeping flight through the minds of thinking men at war with themselves, a war that lingers long after she's gone. I pronounce it slightly like "hilt" because the T adds a secondary meaning, that of a sword, because if someone is lucky enough, she can be a handle and a guard against the loveless and the unloved."

Chloé pulled my arm back and I wrestled free and got real close to his glazed eyes that had never seen past that gargantuan nose, "Call her an elf again and I'll cut your legs off at the knee, put it on a canvas and title it "Johann's heel, and paint some sculpture in the background. I'll sell it for good money too. Then I'll buy her something nice and elegant for her birthday, maybe an Hermès shawl or something..." my whispers must've frightened him because he started backing away the second I stopped talking.

"Sorry sorry," he bumped into someone, "Sorry," he apologized to the waiter for no reason, "I mean thanks," and put his drink on the tray and disappeared into the crowd.

Chloé's eyes hadn't changed; could she hear what I was saying?

"Let's eat something. I'm hungry."

"Yes." I was ready to leave as soon I came in but I wanted to support Chloé. It was the others, those around us laughing and snorting nothing of significance and boasting everything of insignificance. No amount of glib charm impressed me or made me trusting of such hollow words coming from empty heads. I wanted the unwanted: the sterile and paining truths of the cosmos. Of course, after recent events I'd realized that trying to be an *artist* and thinking in this pedantic way made me tediously flawed and paradoxical. I was aware of this irony and there was nothing I could do to change it. Space and time created me, and the time will come when I would no longer occupy any space.

"It'd sell too... isn't that disconcerting?"

"What would sell?"

"The painting..."

I gave her a vexing look.

"... Of Johann's legs," she laughed and it sounded better than the music she played. No, dearest reader, of course it didn't actually *sound* better than her hand gliding across that instrument creating divine waves; it's a metaphor. Are metaphors still employed? Perhaps ideas are compared some alternative way in the modern world. Her laugh. What did her laugh sound like? The straight lines of vibrating grass during a summer breeze, or the song of crickets in the foreground of the harmonious whooshing from soft winds over an inlet at night. *That's* what her laugh sounded like.

"Hild said we had reservations somewhere?"

"Pfft," she scoffed, "I know a killer sandwich shop up the street. I'm not going to a place that's going to play botched Chopin or a Mozart Divertimento while we eat."

"Fair enough. Must be a curse not to be able to enjoy such music anymore."

"Why do you say that?"

"Because you're gifted to see the flaws of a misplayed piece."

A beer belly with a thinning hairline in a pinstriped Brooks Brothers suit brushed by her on the way down and she tried to place his face. "By the way, you want to hear something weird?"

"Always."

"Someone offered to buy my cello before the show tonight."

"Your cello?"

"Yes," she nodded.

"I'm just trying to wrap my head around it. Someone tried to *buy* a Stradivarius?"

"Yes. It wasn't you was it? I got a note in my dressing room that someone was willing to make an offer on it. I thought of you... it's so out there I thought it was your way of saying 'you're more than an instrument.'"

"Is money that valuable now? Someone can *buy* a Stradivarius?" I shook my head, "No Clo. You think too much of me."

"Okay. The note gave me chills. No name, no nothing. Just a number with "For your cello" scribbled beneath it."

"You still have the note?"

"What are you ... *going' to investigate it?*" she faked the Bogart transatlantic accent, "It was cuz' of *her*, that woman who in that dark hallway," she talked with her mouth slanted to one side, "Told me about that cello. And I'm here cuz' of a god*damn* cello."

"No. Information is knowledge, and knowledge is power."

"You're not a private investigator."

"Forget I said anything," I followed her down the stairs happy to be free of this responsibility. As sarcastic as she was being, she was right. I wasn't going to risk anything over a cello... no, over a woman, and with the way she was describing the whole thing, it sounded serious enough to end bloody.

Two steps from the bottom the wood creaked when she turned back, "It must still be in my dressing room."

I reached into my pocket for a Davidoff, "If you find it," I lit it right when we walked outside, "Send it to my hotel. I'll find out who sent it," and took a drag.

She took the cigarillo and looked at me. A silent background to the city's screeching loudness surrounded us. Without warning she slapped her knee and roared with laughter, glowing in the yellow lamppost above us. "Stop it! I'm going to cry," she continued snickering, her flat stomach expanding and contracting rapidly. "Oh my God!" and she started laughing again.

"What's so funny?"

She calmed down a few seconds later, "YOU!" and started laughing again.

I watched perplexed faces walk by and watch us as if we'd just escaped from Bellevue.

Her cheeks turned red and she covered her mouth. She pretended to reach into a pocket and take out a cigarette, "If you find it," and pretended to put it on her lip, "Send it to me," and blew air out of her mouth and laughed, "I can't do it! I can't!" she pretended to take a drag and blow air out again, "I'll find out who did it. ... You really are a... a... character out of a movie or a book."

"Yeah yeah yeah. Laugh it up princess. Don't sell that cello and quit your day job."

"It's this way," she kept laughing and moving down the street.

"Everyone's a comedian."

"Thanks Michelangelo. I mean that... I do."

"For what?"

"For the laughs. I know you don't mean to and I rarely get an opportunity to laugh like that but you're just so funny. ... I'm not laughing *at* you. It's a compliment."

"Don't worry about it Clo. I love hearing you laugh anyway."

She stopped as if she'd never laughed in her life, "What?"

"I..." Stuttering. Sweat. Exhaustion. I yawned and so did she, "The sound of a beautiful woman laughing is better than the best song never heard and the most delicate poem never written."

The laughter started up again, "You're doing it on purpose now. You're not really like this..." she stopped and looked back at me, "Are you? ... No! No one is."

The city quieted down for a second and I heard crickets. She stood under the night sky, lit up by the building lights and the streetlamps, bathed in Tuscan yellow.

I felt someone quickly approaching behind me. I stuck out my elbow and grabbed him by the arm, "Oh. What do you want?"

An out of breath Johann wrestled free and wiped his jacket where I'd been holding him, "Alfhild said you speak Nordic. Do you?"

"Nordic is not a language. Do you mean Danish?"

"That doesn't help," he chortled.

Chloé started walking back, "What do you need?" the wet parts of her hair sparkled through the night air.

"I want to say 'You're hot' in Nordic."

"Nordic is not a language Joe. Norway has two written forms: Bokmål and Nynorsk. If you want to *say* it and not write it it's just a matter of dialect."

He looked at her like a child lost in a forest just before dusk, "Uhhhh. Yeah I want to say it."

Hild was Norwegian so I figured he did something and had to make it up to her. "Norwegian and Danish are relatively close; in Danish it's 'Du er smuk.' Du is you, er is are, and smuk is beautiful," I cringed when I had to say 'beautiful.'

"I think it's a different word in Norwegian Michelangelo," Chloé nodded.

"Beautiful?"

"Yeah."

Johann watched us like a mechanic in an operating room, with wide and empty eyes.

"It's *vakker* in Norwegian Bréanainn," she continued.

"Vakker du smack. GOT it. Thanks!" and he ran back onto the rain towards the entrance of the lounge.

"He's lucky he's rich," Chloé chuckled.

"Yes," I closed my eyes and breathed in the cool air. When I opened them, Chloé's ad appeared on a board under a parasol of a store's patio.

"We love Chloé Lysettensen!" someone had written in white chalk.

I took to studying her name and how unique it was. It wasn't Chloe; that would be too bland. No, it was Chloé, with an accent over the E, and no one I'd encountered had ever omitted it.

Why? What did it mean? It wasn't pronounced any different as if it were Chloe.

É. Why the accent? That small simple line over the letter. Was it because she flew over everyone else with the music she played? The way she seemed like she floated over the asphalt when she walked? Her imaginative voice when she talked?

É. Was it a slide from above that would fall when it got to the edge to the letter or was it a set of stairs you could climb if you got above the straight vertical line of the E?

It was like an uncompleted halo over her name, like God got lazy when sculpting her and went out for a smoke, and then someone else stepped in and finished what he started.

The accent was driving me no more insane than she was. I looked over her head and she was just looking at me, not staring, but just looking at me, until finally she saw me gaping at the sign and turned back under the sound of the torrential downpour.

"It's a biblical cataract," she paused and listened to the rain to break the tension.

Hvordan kan du elske hende? It'd been a while since thoughts came to me in Danish and *I didn't know* why they started up again.

"Clo, we should look for a cab," I looked at her heels nearly flooded to the top, "Hop on my back, your shoes are getting wet."

"When it rains…"

I turned around and signaled her to jump on.

"You want me to ride you? … I mean like a horse? … I mean on your back. I mean…," and she just stopped.

"We're not kids. Just hop on."

"I didn't know you spoke Danish," she took off her shoes and held them and hopped on my back.

"My family is originally from Denmark. I just picked it up around the house and reading Kierkegaard."

"That's heavy," she clutched my shoulder and neck, "THAT WAY YOUNG PRINCE! GIDDY UP!" and saddled my hips with her bare feet.

I moved towards a couple of taxis parked in front of the doors we'd left. Someone whispered, "This loser is *deep* in the friend zone bruh!" and I barely understood what he meant before Chloé rasberried at them and pecked me on the neck.

"Don't kiss me out of spite for others. It's insulting," even though it was the most pleasure I'd had since I visited my father's grave.

"More often than not, most people get together out of spite for others who say it's impossible."

"And more often than not, those that seem perfect for each other are often horrible to each other."

"They think we're perfect for each other."

"Who?"

"Everyone: Hild, Wolfe, even that ogre Johann."

"It vexes me how he's able to invoke the dislike of even the most refined and elegant woman."

"Even Hild barely tolerates him," she eased her grip on my neck and jumped off on the carpet in front of a hotel.

"Yet she warms his bed."

"Don't be fooled by appearances. I think it's more political than that. She comes from a prominent family; he comes from a prominent family."

"What is this?" I watched her put her shoes on and massage her right calf, "The Italian Renaissance? What? ... Is a Medici to wed a Borgia to end a feud?"

"Didn't you say *nothing changes with time* once?"

"I don't recall."

"I think you did. We've come a long way from the renaissance but not much has changed."

"I guess not," I lit a cigarillo, "You want one?"

"Sure."

* * *

I got back to my room at around 11 but I felt the insomnia taking me by the throat and squeezing until I was forever awake. The cracked open window ensured that the canvas facing the wall in the corner fiddled back and forth with every mild gust in its direction.

Where and how was this going to end? Is there some pleasure in getting lost in the woods? Some euphoria upon standing alone on the sand in front of the sea?

"You're listening to Late Classical FM. It's 11:25 and we have some Chloé Lysettensen for you. The beautiful cellist playing beautiful music."

I was tired of hearing of Chloé, I walked over to the radio to turn it off but then it started: the notes carried a dim melancholy across the room through high and low waves of agonizing elation. I stared at the back of the empty canvas. In a society that requires of its citizens only that they perform competently their specialized social function, be it their industry or relationships, people are equated with their ability to perform this function, and the remaining parts of their identities are simply permitted to subsist as best as they can. Unfortunately this means it's relegated below the void of consciousness and eventually forgotten. The arts are thus forgotten because they are labeled as unproductive and inefficient; they have minimal profit other than their narrow use as investments for the ruling elite.

Hild had said she would help me get to sleep so after a few tries I finally got her on the line.

"Is something wrong Michelangelo?"

"I couldn't sleep."

"Oh," she yawned, "Does that happen often?"

"Yes."

Silence.

"Hild... can I ask you something?"

"Yes."

"It's personal."

"It's quite all right. What's bothering you?"

I walked over and fiddled with the canvas and looked down the city at a dog digging through trash, "What do you see in Johann?"

She walked somewhere and I heard a door close, "Are you jealous Michelangelo?"

"Not in the least. I think of you somewhere, with some*one else*."

"Who?"

"I won't know that until you answer me."

"Hmm," she sat down and suppressed a yawn, "He's charming and he's a good guy."

"Those are labels. There has to be something specific. If I ask any man or woman what they think of the person they love they'd answer exactly as you answered it. How do you come to this understanding? Where does the unity of a relationship come to an apex? At what time, *where*?"

"It's because you think about these things. *That's* why you can't sleep Michelangelo. ... Let it go. You won't... No; you *can't* understand everything."

I sat on the armchair near the window, "My goal was not to make it personal and or offend you. What do you think of Lord Byron?"

"Lord Byron?"

"Yes."

"Bit of a romantic for me. Melodramatic maybe. He said something about sleep didn't he?"

How clever of her, "*Death, so called, is a thing which makes men weep, And yet a third of life is passed in sleep.*"

"That's it! You Foolgled it didn't you?"

"What's that?"

"You don't know what...? Never mind. Impressive recall Michelangelo. What's it mean?"

"I wish I knew."

"You're a poet! Take a guess."

Thinking about the poem my eyelids felt heavier and heavier and just as I was about to drift into uncomfortable territory a knock at the door threw me awake.

"I'll call you back," I hung up and opened the door.

"Chloé..."

She pushed me into the bed and we fell into it because I held her hand.

"What are you—"

She put her finger over my lips and shushed me.

I moved closer and kissed her, thrusting my mouth so hard into hers our teeth touched; I picked her up and threw her on the bed while she moaned under the pearly glint of the dimmed nightstand light. I kissed the pink of her knees and looked at the strands of her yellow hair in lines on the white pillow.

Deep inhale. Where am I? "How childish to dream of such things."

I dozed off again. This time it was Hild tucking me into bed and pecking me on the forehead. She did a double take before she got to the door and leafed through my sketchbook on the TV stand. In a haze I saw my phone with Hild's name highlighted green and hours elapsed on the minute counter.

I awoke to the somber, long-winded melody of Fauré's *Élégie* (Op. 24) in C minor with the sound of the cello carrying the main theme as the piano provided a harmonic accompaniment. I just laid there, still and motionless in bed. Could I lie here forever? Only when I heard a dog bark outside and the major-key middle section of piano bore the melody before it passed it to the cello did I rose and looked outside. The sun had just begun to rise in the distance and in haste I grabbed my sketchbook from the nightstand and tried to catch the purple and the orange and the green before the clouds oppressed them in dulling gray. Under it all, an old woman with a dog walked towards Central Park followed by a middle-aged businessman walking east.

"That was Fauré's Élégie in C minor from 1967 with Leonard Rose on the cello accompanied by the Philadelphia Orchestra conducted by Eugene Ormandy. Up next we have Tchaikovsky's fourth movement of Symphony No. 6, also known as the *Pathetique*, conducted by Myung-Whun Chung and performed by the Orchestre Philharmonique de Radio France. You're listening to Classical—"

I turned the radio off.

XX
SEEKER OF TRUTH

A phone rings. Death calls.

The clock buzzed 3:45 A.M. "It's not even four yet."

"I know. There's been another murder."

Britten sat up from beneath the blanket and the cool night air made *goose flesh* over his body. "What a day..." he used the table as support because his knee had recently started bothering him; some of the unsolved murder cases on the table slipped off.

"What... a... day," he grabbed his knee as he picked some of them up. One tabbed "1998" slipped back out again and the pages feathered onto the floor.

"What a day what a day what a day," he stepped on the picture of the victim; the abusive, hard drinking husband and father in a fitting wife-beater stained with booze and sauce. "Straight out of a comic book." Justice demanded that he treat this case like any other and solve it. Humanity demanded that he didn't. He hadn't decided yet.

He filled a cup with lukewarm water and put it on the nightstand outside his bathroom before he stepped into the shower. The hot water eased the tension on his knee.

Drying his hair on the way out he knocked over the glass with his towel and the water saturated the face of the 1998 murder victim.

He stepped over the glass, reversing the painkilling effects of the hot water.

"Taxi!" he called on the street as a cab whizzed right by him. He walked into the subway and towards the scene Alicia had closed off for him. "Another day. Another death." he tapped his knee.

An old woman begged for change before he entered the lobby of the Dark Château. He kept his gaze on an overworked security guard and a caretaker who kept stretching his back and holding his hip.

"What is this place like during the day?" the people that roamed these floors were people he always avoided: women who whored their souls as secretaries of balding, inelegant men with self-aggrandizing chuckles. Masked by the middle-class as patriots in the eternal fight against a shadow enemy created to fill the void of heroes. Reds. Nazis. Terrorists. Muslims. Freethinkers. Whatever they call them now. He wanted to be out of there before these vultures began their religious thieving.

"When do they open?"

"Good morning to you too! ..." she looked around, "Where's my coffee? I told you over the phone didn't I?"

"I... forgot it," what a day, "We can't have people marching in here and trampling all over this place."

Let them all stay home, he thought; they would be happy in a lavish basement with unlimited Maker's Mark and cheap homemade pornos. These people who think that subtitled foreign films have too much reading; he wanted to hunt them like they pay to kill big game under controlled environments. Let them loose in a jungle, naked to the bone and see their empty heads and full bellies flop left and right and up and down.

Alicia laughed and tapped him on the shoulder, "Yeah. Let me just call the president. ... *Close down* the offices of one of the world's biggest banks on a market day because some woman got killed."

They walked past the security desk and into the elevator where the elevator attendant hummed a song as they made their way up to the 36th floor, "You see anything? Anyone stand out?"

"Probably. Thousands of people come in on any given day sir."

"That's what I figured."

Uniforms and CSAT crowded around a doorway about halfway through the corridor.

"Who is," he corrected himself, "Who *was* she Alicia?"

She swiped the screen on her tablet, "Kara Næss. Worked for Minitar insurance. They appraise and insure artwork and investments."

"Insurance on investments? Even when they're wrong they're right huh?"

"We're going through her calendar but so far nothing..."

"Boyfriend?"

"We don't know. We've tried contacting her assistant but we've received no response."

"This is the only office Minitar rents?"

"No. A..." she swiped on her tablet again, "Mia Søvner also works next door but we can't get ahold of her."

"Is that her assistant? ... This Mia?"

"We don't know. Files are hard to come by. We got a call from their lawyers that demanded a subpoena, they're subsidiaries of further subsidiaries that's not even a parent company."

"What's going on? What do we know Alicia?"

"We have stab wounds to the abdomen and chest. There was a safe behind the painting in there. Empty now, and two glasses on her desk. Other than that everything seems normal."

"What was the painting?"

"What?"

"The painting. What was it?"

"I don't know Ben."

He chuckled, "Okay. We got a dead appraiser... excuse me," he squeezed into the office, "Two glasses on the table, and an empty safe. Insurance scam?"

"Maybe she uncovered fraud or something."

"Maybe..." he looked around the door and everyone quieted down. "What are you thinking?"

He looked at the smog line outside the window, "I'm thinking... these are wine glasses. Why? She had no appointments. Unless she didn't register the appointment on purpose... or did they appraise something important recently? One that would be a cause for celebration?"

"No. I don't think so."

"Hmmm," he walked over and sniffed the glass, "*Red* wine. No cause for celebration."

"Can we dust these for fingerprints please," Alicia called into the doorway.

"Sure ma'am," a technician walked in and registered the evidence and began dusting for prints, "He's the golden boy; always finds what's there."

"Don't talk about me like I'm not here," Britten heard an officer telling someone they can't go in, "Who is that?" he exited and saw a custodian nodding to the commands of the officer, "Excuse me officer," and then he addressed the woman, "Good morning Miss. I am Detective Britten, do you work in these offices?"

"Good morning detective. I clean offices once a month," she had a slight accent, "I have to get in to clean or I no get paid."

"Well. This is a crime scene. No one can go in or out if they're not authorized but don't worry, when we're done we'll clean up a bit and let you in."

"Okay, gracias."

She turned around with her cart towards some of the other offices.

"Wait," he ran up to her, "Can you get into this office?" he tried turning the locked knob of the other Minitar office.

"Yes of course. That is Mia's office. She very nice."

"I bet she is."

Keys jingled and the door squeaked open to an organized and compulsively kept office.

"Thank you. I'll let you get back to it."

"Habe a nice day officer."

"And you as well," what a day.

"Ben? What's going on?" Alicia appeared behind him, "The scene is in the next office."

"This is a Minitar office too," he approached the window, "Do me a favor, touch that piece of paper right by you."

"What?"

"That folder there, just grab it for me."

"This one?" Alicia picked up the folder as dust flew into her nose and she sneezed twice. "Not as clean as it looks."

"Bless you!" Britten moved towards the desk, "Wouldn't you say that someone who is near compulsive about their office would also take the time to dust it?" he pointed to the papers and the phone in line with the edges of the table.

"Yes I would say that."

"Then can we conclude that there being dust in an office such as this following a person such as the image we've created of her, that she hasn't been in her office in a while?"

"Yes we can conclude that."

Britten opened the top right drawer of her desk, "Nothing but files and papers," then he stopped suddenly and looked up.

The uniform officers scampered across the office to watch him.

"Ben what is it?"

He sniffed, "That smell... I've smelled it before," he started going through the drawers in the desk, and then the file cabinet before he froze looking at a picture frame atop the file cabinet in the corner.

"Ben?"

"What... a *day*."

"Ben what is it?"

"It's the victim from the Slender Thighs. Our Jane Doe."

"The Málaga victim? From Spain? ... She works here?"

He clicked the blinking light on her phone.

"First new message. 'Hi my name is Kane Ventoni. I'm calling on behalf of a client who would like to insure their 1709 Stradivarius. Give me a call back so we can arrange it down at your offices.' End of first message. New message. 'Hello, it's Ventoni again, I wanted to follow up on my message, since we haven't met I can only assume you're not interested in my offer.' End of message. Last message. 'Hello. I vant to let you know you make big mistake not seeing my man. I see you soon.' End of message." there was an obvious accent in the final message.

"The first message. Ventoni. We keep hearing this name."

"The second victim? So Søvner and Laukkanen are linked?"

"We're getting somewhere. Someone is tying up loose ends. Look up that cello this Ventoni guy is talking about. That's a lead right there. There can't be that many rare cellos in this city. And that last guy... his accent was familiar."

"What's going on here Ben?"

"I don't know... I bet this Kane knows though," he addressed the admiring eyes of his colleagues standing in the doorway, "Bag and tag everything ladies and gents. And call me when those prints come back from the fingerprints on the glass we found in Næss's office."

"Yes sir."

"Come on. Don't call me sir."

"Okay sir. ... I mean, Detective Britten."

He heaved and caressed his knee when he finally got outside, and the first of the suits, the moguls of lower management hoping to one day become the boot that suffocates the neck of the lower class, started revolving through the doors behind him.

The woman who asked him for change at sunrise was still there, asking a suit for money for a coffee, and when he refused, wanting the newspaper he held under his arm. The suit screamed no and threw the paper in the garbage behind Britten.

"You're wasting your time sister."

"Who isn't?"

"You know how they afford those suits? They steal them. Thieves never share their spoils."

She laughed through her missing teeth.

He gave her three dollars for a coffee. An act of the so-called *good* to absolve the conditions of their fellow men from the haughty to the helpless to the dead. How can something be built on a broken foundation? No matter how much cosmetic pampering is applied, the foundation rots and rots until it finally... gives.

XXI
THE RAVEN

The fraud unit had brought in a psychic to help locate Ventoni. They need psychics to find lawyers. Dirty money can be swept for only so long.

How could these officers "keep an open mind" and listen to these people who declare openly that they've streamlined the secret truth to the existence of all things? Quasi-philosophers, with *profound* meditation tactics in their luxury flats, full bellies, and exploding wallets contemplating life and death and the eternal problems we all face. Relationship trouble? Money trouble? I can help. With the police it's always locating someone: a missing child, a runaway teen, a disappeared suspect. They're always near water and in a closed space, and even if the person is found on the rooftop of the Empire State, they'll say that the sewer and water mains run right under the building and the *enclosed* space is an allegory for the suffocating city.

"Boss," someone handed Britten a folder.

"What is it officer?"

"We found that cello you asked for. It's a Stradivarius right? From the early 1700s?"

He nodded.

"I see water. He's near dripping water," the woman-psychic pretended to almost faint.

"He's near a faucet? WHOA! Pay the woman *detective*," he had enough of these games.

"You are skeptical sir. You've lost someone," she looked at Britten.

Sophistical appeals to virtue and honor and prophecy; God chose to bestow *me* with this gift because I am these things. Sometimes they deceive themselves into thinking they know something about the universe or the stars, and how closely it's linked to human destiny. Blasphemy. Heresy. Though Britten often couldn't pinpoint *how* they commit heresy for it has nothing to do with him; religion and divinity is often individual as each person has their own soul and is responsible for it.

"Yes I see him," she fell to her knees in the middle of the squad room, "I hear music. Classical music."

She would've heard the officer talk about the 'early 1700s Stradivarius.' No one said they weren't smart. They are merely buffoons though they're ignorant of it as is everyone who believes their lies but rarely does anyone laugh at them or get pleasure from their delusional ignorance.

"We have the address," the officer pointed to somewhere on the sheet Britten was reading, "There's only one from that year in the world boss. This has to be the girl."

Why is it, Britten wondered, that astrologers and psychics always concur with the opinions of their clients, "We think he's in hiding," as obvious from their required assistance. Perhaps it's the people around them. They profit from the words they spew, that they have the universe's blessing and the stars speak to the favor of the client's goals.

"What's going on?" Alicia entered the room and walked through the psychic and the two detectives from the fraud unit towards Britten and the officer.

"We're going to the Ritz," he said to Alicia. "Officer Baldo, would you please go down to trace and forensics and breathe down their necks for those fingerprints?"

"Yes sir—I mean Detective Britten."

"Excellent."

They drove by a club where more of the ignorant bathed in each other's indolence. A beautiful woman stood alone in a lime green dress away from the crowd. Britten looked up from the file he'd been reading and spotted her. She was talking on the phone but she was crying. People are beautiful but they're also fragile. Others brushed by her and screamed and woo-ed and hollered but no one noticed her pain, or they did and didn't care. She hung up and for a second, only a split second; she caressed the screen with her thumb. A tear landed on the thigh of her dress, camouflaging itself with the rain but he saw it. Britten sees everything.

"This city..."

"It's a little late Ben. Shouldn't we wait until tomorrow?"

"We push everyone away because we live in eternal fear that we'll feel something. And we're so attached to technology and our robotic counterparts that feeling some*thing* for someone else is an abandoned idea of the foolish and archaic."

"What?"

"No. I think we're dealing with a time-sensitive issue," he flipped the page to the autopsy of Søvner, "The dead exceed all that ever lived. There is more night than day."

"What?"

"Nothing."

"You know, you've been acting kind of odd recently."

There was silence in car for a little while, "By the way," Britten finally broke it, "What's with all the guys squeezing in the doorway whenever we arrive at a scene?"

"They like to watch you work. You've asked me hundreds of times."

A porter opened Britten's door and he instinctively went for his piece.

"We're here."

The Ritz. Britten tipped the valet and they made their way into the lobby, "We're looking for a Chloé Lysettensen."

"I'm sorry we can't give out information about our guests."

Britten sighed and flashed his badge.

"I'm sorry we can't give out information about our guests," he repeated.

Britten turned to Alicia, "Call the judge. Get a writ. Let's shut this whole hotel down. Make all these guests find new rooms."

"Sir? I am the hotel manager. What's the problem?" another man in a fine-pressed suit stood next to Britten across the counter.

"I need to speak with Miss Lysettensen. It's for her protection. She may be in danger. We have reason to believe a crime may take place here or near her."

"Is it in the interest of her safety?"

"We wouldn't be here at this time if it weren't."

The man nodded to the concierge and after a few keystrokes he handed Britten a keycard, "Miss Lysettensen is in the Premier Suite. You'll need this key to access the elevator."

"I will join you as well," the hotel manager walked behind them.

The elevator doors beeped up to the 19th floor, where Britten heard voices coming from the door they were about to knock on.

"The light isn't right! This damn rain!"

"Don't get upset with the rain," a woman's voice answered, "It can only fall the one way."

The manager knocked on the door, "Miss Lysettensen?"

Footsteps approached the door and a woman answered, "Good evening."

"Good evening Missus Lysettensen, I am very sorry to disturb you but they're from the police and they believe you may be in danger."

The word 'danger' hastened someone's footsteps towards the girl.

"Danger? Me? … Please come in."

The doors opened to a 100 square foot suite with a gratuitous view of New York City. Britten approached the window and looked down at the city, "Almost makes it look calm doesn't it?"

"The orchestra has put me here," she said, "I'm sorry, I never got your name."

"I'm sorry. I am Detective Benjamin Britten," he extended his hand.

"Like the composer," she giggled.

"Yes."

I approached the detective from the side, "We meet again Detective Britten."

"Mister Eycsüp. We always seem to do so in the oddest circumstances."

I had paint on my hands, "I'd shake your hand but..." I showed him my fingers: blue and orange from the acrylic base of the canvas sitting on the easel near the window.

"Please. Sit," Chloe guided everyone to the maroon leather armchairs around the main room of the suite, "Would you like a drink: juice, coffee, tea?"

"No thank you. ... I'll get right to it Miss Lysettensen. You're the owner of a 1708 Stradii...Stradi... Stradivarius... that's a mouthful... are you not?"

"You can't own a Stradivarius detective. It's on loan to me," she guided his eyes to the opposite corner of the painting, where her cello sat in mild night.

"Has anyone suspicious approached you? Anyone trying to buy it in simple ignorance or even anything really out of the ordinary worth mentioning?"

She paused for a second, "No. ..." wasn't there someone that handed her a note or left a message?

"Wait," she recalled. "Yes, someone approached me after one of my shows. Wanted to buy it. Can you believe that? *Buy* a Stradivarius?" she laughed.

"People will try to buy anything these days," Britten fiddled with his notebook, "Did you get a name? Anything that would help us pursue the person? Did you see him? Maybe we could have you sit down with our sketch artist and work on a composite."

Something didn't add up, "Two detectives and the hotel manager of the Ritz enter a room late at night to ask questions about a possible cello purchase?"

"You're too smart to be an artist," Britten chuckled, "This lead turned up in a murder investigation. We're just being extra careful and following every lead."

"Is she a target? ... Is she safe?" her beauty, her hands, her fingers.

Britten turned to me, "We have no reason to believe she's a target. Her name showed up in an insurance firm and like I said, we're just taking precautions..."

"And doing our due diligence," the woman finished Britten's sentence.

Insurance firm. Minitar? "Okay."

Thunder hit the window and the wind shook the easel; I scrambled to save the canvas from falling and barely caught it by its corner. Britten ran over and helped me and looked askance at the two little hooks at the bottom of the canvas missing the chain in between.

"You should get a new chain."

"It's around here somewhere; I must've lost it."

We put the canvas back on the easel further from the window, "Well I won't take up any more of your time. Thank you for everything." The manager apologized again for the interruption when they left.

"What's going on Clo?" I walked where Britten had looked down at Central Park. Twilight would eventually slant towards the trees, bathing them in royal gold. The light of the city danced through the creases of the aged elm, and poetic words dissipated with the downpour while the wet leaves vibrated in the wind with purpose.

She walked over and connected her tablet to the room's speaker system. The lamenting notes of a single piano filled the room. "I was in Almería, it was late. I was walking through the streets after a rehearsal, practically running really, I just wanted to get home. When I walked by this lounge or restaurant or bar with one person in it... she wasn't doing anything, just sitting there. Quietly. I could only see her face staring at her wine glass because of the candle on the counter. Then this piece started to play," she closed her eyes to listen to a series of low tones increasing in tempo, "The single piano. Lonely like the woman at the counter, took me over like a wave, and everything started moving through me in slow motion. I heard this piece rushing home; the person inside was hearing it while musing alone at a bar. Some will be walking, others in a car travelling or on a bus or an airplane, maybe even laying down on a bed. Wherever they are, whoever they are, are they all hearing this piece? Can we see another listening to this piece with the same incorrigible effect as us? To see the piece and our lives through another's eyes, in slow motion. Where was the person sitting when they composed this piece, what were they thinking about?" she took a breath.

"I think we're blind sometimes because things happen to us in our lives, and some of those things require an action we'd never imagine ourselves performing. But here we are, after having done the thing we vowed never to do. So now we have to come up with ways to deal with it."

She hovered towards me, "Living, modern life I think, is done somewhere else. We're born, we grow, we study, we go to work and take care of our family. We never realize how short time is, so we always have this sense of urgency about our actions. To keep moving faster and faster, and we fail to see that by zooming past everything faster and faster, we miss the very life we're trying to live."

"Exactly. It's a fear of time," I took a step towards her, "The fear of an ending time, of our time, of death. Maybe some people, like you hearing this piece, can overcome that fear and calm it, so little moments in our life can feel as if they're slowing and we're free to feel whatever we please without any fear," if the strings of her cello could vibrate with the melancholic passion of every lost soul like me, I would want to be one of them until time comes to a stop for us all.

Just as the ivory sound of the piano keys faded out and the sound of the rain became once again, the ambient noise of this city's allegorical purification, she held her hands out and I let myself fall into her arms. Her lips were iced with flames, freezing the veins in my forearms then immediately warming them.

XXII
THE SORROW OF LOVE

"For only $36.99 per month, upgrade your music subscription to be free of ads. ... It's June 18th. Where are you? You're stuck in your dead end job going nowhere. You wish you were somewhere else. That's possible. Take a vacation with Vacair. Don't waste your money on stuff you'll never use. Use it to experience *paradise*."

Chloé pulled away and walked over to her tablet; the screen lit up her face in eggshell yellow as she swiped left and right.

"What is it?"

"It's a news bulletin. A lawyer's wife was murdered."

I'm supposed to mourn the death of a lawyer's wife? "Someone gets killed everyday Clo."

"Not like this. They report that she was tortured in her living room. They found cut pieces of her Persian rug down her throat. Pieces of rug! Until she choked."

"What in the—" I walked over and looked at the screen over her shoulder. I could smell the perfume on her neck; it was a toss-up between Dior's *J'adore* and Dolce and Gabbana's *Eau de Parfum.*

The ex-wife of prominent attorney Kane Ventoni was murdered yesterday in her house in the Hamptons. Police have reported that there are numerous leads and suspects in the case with potential ties to organized crime. Robbery has not been ruled out but the lead detective on the case has reported that the medical examiner found pieces of the former Mrs. Ventoni's rug in her stomach and throat.

"The most innovative field."

"What's that hon?"

"Death... is the only thing humanity has gotten better at during our existence. We've gone from wooden clubs to unmanned drones. We have more *creative* ways to murder each other than we have ways of filtering water or making love."

"And both those things are better than death," she walked over to the cello and took it off its stand.

"Are you going to play something for me?"

"Not Misty, that's for sure."

"Clever."

"I have to practice Michelangelo. I didn't just wake up one day and realize I was gifted at the cello."

I sat down where Britten had questioned her and turned the chair facing her foliage green dress.

F-sharp, D, G, C, she turned the pegs. Then she stopped below the middle C and looked at me, right at me, while the cello rested on her thigh.

"Can I ask you something?"

"Yes," a new compact binary candidate for a supermassive black hole was recently discovered at such close orbital separation that we *may* discover something about the merger of supermassive black holes; but nothing in the universe would stand in my way to immortalize the spaces she'd occupied.

"What'd you think of me when we first met?"

I was caught off guard, "Pardon?"

"That first show; you were in the mezzanine right? In the dark suit? I saw you when I walked in. You were there but you weren't really there."

"There's no way you saw me. There were thousands of people."

"You were sitting next to Hild. I saw the glare of someone's phone beside her and you sat on the opposite side. The screen lit up your face a little bit. I *could* see you," she let the bow slip down through her fingers.

"What would you like to know?"

"What was your first impression? Of me I mean. Had you heard about me before? What was it like when you saw me for the first time?"

I tried to imagine the moment in my mind like a painting long faded by history and memory, "I wanted to meet you after the show and saw you being congratulated through receding hairlines and champagne glasses.

'There *she* is,' Hild said. I looked over and saw your hair, bright and radiant. The temporality of the moments that had lined up to form my life was sundered. You occupied a perfect space in that short time. Immediately and almost unconsciously, I was envious with the poison of rage at the Michelangeli of the other universes that had met you or the ones that would meet you because I wanted you all to myself. In equal probability, I lamented for the Michelangeli that'd never meet you; I pitied them because they'd never be as good an artist as the ones who'd seen you, felt you, and talked to you. I began to loathe timelessness.... Even me, this Michel, wasn't and probably isn't a good enough painter to express these ideas. It would be foolish to even attempt it," I'd been an appraiser for mere hours that day but I knew deep down, none of me in any universe could ever be worth *any* of her in one.

B, C, G, "You thought about a lot," she smiled and started playing.

The notes went up and down in anguish and glee, stretching through the air like a summer breeze and floating among the winter clouds. Lifetimes walked through the smoke but the tempo was blue and green and yellow and red. Colors were different now; I could *hear* them. Different hues and shades and from different perspectives. Roses were redder because I heard them bleed when they failed to kiss the sky. The sun's yellow was warmer in the breeze and cooler in the heat because I felt its color in my soul. The roots of old trees in abandoned fields were like silent wisdom passing through my mind. And the sky's blue, oh the blue; it was like seeing it for the first time each time I saw it, and it was still less blue than her eyes.

The beauty of the notes meshed well with her personal beauty. I had trouble separating the two. It was as if two became one. She *was* the music and the music was Beauty.

Are those that pursue simple beauty happier because of their pursuit? Throughout my life I've tried to seek it with pleasure but I am almost always apprehended by its tyranny. The horizon has never penetrated my soul; the sky has never parted its clouds to illustrate its magnificence. My eyes do not grasp the depth of its ardor. Could it be that my pursuit is in vain? Everything I have touched, felt, or seen has been imperfect and incomplete. My paintings are filled with anguish and everyone will feel its pain and incomprehensibility. None of my creations could be beautiful because I am competing with some*thing* superior to myself and thus all I create is fated to be ugly and incomplete. The more I thought about it and every time I used the word I seemed to diminish its qualities. If I refer to all of these things as beautiful... it'll lose its panache and if I come face-to-face with real Beauty I wouldn't recognize it.

Nightfall dimmed the sky's grape-purple hue, a dusk of oranges and tangerines and grapes as if it belonged to Dionysus. Chloé had lit some candles in lieu of the electricity. They sizzled and its drops crystallized as it wrapped around the stick like a spiral. Somewhere else, fire cackled and lit up the night for a few seconds at a time. A snake hissed at me and slithered along the grass. It stopped, turned back on itself and swallowed its own tail. I backed away among dead winter trees and bumped into Chloé shivering at the base of a distant mountain.

Desolation avalanched through me. The snake weaved in between my legs and worked its way up to my arms. I reached and touched her hand and the snake slithered onto her palm and rotated around her neck and looked at me. Suddenly she's holding an apple. She bit it.

"Whoa," I opened my eyes to the sound of Chloé munching on a Granny Smith.

"No electricity yet," the grey sky lit up and glinted across her supple nose. She tossed it at me, "Try it. It's good."

I caught it from under the blanket. "It's not peeled. ... Where'd I get the blanket? When did I even fall *asleep?*"

"You ask too many questions," she sniggered.

I bit exactly where her lips had been. It was sweet and delicious and I wanted more. She tapped something on her uPad.

I wallowed in its taste, "You know, in a parallel universe, that kumquat could be an apple."

"You and parallels. There's no such thing. This is it," her eyes pierced my chest and I felt slimy.

"That can't be."

"Deal with it. It probably is," a cello variation of an étude played through the speakers of her Kumquat.

"You should charge this. You're only at 6%."

"Maybe you didn't hear me. There's no electricity."

"We're at the Ritz!"

"The Ritz still needs electricity Michelangelo. The storm knocked out some towers and some cables or something."

"The Dark Ages cometh again."

"The Dark Ages neveth lefteth."

I wasn't awake enough to fully appreciate her.

"You need an espresso!" she walked towards the phone before she realized there was no power, "Right," and headed for the door.

"Hello?" someone knocked just as Chloé approached the door.

"Yes?"

"Chloé. It's Alfhild."

She opened the door to be face to face with Hild's Burberry jeans, Hunter rain boots, and Prada biker jacket.

"You guys don't have electricity either?"

"No," Chloé opened the door further and Hild entered and saw me.

"Michelangelo. You *slept*?" she looked at Chloé for a second then back at me.

"I don't know how it happened."

"Doesn't he look at peace when he's sleeping?" Hild asked.

When had she seen me asleep?

Chloé nodded.

"When have you seen me asleep?"

They both laughed.

"Let's go down for breakfast."

"I need to get cleaned up," I got up and stretched. The water swirled through the drain and made that weird noise when it fell into the pipe. I could see the corner of the white marble counter by the candle Chloé had lit. I watched it burn for so long the water turned cold.

"That was a long shower," Hild tapped her Hermès umbrella on the floor.

"I... by the way Hild, did you know where was a murder at Minitar?"

"A murder?"

"I don't want to talk about this," Chloé came out of the shower drying her hair, "You used up all the hot water Michelangelo. It's too morbid. Let's talk about something else."

The music cut out, "Battery's done. We're on our own. No technology! The apocalypse is here!"

They laughed.

People complained in the stairwell for their inability to use the elevators.

The ladies convened to the restroom before we sat down and it was just Wolfe, Johann, and I. There were some lights on in the center of the room, perhaps from a generator; otherwise little gas lamps that gave the room a bluish-yellow vibe lit up the whole place.

"PSSSSH," Johann made an explosive sound and rounded his fingers further away, "SO ... SOO... what's the word? TAPPABLE! ... SHHH SHH SH."

A young woman came up to our table, "Hi," she looked at Elroy and I, "May I offer you some breakfast?"

"Yes," Wolfe nodded, "I'll have the Eggs Benedict and a large OJ please."

"And you sir?" she asked me.

"Double espresso and a glass of warm milk please. Not the milk *in* the espresso but two separate cups."

"Okay," she scribbled in her pocketbook, "One OJ with eggs benedict, a double espresso, and a glass of warm milk; anything else?" she didn't look up.

"Martini. Extra *dirty*," Johann tittered.

She looked at the clock in the corner: 8:07 A.M., "Okay."

"Brrr," he wrapped his shoulders in his arm, "Is it just me or did a chill just walk through this place?" Johann laughed.

At the same time, Chloé and Hild were coming and I eavesdropped the last part of their conversation, "He'd pick a fight with the moon if it didn't shine right on his canvas." Hild laughed.

Johann slumped in his chair when he saw Hild.

"Who was that?" Hild asked.

"Who? Nobody." Johann pulled his chair in.

"The origin of David and Goliath," I whispered.

"I'm sorry?"

"When the giant cyclops Polyphemus met Odysseus on the island of Sicily and asked his name, Odysseus said his name was *Outis*, which means *No man* or *Nobody*."

"Odi-who-now?" Johann twirled his index finger around his temple and mouthed *I don't know* to Wolfe.

I ignored him, "Now, Polyphemus scoffed at hospitality and trapped Odysseus's men in his cave and kept eating them. Eventually after passing out from the wine he was blinded by Odysseus with a hardened and large wooden stake. He burst awake and asked for help from his fellow giants... but when they asked him for the name of his attacker, he could only say..." I looked at Hild.

"Nobody!" she answered.

"And his friends thought that divine power was seeking retribution for his sins and recommend that he pray for a cure."

Johann was whispering something to Elroy and he stopped when he noticed all of us staring, "Oh... are you done with that *marvelous* story?"

"Yes."

"What was the point of it, if you don't mind *me* asking a question for once."

Hild tried to say something but I didn't let her.

"Well Joe... Sometimes *Nobody*, is the main character in a story."

"Interesting."

I got up, "I need a smoke."

"I'll join you," Hild said, "You're going to need this anyway," and handed me her umbrella.

We walked outside and I popped open the orange Hermès umbrella and watched people run from A to B in haste, "It never ceases to amaze me."

"What?"

"People running in the rain. Do they think running faster lowers the chance of getting wet?" I lit two Davidoffs and handed one to her.

"You knew those guys hadn't read the *Odyssey* right?" she asked as soon as she'd exhaled smoke.

"Elroy has... besides, I don't like people who pretend to be well-read or educated while bordering on quasi-intellectual babble. Never discussing anything of importance past how a dame looks or whom they've bedded," I forgot who I was talking to for a second; she was his girlfriend and I immediately regretted what I'd said.

"Fair point," she ignored it. It was silent for a few drags barring the pattering rain and the sound of its drops landing on the umbrella above us. She moved a small step closer to me, "You know Odysseus reveals his name to Polyphemus right? Once he thinks they've snuck out of the cave and are sneaking away."

"And Polyphemus prays to Poseidon to punish them and they barely escape. I remember the tale."

"Just making sure you're not a quasi-intellectual babbling nonsense and thinking about women."

My cigar slipped through my fingers and landed in a puddle near my boot, "Fair point."

She watched it doused in water, "Aren't you going to light another one?" she raised her eyebrow as the final haze of smoke from the cigar rose to my eyes.

"No. I've had enough for one day."

A man holding a newspaper over his head in a trench coat and brogues ran by us and inside the lobby but then stopped and turned around.

"Mister Eycsüp."

"Detective Britten."

Hild put out her cigarillo and stood there.

"I'll be right in Hild," I held the door open for her.

She walked inside.

"It's never going to let up huh?"

"I guess not. ... Mister Eycsüp. You mind if I ask you a few questions?"

"About what?"

"Minitar."

"I'm not sure how much help I can be but fire away," I started walking inside and we stood near the door.

"Did you know a Kara Næss?"

"I didn't *know* her, no. I was at her office a few days ago to discuss Minitar's work on some appraisals done on some paintings I'd purchased for a client."

"And the lovely young lady that was just with you is your client right? The same one who was at the auction? Countess Baldure?"

"I shouldn't say detective."

"Not a problem. We found some evidence that places you there. You should know we think you're the last person to see her alive."

He was gauging me, "Other than her killer you mean."

"Of course. So I am to understand you were at the office on business?"

"Yes of course."

"You don't have a relationship with Miss Næss outside of this appraisal stuff?"

How many times is he going to ask the same question? I scoured my memory for this so-called evidence because I was ready to call his bluff. Something told me he wasn't bluffing.

They had me at the scene and they think I was romantically involved with her. That's motive and opportunity. Evidence is knowledge around these parts.

"Mister Eycsüp?"

"Oh I'm sorry. Yes detective. This evidence you say you have. It's not a fingerprint on a wine glass is it? That was on her desk when I arrived. I pushed it aside when I sat down.

"That is certainly one explanation. Well listen I don't want to take up any more of your time. Please let us know if you plan on leaving the state."

"I might be heading to Barcelona in the next few days if that's all right."

"When exactly?"

"I don't know yet but it is possible."

He handed me his business card, "Just give me a call before you do. Everything should be fine as long as I can reach you."

"I'll certainly let you know."

I started walking towards our table.

"One more thing."

"Yes?"

"Have you ever been to Málaga?"

"No."

"You sure? Because passport control and customs show Missus Næss and Missus Søvner in Málaga around the same time you were in Barcelona. They're close to one another aren't they?"

He knew I'd been to Spain, "I wouldn't know…. Who's this Miss Søvner?"

"She's Miss Næss's assistant; so you've never been to Málaga?"

"We have all been to Málaga and yet none of us have been to Málaga."

"Is Málaga the fringe zone then?"

"Any timed vacant space has the ability to be *fringe*, as you say detective. Space is always in flux so we have all occupied such a space at one time or another."

He chuckled, "Very well. Thank you for your time," and extended his hand

"Finally. They say know a man by his handshake," I shook his hand.

I got even wetter than I was on the way back to the car, "It's not him."

"Everything points to him Ben. We have him *at the scene*. He was probably involved with her. How else would he hang around these princesses and rich boys? He barely had enough to pay rent in Barcelona before that princess paid him for his commission. If you ask me… he's probably banging her too! Look at the file Ben!" she threw the papers towards me.

"She's a countess."

"What?"

"She's not a princess. ... You didn't talk to him Alicia. There's something about him. He didn't do it. The way he moves, the way he held the door for her. I don't think he'd hurt a woman. *Especially* if the premise that they were romantically involved is sound."

"The way he moves? Ben you know I trust you. You've never been wrong but there's a first time for everything. It's like you have tunnel vision with this guy!"

"I'm following the facts and analyzing his behavior. He doesn't fit in. He's weird yes, but he doesn't hide it. He stands out. He's smart. He's smart enough to know that to evade detection you have to blend in, you can't stand out. But he does. He doesn't hide himself. He's not masked like everybody else."

She looked at me like I was insane.

"I don't expect you to understand," I couldn't unmask him and no one has ever been able to hide their true face from me. I had to believe that Eycsüp wore no mask.

"Okay Ben, you want to talk behaviors? Look at the profile the federal agency sent us," she reached into the backseat and put a folder on his lap.

I didn't even need to open it, "Let me guess. Killer is 28-40. Well educated. Well trained. Possible involvement in law enforcement or the military."

"He's in his thirties. He has a doctorate in physics. He was in the infantry."

"1994. 13-year-old dies in his mother's basement. No evidence."

"What?"

"We found nothing. No evidence of anything. Of anyone else anywhere in the house. He had some sickness; this disease that ate away at his body. Profiler said it was the boy's mother. Munchausen by Proxy. We arrested her. Twelve years later right? Exact same case. Same thing happens. Profiler says the same thing. We arrest the mother again. Something doesn't sit right. Captain says to look into it some more."

"Ben what are you—"

"Turns out they had the same nurse. She came into their houses sometimes to take care of them. The kids were dying anyway but she was an angel of mercy or something. Gave them something that didn't show up in any of the tox screens. That first mom was innocent. We sent her up, pressed and dressed and commended for our investigative abilities. 12 years Alicia. 12 years in the rabbit hole."

"I get it. Profiles aren't always right. Nothing's perfect."

"2005. Two teenagers die in a field somewhere. A lover's point of the neighborhood up north. I was vacationing. Multiple stab wounds.

Really gruesome stuff. Entrails hanging out. Bodies were just mutilated."

"Stop it."

"He was so weird. The girl's ex-boyfriend. He owned a bicycle repair shop. His brother had run over a deer on his motorcycle and the ex was cleaning the bike. He got some blood on his clothes. Profile said it was full of rage. It was personal. We arrest him. He fit the profile to a T. Isolated. Introverted. Peculiar. Interested in taking things apart. He maintains his innocence throughout. Right up to the point where the Aryan Brotherhood stabbed him for protecting a black guy against an assault. Race traitor he turned out to be."

"So?"

"A year later. Same day. A couple dies in their house a couple of towns over. Multiple stab wounds. This time they said it was a hitchhiker. Deputy on the case called me because I'd been up there before. Turns out to be a 20-something-year-old. Serial killer. They were his sixth and seventh kill. His first was his girlfriend. He'd opened up her femoral artery. Cut it out and played with the parts of her leg. He was impotent so that's why there was so much rage."

"You've made your point."

"I see things as black and white. I have to. There is no choice. We investigate the horrors of humanity. A good day for us is a married couple threatening to kill each other, *threatening* but never acting on it. But these things: profiles, psychic readings; they're always just vague enough to bias your opinion when you come across a person you don't like, and just general enough that if it doesn't fit you can point to some attribute or quality and explain why it's negated. Even a broken watch is right twice a day."

"But they are right sometimes. Brussel in the 40s and 50s. Right down to the double-breasted coat, buttoned. They caught the Mad Bomber because of him."

"A cheap illusion. Even that profile, the *actual* profile, is veiled with such ambiguous language that any inquiry or interpretation could be right or wrong. If you make enough predictions fast enough, eventually the ones that are wrong will disappear and the correct ones will make you a part of history."

"That's bad induction Ben. Because they've been wrong before, and even when they were right they got *lucky*, so you say, or were ambiguous... or whatever, they'll be wrong again in the future?"

"No. That's not what I'm saying at all. This is not a lesson in Hume. I'm saying the probability is incredibly high, to near the point of certainty, that they'll be wrong, so it'd *probably* be a waste of time to pursue this method of investigation, especially considering our own method of investigation is more probable to yield *accurate* and *true* results. We're not after results, after *an* arrest. We're after the *right* results and *the* arrest."

"That's backwards logic. What you said about him. The way he moves and the way he held the door open for the girl. That's profiling too."

"I know him though. It's not a standard template of this crime. That's what they say about all these crimes. Military experience. In his thirties. Lonely. Everyone is different Alicia; everything is a person-to-person, case-by-case basis. Based on what I know, *my* past experiences, the people I've met, and the cases I've worked. They're wrong here. It's not him."

"We only have so much time before the captain orders us to move in anyway. We have motive and opportunity."

"Our motive is circumstantial. That's what I'll report. The bureaucrats can try to pressure me all they want but I'll be the Boy Wonder if I have to. I'll go to the press if they give me no choice. I won't make the same mistakes I've made. If we do establish that they were romantically involved or there was some other motive attributed to Eycsüp, then I'll move in, not a second before."

She turned the ignition, "I expect nothing less from you Ben," and we drove towards the sky where the rain had broke.

"Besides, who's this Ventoni guy? And that guy with the *big mistake* accent on Næss's answering machine? We have other viable suspects," I could finally see a tint of sky.

PART TWO:
REDEMPTION

FALL

I
BETSY

I slid the chair across the table and sat next to the suspect. People are simple creatures. Lions kill because they're hungry or because someone is infringing on their territory; we kill because we can and we're the only creature that enjoys it. What comes after is what bothers us: the social conditioning. You've done something wrong. Religious absolution or redemption. Every man or woman, even the good ones, wants to be redeemed. Most of the time they don't even know why they *need* to be redeemed. They've just been told they *can* be redeemed so they pursue redemption despite never needing it.

"It's not like I don't understand Frankie. Can I call you Frankie?"

His hands shook as he nodded.

"I understand Frankie," I moved closer, "It was her fault right? Her mom had cancer and she passed it on to your little baby girl."

"I couldn't stand the pain. That stupid bitch had to go! But my daughter; it was an act of mercy, I can't be punished for that right?"

"No you shouldn't be punished. Look, *off* the record," I turned off the recorder on the table and he looked to confirm the tape was no longer spinning, "You're a hero. All the guys behind that glass," I pointed to the two-way mirror, "You're a hero. Who doesn't want to give the old lady a little tappin'? Put them in their place? ... I tell you we've all thought about it."

"Exactly. I go to work; I come home, all I want is my daughter to be quiet and a big fat steak on the table by my wife. Is that too much to ask?"

"No. That's not enough to ask actually. I bet she didn't even have the decency to massage your feet after a long hard day in those work boots."

He curled his toes in his shoes, "I pay for her to go to the salon and get herself done 10 times a month!"

"Wow, and she's still so ungrateful!"

He scoffed and shook his head.

"They'll never go for that. You have to forget that," I turned my back to the mirror, "You tell them you did it out of love. It's obvious you loved your wife."

"I... did. I did all I could for her."

"And you obviously loved your daughter."

"More than anything."

"There you go. They'll hang you if you tell them you did it out of rage. You have to tell them you did it out of love. They'll forgive you. They're good people," the trick is to offer redemption. Give them an *or* option like a child. 'You can't tell them you did it out of rage; tell them it was out of love,' and he forgets the option to not tell them *anything* still exists.

"It was... it was out of love. I'd been drinking with the boys. I got home and she asked where I'd been. I just snapped."

"So it *was* out of love... and your daughter... your daughter would've passed away anyway. You spared her pain. You're a good father."

Tears flowed through his murderous eyes, "I am."

"You killed them out of love."

"It was out of love."

I pushed the notepad and pen towards him, "Write it down. They're good guys. They'll take care of you," I wanted to take out my gun right there and splatter his brains all over the notebook.

"Thank you for the assist detective. You're every bit as genius as they say."

"They're wrong."

Two more people thanked and praised my interview technique when I walked by the media room. I watched the suspect from one of the six monitors write his proclamation of love for the people he'd killed. It's a good thing murderers are idiots but I guess they wouldn't be murderers otherwise.

Alicia was browsing the net on my computer when I walked into the pit, "What's with all these unsolved murder cases and files set as your homepage. That's morbid Ben."

"There's so many names... why are there so many names on that list?" my phone flashed with an update for an Amber Alert. Green late 2000s Ford.

A woman with a khimar was saying something to an officer near me and I watched them. The officer said "I can't help you Miss. I wish I could but I can't. You have to go to your *local* police station. Not here, your LO-KEL station. Near where you *live*," he mimed a pillow with his hands and put his face on them.

"Let's go Alicia. I need to go for a walk."

We bumped into the officer near the elevator.

"That woman, with the head covering, what'd she want?"

"I don't know! Something or other. They come to our country as refugees and want things from us too!"

"Hmmm."

"We got a problem here? You an eyraab lover?"

I looked at him, head-to-toe idiot but malleable, "We make our money from the sale of small arms officer. We went to war and destabilized the region to sell weapons to the same rebels that have taken over. Now we have to train new rebels and sell them weapons to save the old rebels. See the pattern? Woman like that... gets caught in the middle. She has to come to a country where everybody hates her and she can't speak the language and kiss the ass of the people who've murdered her family and destroyed her country."

"You're Detective Britten aren't you? You're famous man!"

The doors opened, "Find out what she wants Officer..." I read his nametag, "Yates. We owe them that. We owe *ourselves* that."

"Yes sir."

"Don't call me sir," I walked out into the parking garage towards the car.

"You think he'll listen?" Alicia paced to catch up to me.

"No. But I have to try."

"I thought you said we're going for a walk."

"Yeah... let's drive to the park. I need some air."

Rain bounced off the metal of our Suburban as soon we came out of the garage. A BMW veered to the right and splashed water from a puddle onto a homeless man standing in the corner. Most New Yorkers are zombies; they wander the streets and consume each other's brains with analyses of the political and the useless of the city, mimicking like monkeys whatever the economic magazines say. Some New Yorkers are borderline psychotic, insane with the idea that money isn't everything. They avoid Fifth Avenue and Madison in search of the transcendental and the real rather than the tangible and the useless. They are mad with love and insane with creation. In this city, hustlers of the intellect compete in a tug-of-war with hustlers of wicked laws and banks.

"Is this really the best city in the world Alice?"

"You haven't called me that for a long time," she honked at a cab that stopped abruptly for a fare in the shape of a wet suit, "How are we going to go for a walk in this?"

The city stands alone as the purgatory of the universe. ... Angelenos share a glint of hope in their eyes because they relate to one another. They all fathom themselves undiscovered actors, rock stars, and avant-garde artists... the kind of people who have their farts described on the front page of modern newspapers. This is the dream of nearly every person who ever lived. Londoners can be arrogant but they are well bred and well read, blaming all their problems on either the immigrants or the French. Torontonians, in fear of being compared to New Yorkers or Londoners suffer from an inferiority complex that presents itself out of need to be better and more elegant. A need to be different. Unfortunately they never shut up about it and thus come off as more pompous than the Londoner and more quasi-intellectual than readers of the *New Yorker*. The Dutch stand apart. They take their children to the museum and discuss literature and politics at cozy cafés.

They are a wonderful people. They smile and treat each other with respect and the utmost cordiality. Their only problem is tourists who visit their country for the legal prostitution and marijuana.

New Yorkers... mostly talk about how great their city is by pointing out the quantity of CosmicLoots cafés around every half-block and the inflated real estate rates which to them implies a higher-than-deserved socioeconomic status. A New Yorker's best hope, if he or she can dig deep enough to find any, is to die from consumption and be buried in the Hamptons with a view of the skyline and be read about by sniffling readers of the *Wall Street Journal*. Most of them simply exist... exist in the land of the lonely and exiled overwhelmed by the banality of their souls traversing the streets and brushing past one another with no empathy.

It took us a half-hour to go six blocks and get to Park Drive. Two workers in uniforms had blocked off one of the roads and were sawing pieces of trees.

"Stop."

"What?"

"Stop the car Alice."

I ran out into the rain, "Hey, what the hell are you doing?" I screamed over the sound of the storm and the saw.

One of the men turned around chewing tobacco, "Who in the devil are you?"

"Stop cutting these trees," I flashed my badge.

He spit on the ground next to me and laughed, "Detective huh? Why don't you go detect some shit? We have a permit. These gotta go down to make room."

"Make room for what?"

"Devil if I know. All I's know is, they call me up and say 'Paul, be here at this address and cut down these trees. Rain or shine.' And so here I am."

"These are historical landmarks. Let me see your permits."

He walked over to a box a few feet from him and held a piece of paper in his jacket to keep it from getting wet, "It's got all the signatures and everything."

"*Daskapeetal Realty*. I've never heard of them."

"Don't worry, we'll leave some of them. It's only these ones here," and he seemed to point to all the trees in the general vicinity.

Water trickled through my hair and I followed one of the drops to a *Post* overhead beneath a puddle under my boot: *Remains of homicide victim stolen from local morgue after burglary upstate.*

"Drive."

"Where?"

"Away from here."

Given the choice, I would've preferred seclusion from the demands of society but I knew I couldn't sail through the sea of life alone. I had to socialize. So what if the world is comprised of stupid people basking in meaningless chatter? Saying nothing of value but believing their individual existence to be of vital importance to the betterment of the planet? This meant nothing to me. I liked hearing the birds tattle me awake in summer mornings and watching volts of vultures squawk useless tidbits of information at cafés. Which celebrity was spotted at which bar and with whom? I liked observing the sheep baa about the *profound* implications of a certain president arguing why his country should go to war and bring democracy and capitalism to regions devoid of it. Freedom is non-negotiable. Without these *social* trips I'd lose my edge; I wouldn't know the layman's take on a certain subject matter and I couldn't do what I do. People should never be by themselves *all* the time. Our existence is profound specifically because other instances of an existence appear one after another.

Living in isolation is melancholic not because you're alone but because you no longer gauge time the same way you would in the presence of others.

This was what I told myself but the truth was simpler. I didn't want to be alone in darkening solitude because in the pitfalls of my soul, among murderers and rapists and thieves and drug-dealers, the only thing that kept me sane was Alice. I hated admitting it. I wanted to know everything about her: her secrets, ambitions, fantasies, and dreams. I wanted to contemplate her existence and how she became the person that sat next to me and talked to me; how she faced adversity. I wanted to appear in front of her soaked from a thunderstorm and whisper 'I love you.' I wanted to be near her all the time and be in the radiance of her seraphic gaze for the rest of my life. I wanted to be secluded somewhere with her. I wanted to run away with her to Spain or Italy or Denmark or Portugal. I was insane and I knew it. I dreamt of these moments and if these were dreams and that's all they were, nothing was true and the case of my soul would forever remain unsolved.

Some days she was all I thought about. She was with me when I ate alone over the sink, when I laid my head down on my bed, when I walked to the nearby dive and ordered a bud. She was always with me and yet she wasn't. She listened to me talk about nothing of importance. Men love to talk about nothing; it's all we really know. Women on the other hand, talk very little about everything. Which was preferred was a matter of sheer preference.

Was it insane that I was more comfortable talking to killers and drug peddlers than I was to the woman I was supposedly in love with?

"Want to get away for a while?" I asked while I noted the colors of a few cars driving past us.

"Where?"

"Lisbon."

"I was thinking Berlin."

"Okay."

"Just okay? No argument? No *enlightening* me as to why Lisbon is the better choice?"

"I'm tired Alice. Exhausted by pretense and cynicism veiled by sycophantic smiles," I looked through the moon-roof just as the sun reddened the sky like blood spilling in the center of a lake... and with this blood that beheld the dewy grass and damp trees, two storm clouds neared and eventually consumed a white one fluffed with pandered glee. The lighter something is, the easier it is to darken it.

"SHU-1 come in," the dash radio garbled.

My phone vibrated.

"This is SHU-1. Go ahead dispatch," Alicia responded.

"Officers responded to a 10-11 called in at a residential address. It's turned into a 10-10, a possible murder. Please advise."

"What's the address on that 181 dispatch?"

"Yes captain. Right away."

"SHU-1, it's on East 72nd street just before Madison. Units are already on scene."

"That's a 10-4 dispatch. Detective Britten is on the line with the captain now. Have CSAT lock the scene down. No press."

"That's a 10-4 SHU-1. It seems right up Detective America's alley. Uniforms and homicide said they have no idea what's going on."

"That's a roger dispatch. We'll be there momentarily. Over and out," she put the receiver back on the dash and turned to me, "Cap called you?"

"Yeah. He wants us there. Vic used to be a cop. He wants it done right."

She turned the radio up to drown out the horns and the insults hurled around by those in a perpetual state of road-rage. We caught the end of a modern classical piece.

That was the lovely Chloé Lysettensen. Up next we have—

"Lysettensen. That name sounds so familiar," Alicia turned on our police lights in an attempt to beat the traffic.

"The cellist. Remember last spring? We were chasing that lawyer tied to the mob? Someone was trying to steal or buy her rare cello."

"Right. Wasn't it linked to that other case?"

"I don't remember. I have the file at home."

A silver Pontiac cut Alicia off and I stuck my head out the window, "HEY!" I pointed to the siren lights on the dash, "You see the light?"

"Go stuff yourself!" the woman flipped me the bird.

"That's ladylike!" Alicia snickered then turned to me, "You have a way with women."

It took us an hour to arrive at the scene. Two officers in full rain gear guided us inside the house.

"When did this happen?" I asked the first respondent.

"Neighbor called it in. She saw someone inside the house through her kitchen window and the owner lives alone."

"The victim isn't the owner?"

"No sir—I mean, Detective Britten."

I looked through the kitchen window stained and wet by the rain sloshing all over it, "How'd she see it through this rain?"

"Owner's a woman. She's been away for a few months. No brother or boyfriend in her life. She said..." he flipped through his book, "That... there was a man inside that looked suspicious. To be honest detective she was right. He tripped the silent alarm. Almost as soon as we arrived two security guards from the alarm company also arrived. I got their information but they said someone had entered without the proper code and no one answered the phone to provide the password."

"Cap said he used to be on the job. Now retired. We can rule out a prowler or robbery as motive. Take me to the scene."

CSAT's camera flashes were going off all over the living room. Everyone parted to the side and opened a path for me as soon as I entered.

"SHHH. I want to see this," I heard one uniform whisper to another.

"Victim's name?" I called into the sea of blue standing around the room like the house's wallpaper.

"Uhh..." the first respondent's partner stepped forward, "He's retired Detective Sergeant Hartmann, Cynebald Hartmann. He spends most of the time telling stories to rookies at cop bars and bowling."

"So..." I knelt down near his head, where his neck was contused with little oval shapes all the way across, "Detective Sergeant, why did you break into this house to be choked?" leaves rustled under the rain outside.

"Have we canvased the neighbors?" Alice called out.

"Fantastic idea. And find out who the house belonged to."

"We already know that sir. It belongs to a company called the Anschein Group. They're a parent company for some other companies. We're having Research Investigations follow up but we're getting the run around from their lawyers. They say this is registered to an employee that worked for one of their companies but they won't say which company and who."

"Keep at it," I leaned closer to Hartmann's hands, "Get their address if you have to and I'll stop in."

Someone in the house next door craned their neck through the kitchen window and I caught it in my peripheral.

"Where are you going? ... BEN!" Alicia called out.

I was instantly soaked from head to toe, "Hello?" I knocked on the neighbor's door.

It took a few seconds but an older woman in eyeglasses answered the door, "One moment."

"Good afternoon miss," I flashed my badge.

"Please, step in detective. You're getting wet out there!" the brooch on her blazer matched her earrings and necklace.

"Thank you."

She walked deeper into the house and handed me a towel, "You'll catch a cold."

"It's not necessary."

"Take it. You'll catch a cold."

Alicia knocked on the door out of breath followed by a uniform wearing a plastic bag holding an umbrella over her head.

"This is my partner. May I ask you a few questions about your neighbor miss?" I dried my hair with the Ralph Lauren towel she'd handed me.

"Yes. I was the one who called the police. I'd never seen a man inside Karin's house. He looked like he was rummaging through her things."

"Karin? That was the victim's name?"

"No. Her name was Kara; she told us to call her Karin."

The hairs on my neck tingled, "Kara... what else can you tell me?"

"She was really nice to everyone. She baked a cake when she moved in and invited everyone over to her place."

"It was just her in that house?"

"Yes. She said her company had rented it for her. She worked near Wall Street."

"Any friends or boyfriends you know of?"

"No. She was a quiet girl. Do you know where she is? I haven't seen her in a couple of months but she told me she traveled a lot so I wasn't worried."

"What was her last name, do you know?"

"It was difficult to pronounce. Naught; Nice; Naice. I can't remember."

"Næss?"

"Yes that's it!"

"Thank you for your time miss. And the towel," I handed her back the towel.

"Is that the same girl—"

"From that case a while back. Yes. This is her house. That's why we couldn't find out where she lived. It wasn't under her name. It was under her parent company. I'm willing to bet this Anschein owns Minitar."

"Boss they're still giving me the run around," an officer held a phone up as I walked back into the scene.

"Tell them to send us everything on a company called Minitar. This is a triple homicide, or the press will find out that Anschein isn't cooperating with murder investigations; their stockholders and investors will sure love that."

"Sir," the officer said into the phone.

"I heard," the voice returned, "We'll fax it to your office detective..."

The officer handed me the phone, "Britten, Ben Britten," I tossed the phone back to the officer.

I roamed the living room and sniffed, "There's no blood."

"No detective. He was strangled."

The examiner came in, "Sorry I'm late. Traffic in this storm," and began going over the body.

"Alicia," I turned around and she startled me, "Whoa! Can you do some forensic accounting? Find out what you can about this Anschein, what they own, *who* they own. Minitar too. This feels... big."

"Sure Ben," she pulled out her phone, "I'll see what I can find on the web. Then back at the office I'll go through the business files and registrations."

"Perfect," I sniffed again, "Alicia wait."

She looked up from her phone, "Yes."

"Help the examiner. See if he bled anywhere."

She walked over and they turned the body over and examined it. "No, there's no blood."

"I smell blood. Where's it—" I threw the couch cushions down and searched between the cracks. Nothing.

"You smell blood?"

"There's blood," I looked under the couch and saw something shining in the corner, "Forensics! Lift this couch, there's something under it," I put on a latex glove.

Two officers lifted the couch and pushed it to the side.

"Easy gents."

A bloody hunting knife rolled against the floor.

"It can't be his blood," Alicia walked up behind me and we examined it.

"It's not. It's Kara's."

"Kara's?"

"Yes."

"Wait wait wait. Hartmann killed Næss?"

"Look at his hand. The entire narrative is right there. Choke me." I stood over the body, pretending to hold a knife. Alicia started to choke me, I struggled, and when I fell I opened my palm and the invisible knife fell in the proximity of where the knife was.

"If Hartmann killed Næss, who killed Hartmann?"

"I never said Hartmann killed Næss. Someone wants us to *think* Hartmann killed Næss. The greatest cases of criminal mastery are not the cases in which the killer is uncaught or dead. They're cases where we make an arrest and someone goes to jail. We pat ourselves on the back and never obsess over the details of a killer gone free; we've got our man. Case closed. Here, they make it look like Hartmann killed Søvner and Næss, and then some vagrant or addict will come in and confess to Hartmann's murder."

"What other alternative is there then?"

"One person killed them all, or least Hartmann and Næss, then made it look like Hartmann killed Næss. But what'd be the motive... why was he here?"

"Detective I just got off the phone with the captain. He says Hartmann had a P.I. license. It was expired but he renewed it two weeks ago."

"Did he have an office or apartment? Where did he work?"

"I'll find out. Captain?" he said into the phone, "Yes. His address," he nodded to me.

"So someone kills Søvner in Spain. Næss at her office, then a P.I. in Næss's house. No one hears a thing."

"Don't quote me yet detective," Alicia's assistant stood up from the body, "But it looks like strangulation. There are contusions on the neck. Little ovals that could've been metallic. I won't know where until I've opened him up."

I looked to the corner of the dining room, where a painting sat on an easel, "Alicia, could it have been a chain?"

"No, it's too thin for that."

"Not a bicycle or motorcycle chain, but an easel chain. I walked over and disconnected the chain from the easel, "Like this."

She took it and put it close to the victim's neck, "Yes it could be. But it's not this one. This one is too thick."

"So a smaller easel."

"Yes that could work."

"These were cold cases. We'd practically given up. Why the sudden surge? Hartmann must've found something. We have to find out who hired him."

"Remember the Søvner case Alicia?"

"In that sleazy hostel slash motel in Málaga?"

"Yeah…"

"How'd she die?"

"Stab wounds. She was tortured. It was difficult to establish a cause of death."

"He likes knives. Guns are too loud. Difficult to explain away if you're caught. A knife? *Why officer I'm a hunter.* No one bats an eye. He's good. This bothers me. Why is he good at this? Why is he good at taking something that shouldn't be taken?"

"Ben," she kept me from spiraling.

"I need Anschein's address in case that 'fax' gets lost officer. And send me Hartmann's office and apartment addresses as well."

"Sure thing detective. I'll send it to your phone."

I waited for Alicia in the car and watched the rain swim down the jerkin roofs with old French cornices, "Damn it," I ran back inside, "The painting."

"What?" Alicia was getting ready to walk back out.

"The painting. On the easel. It's signed Monet. It's a fake. It's probably there to be appraised. Photograph it."

"Yes detective."

We ran back to the car.

"Drop me off at home Alicia. I'm exhausted," my bones ached with fatigue.

"It's the weather."

"No…" I thought about the list of unsolved murder cases on that webpage and the long list of cold cases on my nightstand, "It's not that."

"You okay Ben? You look like you're getting ready to retire," she hit the breaks when a pedestrian jaywalked across Fifth to cram inside a bar.

"You think about the victims Alicia?"

"What?"

"The dead. The passport or driver's license pictures of those long gone from our world."

"What do you mean?"

"And when we ask their families for a picture; it always takes them so long to give us one. They go through thousands of pictures trying to find the perfect one. No matter which one they give us they regret it. We're always the antagonists in the worst day of their lives. We're the ones who told them their son or daughter, husband or wife, father or mother… is gone."

"That's our job."

"Our faces are etched in their nightmares. They never forget what they did that day, right up to the moment I appear at their door."

"I think about the ones we couldn't solve sometimes. I'm not as obsessive as you but yes I do. That case in Málaga for example, and even this Kara woman. I can't help but draw parallels. Young professional women in male-dominant fields."

"Sometimes I dream about them. I see the murdered. They're always quiet, sitting somewhere around an aura of depression. Presumably the complete opposite of what they were like in life. I always stand far away; I never approach them. I would've never known them in physical existence and I have to know them in death. They appear in the weirdest places sometimes. Places they don't belong. They'll appear in my office at the station house, your apartment, even my own house; places they could have no external knowledge about. Sometimes they'll be sitting on my nightstand or on my table, or on that huge faux-chandelier thing I have above my dining table; you know the one."

"Yeah… the little wooden one."

"That's the one. They'll just sit there. Silent and meditative, frowning at a spot on the wall or at the folders I keep on the nightstand. Their faces hide a grimace like their mask of consciousness has slipped away, as if their deaths weren't supposed to happen and my failure to avenge them is *my* shame. It's not them; I know that; they're just dreams. Dreams mean nothing…."

"But?" she pulled over and looked at me.

"When I'm wide awake; sharp and keen and searching for the details that make or break a case, or even a moment of happiness or sorrow, at the apex of conscious thought; I can't help but thinking that mortality has a chance to see through its limits and expand upon itself. But even from this Ivory Tower, this roof of a castle I've built, I feel like I'm trying to see through a fog, and somehow this blissful feeling is also a mask, and behind the fog is death waiting for me."

"We all die Ben. You shouldn't think about it like that. Life is a river. While it does flow only the one way and it might even flow below or above rapids, it flows nonetheless."

"What do you think happens when we die?" the rain let up for a few minutes.

"I don't know Ben. I'd like to hope we go to heaven. Somewhere where your favorite films, books, paintings, and songs are available at your leisure, and you're completely unbound. A place where people you admire and respect and love appear to you not only in dreams but manifest clearly in front of your eyes," she tapped her index finger near her eyes. "A place where you could eat whatever you wanted and retain your health, and you ate and slept only if you wanted to... but if you chose to sleep... the dreams, oh the dreams you'd have."

"How lofty," I sneered, "What if you don't go to heaven?"

She glanced pensively at the sun and the sky, paving the way through the stars, "You stand behind a one-way mirror and watch the people you love live in heaven without you. ... At least I hope," she crossed herself and kissed the gold cross necklace her mother had given her on her 18th birthday.

The more I thought I loved her the more I *knew* I hated her. Hope. I loathe hopers; I detest their existence. To hope is to be self-deluded and there is no greater sin than one of pride in delusion. It is not real. These thoughts are a fantasy. She crossed herself, the audacity. Hope is ridiculous on its own but religion? Even atheism? Too far and too few in between. I tried to understand religion, I tried my damndest but I couldn't get past the idea that I could do whatever I wanted and still be redeemed. If you believe in God and that he created all things, even if He's wrathful, He created you; He has no choice but to forgive you. He made you the way you are. That means that people aren't good or bad but that their actions perpetuate their goodness or wickedness. Then what good act would redeem someone who is consistently wicked? Are some actions irredeemable? The killing of another person for example. What if the victim was wicked themselves? And what of the good? I'm supposed to compete with the Lord's son in units of goodness and sacrifice? What if I've been consistently good throughout my life but then have to commit one of those irredeemable acts?

Someone whispered my name.

Hasn't God forced my hand? He has to know I'd eventually perform this act; was I always bad even without knowing it myself? What's the point of resisting temptation if I'm hoping to be rewarded for it? And if it's presaged that I screw up somewhere and have to watch Alicia through a one-way mirror with— wait. What am I saying? Do I love her?

There it is again. The whisper, "Ben," carried into the night.

Anyway, what's the point of resisting temptation if in the end I'm still going to be forced to watch my beloved love another?

'You have many questions,' the kind Father Antonini said after he caught his breath, 'It is more important to have faith, and *hope*.'

I loathe hopers. Religion is treacherous and corrosive to the very souls it claims to save.

The so-called *liberal* students holding smartphones and whining about the dangers of capitalism on their unlimited data plans all over the

Internet will have laughed and mocked the dogmatism of traditional religion by joining a niche cult of dogmatism hell-bent on eradicating every religion but their own. These are the modern crusades.

The whisper got closer.

Be intolerable of religion and God or you're an idiot... they are worse. They are hopers of the intellect rather than the religious who are hopers of the soul. I abhor hopers. They are looters of truth, plunderers of reality, and sophists of the imagination. I want to drown them in seas of lava as payment for their indolence.

"Ben," the whisper nudged me.

"WHAT IN THE?" I shook my head awake, "When did I fall asleep?"

"Right after I told you about dreaming in heaven," she held the passenger door above me as her necklace refracted the blue CLOSED sign of a storefront window.

"What time is it?"

"It's late. I had to take a detour because of construction and then there was traffic because everyone had to detour."

"You want to come up? You can take the bed. It'll be morning by the time you get home."

"That'd be nice."

I threw the cold case files off the bed, "Excuse the mess."

She looked at the light fixture above my dining table, "It's fine," she picked up one of the files, the 1998 cold case stained and wrinkled with water, "This one is from 1998."

"Yeah," I got a fresh set of sheets and blankets.

She picked up another, "This one is from '88. Are these all cold cases Ben?"

"Yes they are."

She pretended not to be surprised, "You live in the minds of the murdered, searching for an ingress into the minds that murdered them."

"Here's a blanket and some fresh sheets. ... And let me get you a pillow."

"Let me take the couch Ben."

"Nonsense. You take the bed," I had no couch.

"Ben?" she touched my hand when I gave her the pillow, "It's okay."

"What's okay?"

"You can't solve them all. ... No one can. It's okay to leave things in the grey. Not everything is open and shut."

"Good night Alice," I turned the light off and laid down on the floor of the main room.

She shuffled on the bed. The dead permitted me no sleep.

II
JILL-LYN

I went for a walk just after sunrise.

Time doesn't exist in this city; 4 A.M. is the same as 4 P.M.. Thieves in worn out clothing rob the natives who rob the tourists who rob the city of its identity, and the conmen in suits rob them all.

A woman brushed past me and walked over to the corner of the sidewalk and stopped. Another pregnant woman walked by us both and I was taken aback by the required hubris to further this existence. The arrogance to think that children will bring forth a better future and forego everything we've done to everyone we've ever met. I saw a green car and for a second thought it was the one from the Amber Alert but then a dad got out with a Labrador and what I assumed was his daughter frolicked and played with the puppy. I imagined him having two lives. One where he's a great family man where he takes his kid and dog to the park and goes grocery shopping and loves his wife, and one where he's a kidnapper and rapist. Which would be his real life and which the mask?

Most other cities have a sense of belonging or an odd sodality that arises from a need for companionship. Here, everyone's hustling each other so there's no room for loyalty. The pregnant woman disappeared down an alley to my left.

"Spare some change?" a voice asked.

I reached into my pocket and came out empty, "Sorry friend."

He thought I patronized him. This city should rot; its rivers should dry and its sky turned black forever. Its buildings should be torn down and every hustler should be left to burn with them. Maybe people can change, maybe one day these hustlers will wake up next to their coked up escorts in their penthouses, look out towards the skyline, and say to themselves "What have we done?"

Someone honked and a man got out of his Hyundai Sonata, manic with venomous rage and walked towards a cabbie that he thought had cut him off.

A siren in the distance drew closer. People don't change. Nothing changes, not even ideas.

The world is a non-stop party train. Last stop: Hell.

I ordered Alicia her one-pump chocolate, low-fat, vanilla bean macchiato from CosmicLoots. I had to wait in line for ten minutes but everyone in front and behind me thought it was worth it.

"Are you a titanium member?" the barista asked me after I'd placed my order.

"No. How do I get that?" For Alicia.

"Well if you make 100 transactions a month, you get this awesome card," he showed me a template, "And you get free refills on your coffee and juice."

One... hundred transactions? "You actually have *titanium* members? That's nearly three times a day of coming to this place!"

"We do! Everyone loves it. So that's a special-order macchiato with a pump of chocolate and low-fat vanilla bean and a black coffee. You sure you want that dark roast black?"

"It's coffee isn't it?"

"Of course! That'll be $8.67"

I don't remember ordering gold, "LordCart."

"Go ahead."

I swiped the card on their terminal.

"You can just tap it you know. LordCarts have PayNow. Just wave it over the machine."

"Next time."

"Can I get your name for the order?"

"Ben."

He wrote my name and handed the cup down the line of employees all in black and purple uniforms screaming orders and making drinks.

I walked to the side and the person behind me flashed her titanium card and ordered a coffee "Filled halfway because I like a lot of cream," the blue swirled and got sucked into a dulling grey in the sky behind her.

"Ken? Ken?"

I followed the gaze of the employee, what a great name to have.

"Ken?" she looked at the name of the cup, "Black dark roast and special-order macchiato."

"Oh. That's me. I guess I'm Ken."

I turned the cup, *Ken* written in bold permanent marker.

The girl behind me pointed to the cup, "You should take a picture of that and put it on *QuickPic*."

"What's that?"

"It's an app. You take a picture and upload it," she pulled out her smartphone and showed me the app, pictures of food and women in tight bikinis populated the screen.

"Then you can tag CosmicLoots. Look," she searched up the CosmicLoots tag and nearly 6 million 'supporters' showed off the company employees misspelling their name. "See, there's 387 tags nearby! You're not alone," she smiled through her white teeth and pink lips.

"We're all alone. We just like to think we're not."

She ignored what I said, "You should get the app, it's good. And you can *support* me. My tag's everyone loves redheads!"

"I'll look you up."

"It's Every, then the number one, L-U-V-S, then redheads," *Welcome Every1luvsredheads*, I read on the screen when she turned it towards me.

"Nice."

A guy wearing wayfarers and jean shorts with matching spray-painted Converse All-Stars held the door open for me on the way out.

"Thanks. It's supposed to rain today, are shorts a good idea?"

"I don't get cold. You should'da gotten that biddy's number. She wants the D, telling you to add her on QP? You're in man. Just message her and wham bam thank you ma'am."

"I didn't understand a word you just said."

He laughed and walked inside.

I knew then why he'd wore shorts: a tattoo of a pelican on his right calf with the words, "Free Hunter" inked above it.

The pursuit of the ugly is never-ending. I thought about the Næss case and that artist everyone thought was the killer because of the fingerprints.

Back at my apartment Alicia had stepped out of the shower and was drying her shoulders.

I put her coffee on the bed and walked towards the main room, "Alice where are my files?"

"I took them," she appeared from behind the door with her titian hair damp like a bottle of cool red wine.

"Why?"

"I put them in the empty drawer Ben. It's unhealthy to obsess like this," she took a sip of her coffee, "Thanks. You remembered the chocolate."

"You're welcome. Say, you know what I was thinking?"

"What?"

"The fingerprints we found in Næss's office remember?"

"Yes. They belonged to that expat who lived in Spain."

"Yeah him! Let's run his prints through all the various military databases, VICAP, the feds, the whole works. We never did that back in the day."

"You were convinced he wasn't the killer."

"He didn't kill Næss but there's something about him."

"I couldn't sleep last night. I logged on and looked up Anschein."

"What'd you find?" I sat down at the dining table.

"They're multinational. A huge corporation based in Germany; they own around a hundred subsidiaries and shell companies. Insured by none other than... I'll take the labyrinth for 200 Alex."

"Minitar."

"They own the insurance company that insures them? How does that even work?" she looked up at me and reached for her macchiato.

"I have no idea. Maybe Minitar is itself insured by a third-party shell company."

"Their realty and development firm was hidden among other shell companies and you've already had a run-in with them."

"Who are these guys?"

"That's not the break Ben."

"There's more?"

"Yes! They have a Manhattan firm owned by the *Seventh Circle Representation* on retainer."

"And who are they?"

"Seventh Circle is a bunch of law firms, but one of them is... drum roll please... Ventoni, Kalumnia, and Van Couperville."

"Ventoni. He's the key to this. There was a psychic a while back. Did she help the fraud unit bring him in?"

"Don't ask questions you know the answer to!" she put her jacket on.

"I'm practicing for when we talk to these lawyers," we descended the stairs onto the road.

She laughed. "I got Hartmann's address. His apartment doubled as his office."

It'd started raining, "Perfect. Let's go," we ran to the car across the street.

III
JENNIFER

Hartmann was a living cliché and that hadn't changed in death. His apartment had the feel of a man alone with no hope. Blinds drawn on all the windows for a dark atmosphere, half empty bottles of bourbon on tables and counters, and papers and files of unsolved cases. I was frightened of the papers. It was a vision of my future.

It's unhealthy, Alice kept saying but how do you change who you are and what you do? An altruist doesn't just become a banker any more than an honest, hard-working gentleman becomes a lawyer. People do what fits their personality and essence.

A bourbon ring stain on an unsolved robbery page caught my eye and I stared at it. I stared at it so long that Alice walked up to me, "What is it. Is it important?" she looked at the paper.

"No. It's nothing."

She walked behind his coffee table that he used as a desk judging from all the notepads and loose leafs of paper. "Nothing on his calendar for the past month."

"Maybe he didn't write it down."

"There's nothing here," she moved some papers around and a printout of museum exhibits fell on her lap.

"What are those?"

She looked through them and read them, "It looks like he went to museums to see some paintings, and then these," she looked at some other papers, "Are appraisal forms for a set of paintings bought at auction."

I pulled the curtains behind her. It was day but night dwindled in the sky; this city howls for prey all day and feasts like a wolf at night. If you listen you can hear the howls and the screams of the lonely and forlorn. The city is a monster and it survives on a refined diet of the just and honorable and the beautiful and naïve. You feel it around you; you feel it when you pull the curtains of a dark apartment or when you walk outside through a revolving door.

"Thanks. Now I can see," she looked back.

"What were the paintings?"

She looked at the paper again, "This one here is for one called: *Sunset, Deer, and River,* by Albert Bierstadt. There's a bunch more."

"Where's that painting now?"

She did a web search on her phone, "It's in a private collection. But these numbers here, for this appraisal don't make sense."

"What do you mean?"

"The numbers are either incredibly deflated or too inflated to be a reproduction."

"Inflation makes sense. Check the ones that are deflated."

"We have the appraisal numbers here. There's 3 here: MTR3576, MTR8760, MTR6701."

"The letterhead," I guided her eyes to the top of the page.

"Minitar."

"Who hired him?"

"I'm looking for something that resembles a contract but you see this mess!"

"Yeah," I sat down on the couch beside her and closed my eyes.

"Ben?"

"Let me think. — I come in. I work here," I looked around to the bottle of bourbon on the counter. "No. I don't invite my guest here. It's not presentable," I move and sit at the kitchen table, "No. Not here."

Alicia watched me from the main room, "Why not?"

"Dirty dishes piled up in the sink."

I walked to a corner where a small desk with a chair faced two others, "Here," I sat on the single chair. "They sit there. There's no booze in sight. I sit down and they tell me their problem. *Your wife is being unfaithful, I'll look into it*," a bottle of sealed top-shelf bourbon sat under the table in the corner, "They're happy with my progress. One of them notices I like bourbon. He brings me a bottle. This case is important to me. I put all the files on top. It brings me borderline out of retirement."

Alicia's footsteps follow me to the bedroom.

"I put it in one of the drawers of my nightstand. I keep it close to me. I never bring women here so the drawer is empty except for mementos of my past."

"The contract?"

"A chance for catharsis. I'm a cop again. It represents every case I could never solve," I opened the drawer.

Alicia crowded over my shoulder, "I'm curious."

There was a file there along with a faded picture of a young woman from the 60s.

"Jesus Ben. It must be exhausting in your head."

I opened the file and scanned the page for the client's name, "Alfhild Baldure."

"The princess?"

"No. Not a princess. A *countess*. It says she came with someone else. He never gave his name."

"Is there a description?"

Alicia's phone rang and she took it in the main room.

"So why would a countess come to this has-been's place? She probably has bodyguards and investigators on retainer?" I sat on a stool near his bed and rubbed my knee. "You didn't want anyone in your family to know what you wanted investigated. Mistrust. Then who'd you come with? You came with someone you trust. Boyfriend? ... No. He'd probably talk you out of it. Say you're being paranoid. *They're only paintings* he'll say. Probably."

"What?" Alicia walked back into the bedroom, "Your knee okay?" she put her phone back in her pocket.

"I'm fine."

"That was the research department, they got in touch with an art professor who can lend his expertise. He'll be going in today to talk about the paintings. I forwarded them the details."

"Okay."

"What'd you find out?"

"This is convoluted Alicia. Nothing makes sense individually but it all makes sense when you step back."

"Ben... talk to me. What you just said made no sense."

I chuckled, "Baldure. She has people on the payroll that could do this, right?"

"Probably."

"So why come to Hartmann?"

"I don't know. She didn't want anyone to know?"

"Or she didn't trust anyone other than the guy she came with."

"Who's that guy she's dating? It was in the Dutch tabloids some time ago. Some scandal."

"Brahms."

"How'd you remember that?"

"Our namesakes were musicians. I thought it was amusing when I first heard about him."

"Oh," she laughed, "Right."

"So she came with Brahms?"

"No I don't think so, and I don't know why I don't think so."

"We'll follow up with the paintings and this professor then."

"That sounds good."

"Oh... and Minitar got back to us. Yates just emailed me some of the forms. They've sent us 18,000 pages!"

"They're going to bury us with paperwork. Send them those exact appraisal numbers. It should send up some red flags. Tell them we'll shut down their offices if they send us more than 40 pages or something."

"We can't do that."

"Their lawyers are under investigation right? They don't want to call that bluff."

I flipped the page of the folder, "His notes on the initial meeting. He has a description of the guy that accompanied Baldure."

"The cop instincts. ... What's it say?"

"It describes him as thin and tall. Well mannered with broad shoulders. He... pulled out her chair when they got up and he was carrying *The Analysis of Beauty* by William Hogarth."

"Add it to the file. It doesn't help us much unless he... check the other pages, maybe he did a composite himself."

I flipped through the pages, "No. But it does help. There was an artist. He held the door open for her. Remember?"

"Not this again."

"It's the same guy."

"You can't be sure."

"Can you track them down? This artist, Baldure, and that cellist?"

"I can't just ask to track down an *artist* Ben."

"I have his name in my files. It's Raphael like the painter or Michael like the archangel or something."

"Finally we're getting somewhere."

"Ventoni was bullying the cellist into selling her cello. Baldure's paintings are insured by a company represented by Ventoni. How's this Raphael fit in?"

"Maybe they're friends. All of them I mean."

"Maybe. That's a lot of leads on a cold case. Let's follow up."

"Too bad the price was a life."

"His existence glided across the edge of a blade into non-existence anyway. Look at this place. Whether he lived or whether he didn't exist mattered to no one but him. It doesn't matter now that he's gone."

"Life is important independent of that isn't it?"

"I don't know. I know life's unfair, and for the people of this city, that's a good thing."

IV

LINDSAY

Back in the squad room I looked up newspaper articles on Minitar and Daskapeetal while Alicia followed up with the cellist.

I found nothing. I found less than nothing. Journals raced to be the first to write about Daskapeetal's philanthropy, donating to numerous charity organizations and funding halfway houses across the country. Every single one of them was declared and used up to the maximum allotted tax break. Their 1040 Forms even had the chairs and tables itemized under Schedule A. I couldn't find one T uncrossed. With their larger donations, like new computers for inner-city schools or a library; appraisals couldn't wait to sign off on their 8283 forms.

Ventoni was good; I had nothing on them except a gleaming reputation for trying and succeeding to rebuild a corrupt city for *future generations*.

"Ben?"

"Yeah?" I looked up from the screen.

"There's a woman on the phone looking for you."

"A woman? What's her name?"

"She'd only talk to you."

"What's she sound like?"

"Rich and sexy."

"You sound jealous Alice."

"Line 3," and the door shook on her way out.

I pressed 3 on the phone, "This is Detective Britten."

"Ben? It's Henrietta."

Henrietta Clotho Corna, one of my confidential informants.

"Henrietta, are you okay?"

"I'm fine. Can we meet? I heard something and I want to speak to you."

"Sure."

The rain lightened outside; the sky tired of paling and ruling over this already-dead city. A gust caught Central Park leaves in spirals and chased them down Park Avenue. The wind was now the nemesis of the just and unjust alike; it broke umbrellas in women's hands and the drizzle jump-started their dry and broken hearts. I tried to light my Marlboro but wind always beats fire. I stopped at a corner and steepled my fingers until I finally lit it. A woman ran by me into a salon.

Henrietta sat at the back of a Turkish sandwich shop with her Tärnsjö Garveri briefcase on her lap. I caught her with cocaine once and let her go. She was young and on her way up. Ever since then she had a soft spot for me. She helps when she can. I hadn't heard from her in years; it must be important. "If you're trying to blend in; you picked the wrong place. We would've merged better with the crowd at the Intercontinental or Trump Tower.

"I could bump into somebody I know over there."

"ORDER UP!" the owner yelled and it startled Henrietta.

"Hey... it's okay," I sat down, "Are you all right?"

"You've caused quite a stir, with that partner of yours?"

"Alicia?"

"No. The old fat guy. Said he wasn't a cop but then he starts asking questions and I suddenly read in the paper he's been killed in a woman's house."

"Hartmann?"

"Yeah! I work at Cocytus Mutual now," she clutched her briefcase.

"I can tell you're doing well," I winked.

"Stop joking around," she exhaled, "Just listen."

"Henrietta, stay calm. I'm here now. Tell me," 'I'm here now. Nothing to worry about.' What a cliché my existence was becoming.

"Anyway, we own a construction company, Lethe—"

"Yeah I've seen their trucks all around town."

"Precisely. Anyway, these Lethe guys are real shifty. They give me the creeps. I think they're mafia or something but not Italian. And he's scared, now nothing spooks him. Generally I avoid them."

"But something happened."

"Yes. The other day, one of these guys, Phillip, who has a huge scar from his left ear to about halfway down his chin. They say around the office someone tried to cut his throat and he woke up halfway and survived..." she dozed off.

"Henrietta! Focus."

"Oh Ben... this guy is talking to my boss about one of the lawyers they have on retainer an about some painting appraisals. I asked my boss about it later and he clenched his jaw and told me not to worry about it."

"Henrietta. What'd you do?"

She loosened her grip on the briefcase, "I took... some files Ben. Everything is logged on our servers. I think they know I have them. It's about an insurance company named Minitar; we own them too. It talks about some painting appraisals. Only the files don't make sense. They appraise paintings bought at auction, then they're lost or stolen or something, and the beneficiary is always listed as a donation to Acheron Homes."

"Acheron Homes? Their name came up in my research into Daskapeetal."

"Daskapeetal is itself a subsidiary... Acheron is one of our charity organizations. They're all owned by Anschein."

"What's in the files?"

"It's Minitar's and Lethe's investment portfolios."

"Jesus Henrietta. Why?"

"They were talking about the murders of some Minitar employees a while back. Then I read someone just died and they were talking about how insulated we are... this Philip guy gives me the heebie-jeebies. And when I read someone had died and you were investigating it and I had access to the files... I printed them."

I handed her my keys, "I don't think it's safe for you Henrietta; go to my place. You'll be safe there."

"No I won't! That's part of the reason I wanted to meet. They know about you Ben. They know who you are. I met you to tell you *you're* in danger. These guys don't care. Find Johann Brahms Ben."

"Johann Brahms?"

"Yeah... I knew him a while back. It was after you and I.... Johann has access to a lot of capital through his girlfriend. I think he had something going on with the appraiser at Minitar. I think they were into something Ben. They tried to stick their hand in the pot and make some money. I think these guys found out and now you're going to be caught in the middle."

"You know anything about a lawyer named Ventoni?"

"Yes he's a partner at one of the law firms we have on retainer. I've heard his name around the office."

"I think he's involved."

"He's missing too. I think he got tasked with cleaning this up and he screwed up."

"Who had the chicken and beef combo?" someone called out and it startled Henrietta again.

I put my keys in her palm, "Listen Henrietta, go to my place. They're not going to ice a detective."

"No Ben!"

"Just listen please. For once, listen to me."

"I always listen to you Ben," she lifted her hand off the briefcase and touched my finger holding a pen.

"Go to my place. Right when you enter look to the left. There's a bunch of keys there. Take the one with the red keychain. It's to my mom's place in New Hampshire. You'll be safe there. No one knows about it."

"I heard. I meant to call you. I'm sorry Ben."

"Will you go?" I touched her nail and then her finger and she handed me the briefcase.

"Yes," she pecked me on the cheek and I sat frozen in the restaurant with steam and order numbers filling the room.

This is exactly the type of case that gets you killed. Murderers, serial killers, rapists; they're all people with their own distorted code. Serials kill particular people. Murderers kill out of passion or profit. Corporate honchos have no code. Being on the wrong side of this case meant being on the wrong side of existence.

V

HELEN

I can't stand cops in entertainment or stories. They always seem to solve the crime and do it in the coolest way. They always follow some prolific montage of sorting the evidence in a visual way and when the plot has advanced as far as it will, they see that key detail that solves everything. It's like a silent conspiracy against actual police work. They never show the hours on end you spend reading accounting reports, looking at pictures of dead bodies, or reading the life story of sadists and killers. They don't tell you that sometimes a pretty dame hands you all the evidence in a foggy restaurant and you're still too stupid to put it together because fancy men in suits have convoluted the law to the point where every professional's ambition is to find the loophole that circumvents it.

A raven sat on the tree and covered its eyes from the rain.

"Where have you been? Alicia walked into my office after me.

"I got it Alice," I showed her the briefcase.

"Where'd you get that? Your '*informant*'?" she air-quoted.

"It's all there, everything."

"We'll read it on the plane."

"Where are we going?"

"I got a guy at Minitar who didn't know he was supposed to give me the runaround. I got all the appraisal forms. We have Kara's signatures on *all* of them. I tracked down the client on these purchases: Alfhild Baldure."

"The countess? Why would she be involved?"

"I don't know. Let's go ask her."

"The captain signed off on the trip?"

"Yeah... I already talked to him. Our other lead is there too. Remember that cellist? Lysettensen?"

"Yes. With someone trying to nab it?"

"She's there too."

"And the fingerprints I asked you to run through all databases?"

"Results aren't back yet. There's a backlog but I told Julie to email to me as soon as she gets them."

"Where are we going?

"Barcelona."

"It'll be beautiful this time of year."

"And we can get away from this rain."

I hoped Henrietta had gotten the key and was on her way to New Hampshire. There *I* was now, hoping like the rest of these deluded creatures.

Yates gave us a ride to JFK and even though the traffic was horrible, Alicia thought ahead and checked us in online. We had our boarding passes and no luggage to check so it was straight to security.

Hours well wasted. The line to get to the security checkpoint snaked around 16 times.

"Have your boarding pass and passport ready. Empty your pockets. Take off your watches and your belts and any other metals and follow the instructions given," the agent in charge of permitting you to the security line droned. He beckoned one person to go to one of the three security checkpoints behind him. A young girl travelling alone was absconded by another agent for a random search but no one batted an eye because she was white. Not even the civil rights groups or the feminists or the profiled Muslims hell-bent on equality. No one cared about anything anymore as long as it didn't interfere with their Comedy Central political commentaries late at night and their freedom to line up for Kumquats during the day.

I threw my badge in the bin when the guard asked me if I had anything in my pocket, "I didn't see that girl do anything wrong by the way. I've noted your badge number."

The failed-cop now turned security guard drunk with what little power he had over his fellow man tried to stare me down, "Step through the machine sir," he pointed me towards the x-ray.

"I say something you don't like so I must be a terrorist. You embarrass me as an American."

"Sir step through please."

Nothing beeped when I stepped through.

"I still have to search you sir. Please hold out your arms."

He patted and prodded me for minutes on end.

"Come on, he doesn't have anything. We have flights to catch," finally someone behind me in the line called out.

He let me through once his inferiority complex had been adequately satisfied.

Alicia waited for me near the international departures gate.

"Black right?" she handed me a CosmicLoots coffee cup.

"Thanks."

We sat on the overused gate chairs flattened by the endless sea of full bellies and fat asses.

"Things are coming along nicely Ben. We're getting away like you wanted."

I clutched the briefcase Henrietta had given me, "This isn't what I meant. We follow Death's footsteps."

"What?" she whispered along to Ryan Adam's cover of Wonderwall playing through the speakers near us.

"I'm a homicide detective. You're a medical examiner. We clean up Death's messes. Every time we're called to a place, every, single, goddamn time, someone or some people have died. And there we are, like darkness after sunset, every time. To solve it, to listen to the dead, look in their eyes, touch their cold bodies, and read their now unconscious minds."

"Stop it Ben. It's just a job."

"We work forty hours minimum Alice. Minimum. We pull in eighteen-hour days most of the time. We spend 80% of our life with death; I've never held a baby; never touched life; never experienced a love so profound it stirred me out this job."

"We are not what we do. We don't deal in death," her necklace popped out from under her shirt.

How does she say it so simply? She cuts open dead bodies from morning to night but with a delicate "It's just a job," she negates everything I've been thinking about this past year.

"I'll be right back," I walked over to a FlynRead store just ahead of us.

"We'll be right with you," one of the two ladies at the counter was cashing out a guy buying an issue of *the Healthy Man*. He bought an Everest energy bar and left. "How may I help you?"

"Do you have the Analysis of Beauty by Hogarth?"

"I don't think so, that sounds like an obscure book. Let me check the computer. We might have one in the bargain bin."

"I'm looking for that book about the rich man with the hot girlfriend, with all the sex? My friend told me about it but I don't know what it's called," a woman behind me called over.

"Yes," she pointed to an entire shelf under *'Bestsellers'*, "Right over there."

"Thanks."

"Sir?" the employee caught my attention.

"Yes."

"We actually do have one in stock. It's a Dover reprint of the original 1908 edition."

"It'll do."

"I'll ring it up."

"Thanks."

She scanned the book and 57.42 appeared on the screen. The woman buying the porn novel paid 12 bucks for hers and left.

"May I scan your boarding pass?"

I showed her the boarding pass Alicia had sent to my phone.

"Are you an artist?"

"I'm sorry?"

"Are you an artist?"

"No. Why do you ask?"

"This is an art theory book. I thought you were."

"No. It's for a case. I'm a detective," I showed her my card and tapped it on the terminal.

"Anything can be art. You can be an artist in painting or sculpture or food or accounting. You can be an artist *and* a detective..."

"In a way you're right."

"Where are you travelling to?"

"Spain."

"For a vacation?"

I wish, "No. A case is taking us there. My partner and I."

"Not bad. Must be a difficult case."

Death never takes a holiday; that's a good thing, "Yes," I grabbed the book off the counter, "Thank you."

"Good day. Have a nice flight. Enjoy Spain!"

I waved and sat back down next to Alicia.

"What'd you buy? Something for the flight?"

"Not really," I showed her the book, "It's the book Hartmann said the guy had."

"Oh that's a good call."

"I want to get inside his head."

"You think it's Eycsüp?"

A flight attendant walked over to the counter at the gate and everyone who ever skipped a lesson in listening and class etiquette barged towards the doors to shove onto the plane.

"Probably. It's hypocritical isn't it? Reading about beauty and being an artist while being involved in this?"

"Art has nothing to do with being an artist."

A woman walked straight by someone in front of her.

"Ladies and gentlemen boarding on flight A3415 to Barcelona we are ready for general boarding; we're sorry for the delay. At this point we ask only passengers who require special attention and those travelling with children to come forward."

People only heard what they wanted to hear and moved towards her anyway. One by one she had to tell them to wait until she called them for boarding.

"Yeah I guess it is. But people are people; I mean we can never predict what someone will do or what someone is like."

"Are past behaviors a good indicator of how someone will act in the future?" I cracked open the spine of the book. We were already delayed 25 minutes, and with these ogres who knew when we might take off.

"Ladies and gentlemen please do not approach the gate unless you require special attention or are travelling with small children. We also request all passengers from rows 45-49 to start boarding now," everyone moved closer like an elephant stampede, "Sir you have to wait; we're only boarding rows 45-49 now. You're sitting in row 36."

An Asian lady pushed a lady aside and shoved across to board, "Madame you're in row 26, it's not your turn to board yet."

"Jesus Christ," Alicia shook her head.

"Where are we sitting?"

"47."

"They're boarding us now!"

"I completely gapped it," we got up and had to elbow our way through the line.

The woman in row 26 complained and nagged why Alicia and I got to "cut in line" and the attendant told her to step back until her row was called.

We squeezed through the rows towards our seats and the smell of body odor, sweat, and diapers festered in the air.

Her phone chirped but we were too squeezed for her to check it now. Finally we got to our seats.

"You want window or aisle?"

My knee shook, "Aisle."

"Sure."

I put our bags in the overhead compartment and we sat down.

She checked her email when we sat down, "The fingerprints are back from the military."

"What do we got?"

"It's a match to Eycsüp in Næss's office."

"We know that, what else?"

She scrolled down, "There's another match."

"To what?"

"A cold case. From 1998. An Ingolf De Geest was killed and his remains were found buried close to a lake in the country. It's a closed case though."

"So then it doesn't matter,"

"This is weird."

"What?"

She tapped away on the screen and a person opened our overhead compartment to look for a place to put her bag, "It says the file was checked out.

"By who?"

"By you!"

"The 1998 murder of the abusive alcoholic?"

"Yes!"

"What the hell would someone like Eycsüp have to do with some insecure redneck in Notown Mississippi?"

"It says the case was reopened recently. The suspect had originally confessed in exchange for consideration against the death penalty."

"Killers afraid of dying... how indelible."

"Some innocence project lawyer trying to put something flashy on his resume looked the case up, and with modern technology demanded that the fingerprints on a shovel found at the scene be tested."

"And it matches Eycsüp?"

"Yeah..."

"Could be anything. Is this Anschein?"

"It's worth checking out. Maybe they know something."

"Of course. I have a feeling we'll see him in Barcelona."

"Why?"

"He hangs around the cellist and the countess doesn't he?" I opened the book again.

"Yeah..."

"Ladies and gentlemen this is your captain speaking. We're sorry for the delay. We'll be flying against the wind and expect to land a little later than planned. We're going to start taxiing in a minute so make sure you're seated and your seat belts are fastened. We welcome you aboard. We have loads of movies and music for you on the in-flight entertainment. Please direct your attention to the cabin crew for the procedures in case of emergency landings and safety."

A woman sitting at the emergency exit, who had more leg room than the first class seats stopped the attendant on her way to her seat, "Excuse me is there no in-flight entertainment for this seat?" the entertainment T.V. was connected to the seat in front of you so the trade-off for the comfortable leg-room was to be without Internet and Follywood for 5 hours.

"God forbid these hairless apes have to live without Foolgle and NovelFaces for a few hours," I turned to Alicia while the attendant gave some stock answer to the woman and proceeded to her seat. "Can you pull the file on the guy doing time for the murder of De Geest? I want to read the file when we land."

"It's at your house Ben."

"There's a digital version isn't there? I want to be appraised in case an opportunity arises for me to bring it up to Eycsüp."

"Okay."

"Thank you Alice."

"You're welcome Benjamin."

"I hate it when you call me that."

VI

LINDSAY

We landed behind schedule.

A flight attendant told a guy to "Sit down until the aircraft has come to a complete stop," and when it did, everyone stood up all at once and hastened to bring their overhead luggage down. The doors hadn't opened yet so they stood in the narrow aisles, bags in hand waiting for the doors to open.

"You were asleep. You missed it Ben."

"What'd I miss?" the dead couldn't rise and get me up here. I needed the shuteye.

A guy slammed his carry-on into my knee and the pain crawled up my leg, "Watch it!" he turned back.

"How rude," Alicia shook her head, "You missed it. I looked out the window when we were coming into the city and the design and the architecture...."

"Most of it is designed by Gaudí."

"Oh that's right. The Modernist."

"Yeah. So it was nice?"

"No skyscrapers, and all the suburbs were in line, like at the same height," she moved her hand across her chest, "The urban planning is... is, like the roads were perpendicular and diagonal; the neighborhoods were wide and most of the windows and houses had big windows facing the east."

"The sun rises in the east here. That's smart."

The line had started moving so I got up and took down our bags.

"I think I want to live here one day," she took one last look out the window at the tarmac and the planes around us.

People die here same as everywhere else, "How many unsolved do you think they get every year?"

"Stop it," she walked ahead without me, off the plane and through the terminal while browsing her phone.

Despite having no checked luggage it took us half an hour to go through Passport Control.

Alicia walked up to a woman holding up a "Shea" sign when we walked through customs.

"I'm Alicia Shea."

"Hello Miss Alicia, I am Inspector Montse Caterina Pavia; everyone calls me Cat."

"Hi. This is my partner Detective Ben Britten."

"Your middle name is Caterina?"

"Yes but please call me Cat," she smiled and tossed her hair back, "I came to give you a ride to your hotel. You know where you're staying correct?"

"It's this hotel here," Alicia turned the screen of her phone towards Cat, "It's on Ronda Sant Pere."

"Yes yes. Lower side of Dreta de l'Eixample. Main thoroughfare. Good neighborhood."

"We're here to work," I chimed in.

"Of course. I park closeby. You have no luggage?"

"No."

We followed her to her car: a four-door Peugeot 208.

Cat, short for Caterina; I'd known Alicia for 13 lucky years but I'd never asked what her middle name was or even whether she had one.

Are these facts, facts that make her the person she is, relevant if I consider her someone I love?

The sky was bluer here. I saw it when Cat drove out of the garage. I was slightly colorblind but I was sure I was right when Alicia blurted out, "Wow. Your sky is an azure blue."

"It's nicer in summer. What color is New York City sky in Fall? ... I mean we all know it must be beautiful. America is the Promised Land," she shifted gears and took the second exit on a roundabout onto Avenue de l'Aeroport.

I sank into despair; our money obsessed and quasi-cultural, bullying nation that oppresses under the guise of freedom is the Promised Land? "Fall is a gift for the corrosive poison of New York's other seasons. The harsh winters from the north with their knee-high snows and freezing flurries ice your body in place. The mildew and perpetual rain from overcast clouds of spring hover over bank offices before the summer. Summers force out the stink of garbage and sweat and piss; summers that force even the unkindnesses of ravens upstate in pursuit of disappearing shades from dying trees. Beauty avoids New York for good reason. We've corrupted it beyond repair." Damn that artist. Damn him.

"Don't mind him," Alicia slapped me on the shoulder, "America is great."

"Yes. What is your president always says?" another roundabout put us on Carrer del Garraf before we merged onto the C-31 highway, "God bless the United States of America."

"Indeed," God bless America; God bless the freedom to lie to your electors; God bless the rich and the dishonorable and the corrupt and the demanding and the entitled and the intellectually impoverished. God bless the lawyers and the banks and the politicians and the lobbyists. God bless them all.

Cat merged onto the left lane towards Gran Via de les Corts Catalanes. The radio broke song and a man chattered in Catalan. At some point during the broadcast, Cat crossed herself, "Déu meu!"

"What is it?" Alicia felt for her necklace.

"Murders. Many murders happening in last two weeks."

"Are you investigating it?" I asked.

"No. My colleagues are. Someone killing old women. Seniors. This is the fifth murder in 8 weeks," Chingón's *Bajo Sexto* played after the news alert.

"Five *seniors* dead." Clouds greyed the sky. "How's he picking them?"

"My friends have no ideas. They are all strangled in their apartments. All over age of 70. All women."

It's a curse. They don't show you this in crime novels or books. They don't show you the psyche of the investigator past his abilities to tie up and merge clues leading to the killer in the climax. They don't show you the erosion of his mind and body, death here and death there wearing him down with each passing second. They don't elucidate the fright of the investigator, the fright that comes with the ease of understanding a killer. Why do I understand it so easily? Is it in me too? Death? Waiting?

"Check where they bought their groceries or bought their bread or fruits. It's probably a young guy. Just starting out. Maybe he's had petty thefts in the past, maybe not. He picks old women because they're weak so he can overpower them easily. He probably offers to help with their groceries. Old ladies are courageous and gentle; they'll drive young men places and offer them hot tea if it's cold and lemonade if it's hot. He gets in... and external motivations provoke his rage. Their kindness fills him with anger." What a stupid job I had. The necessity of its existence directly opposed our collective instinct as a species to survive. We have perfected killing to the point of training unmanned computers to kill others of our species because of the color of their skin or their internal belief system.

My knee burned in the backseat.

"My friend in Interpol said you were good."

"He's too kind. We worked together in Málaga."

"Is that the case that brings you here?" there was another roundabout but we stayed on the same road.

"In a way," I took out a Marlboro, "May I smoke?"

"Yes of course. I am glad you mention," Cat asked Alicia to hold the wheel and took out a cigarette of her own.

Alicia was taking pictures of the buildings and streets on her phone as we hit a little bit of traffic, "This is a beautiful place," she took a picture of a stand selling fútbol kits.

I tapped the Hogarth book in my bag and took a drag.

The dead walked. They walked everywhere. We are all dead; it just takes one lifetime to realize it.

Someone startled Alicia's shutter-bugging by screaming something and when I looked I saw a pickpocket running down the street and a man jogging behind him with no hope of catching the thief.

"I wonder what he took," I put my head on the glass.

"Probably his phone. Be careful with your laptops and phones and wallets here. Especially on the metro," she flicked the ashes of her cigarette outside.

The Promised Land, consumed by the darkness of possessions and desolate technology passing for importance and purpose in beings devoid of meaning.

We turned right onto Carrer de Bailèn.

"We're almost there. I will tell my partners about your theory on the killings. It will help."

"Keep me updated. I can help," I flicked my cigarette out the window as we turned onto Ronda de Sant Pere and came to a stop.

Alicia got out, "Thanks for the ride!"

Cat reached over and handed her a card, "Call me if you need a ride anywhere or for anything. I can help you guys for your investigation as well."

"Thank you," I limped out.

"You okay?" Alicia tried to grab my hand.

"Yeah. Thank you Cat."

We walked into the lobby.

The receptionist was talking on the phone and continued her rather, personal conversation judging from her smile and intonation. Finally she hung up and looked up at Alicia.

"Hola."

"Shea. We have a reservation."

She took a piece of paper and read through a list of names. "Oh yes. Shea. One room with a king size bed."

"There must be a mistake. We called in for two rooms with twin beds."

"No. It says one room with one bed."

"Can we book another room?" I asked.

"It's not possible. We are overbooked this week. It is El Clàssic."

"What's that?" Alicia asked, "A festival?"

"No. It's the Barcelona Madrid game."

"It's a soccer match — sorry. Fútbol match Alicia."

"Oh."

"Yes. If Barcelona wins they will have a good chance to win the league later in the year."

"Okay then. We'll take the room," I need a hot shower to divert the pain out of my knee, "We have to work anyway. There's a lot of it to be done and I have to go over the contracts and stuff again."

The receptionist checked us in and handed Alicia our two keys.

"Call Cat later if you can please Alice. See if she can track down Baldure and Eycsüp. If Lysettensen is here too all the better."

"Will do. I'm going to need some shuteye though. I'm a little jet-lagged."

"I'm exhausted too. I'm sure there'll be a couch. We'll work something out."

"Don't be ridiculous. With your knee, I'll take the couch."

"It's quite all right. A hot shower usually cures this old boy right up," I tapped my knee and it hurt worse than it does in the morning when it rains.

VII
Morgan Dana

I dreamt I was dead. I was killed and I watched Alicia and others flop and twist looking for my killer. Through it all I felt free; I saw an orange scarf somewhere. I hovered above myself and watched everything and met others like me. Some of them were wrathful and wanted the blood of those that robbed them of life; I think these were the atheists or the skeptics. They were still tied to their physicality and wanted their killers to suffer as they did. I knew better. I towered above them and flew towards the clouds; the higher I flew the lighter it got until it turned absolutely pitch black. After a while I heard weeping and followed it through the stars. A sort of *thing*, I wouldn't even call it a being, but a *thing* made of light hovered in the air gulping what seemed to be wine but for all I knew could've been anti-matter. I thought I heard it whisper and mumble numbers and equations.

"You're the first *person* up here," a voice boomed.

"Am I dead?"

"From the beginning everything had been ruined. Humans were supposed to become humans *there*. I wasn't meant to be a source of suffering."

"I'm dead. Is this heaven?"

"They're the only ones who screwed everything up. Filthy *people*. It's my own fault. I had hundreds and thousands of plans to cope with the love but all of these plans were ruined by your decadence," it sobbed and put a cigarette to its lip, using its burning finger to light it.

"So fix it."

"I can't. I gave them wisdom to know who created their world and the free will to choose how to live in it. I can't intervene anymore... I shouldn't have given you both. I would help if you didn't *know*. If you weren't free to think what you want... I'd implant wisdom and truth into your minds."

"... God?"

"I hate that word. I have my own problems."

"How does the morality of something, whether or not you really are you, play into it? Isn't that something we— wait, what problems do *you* have?"

"Who created me?" it threw its cigarette behind me and when I looked it spiraled around the Earth.

"Ben!"

"Huh?"

Alicia stood over me in a long Hawaiian shirt and shook me.

"What's going on?"

"You were talking in your sleep!" she rubbed her eyes but pulled the curtains to let in the light.

"I was? I think I was dreaming. What was I saying?"

"Something about shooting stars."

"Shooting stars?"

"Yeah... and a sanguinary river."

"Must've been a weird one."

She picked up her phone, "Yates and Cat sent us the info."

I was still half asleep, "What info?"

"The address for Eycsüp and Baldure."

"Where are they?"

"You're not going to believe this."

"Try me," I got up and limped towards the coffee machine, "Where's that damn coffee?"

"Wait I'll get it," she checked the drawers and the minibar and started the coffee machine.

"So... where are they?"

"They're all at the same place. All three of them: Lysettensen, Eycsüp, and Baldure. God smiles upon us today."

Somehow I doubted that, "That's interesting. Where are they?"

She tapped her phone, "They are in..." and the screen lit up her eyes, "Diagonal Mar, at the main tower: Illa del Llac."

"Perfect."

The coffee machine chimed.

"I'm going to take a shower," she took a towel.

I poured myself some coffee and sat on the bed. Radio 1 was playing "American Music" so I turned it up. A song played while I looked towards the Sagrada Familia off in the distance with each of its tips trying to pierce the sky.

"That was *the Humbling River* by Puscifer, from their album *Sound Into Blood Into Wine*. Next up we have—"

I turned the radio off and looked at the center of my coffee.

"It's all yours," Alicia snapped her fingers, "Are you focused Ben?"

"Pardon?"

"Focus. You seem out of it lately."

"I'm fine," I headed to the shower.

The water pressure helped my knee and I pressed myself to remember the facts of the '98 cold case. Eycsüp would've hardly been 18 or 19 at the time. Why were his fingerprints there? I didn't have all the facts and I didn't want to jump to conclusions about an old case.

"Should've asked him who the killer was," I whispered to myself when I got out of the shower.

"Asked who?"

"Nothing."

"One of the guys emailed me the file from '98. The one that's at your house."

"Fill me in."

"I got your back Ben, you know that right?"

"What are you talking about?"

"If you decided not to pursue the case... I'm okay with it staying cold."

"I thought it was closed anyway."

"You know what I mean."

"No I don't. Alicia, what's going on?"

"It says De Geest was a regular scumbag. He was an abusive alcoholic. He beat his wife and daughter every day."

"You mean we should somehow get the best friend out because De Geest deserved to die?"

"There's more."

I sat down on the chair and opened my carry-on.

"It says here it wasn't the first time the officer had responded to the house. One time," she swiped the screen, "Oh Jesus. His daughter, his daughter..." her eyes widened.

I just remembered why I used the mugshot of this guy as garbage, "Take a breath."

"It says him and his friend came home one day after drinking. This is wrong right? It's his daughter!" she shook the phone and I took it out of her hand.

Him and a friend raped his 19 year-old daughter. Two days later he was dead. Her and her mother were freed and his friend was in jail for his murder. It was the investigating detective's belief that De Geest's friend killed him for his wife; that they had an affair and his friend's daughter probably reminded him of her.

"What pieces of filth," she snatched the phone back and her eyes went left and right reading the coroner's reports and the victim's report and the witness reports.

"So he kills his best friend after raping his daughter together. Why kill him?"

Alicia didn't look up.

"Alice!"

"Hmmm? Sorry."

"The motive."

"Maybe he thought De Geest would turn him in."

"But De Geest was complacent and a collaborator."

"I don't know," she walked over to her bag and grabbed a change of clothes.

"And we're assuming the friend *was* in fact the killer."

"Can we just let this one slide? It's a cold case. It's done. It's a *closed* case."

"We don't choose the victims Alice. We can't choose which ones to solve because the victim is garbage. It's more than that."

"More than what?"

"It's about justice. Murderers have to be punished regardless of who they're killing."

"His daughter…" she shook her head again.

"Where were Eycsüp's fingerprints found?

"They were…" she swiped up, "Found on the handle of a shovel near the scene where De Geest's body was buried. Fingerprints were preserved somehow. Don't know how. The shovel rusted and just stayed there. Campers found the body seven months later. But by then the friend had already confessed and the case was closed."

"And fingerprinting back then was expensive so why bother? They probably thought it'd match their suspect anyway."

"Well… they had a confession."

"Maybe he was framed and he confessed because he doesn't want the death penalty."

"That's what it says here too but I don't know."

"What's bothering you?"

"Well… for one he's clearly a scumbag. Not just De Geest but his buddy…"

"What's his name again?"

"Larry Krazimox, he's a scumbag too. In and out of prison since he was 16. Couple of assaults and thefts, he has a charge for pimping."

"So they're both garbage? What's hard to believe about him being setup by someone smarter than them?"

"It could've been an accident Ben. What if Eycsüp was walking by later and he slipped or something, and his hand touched the shovel only he didn't know what he touched and he moved on. Maybe he was camping or hiking."

"It's possible. Is he connected to De Geest?" Two times this guy's fingerprints end up somewhere by coincidence? He must be either the unluckiest guy on the planet or the most intelligent. Since I'm the unluckiest… it's not coincidence.

"They lived in the same town but I don't know."

"How old was Eycsüp at the time?"

"I have his birth date here," she flipped through some papers from a folder in her briefcase, "19," she looked up at me.

"So it *is* possible they knew each other. … Where's she now?"

"She's been in and out of rehab clinics since... always used the spousal military benefit. Two drug convictions. It ruined her life Ben."

"Does it say where she is now?"

"It does," she covered her mouth with her hand.

"Alicia?"

"She committed suicide two years ago."

Someone once said 'You are what you do,' and I wondered how I could hate what I do and not hate myself. I was supposed to catch the guy that killed De Geest; if Krazimox was innocent I had a duty to free him. If Eycsüp was the killer. I had to put him in prison instead of Krazimox. I wasn't supposed to have any feelings about it. It was black and white. Point to the killer. Arrest him. Put him in jail. It's simple. Then why this gut-wrenching feeling that I should leave everything be? I could see, definitively and without any doubt that De Geest and Krazimox contributed to events that directly led to her death. She wouldn't have committed suicide without their existence. They have to suffer and I hated the doubt creeping through me, the doubt whether I was going to free Krazimox knowing he was innocent.

"They didn't even give her a proper burial Ben!"

"What?"

"Suicide is a sin," she tapped her necklace, "They didn't even bury her in the church cemetery."

"Where's she buried?"

"Under a stone marked plot near her family friend's cottage."

"That's good."

"What is?" she shook her head.

"The stones. People used to put stones on graves."

"Why?"

"To keep the dead from rising into the physical land. Same principle as tombstones. Only now they're quotable totems for the living: *here lies a great father,* so on and so forth."

"We do it for ourselves. Not for the dead."

Like everything else, I thought. "What was her name?"

"Mædeleine."

VIII
AMBER ALYSSA

It must've still been early because the streets were relatively empty. Alicia hailed a cab and the driver understood where we wanted to go. The language barrier isn't as bad now that we have technology. Alicia's Foolgle Map showed the driver exactly where to take us. He turned the radio down but Alicia told him not to worry.

Clouds hovered through the air and hid the sun. It tried to shine through and the colors of the clouds mixed with its rays. I watched people walking up and down the streets preparing for the game; tourists took pictures of everything from the cement in the floor to the flickering tips of light poles to the graffitied garage doors of old auto shops.

Amore Pertudo by José Careccas played in the background of my thoughts.

"Do you have a middle name Alicia?"

"What?" she turned from the window and looked at me.

"I don't even know if you have a middle name."

"How long have we known each other?"

"13 or 14 years I think."

"Wow. 13 years."

"And I still don't know. Do you have a middle name?"

"I just... don't remember if you've ever asked me a personal question before," she rolled the window down and the breeze rifled through her hair.

"I'm stupid. I'm sorry. I'd like to know."

"Yes Ben. I have a middle name," she looked up from browsing her phone.

Games. She was playing games with me, "What is it?"

"You really want to know?"

"I wouldn't have asked otherwise."

"I thought you were making small talk."

"Since when have you known me to make small talk?"

The driver yelled something at a cyclist who'd cut him off and they vented their frustrations with the world at each other.

My forearm grazed her fingertips when I reached over to cradle my knee. The color of her cheeks had started to mystify me, darkening and lightening depending on what she saw outside. I wondered how young people connected these days with technology and the evolution of alienation; how did they come to know the other person from the inside? The captain had to issue a statement recently that young teens sending out nude photos of themselves, even to one person, would be pursued and charged as a distributor of child pornography. Is that how they connected? From milkshakes and burgers at the drive-in theater in little dresses to smoothies at the cinema in slim-fit jeans to frozen yoghurt naked? Eycsüp said he'd been to Spain and he'd never been to Spain; both of these can't be true so what did he mean? That there's a choice in never having a choice? Are we all living in a river flowing the one way? A sanguinary river of everything great and wonderful?

Our driver pointed to the Arc de Triomf and with great difficulty explained how different it was from the Parisian one.

"It was the entrance to the 1888 World Fair," Alicia nodded.

I looked at her.

"It's right here," and she pointed her phone at me, filled with details about the gate. Facts like the name of its architect being Josep Vilaseca i Casanovas and the red brickwork being in Neo-Mudéjar style. The "Barcelona rep les nacions" on the front frieze meant "Barcelona welcomes the nations" but no amount of drab information or facts compared to seeing it with my own eyes. The red bricks brightened as they went up towards the sky like Alicia's cheeks and darkened as they neared the ground like my hope.

"I'd like to come here if we have time."

"Don't you want to work?" there was a look of shock on her face.

"I want to see this arch up close."

"Okay," she tapped the driver on the shoulder and he navigated out of traffic and dropped us off.

Excitement washed over me. I felt like an insect crawling towards something monumental when I approached it. Feeling the brick on my fingers pulsated my hand. The wind blew through Alicia's hair and the sound of ruffling trees caught the air in a circular dance. There was nothing on the planet at that moment except Alicia walking under the gate of that arch and me watching her.

"Why are you looking at me like that?" she looked back.

"Like what?" it took me ages to navigate to the camera on my phone but I finally did, and I took a picture of her walking towards me from the arch.

"You have a look."

"What look? ... No I don't," I never noticed her eyes before: shades of green and brown and orange getting progressively lighter as they traveled outwards from her dilating pupil like foreign jewels. Is this how Eycsüp saw people when he looked into their eyes?

"You do. There's a look. I've never seen it before," she walked over to the street and tried to hail a cab.

"What look?"

"I don't know. When I looked back there was something in your eye," she waved at a cabbie who dropped off some tourists then made her way towards us.

"What? Maybe there's something in my eye," I rubbed my eye.

"No," she scooted into the cab and showed the driver the map of our destination.

"You like the arch?" the driver looked at us through the rearview.

"Your city is beautiful."

"Are you on honeymoon?" she smiled.

Alicia laughed, "No. He's a detective. I'm a doctor and mortician. We're on a case."

"Oh. So sorry. Barcelona brings a lot of people on the honeymoon. It is very romantic city."

"It is," I blurted out and Alicia looked at me.

"You've been really weird lately Ben."

"Everyone keeps saying that. Why does everyone keep saying that?"

"You just seem different. I don't think anything has happened so I just don't know."

"I'm myself. Do people notice gradual and subtle changes in themselves? Do you notice yourself change over time or do you notice it only after someone has pointed it out?"

"What are you asking me Ben?"

The city woke with zest. People walked outside and I watched a woman sweep the ground outside a quaint café.

"Is it possible to understand the mind of a killer and separate yourself from the understanding?"

"Surely. Otherwise most investigators would be killers wouldn't they?"

"Don't we kill though?"

"If it warrants it, yes. Sure. But you're not a killer."

"How do you distinguish killers? Is someone more justified in the taking of a life than another? It makes me less of a killer if I traveled through time and killed Hitler or Stalin, than say, that guy, or that girl, or that girl," I pointed to people we drove past on the street.

"Moral absolutism is flawed."

"It's very Kantian. It's *all* wrong. Even the one that says the greater good for the greatest number. How do we define the word greater and greatest and even number? Are people equal?"

"Since when do you care about whether or not something is intrinsically right or wrong? You said to me 'a murderer has to be caught. We don't choose the victims' didn't you?"

"It's true. I did say that."

"What's changed since you said it?"

"My perception I guess," I still didn't know her middle name.

IX

THE DOLE OF THE KING'S DAUGHTER

Blue ran from the sky when the clouds descended upon the skyscraper. These buildings that steal a piece of the sky and shift the wind that so rightfully belongs to the air; where's the justice in that? Can the sky sue these buildings in a court of law and ask for a continuance from the wind?

"Here we are. Your conversation is interesting," she handed me a card, "If you need anyone to drive you anywhere please give me a call."

"Thanks."

We walked towards the main tower of the Illia del Llac in silence. We walked into the communal area where a concierge greeted us and security guards roamed. There were signs for the pool, the change room, and the gym. Opposite these signs were arrows directing you to a tennis court, a squash court, and a general basketball court.

A man in a tuxedo approached Alicia, "How may I help you?"

I flashed my badge, "We're with the police. We're here to see Countess Baldure and Madame Lysettensen."

"That is an American badge."

"We need to speak with them all the same. Your precinct knows we're here."

"Are they expecting you?"

"No," Alicia said, "It's about an ongoing investigation."

He walked over to a counter and typed something on the screen and then spoke with some people on the phone.

"Mademoiselle Baldure is not in," he put the phone on his shoulder.

"Miss Lysettensen?"

He talked through the phone again, "No. Sorry. ... One moment please. What are your names?"

"Ben Britten and Alicia Shea."

"Ben Britten and Alicia Shea," he said over the line.

A security guard walked over to us. "You may go up," the concierge walked over, "My colleague will accompany you to the door."

"Thank you sir," Alicia walked behind the security guard to the lift.

The elevator doors opened to a duplex on the 21st floor at the top of the building. The living room ceiling was six meters above us. Glass walls around us made it easy to see the city of Barcelona and the lake, cityscape, a park, and the Catalan mountains surrounding everything else.

"Hello?" Alicia walked through the lounge of the first floor, where someone was smoking on the terrace.

Eycsüp turned around, "Detectives. How peculiar to find you here."

226

"I'm not a detective sir."

"Don't call me sir please," he walked by and glanced at a canvas near the corner of the room. I chuckled.

He walked inside and through the marble floor back to the lounge and sat down on one of the chairs, "Please, join me. May I offer you a drink or some snacks? Tapas perhaps?"

"Tapas? What are those? We heard of Tapas bars in Málaga but never had the pleasure," Alicia sat down across him.

"Tapas are delicious. They're appetizers. You can get them cold with olives and cheese, or hot with squid and meats and such. They're like our hand foods back home but more delicious and sophisticated."

"Sure. I'd love to try some," Alicia nodded to me.

He walked over to the counter in the kitchen and picked up the phone. "Sí..." and then he chattered in Spanish or Catalan (I was unable to distinguish them), "Yes. From Cachitos. It's on Rambla," he hung up and sat back down.

"What'd you get us?" I asked and walked over to one of the windows and looked at a river in the distance that led to the sea.

"I got the assorted mix. A bit of everything from *Cachitos*; it's one of the best places to get tapas. It should be here soon."

"Thank you," Alicia walked over to the terrace and looked at the view.

"It's nice to see you again Detective Britten. What brings you to Barcelona? You're not a fútbol fan are you?"

"No."

"Because it's El Clásico this weekend."

"I heard but no. I'm here," he looked up and saw Alicia across the room looking at the canvas and the view through one of the glass walls, "Can I ask you something Mister Eycsüp?"

"Please call me Michel. And of course."

"Do you remember the time we spoke at the Ritz?"

A sly smile flashed across his face, "There is no such thing as time," he walked over to the canvas and I followed, "The light isn't right," he whispered.

"That's what I wanted to ask you about. You said 'we've all been to Málaga and none of us have been to Málaga' ... what'd you mean?"

He lit a cigarillo and stroked the canvas in exacting brush strokes, then he put the brush down and looked outside.

"How was your summer?" I asked when the silence got uncomfortable and looking down at the bottom of the easel, I saw no chain.

"Summer is a season too beautiful to exist. Any depiction or experience of it is an inferior image of a reality that exists somewhere, and that somewhere isn't here. ... I'm sorry, what did you want to ask?"

"What'd you mean when you said we've all been everywhere and yet no one has been anywhere?"

"It's true that space is finite. I can't occupy the space you're standing in right now unless you move but this is limited to human capacity; the vastness of the universe, with us as a little dot means we can never evolve enough or understand enough to comprehend concepts like space and time."

"And so nothing has ever happened and no one has ever been anywhere because people can't understand these things?"

"You'll ruin yourself thinking about this stuff," he put his cigar down on the ashtray and looked outside.

Again silence reigned until I couldn't take it, "Mister Eycsüp. Focus."

His head lifted up and down and turned left and right.

"Mister Eycsüp?"

He tilted his neck towards the canvas and I watched his eyes focus on a point in the corner.

"Michel."

"The light isn't right!" he snapped looking outside towards a cloud moving towards us.

I hadn't seen the painting yet, "And what are you looking for? A *different* light?"

He looked at me as if the answer was obvious, "Of course not."

"What are you looking for?"

"God."

"You're looking for *God*?"

"Aren't you?"

"Not anymore... Wait. You're a physicist!"

"So? Being a physicist has nothing to do with playing with dice."

"I'd like to believe that."

"Then believe it. Your beliefs are easy to change. We've just told ourselves it's hard but it's not, all it takes is a moment, a touch. Anything can change everything. Not believing in something doesn't mean you can't search for it."

"You just said moments don't exist."

"Don't engage in wordplay detective. We both know I meant metaphysically or conceptually, not literally... otherwise we've never had the conversation we're having right now."

"Right..."

"What's stopping you? From believing in such things?"

The wind near the roof of the penthouse caught Alice's hair out on the terrace and I shifted my glance towards Eycsüp's, "The pile of unsolved murder cases on my desk. What changed? For you I mean."

"I don't remember the exact moment the alteration of the belief took place, it befell me so gradually that I hadn't even noticed it had happened."

"Then how do you know you even changed?"

"Because it's a fallacy that the prophetic moments of a life, when changed or changing are symbolized by drama. Those are moments you know and remember because you've chosen them. The true moments of a changing life, be it through fate or randomness, is marked by a divine silence, and often we can't notice them because we're paying attention to something else, until a seed planted in our consciousness starts growing and growing until it's become a tree bearing fruit, and the moment the first piece ripens and falls into our mind, we've changed and now we find that not only we've changed, but there's a tree there we hadn't noticed before."

"Now that you know you've changed... what were the moments leading up to that initial moment that would eventually lead to the change? Random? Or fateful?"

"I still don't know," he walked around the canvas again and looked at it.

The door creaked closed. Chloé Lysettensen walked up and completely ignoring both of us, walked behind him facing the canvas, looked at it, and nodded.

She greeted the canvas and not the man, and even that wasn't the weirdest thing. The clouds had since greyed the entire penthouse but for some reason he started painting almost as immediately as she'd nodded at the canvas, as if a dog called on command.

"Miss Lysettensen."

"Where are my manners? Hello Detective... Britten. I didn't see you there."

"I'm impressed you remember my name."

She smiled then walked over to the other room, "Excuse me, I'm going to freshen up."

"There are good things detective," he put the brush on the easel and walked towards me, "You look so despondent."

"Just last spring you were the most malcontent person I'd ever encountered."

"I still am; I just wear a mask now," he picked up a different brush.

"Masks... you're telling me the Venetians were onto something?" There was scarcely a need to depict these ideas and elucidate alienation, narcissism, and evil, and treat it as if it were original and avant-garde. It was beneath me to illustrate a dystopian *future* if we continued down this path; it is happening now and people have closed their eyes in either conscious, or unconscious regard. I looked outside and saw it everywhere and I couldn't help but wonder how people have learned to cultivate the masks they wear for one another. Was it like a piece of clothing that we must wear in society? A pair of pants, shoes, a shirt, your mask. I was naked and everyone could see it, and in seeing it, they are afraid; I frighten them, but really they are afraid of themselves.

"Maybe."

"What's good about the mask? ... I'm curious," I looked over to the coffee table and saw a copy of Hume's *Four Dissertations*.

"Well..." he put the brush down again when the clouds parted for an electric blue, "Compared to New York? A lot of things, but I mean the modern-man regardless of his location. His intellectual purgatory must be a haven in your profession when you consider technology."

"What do you mean?" I reached and opened my detective's notebook.

"An example? Well off the top of my head... identification of suspects and victims. The modern citizen is too much of a self-satisfied narcissist... that if he dies in this garbage dump of a world, you'll surely find a picture he took of himself. So to identify a victim without identification means less than it did in the 80s or 90s."

"And the suspects?"

"Big Brother has insured that all social media, depending on which one or how many your suspect uses, will provide your profile to you. What food they eat and their exercise habits: QuickPic; which art form they enjoy and how much they enjoy it: ReadNow; who their friends are and how sheepishly they think of political issues: NovelFaces; their professional interests and CV: LinkUp."

"If they teach rookies to use these things I'll be out of a job!" I chuckled.

"Rookies do use it. Nearly everyone uses at least one and there are hundreds of these services out there. Soon even those rookies will be out of a job. You'll all be downsized because we'll program machines that'll compile profiles and procure who's most likely to commit a crime and even *which* crime."

"Say I'm looking for someone who's killed once, just once, and he/she thinks they got away with it. I can't use what you told me to find him. Because he's not a psycho."

"He killed once a long time ago?"

"Yes."

"Well... if I were the killer," he took another cigarillo out of a white tin case and lit it, "I'd make sure the case was already solved. The perfect crime is not the case that remains open but one where the detective sleeps soundly at night having caught the *killer*, convinced as he may be in the belief that who he has is in fact guilty. The perfect crime is to set up a formulation in which the investigator follows all the clues and sequences in perfect logic to the wrong man."

Smoke filled the air.

Alicia walked back inside, "Was that Chloé Lysettensen?"

"Yes," Eycsüp answered.

"Is Countess Baldure here by any chance?"

"No I don't believe so. Is there something wrong?"

"Not at all. We just had a few questions for her regarding some paintings purchased last spring."

"I purchased those paintings for her. I briefly spoke with Detective Britten about it," Eycsüp looked at me.

The phone rang and ticked.

"Michelangelo?" Lysettensen called from the top floor, "Your order is here. Someone is bringing it up."

"Our tapas! This'll be delicious."

He stood at the counter organizing the food into plates, "Is she a vegetarian?" he asked me, looking at Alicia across the room.

I didn't know. What a failure I was as a friend and even a co-worker. By the bare minimum of human interaction required of someone who sees someone else everyday I fell short.

"Uh..." I shrugged my shoulders and he looked at me with a weird gaze penetrating the entirety of the space between us.

"The way she looks at you and moves around you. You should know..."

"What do you mean?"

He walked by me towards Alicia, "Are you a vegetarian?"

"No."

"Nice view isn't it?"

"Very. The urban planning is wonderful; I was telling Ben on the plane."

"It's designed by a man named Cerdà. He based it on a grid planning of larger blocks than usual. The blocks were larger than any Greek or Roman setup before it. He created bigger interior spaces and most of the places face the east to allow ample sunlight IF IT WOULD SHINE," he burst towards the terrace at the sky and then looked at the canvas, "I apologize."

She cracked up, "I know the feeling. It's horrible in New York right now. Constant overcast and rain."

"I remember," he walked back towards the counter and Alicia followed. "Excellent," he opened the bag and examined its contents,

"Soldaditos de pollo," and then separated some chicken strips onto plates, "Canelones con foie y trufa, pimientos de Padrón, coca de pan con tomato, queso manchego, gaspacho andaluz. Hmm, is that it?" one by one he listed them and one by one he carefully arranged them on plates. He *was* methodical but I couldn't get past the idea that there was something beneath it all, something about himself he pieced together as he went along.

"Did you order tapas again Michelangelo?" Lysettensen appeared from above, "Let me guess, Cachitos?" she loaded some pods into a fancy-looking coffee machine and put some espresso cups on the counter.

"It's the only place."

"Do you still play Miss Lysettensen?" Alicia asked and sat down close to her.

Eycsüp organized the plates around a glass dinner table near one of the walls overlooking the park, "What did you want to ask about the painting detective?"

I was weary about revealing too many facts but anything he said would help me, either as a suspect or an interested man with an understanding into what makes us ugly, "The appraiser that handled your paintings and her assistant have been killed. Madame Baldure hired a private detective to investigate some discrepancies in payouts received for some other paintings that went missing. We can't find any evidence of how these payouts occurred and where the paintings went missing. We only have the word of these insurance firms to go on and they're not really reliable."

"Bon appétit," he put the plates in front of us, "I was with Madame Baldure. She hired Hartmann on my request."

"Really? May we ask why?" Alicia reached for one of the olives.

"The worth of the paintings didn't make sense to me either. I asked her to follow up because I purchased some paintings for her, then *someone* appraised them citing transfer of ownership and then the paintings disappeared and I assumed there were some payouts."

"So Madame Baldure didn't know?"

"No of course not. It wouldn't make sense for her to have known about it; why would she open an investigation that would lead to herself in the end when secrecy would insure success?"

"Maybe something happened," I reached for one of the meat skewers, "And she wanted to deter suspicion from herself."

"She's not the type. I know her. Believe me detective. I know you won't take my word for it but investigating Contessina Baldure would be a waste of your time. Besides, I assume you found all the files with her signatures and our purchase of most of those paintings are on record at the galleries. For her to be involved and wanting to deter suspicion from herself would require a collusion from the highest levels of these galleries and companies, specifically with the intention that you don't get the evidence you have in your possession."

"He's right," Lysettensen dabbed her mouth with a napkin that had a treble clef design on it, "I've known Alfhild all my life. She's naïve because she grew up in a somewhat closed environment."

"So she's trusting?"

"Yes. She's not stupid but she can be quick to trust and can be taken advantage of if that person's intentions aren't pure," she got up to turn on the espresso machine.

"These are delicious. Thank you Mister Eycsüp," Alicia chewed one of the truffles.

"You're most welcome."

"May I ask you a personal question?" I put down my fork.

"Yes."

"Is murder wrong in all circumstances?"

"I'd like to believe so but humans are so complex things are rarely that simple."

"So it is possible to kill for the right reasons?"

"In an ideal world yes. But our issue is the way we use words to communicate with others. What and how would we define these so-called *right* reasons? Some can argue for profit of the whole and somewhere down the line the whole would be transferred to the self. Some would argue for the oppressed but that makes us oppressors of the oppressors in idealistic attempts to free one set of the oppressed by oppressing those that shackle them. ... In the end becoming tyrants ourselves."

"Please don't get him started," Lysettensen shook her head at me.

"Think about religion detective," he looked at me, "It's too late Clo," he glanced at Lysettensen but let his eyes linger on her face for a second.

"What about it? They're oppressors as much as they want us to think differently."

Alicia gripped her necklace but didn't say anything.

"No matter how much you loathe God or can't reconcile the Epicurean paradox between benevolence and omnipotence, go to the Cathedral in this city, or the Sagrada Familia. Breathe the air and watch the people come in and out of these places. It would be a frightening world without churches, synagogues, and mosques; hipsters would have us tear them down because they represent tax-exemptions; they'd have us build cold, sterile laboratories in their place but they misunderstand the symbolism of its tall steeples."

"Hope," Alicia put her necklace under her blouse.

"I saw your necklace but it's not *just* hope. Does a laboratory give us an ethereal divinity against a world destroying itself? Does it reflect the infinite colors of stained windows on your face at dawn, and burn in fierce candlelight at dusk? Colors that should be used to combat corrupt militaries and their black weapons built in laboratories? Is the silence of a laboratory, panicked by fear of a result against your favor and losing your funding, the same as the silence in a temple? The silence that should combat sophistical politicians and the yes-men of middle management in banks? Listen to the sound of a hymning violin or cello," he looked to Lysettensen, "Surround and fill the walls of a symphony hall and try to recreate it using technology built by science. Can science stop the façade of democracy? The farce of voting for one of two political parties each yearning for the opportunity to fill their own pockets? Sit in the Barcelona Cathedral and watch those praying for themselves or their loved ones or even the damned; can science battle the sweet venom of the shallow and the unthinking? Their lackluster and deep-rooted motivation to equate the methodology, experimentation, and dulling causal efficacy of re-experimentation in a lab with truths about the physical world that can better help us understand the non-physical? Read the words of holy books, of philosophy, literature, and art; read the surreal power of poetry. Memorize it against the dilution of truthful language and the meaningless aphorisms of social justice causes popularizing themselves for personal gain. A world devoid of these thoughts is a world already burning."

Alicia leaned in, "That's beautiful."

"If we believe that, we have to believe that souls are eternal and timeless," I ate the last of the olives.

"Timelessness and immortality are curses if they hold true."

Lysettensen tilted her head and Alicia was offended beyond regard.

He lit a cigarillo and leaned in, "Demands are made of us to *vote* for oppression under the guise of choice. We're told to love the boot that suffocates us as its metal slams through the streets we've built and if we should so expose such facts, the boots deafen the silence with catlike steps behind the oppressed just before they're stabbed in the heart," he breathed in the smoke, "The praying people, the absurdity of a kneeling man is being told to forgive and love their oppressors."

"How vague and ambiguous the language of the oppressors must be to be able to perpetuate the circle," Lysettensen blinked.

"Exactly. Only in a world previously agreed to nurture a collective self-delusion could such ideas thrive. The *true* golden rule devised by wise men and women to love your enemy is bound to lead to disaster. It robs the lover of his identity and self-confidence, buttering them in the hands of wolves disguised as beloveds in fancy suits. The lovers will never have the strength to stand up to them even with power of force or use of weapons..."

"Because they can never get past the belief that they're doing wrong," Alicia clenched and unclenched her fists.

"We love the *idea* of God but we can never love Him as a person. How could we? He is more like us than we are. How do we love a being that demands you kill your first-born son to prove your loyalty? A God that punishes those who question his power like Lot's wife or Job, who are created to be ignorant. Did God not create them like that? How can we ask questions if we are unable to be curious? Even scientifically? If our questions do not line up within the rigid framework of a discipline's methodology? How can we doubt ourselves when doubt is seen a weakness and we are told to always remain strong in the face of adversity? What a shoddy God... to demand slavery of us and want us to abide joyfully and gratefully, and be offended when some of us refuse. If he is omnipotent, He's with us every second. He notes our thoughts and motivations and intentions. How can we be ourselves when we are imprisoned with the foreknowledge that these motivations and intentions can never be hidden? What are we without the hidden facts that make us who we are? These facts that He knows? How much must He hate us to render our souls immortal? And we come to your point now detective. Why do we love immortality? Without death we would no longer need time; nothing could be missed. There'd be no need to ever do anything. Doing something now would mean nothing. There'd be no sin or wicked moment we couldn't relive because there'd always be time to make up for it. I need only point to the creations of His creation in our infinite libraries. Books like *All Men are Mortal, Death with Interruptions, the Immortal, Death Takes a Holiday...* so on and so forth. These show you how absurd immortality would be. And these are concocted scenarios of the physical by the creations! This doesn't even begin to graze the absurdity of immortality in some abstract. It would be impossible to be a Buddhist and live in the present because enjoyment of a moment comes from the love of its passing in retrospect. Kissing the loves of your life today is the same as kissing them tomorrow. But you don't want to kiss them tomorrow, you want them today because you know you're going to die someday. So why are we so happy in accepting the immortality of the soul knowing this? This instant, and every instant after this one; if we were timeless and our souls were immortal, I could never want them. Metaphysically, a conceptual requirement of desire is timed—."

"That's enough Michelangelo," Lysettensen rubbed her forehead.

"The passing of emotions and thoughts. They are timed too. You're tired when exposed to too much information at once because the second time it comes it loses its momentary horror or joy. Why doesn't

God understand this? Why does He threaten us with this prison of consciousness while others threaten us in prisons of the physical and the consuming souls of the wicked and the just burn along."

"Michelangelo!"

"I apologize. I get ahead of myself."

"I'm frightened that you're right," I leaned back into the chair.

"I disagree," Alicia crossed her legs, "God gives us the option."

He sighed and took another puff, "But he knows which you'll pick; how is that a free choice? If freedom is the freedom to choose then yes, perhaps we can fool ourselves into thinking we have choices and the freedom to choose between them. But of a freedom not to choose at all?"

The door latched open.

"Hola," a man in dark chinos and a sport jacket walked through the door.

"Wolfe!" Eycsüp stood up, "This is the brilliant Detective Britten, and his lovely partner Alicia Shea… detective and doctor, this is Elroy Wolfe."

"Pleasure. Mister Eycsüp gives me too much credit."

"It's nice to meet you," we shook hands, "But I'm afraid we've taken up enough of your time. We should go," I looked to Alicia.

"Yes," she nodded, "But I will think about what you said."

"Don't," Lysettensen warned, "That's how he wins."

"It's not about winning or losing," Eycsüp chuckled and I think it was the first time I saw him smile.

"Oh, by the way Mister Eycsüp," Alicia stepped towards him, "You went to school in New York right?"

"Yes."

"Do you know a Mædeleine De Geest?"

Elroy glanced towards Eycsüp for a second. Tension built until he said, "Yes of course. I went to school with her. … She passed unfortunately."

"How did she pass? If you don't mind me asking," I wanted to see how he'd handle it.

He put the burning cigarillo down, "She committed suicide some time ago."

Him knowing her fate explained why he didn't want to believe in the immortality of the soul.

"I'm sorry," Alicia said.

"It was a long time ago."

"Well… thank you for your time Mister Eycsüp, and your hospitality Madame Lysettensen."

"Yes. Thank you for everything. The tapas were delicious," Alicia shook their hands, "And also nice to meet you Mister Wolfe."

I shook Lysettensen's hand and smiled.

Eycsüp offered his hand, "No paint this time." We shook hands.

What did he want? Why was he asking me these things? I didn't understand people. I pursued Beauty but the more I dealt with others I realized we were the opposite of what I pursued. They revolted me. I wanted most of them dead and most of the time I had to be cautious so I was not consumed by this rage. I saw through my own time and I knew this passion would burn me.

I walked over to the window and watched them leave. They hailed a cab and drove towards Tibidabo. Looking down the road it looked as if it led to the sky. It ascended until it disappeared into the clouds, which by now rested on the height of the mountain at 1700 feet like a kite floating over its owner. It was wonderful to withdraw from the social and psychological demands of society. I'd forgotten about the ignorance of others here. It wasn't like that with Chloé. It was comfortable to sit in the silence or to watch her practice. With the city at our feet it felt like we were linked to nature and the closer we felt to nature the younger we became. Everything we'd acquired in all these years of existence that led to that moment fell from our souls. We became what we were and would become once again.

The only representation of time in nature is death and because youth is the opposite of death the air enamored us, the presence of one another and the qualities we'd had that we had stopped from flourishing because of societal etiquette finally evolved to what it should've been long ago.

I walked onto the terrace and puffed the last bit of the Davidoff.

This unity came at a price. The closer we came to nature the farther we got from each other; humans aren't natural. We are an irregularity in the evolution of bacteria. We are a virus. I apologize for the melancholic words dear reader; it's almost Mædeleine's birthday.

"Of all days in a year he came today…. Why was he asking about Mædeleine?" Wolfe came up behind me holding his pipe carved with wood from this place or other.

I looked at his mantis green Tod's stretch chinos, "Nice pants."

X
THE LADY OF THE LAKE (EXCERPT)
SECOND CANTOS: PART II

"How's the painting coming along?" he wiped some lint off those ridiculous pants.

"It's not," I lit another Davidoff and looked straight down towards the pavement, "Do you think evil exists? What I mean is, if a good man does evil, does that make him evil?"

"How can a good man do evil? He'd be evil from the start... but more to the point, evil is already in the soul. Matter is a principle of destruction but it can't be evil. If you believe in souls anyway."

"Where does it come from though, this evil? If it's already in the soul?" when did we start talking about souls or matter?

"I don't know. Maybe it's a terminus of desire that destroys all form... like giving in to lust or other bodily desires."

"Then there must be a *relative* reality to what a form ought to be and this form relates to the evil somehow."

"Yeah... maybe it's the absence of a form that ought to be there."

"So something has a form first and evil is privation of that form? What there ought to be is goodness but instead there's evil."

"Something like that. That's where morality comes in I guess. Because you're rational and you can think about things and act on them. So that rationality has to be there... doing harm to others is always being subordinate to this reason because it's giving in to appetites and desires. You do wrong based on profit, ego, false belief, etcetera."

"You aren't what you *ought* to be."

"Do what's *right*, not what you *think* is right."

"How do you distinguish the two?"

"I don't think we can."

I looked at him, "Then what's the point of this damn conversation?"

"Hey, you asked me!"

"I thought you'd have answers."

"All I have are questions," he puffed some tobacco.

"You seen Yohun anywhere?" I asked, "It's quiet."

"I know why you call him that."

"I thought you had no answers."

"It's because he calls Alfhild Alf, and he pronounces it, almost always and especially when he's drunk, as 'Elf.' You pronounce the *Hun* at the end *every* time, like Attila. I get it. It's very clever."

"Isn't that his name? Maybe it's my accent."

"I just want you guys to be friends. He's a good guy."

"So the evil we just talked about, about giving in to bodily desires... you just ignore that altogether?"

"Don't twist my words."

"That's *your* specialty Gorgias. He doesn't interest me," I looked back inside where the light behind me reflected on the terrace door and I could see the faint figure of one of the women walking in the main room, "So if evil is the absence of a form that ought to be there, does that mean beautiful things are also good?"

"To kalokagathia."

"What?" I blew smoke in his face.

"The beautiful and the good, beauty and virtue. All of these belong together. It's Plato. The idea of the outflow from the Good; what is good is also beautiful and vice versa."

"This idea originated from the essence of aristocracy. To be a perfect gentlemen Wolfe."

"That's one interpretation. You should know that nothing is free. Least of all love."

Why should *I* know it? "What idiot thinks love is free?"

"It ought to be."

I thought about Johann having sex with Hild, "I'd rather have money than love."

Shifting his belt and pulling up his pants, he said, "I wouldn't expect that from you. Why?"

"You can buy things with money and the things you lose or gain are bought or lost with money. With love the currency is souls, and they're not as abundant as cash."

"That's funny. I can never tell if you're serious or not."

He was one of the stupidest people I'd ever known but that was why I hung out with him and humored his idiocy. The world consists of two subsets of people: the stupid and the intelligent. The former are far more trustworthy; a stupid person is consistent in their stupidity. They'll *always* do the dumbest thing they can with the most sophistical justification. Always is essential because you'll then know what they'll do and how they'll do it. This makes them easy to control and thereby easy to trust. Intelligent people, though they are by definition smart in their decision-making are thoroughly inconsistent. This is because they have no core beliefs. They have nothing that binds them to any school of thought. You can't rely on a smart man to do the same thing on the same path twice because his rationalization can change on a whim. He may deem it intelligent to trust you one moment but betray you the next. They are never to be trusted.

"I trust you," the sun peered through the clouds for only a second before a hissing sound forced it back to cower behind the clouds. It'd started raining and drops wet the ground in vain hope of trying to wash the blood from this earth.

* * *

I couldn't sleep. I lay in bed fixing my eyes on a spot on the ceiling, attempting to imagine what beauty I could create from it if it were a canvas. I tried to imagine how to fill the empty spaces on my canvas in the lounge and in desperation sought an answer from within myself about whether it was possible still, to love two people at the same time.

Love must be a circle of hell. I couldn't go 30 seconds without thinking of one or the both of them. I relate everything to something they've done or one of them has said. When someone says something I often think, "Oh yes, that's something Clo or Hild *would* have said." I'm mentally exhausted. And when I'm too wiped to fight the insomnia I fall asleep and dream of them, and when I wake I always wake with the thought of their eyes. Four pebbles hidden beneath ocean waves. One time we were sitting at a bar when the Eurosport ticker showed RCD Espanyol having lost 3-0 in the final and I showed the slightest reaction and Clo noticed. She asked me how I felt about her. She had a suspicion something was going on but she didn't come out and say how *she* felt. I detested her for that. I detested her as much as I loved her; she not only never talked about my feelings for her, she just never talked about feelings at all. This was what made her rapturous. Talking has never, not once in the history of animal kind, solved any issue worth solving. It complicates things and makes things dense and abstract and always introduces the possibility of being misunderstood. Most issues, nay, *all* issues are solved in solitude when the mind is free from the obligations of social interaction and emotional suppression. In dark solitude, the body is imprisoned while the mind roams free; this is objectivity. In interactions, especially with people one has an emotional connection, no matter the emotion: envy, anger, adulation, love; the mind is imprisoned with social rules that are mere shadows of actual thoughts. In these cases however, the body moves free. This is why at cafés and nightclubs one sees indubitable numbers attempting fellowships of courtship. In short, I abhorred talking and what better way to embrace this hatred with the refusal to talk to whom you love. That's why I never talked to her; words corrupt, and I loved her too much to corrupt her soul.

The clock hummed until it was drowned out by an agony straining through the walls. Nary a creature nor object could stir in the absence of the sun and its effect was moved by a divine stillness in the crisp night air. I couldn't hear the city. No sound bounced off the concrete and I stopped hearing the pace of time ticking life away.

"Can't sleep either?" she stopped playing when she saw me appear through the darkness.

"Don't stop," the sun was up even if it wasn't. I listened to her eyes talk to me like corked sand floating over waves. God had made her in

Her image. I felt those high cheekbones and slender arms shade the dimming lights of the night.

"You look so fascinated by me pushing hair on a string."

In some distant past, like the fading memory of an old man, whether in this world or a parallel one, I knew I had given in to her a thousand times before and I was bound to this decision once again.

"...What time is it?" she asked when I didn't say anything.

"I don't know. I didn't look."

She put the cello down, "Do you think Hild did what they say she did? Those cops?"

"No," I knew *if* she was involved, it was by the manipulative hand of Johann.

She played *the Lark Ascending* by Nicola Benedetti and the London Philharmonic Orchestra conducted by Andrew Litton through her tablet and I laid my head on the couch. I barely noticed it; it was so gradual the way she floated through the air and sat at the edge of the couch above me.

"What do you think of the painting so far?" I moved up and put my head on her thigh.

She played with my hair, "Your use of contrast and color is grand."

"What about the allegory?" I looked at her.

"You pain yourself when you think of injustice; you can't eliminate it."

Chatter and laughter neared from behind the door.

Hild helped Johann through the door and saw Clo and I on the couch.

"Oh!" she looked flushed, "Hey guys!"

"Look! It's the artists!" Johann giggled, "The singer and the... what are you again?" he flipped his scarf behind him.

I laid back on Clo's thigh. I was too tired for games.

Hild looked at me and kissed Johann; a kiss that lasted so long I could feel my heart tearing but Clo and I listened to the music and drifted through the clouds outside the window.

The nightmare is always the same. A wolf howls at the darkness and laments the absence of the moonlight. Another barks.

Somewhere, a tiger roars and an eagle sings above me. There are animals all around me and I'm sure dream analysts are wetting themselves with excitement. I put no weight in dreams but the eerie part of this dream, the part that makes me tremble with foreboding is the lone crow sitting silently on a branch across my eye line. No matter where I go it's in my eye line. Sometimes the branch just floats in the air and isn't connected to a tree at all. It just... stares at me and says nothing.

After meeting Clo she appears behind me, "Michelangelo?"

I turn and face her, "You're a fictional character," the crow is now behind her with its neck tilted and its eyes looking at me.

"What?" I shake, the reality too much to bear. My thoughts and emotions written on a page somewhere with someone's fingers over the words that describe my deepest secrets even now.

"You're in a novel Michel."

Finally the crow flaps away and I look above me; there are no clouds and no sky, only the black of space until words fill that blackness with a blue that becomes the sky or a yellow that becomes the sun or a green that becomes the grass, and soul and dialogue and character that becomes me.

I fall to my knees when I realize it: someone reading about my life and flipping through my past, present, and future by the simple turn of a page.

Vincent by Don McLean played at a low volume. I awoke on the couch with a blanket over me. Hild stood at the counter cooking breakfast.

"Are you hung-over? ... Wait I don't think I've ever seen you take a drink."

"I don't," I woke up and opened *Four Dissertations* to Chapter 4. It's Mædeleine's birthday and that thought poisoned everything else.

"Speaking of, I bought you a book," she wiped her hands on her apron, "It's on the table there," she pointed towards Chian Hsun's *Six Lectures about Loneliness* on the side table beside the couch.

"Thanks. What's it about?"

"I don't know. I saw it and you popped into my head."

"You see the word loneliness and you think of me?" I got up and stretched my back.

She ground some pepper into the eggs and laughed, "And done! I'm going to take this to Johann. He had a bit too much to drink."

He's had a bit too much of existence if you ask me, "Okay. I have to brush my teeth anyway."

Is love a masterpiece on an empty canvas? Empty in its purity and one that everybody lines up to look at until their legs tire?

"Can I ask you something?" she walked back into the kitchen a few moments later.

"Why does everyone keep asking if they can ask me something; go ahead and ask," my left arm was hurting and kept falling asleep.

"You just seem very closed; the way you look at people, even people you seem to be close to..."

"Hild, go ahead and ask," I repeated.

"You have a doctorate in physics right? ... I looked it up. In the merging of black holes and their gravitational effect on their surroundings?"

"You looked it up?" a smile crept up from behind my throat and I couldn't do anything to stop it, "What's the question Hild?"

"Why'd you get a doctorate in physics? I've seen your verses on memo pads all around and your sketches of scenery. Why didn't you go to art school?"

"I was afraid of being rejected and becoming a fascist."

"Be serious. You could be a professor or a scholar in your field. Instead you did a complete 180 and moved to Italy and then Spain. What instigated it?"

"I thought there was a beauty to physics. At the beginning they teach you the basics and tell you you'll get to the good stuff later. Then when it's later, they tell you the good stuff is everywhere and you have its relation to other things."

"But it's so hard to become a doctor in something! Like I could ask you any physics question and you'd know the answer?"

"I have no answers; I heard that recently," it's funny because I used to laugh at people when they told me about doctorates in physics. What a brilliant idea; how does one become a doctor in the universe when we're such an insignificant part of it? It was much simpler than books or podcasts make it seem. You just have to know the way things behave in *relation* to each other. That's what bothered me. If you have a perfect understanding of the physical world you pretty much have an understanding of nearly everything... but what about things that aren't in the physical world. Do they even exist?

"All my friends went into finance or became lawyers and doctors but none of them really love their vocation."

"No. There is no love. Only what's socially appropriate through an alienation of your job. Each vocation has its own label and its own behavioral designators. Postmodern arteests *all* have the same tattoo and wear the same 'custom' painted Converse All-Stars and they consider themselves nonconformists. Lawyers laugh and think themselves the smartest because they make the most money but they're slaves to corporate law, not justice as their vocation demands. Doctors see themselves as altruists but they're slaves to the pharmaceutical companies. They'll recommend whichever drug pays them the most money. Scientists think themselves the most open-minded people on the planet but try to argue something against their belief-system within the status quo. They're more in love with their beliefs than dogmatists. They'll protect their method to the death rather than listen to the demand of their vocation: to pursue the truth."

"What else is left?"

"Philosophy, but philosophers are among the greatest bullshitters on the planet. So infatuated with the *idea* of being called a philosopher than the actual love for wisdom. It's impossible to argue with a philosopher because they're so dialectically intelligent in their word usage and argumentation. You never know whether to trust them because their argument is aimed at wisdom and truth, or weather they're coloring you blind because they want to win the argument."

"So we've corrupted everything implicitly?"

"Hild don't get him started," Clo walked across the kitchen rubbing her eyes and reaching for the coffee.

"I'm curious. Do you know why he got a doctorate? He won't give me a straight answer."

"Michelangelo?"

"Yeah..." she handed Clo a cup of coffee.

"If I had to guess? ... It's not vanity because he doesn't make us call him doctor. He makes high demands of himself and holds others to the same standard..."

I stopped leafing through the Hsun book and looked at her.

"Am I wrong?"

"No."

"It's out of rebellion," she said it so matter-of-fact, so casually and without any doubt that I myself almost believed it.

Hild poured herself a cup and carefully sipped it, "Elaborate Chloé."

"There must've been a woman involved somewhere. He doesn't do anything without thinking about the 'beautiful shape and color of a woman', but to *get* the doctorate, in physics no less, the highest of the quantum disciplines, and then *not* use it. It's the ultimate defiance against a world that betrays itself. A world with people more impressed by the titles of their positions and jobs than the representations of their jobs."

"That's why he doesn't make us call him doctor. It's aimed specifically at the superficial."

"And in a way, most people are superficial so it's aimed at everyone."

They sat down across me with their coffee cups in hand, "You against the world. Such a teenager at heart," Clo said.

A few seconds passed in quiet, "Well... did we nail it Michelangelo?" Hild asked.

"Like a hammer," I picked up the Hsun book again.

Johann clattered from above and came out with his breakfast tray, "Not so loud!"

244

"You've hardly touched it!" Hild got up.

"I'm meeting Elroy at Tapas 24 for lunch soon so there's no point in eating your eggs."

"I thought we were having brunch later."

"Oh sorry. I forgot. We'll reschedule it," he walked over and turned the TV to BBC. "COME ON! ... What a bunch of idiots."

"Who?"

"PSV! Those punks!" he yelled at the screen, "They lost to Heracles. What a bunch of low-lives."

"Indeed," I chimed in and Clo looked outside.

He walked over to Clo's tablet and played what he thought passed for music, "This is ma jam! ... Babe, have you seen my het Nederlands Elftal scarf?"

"No," Hild answered with her eyes glued to the TV.

"Because they're playing today and I want to catch the game with the boys."

"I don't know where it is," she looked around, "Where's the remote?"

"Don't watch the news. There's nothing important on there except the financial stats anyway."

I looked at the TV where the words "Serial Killer Graciana Ximena Vargas Caught in Barcelona" sat over a video of a man being arrested by officers in uniform.

"Here," Clo reached in the drawer of the side table.

"... *Caught. Vargas worked as a bread distributor to various markets and grocery stores. His attorney has asked for leniency in light of his abused childhood involving his grandmother. 'Leniency? Come on Amy,'*" the shot changed to two people sitting in a newsroom, "*All the victims were senior citizens above the age of 65. It's time Mister Vargas see the full force of the justice system. 'And apparently this was solved by an inspector not even on the case!'*" the woman said, "*Yes. She helped build the profile which eventually led to the arrest.*"

"What a world," Clo walked over to the sink.

"Let them all burn!" Johann took a scarf out of the closet, "I'll be on my way."

"Johann?" Hild looked at him standing in the doorway.

"Yeah?"

"Take it easy on the drinking," she shook her head.

"Yeah yeah yeah..." the door slammed shut.

"You should leave him," Clo was direct.

"I can't."

"Do you love him?"

"I think so."

I opened my mouth to tell her love was an illusion but I refrained.

"What?" she saw it.

"Nothing," I reached for my cigarillo case.

"No," she pulled it towards her, "What were you going to say?"

"I'm not a fan of him Hild but I care deeply for you at the same time. Therefore anything I say will be biased."

"He was going to say you don't love him."

"I do. How would you know that Michelangelo?"

"I didn't say anything Hild."

"He thinks love is a concept and he thinks most concepts are human thought structures designed to infringe on your freedom."

"Well," she looked at me and gripped the Davidoff case, "I love Johann."

"I didn't say anything Contessina. Besides, you don't have to prove anything to me."

"Don't call me that! …Wait, you don't believe in love? That's just wrong!"

Their eyes looked through me and burned a hole in the back of the canvas sitting in the corner of the room.

"No. See that painting there? Sitting on the easel? It's finished and it's not. There is no such thing as time. Nothing occurs and everything occurs. All of it, all of *this*, around us, *in* us, everything. It's all happening on a simultaneous plane. Narratives that advance linearly are done so to profit the feeble intellect, an intellect hoping in desperation to acquire a sense of time. We can only do this linearly. This happened. Now this is happening, and that will or will not happen. It gives us an illusion that we're in control; that we understand. This is a mistake… your death has already happened just as your birth has yet to occur."

"I don't want to have this conversation," Hild stood up.

I knew this was going to happen; people don't want to hear these things no matter how truthful it may be, "Hild… no. Don't go."

"It's not that Michelangelo," she lied, "I have to pick up my friend's daughter and get her ready for dinner."

Clo got up and walked onto the terrace.

"I wouldn't say anything with intent of hurting you Hild."

"I know," she put on her jacket.

"I'll be back."

"Bye Chloé!" she waved towards the terrace.

Clo waved.

The door closed behind her and so did my mind. Stupid. Stupid. Stupid. But now I knew, Hild said he'd do anything for her but now I knew she didn't believe it. For if he did anything she wanted would he risk his life for her? And if he is such a thrill seeker, going out of his way to speed on a highway in daddy's brand new Maserati or flying her family chopper recklessly around her estate, why hasn't he ever been killed or at least injured? He is either blessed or fabricating these grandiose qualities upon himself. Judging from the fact that he was with her, it had to be the former.

"I don't care what you believe. Don't do that again," Clo sat down behind me with her cello leaning against her lap.

"I didn't mean to hurt her; she can do better than Johann."

"Do you know what he does? What his *family* does?"

"Steal?" I blurted out.

She wanted to laugh but didn't, "His dad insures a bank's investments. His great-great-grandfather founded Phlegethon in the 20s."

"Never heard of them."

"They changed their name after the war."

"To what?"

"What do you want from him?"

"Decency. That's not much to ask."

"That's asking everything Michelangelo. *Everything*; being decent and courteous means caring for others and taking their emotions into consideration regarding yourself, that's asking everything."

"Then I'm asking for everything."

The notes of a Nocturne hummed while her hand moved through the air and guided the bow across a piece of wood.

"You know what he said to me once?"

I looked up from the book.

"He thought the best artist in the last *century* was Kanye."

"Orphans of a bankrupt culture." Did he actually think this or had he merely accepted the external caricature of himself, his mask as his real face.

"What?" she weaved in and out of the notes in synchronization, timing our conversation with breaks in the composition.

"He puts more weight on which celebrity is dating whom rather than the lives we've taken for the right of politicians to lobby and not be indicted or bothered by average peons."

"It really is modern feudalism isn't it?"

"Yes, in some archaic way. Freedom is delegated to whoever's funding the lobbyists; you're free to do and say whatever you please and worship whatever God you want and practice whichever culture you find most appealing."

"Why do I *know* there's a but coming?"

"Whichever way of life you find most charming is open to you; all of it is freedom." I looked for the cigarillo case. Where did Hild put it? "… Insofar as it doesn't disrupt the structure's rapt consumerism and couch-sitting time. Freedom, death, peace; the three things politicians use to deceive everyone from the family dog whining for its doggie bones to the Oxford professor peeing himself with excitement over the newest book that argues the freedom to have purchasing power is equal to freeing the slaves of the South."

She started playing then stopped, "You can't have her. You should accept that."

"I never said I wanted her."

"Your eyes scream it every time she's in the vicinity."

"My eyes?"

"The eyes ooze the desires of the soul."

"You can see my desires?" I walked up to her.

"Sometimes."

I moved close to her face, "What do you see?"

She backed away.

"Hvorfor er du bange?" the words came out in Danish.

"Jeg er ikke; alt er et spil for dig," she responded in a Jutland accent.

"Clo," I whispered her name and switched back to English.

"I don't see anything."

"I don't believe that."

She put the bow down and looked into my eyes again, "I see melancholy but also hope. Your irises circle themselves like a spiral originating from your pupils," she moved closer until I felt our noses touching.

"I have to stop by my old studio," I backed away.

She didn't flinch and started practicing again, "Good. I have to head back to New York for the winter. You're more than welcome to join me."

"You just mention in passing that we'll be wintering in New York?"

"No. I mention in passing that *I'll* be wintering in New York."

"Don't be cruel."

"I'm a musician archetype."

"These are just labels: musician, artist, philosopher, communist, capitalist. They don't mean anything. It's demeaning; don't do that to yourself."

She put the cello back in its case and walked up to me, "I already do all I can to myself. I have no time for anything because my life is hours of repetition of the same movements followed by rage when my body doesn't emulate those movements properly, sleeping in king-sized beds in hotel room suites by myself, using weird cellos that don't respond to my touch, and the anticipatory boredom of holding back my tears in patience as I wait for the room to fill up. Then the pressure builds and builds from the moment I start walking onto that stage; all eyes on me, 'the ugly Chloé,' a critic said that about me once—and the conversations I must have with people after the show about compositions and the people who wrote them and the thought that everyone's snapping QuickPics of me and recording me for some video on the Internet where commenters hoard in waves to talk about what they want to do to me in bed and how I fail against some great classical cellist or even a contemporary. Are you looking for this?" she handed me the Davidoff case, "And slowly over time, since I was a child, I came to realize that perfection doesn't exist. Even if I make no mistake, play the notes with angelic perfection I can never live up to an experience somebody had regarding a classical piece *back in the day*. It's all about self-absolution. I absolve myself from having to be perfect but the rage builds nonetheless."

"Against what?" I moved towards her.

"Against the ignorant and idiotic. The Johanns who are too stupid to know better and the Elroys who know too much to know better."

I walked up leaned in to kiss her but she pulled away.

She made me anguish mentally. A woman who pulls away as you go in for a kiss or for a touch of her hand makes you suffer physically. She's pulled away out of an external sense; perhaps she doesn't trust you, perhaps she doesn't know you well enough, perhaps the circumstances of your lives prevent the connection. This is easy to get over. If bros can fathom that some women aren't interested in only the physical. Men simply get over these physical rejections and move on.

The women worth dying for, however rare they are, make you anguish mentally. They do nothing noteworthy but they etch themselves within the deepest and worst parts of your soul and breathe light into it. The realization of this mental anguish is worse than a thousand physical rejections *because* they haven't done anything noteworthy. The mind will circle around looking for solutions like a rat in a mirrored maze, but unbeknownst to us rats, the maze runs circular and there is no way out of the Labyrinth we've created for ourselves by placing this woman on a pedestal. Some women are worthy of this attention but most are not, the ones that are not worthy of this sort of attention do not last since they don't know how to handle the intensity of sincere adulation at the hands of their lovers. In fact, contrary to feminist beliefs, most of these women beg to be mistreated and hated by their lovers and only then do they find them attractive. The tragedy of the genders. The women that do deserve this attention and receive it are fearful of being deceived by the insincerity of passive men that only aspire to physical lust and nothing more, and thus cultivate armors that emulate the physical rejection. After all, since men forget the physical rejections of the many women they attempt to court, these women are happy to fade into the sea of women having rejected a man on accounts known or unknown. This is their way, to fade into the crowd and blend in with the rest of the hallow heads walking through busy streets in the urban metropolis of a man's mind. Chloé's armor was her intelligence shaped like wood and horsehair. She was without a doubt a predator of the intellect; she knew that men were emasculated when their intelligence (and thereby their manliness, since men are so backwards and childish that they think they're still smarter than women *at certain things* which translates mentally into *all things*) was threatened and did everything she could to make these men feel like idiots. She derived the strangest satisfaction from exposing them as the fools they were and always would be. To be fair, almost all of them really were idiots compared to her. All of them except me, or so I thought. This is not to say I read more things than her or had a higher IQ, no. I had built an armor of indifference around myself bordering on perilous apathy. I had simply used up all my emotional powers and was crushed every time so I had left nothing left to give. Chloé was better read, better bred, better spoken, and a better artist, and I knew it. Still, my indifference (and sincere respect transcending the mere physical) had knocked her off her game and she must've thought I was devious and manipulative and absolutely untrustworthy. Whenever she could, she went out of her way to show why I was wrong; this could be something I'd said, my atrocious smoking habit, or a particular technique I'd employed in my latest work. Little did she know, I also thrived on the criticism of the beautiful and the competition of the worthy. This was perhaps why we were so drawn to each other despite Johann's attempts to make me look like a fool and Hild's attempts to make Chloé look undeserving of me because she wanted me bound to furious solitude.

"You smell like smoke," she looked straight at me.

"You're right," I backed away, "I have to head back to my studio for a little while."

"Just bring your stuff here Michelangelo. It's rude to have your landlady hold your place when she could be renting it to someone who can help her."

"Hild gave me a decent sum for those bids, I'm paying. She's not *holding* the place for me; I'm paying rent."

"I'm not talking about the money. I don't care about money."

It insulted me that she *pretended* not to care about money. Women need money. It was absurd to even insinuate they didn't lavish in its possession. Women invest in themselves and men try to purchase that investment; how do you purchase things? With money. Feminists will say this objectifies women but it is worthwhile to note that they have succeeded in equality. Men are objects too. Men are objectified in being rich and lustful and vengeful pigs that desire an object that they think will make them look better or more prestigious or feel better. Women are poisoned by the money men should have whereas men are poisoned by their desires of women. We are all black holes pulling each other towards ourselves and eventually nothing can escape the blackness of anxious tragedy.

"Then what are you talking about?"

"She's old. She could use someone who can help her and make her life easier."

"She has a son."

"I'm too tired to argue. Just bring your stuff here. You can save that money too."

I relented.

"May I take your uMusic player? I have a long way to go."

"Of course. The headphones are by the coffee machine," and after glancing at the canvas just once and shrugging her shoulders, she started practicing and didn't look up again.

When I walked over to pick up the headphones by the coffee machines I saw the plate Johann had put in the sink. The eggs scrambled in perfect circles like the ouroboros with oregano and rosemary centered on the plate. Anger tingled up my left hand when I saw that she'd poured the ketchup in the shape of a heart on the eggs; he hadn't touched it. I used a fork to spread the ketchup around and left.

I heard the notes vibrate throughout the air and even thought I heard her playing in the elevator but that would've been impossible.

It'd started raining while I was in the elevator and I walked out to the sound of the ground begging the cement to part so the water could touch the dirt and life could grow.

"Sir," someone called from behind me.

"Yes?"

It was the concierge, "Please take this," he handed me an umbrella, "Would you like me to hail you a taxi?"

"That won't be necessary," I took the umbrella, "Thanks," and walked towards the door.

The door revolved a young Swedish woman inside and me outside; Hild and an amber-haired little girl stepped out of a matte-black BMW X6.

"Michelangelo?"

"Yes. I have to head to my old studio. I'll be back later tonight."

"You should just bring all your stuff here; no point in paying rent there when you can just live here."

"Okay," there was no point in having the same argument.

The little girl tugged at the pockets of Hild's overcoat and stepped behind her, "Alfhild who is this?"

"This is my friend Michelangelo. Don't be shy. Come say hi."

Slowly she walked towards me, wearing a woman's tie and fall sweater vest and cardigan. She was dressed like an old lady.

"And who is this lovely young lady?" I kneeled down.

"Michelangelo, this is Frøya."

"Frøya. That is a beautiful name. It's nice to meet you."

"Your name is Meekelanjeylo?" she hopped up and down.

Her pronunciation melted my heart, "Yes." Only children are happy; that is God's injustice. We know their happiness is short-lived; that is ours.

"What does it mean?"

"He has to go Frøya, I'm sure he doesn't want to stand in the rain."

I looked up at Hild, "It's quite all right Hild," then looked down, "It means the angel Michael."

"Are you an angel?"

"No," I chuckled, "I'm named after one."

"You don't look like an angel."

I looked at Hild then her reflection in the revolving door, "No I don't."

Hild reached for her hand but she didn't take it, the drizzle bounced up from the ground and hit me in the face, "Do you know what your name means Frøya?"

"No I don't," her tiffany blue eyes glittered.

"It comes from an Old Norse word that means *lady*. It was the name of a goddess."

"Goddess of what?" Hild asked.

"Beauty, love, war and death. She brought the slain in war to Asgard, to heaven, to live with her."

"I didn't know that," Frøya stood on her tippy toes.

"Neither did I. Frøya we do have to go upstairs. I have to get you ready for dinner. ... Michelangelo my driver can give you a ride to your place."

"That's not necessary."

"Nonsense," she pointed to her driver who got out and opened the door to the backseat.

"Thanks. Oh and Hild?"

"Yes?"

"Take that tie off. No ties," I spun the revolving door and they stepped through, "Bye angel," I said to Frøya.

She waved, "I'm not the angel. I'm the goddess; you're the angel," and she tucked on Hild's hand and said something in her ear.

Her driver was standing in the rain with the door open when I turned around.

"Sorry brother," I could hear the dripping sound of raindrops on his hair follicles like in the washbasin of my apartment, "I'll sit up front with you."

We swam through the water and I tried to drive out the pain. I kept thinking about Frøya and how it was Mædeleine's birthday. I had to go back to get my 1000-day chip from the top left drawer of my desk. I'd never needed it but Hild and Clo and Elroy made me feel... I don't know how it made me felt. I just knew I wanted to drink. I never needed to touch it, to feel it, just knowing I had it always seemed to work but sometimes that wasn't enough. Sometimes I had to have it in my hand. Sometimes I had to hold her—I mean it. I looked at a cloud moving across the sky towards the stadium where the spectators of today's game would be rained on and all that would matter would be Barcelona's victory. The cloud merged with another and the sun crept through them, "Happy birthday Mædeleine," I whispered to myself.

We each have a guardian angel and an angel of death. Time and God are Death's children and we are flies without wings walking across their ceiling living room until finally, in their boredom or frustration, they crush us.

"What's your name?"

"Sir?"

"Your name. I never asked your name."

"Do not be obligated to converse with me sir. Madame Baldure and Master Brahms never do so."

Master Brahms... what a world.

"I'm not them."

"Very well sir; my name is Nikolai."

"It's a pleasure to take this drive with you Nikolai. Thank you for the ride. My name is Michelangelo."

"You're welcome sir. I know who you are."

"You do?"

"Yes sir. Madame Baldure often talks about you."

"To who?" I looked at that cloud who'd by now moved in front of the sun.

"Anyone who'd listen."

His coat vibrated, "Excuse me sir."

"Please go ahead."

"...Yes sir... of course sir... right away sir... I'll be there shortly sir... I won't sir... I won't say a thing," he hung up.

We were nearly there, "Everything okay?"

"Yes sir. It's Master Brahms. He wants me to pick up some coffee for him before his dinner date."

"Coffee?"

"Yes sir."

"Why?"

"You know why sir," he pulled over in front of my studio.

"Thank you Nikolai. ... Take care of Johann. You don't have to come back and pick me up. I'll find my own way back."

"I can come back sir. It won't be a problem."

"No it's quite all right."

"Very well sir."

My landlady let me in. Nothing had moved. Dust tangoed on my verses, not because they were old and untouched but because they were dead and buried.

The drawer slipped open and a bottle of Cava rolled to its corner where a description of the Penedès lightened the maroon of the wine.

Where's my phone? I asked myself before my memory flashed to it sitting beside the Hsun book on the nightstand in Clo and Hild's penthouse. I opened the window and saw two people holding hands strolling in the rain on the street perpendicular to mine. The empty Davidoff case amused me. The only thing worse than an empty cigar case was an empty heart, and right then I had both.

I slid down under the window and drank and slurped and gulped the Cava. My hand knocked the broken easel and it hobbled left and right and a piece of paper hovered through the air and landed in front of me.

> "A word is empty and beauty is brief,
> Both are destined to fade out together
> When we realize life is grief.
> Sin, together with fears
> Wallow in our ocean of tears."

Laughable. Simply laughable. How timed my existence regardless of my not believing in traditional time. How different I was before I'd met Hild and Clo and how I'd met them both on one plane of perceivable linearity; why couldn't I have met only *one* of them, and further, why couldn't I have met *both* of them but only *loved* one of them? Why did I have to love *either* of them?

I slumped near one of my other broken easels and read another verse about the beauty of a woman as truth and their beauty in society. Why is beauty suppressed? Why are films that show our society its shame ostracized and amoral? Why are artists and photographers that depict ugly but truthful scenes of bloody wars fought for that elusive black liquid never given the fair credit they deserve? And those that break free from the boot that suffocates them and are given that credit, why are they never happy? Why does gloom surround them? Is beauty and emotion the root of all human misery? Do wars start because of a clash of ideology? And does ideology start because we feel a particular way about a particular something or a particular somebody? If we scrape out the root of the problem: beauty and emotion, does that mean there'd be no clashes of ideology and ergo no war? That'd be great... but I *knew* somewhere deep down that society abolishes Beauty because it's corrosive to the oppressive chains banks use to shackle our intellects, and all that other stuff... is just a happy coincidence.

The unblinking moon glimmered behind the rainclouds until one of them made her close her eyes. The Cava was sweet and delicious rolling above my tongue and sliding down my throat.

A man stood in front of me along the wet pavement down the road. The moment I saw him I began coughing. I hacked and tickled my mouth dry and a thick liquid tinged its way up from my chest. I fell down and my knees hurt when they slammed onto the gravel. I coughed up blood and it fused with the rain on the pavement and I watched it twiddle across the cement and into a manhole. He smiled.

"Michelangelo," he whispered across the road and his words seemed to carry over the sound of the storm, "You're fictional."

More blood diluted in the water when I coughed; I couldn't breathe.

"Michelangelo?"

Yes. It's me. I'm here. I'm Michel and I'm real and no one can take that away. I'm standing here coughing up blood in the rain. That's happening right now and no physics or philosophy could convince me otherwise.

There's no one else standing in the rain but me and the man covered in the fog of illusion. He is the illusion, not me. He's the fictional character, not me. He's a figment of my mind and I am the shadow of the imagination of the divine. *I*, am real.

"Michelangelo... come on!"

The aroma of the cava and the taste of an old Davidoff inebriated me. Whenever I smelt wine, I thought of Mædeleine. That musky smell of grapy liquid; it was all she drank, and the first letter I got on deployment was from her. She said she wanted me to do her a favor no strings attached. The only thing that kept me going in the desert was her face. I should've known then it wouldn't be that simple. When I muse on Mædeleine I think of two things: fine wine... and despair.

I wanted drugs: psychedelics, downers, barbitals.

The back of my head was knocked forward every time a raindrop landed on it. There was a cigar in between my fingers and I couldn't even remember lighting it. I was wearing a blue undershirt because my shirt was across the room for some reason.

My head spun and it felt like everything was on fire when I stood up. I tried to balance my hand on one of my easels but it had no chain because I always lose them. It fell and sketches flew through the air and I stumbled back into my coffee table and hit the radio.

Casey's Last Ride by Kristofferson played while I sipped some more of the Cava and tried to remember where I got the cigarillo fro—

A knock.

I stood still and listened; was I dreaming?

"Michelangelo! Open up!" The door shook.

There was that weird sucking whoop sound when I took my lips off the bottle.

"Yeah?"

"It's me. Nikolai said you should've been back by now!" Hild's voice floated up around my head and into my ears.

I floundered over the coffee table and walked over to the door, spinning through the room like a Spaniard doing the tango.

> Hild, the handle of my sword and hilt of my soul;
> Hild, the green of the earth and the rooted brown of a tree.
> Hild, the gold old men kill for and the thick, black, oil young men
> die for.

Men are fools for pretty faces and hers was a painting. I knew why they ogled her, wanted her, lusted for her, but I couldn't understand them. I couldn't understand the trivialities of these pathetic mortals yearning for something so sophomoric. She was pure elation. She was what you thought of when you thought of the words "bliss" or "paradise" or "heroin."

That's how I felt until I opened that door and realized... how wrong I'd been. Why did I think of her in fits of insomnia? Why was I unable to sleep during winter twilights or summer African sunsets?

She was wearing a designer parka, wet from the rain with pink empty hands and a full heart. The clouds parted behind me and her skin reflected off the table in the moonlight.

I backed away in fright and my hand shook, *once*, when I put the cigar to my lip and flashed to a brother falling in the sand in front of me and bleeding all over the place from a mortar shell.

I knocked some stuff over on my way to the window to look for the clouds that'd been haunting the lighting on my canvas.

"That was hours ago! What are you doing?"

Smoke filled the room.

Her boots sloshed across the parquet. She took them off and her legs rooted to the floor when she opened the fridge, and its light reflected the color of her eyes, "All you have are figs."

"They're from Sicily. Why are you here?" I couldn't stand to see her right now. I couldn't be near her. I didn't want to think about her. In fact, the more I contemplated her the more I wondered if I hated her.

"I love Johann you know. I do. I really do," she took one of the figs and bit into it. It'd certainly spoiled but she was far too refined to spit it out so she gulped it down. "He'd gone to the orchestra today apparently. I didn't even know he liked classical in all the years I'd known him. He always seemed more into indie folk."

The smoke surrounded me and inhaled my being, "That's great. Why are you here Hild?"

"Want me to be honest?"

"I don't want you to be anything other than the sweeping wind that makes you *you!*" I searched in desperation for what she saw in him past his wallet but couldn't find anything; she was rich too. It made no sense to me. Why did she tolerate him?

"*That's* why. Right there."

"What are you talking about?" I started coughing and tasted blood. Cigar smoke misted through the air near her and she walked through it towards me.

She squeezed water out of her hair and it dripped on the floor, "It's raining," she took off her coat to reveal her black Chanel dinner dress.

What an art it is, fashion design. I'd never think this sober. It really is an art no matter how diminishing you think it is to the world but the more I looked at her bosom the less I actually saw despite her skin being displayed rather liberally all around the shoulders and legs.

"Keep your clothes on. In fact... get out," I turned my back to her and faced the window and saw not a soul in the street. The game was probably on.

"You want to know why I really came? ... To pose for you. ... You self-aggrandizing, self-righteous, high-horse-jockeying prick."

The bourgeois capitalist wanting a portrait painted of her, how *Goyan.*

"You came for yourself Contessina and no one else," there are moments you know will break you even if they haven't happened yet. These moments come and they break you with precision and there's nothing you can do to prepare for it. You're unbroken one moment and shattered the next.

I knew she'd eventually break me and I expected it but the moment approached too fast and I just had to accept that I'd be broken and hope that all the king's horses and all the king's men could do their job just once.

"STOP CALLING ME THAT!" she screamed but she wasn't raging; it was more like a desolate yelp.

"You are a countess. Johann is a banker. And I am a paint-splasher. These are the mere facts. Nothing more." It was Mædeleine's birthday today. Why today of all days was this happening? Eros and Thanatos; love and death, why are they so intricately linked?

She nearly fell over, "I... feel like a bird trying to fly in a cage. Help me. Please. Help me," a drop of her hair streamed down her shoulder into her chest and she shivered.

My muscles ached. I was getting a pre-hangover hangover and the Cava was starting to wear off. Each raindrop landing on my windowsill pierced my physicality down to the bare abyss of my consciousness like two black holes merging and their gravitational pull too strong for any light to escape, "I can't."

"What do you mean *you* can't? What are you artists good for if not feeling?"

"Painting is more science than art," I spoke with purpose. I wanted to push her to Johann. She was his responsibility and he was hers. I was just the guy. The other guy. The nothing and I'd always be nothing.

"What?"

"Every stroke, every line, every color, every space, every temporal element; it all has to be calculated. It's simple logic. There's no emotion involved."

"Perché continui a resistermi?" she asked in near fluency.

"Perché non ho altra scelta," I answered.

"You know how I know that? I've been secretly taking lessons so I could impress you. I wanted to talk to you in Italian because it's the language of lovers and haters. It's the language of passion and greatness and poetry and agony."

For the second time in a long time, my thoughts came to me in my native language: *det føltes forkert at stå med hendes hjerte i min hånd.*

I apologize dear reader; your language of choice must be English. What she asked me in Italian was: *why do you continue to resist me?* To which I answered: *because I have no other choice.*

The Danish thought that appeared to me just after that translates in vernacular to: *it felt wrong to stand with her heart in my hand.*

"What? ... You think you can just *wave* me away or stare me down and I'll disappear? You paint all these whores and hussies..." she marched through the studio and found some of the studies and sketches of other women I'd done, "Here!" and she threw them at my feet one by one, "Here. And here. And this one here. ... Oh that's a good one," and she threw the rest of them at me.

"I just can't. Why won't you just leave?" two clouds from opposite directions merged and blinded the moon once again and her face darkened in the Byzantium and violet-blue purple of the sky's lamenting apology for its suffocation of our futile existence.

"WHY?" her screams were still refined but they vibrated the walls nonetheless.

"I won't do it Alfhild," I took a step away from her.

"WHY NOT DAMN IT?!" her scream replaced the thunder that should've came.

"BECAUSE I LOVE YOU!" the Cava blurted out and I took another step towards the window. "I... can't paint you. Go. Please go."

The cigar slipped through my fingers and landed in the puddle her coat had formed.

"You what?" she ran her fingers through her hair in a whisper with her lips redder than my blood on the canvas back at the penthouse titled: "*Linearity of a Still Life Broken by Death.*"

PART THREE:
DESCENT

WINTER

I

THOSE WINTER SUNDAYS

Winters are silent winds of cutting sickles. It was frigid; a deluge of ugly snow and brown slush crawled up your legs whenever you stepped anywhere. You don't really have a negative concept of winter when you're young. They're not *cold* when you're young. Its warmth in your heart is unrelated to physicality or temperature. You dash and crash and fall face first in the snow and laugh at the cold as the slush slides off your snow pants. You ice through winters without a care in the world.

As an adult, slowly and surely you see winter for what it is: the season of death. As we age it becomes a symbol for the inevitable cold that'll consume our bodies. The only control you can have is the warmth of a soul next to you until that winter comes and this symbolism bears with it a silence. A silence that begs of loneliness, for our last winter is sure to be as lonely as it is cold.

Hild had caught the flu. She barely left her room and stayed shivering under the blanket. Johann went back to New York with Wolfe and Clo. I stayed. The great moralist that I'd become didn't know what else to do. There are no choices, nothing but a weaving string of time tyrannizing over space and repressing the thoughts of those swimming against the waves of timelessness. How could I have left her when she was in pain? How could I have left her to whimper alone?

Why do we feel a natural inclination against loneliness and why is this exodus from loneliness universal in everything from animals to people to the sky and even the sea?

Is it not the battle against loneliness that forces the sky to permit the flicker of stars billions of light years away to shine through like scattered embers over dancing sands? Speaking of sand, is it not why the sea rages forth and pounds its grains? Because it's lonely? And in its loneliness knows not a thing calmer than unmoved sand, the dry coarse yellow beaten by the sun to its wet, blue and green waters surrounded by desolate anger? Even black holes, with all their attraction and panache for the lost and aimless, for all their lack of matter and enigma, do they not have the strongest gravitational pull? Do they not pull hope so tightly that its light cannot escape? Is this because God is lonely? Is that why She created us? Out of a rebellious desperation we'll never understand? And for some reason everything She's created exudes a loneliness and thus tries in vain to connect with other things and reconcile its loneliness?

How easy it is for humans to alienate themselves from this divine and tortuous solitude. Death, even lonelier than God, out of spite and anger that he is the anti-creator, damns us to a lonely fate only he understands. How much he must abhor seeing a human couple with the knowledge he can never be with God in all the universe and during all time. In his vast knowledge and tiresome job to take which his beloved creates, how much he must hanker to hold Her in his skeletal fingers knowing he can't touch her, and damned as he is to live outside his grandfather's house, Time, he collects God's children from Her planet be they happy, sad, lonely, or even in love. How much it must pain his soul to collect those in love. They must both eternally lament because being outside time; they know they will never be together.

This is what haunts me, the timelessness… I am Death and they are God split in two.

"Michelangelo?" I heard her cough from the room.

The wind gusted its darkness through the dead trees and the moon was a ghost on the cloudy seas. The pavement was frozen save for the moonlight trying to shine through the rain blocking the sky.

She shivered under the blanket when the door squeaked, "Are you cold?" her teeth clattered when I walked in.

I was shirtless because it was so damn hot and a thick orange ran across my chest because I threw it at the canvas in anger when it wouldn't mix properly.

"Yeah… I'm freezing! Want me to turn up the heat?"

"Liar," her face was paled like a zombie extra in some trashy film and black circles delved through her eyes. God damn you God.

I smiled, "I'll turn up the heat."

"Your smile… I feel better already."

"Stop it," I walked through the door.

She said something I didn't hear because her sore throat had dried her voice.

"What'd you say?"

"I said we both know there's really only one way to warm me up."

"No."

"Of course not. I'm contagious."

"I don't get sick but I'm not crawling in there with you."

"You're so proper. We'll just lie here."

"That's even worse," I took a step towards her, "You have a fever," I put my hand on her forehead, "You're not thinking straight."

With weakened hands she grabbed my forearm and tried to squeeze but she was fatigued so she let go. I walked around the bed and got under the blanket with her. Her legs were colder than space but her face regained some color. She put her hand on my chest where the paint was and followed it across. I grabbed her hand.

"It doesn't mean anything. I know you love her."

"Who?"

"Chloé. I know you're in love with her."

I wanted to laugh. I wanted to burst out laughing and scream at the top of my lungs. Not scream at her but scream and rant and rage at the stars at the cosmic joke we call the earth and its inhabitants.

"What makes you say that?"

"You look at her like you look at the sky when it's blue or a painting you like."

"And how do I look at the blue sky or a painting I like?"

She tried to laugh but coughed instead. I pulled her towards me and held her back to try to soothe her lungs. She took a deep breath, "Thanks."

The wind screamed outside and pounded the window and she twirled her leg on my knee.

"It's just the wind Hild."

"Can I ask you something Michelangelo?"

"After all this time you still have to ask? There is such a thing as *too* proper."

She sneezed.

"Bless you."

"Excuse me."

"What'd you want to ask me?"

"That day when you met Frøya, you said "no ties" and looked at me like a madman at her having to wear a tie to dinner."

"Yes."

"Why?"

"Why what?"

"Why shouldn't she have worn a tie?"

"Children don't like ties. She was in agony. No one likes something around their neck because they intuit the danger. Then as we grow older professional jobs want us not only to wear these nooses but to tighten them willingly every day."

—Something clattered in the main room.

"What was that?"

I got up and snuck towards the living room.

I walked up behind Johann shoving some papers into his jacket pocket from the side table in the corner of the living room.

"I thought you were in New York."

He jumped a few feet off the ground and put his hand on his chest, "Michael! Jesus you scared me. Where's your shirt?"

"I thought you were in New York," I moved towards him.

"I had to meet... a friend. I'm flying down later tonight. I just came to get my Yankees scarf."

"It's in the side table?"

"No. I was just getting some of my papers. I didn't know you'd be here. I thought Alf would be asleep and I could just come in and then leave."

"She's awake. You want to say hi?" I knew he didn't but I pretended to move towards the door.

He put his hand on my shoulder, "Do me a favor brah, can you not tell her I was here?"

"You want me to lie?" I looked at his hand on my shoulder.

"I'd consider it a personal favor," he moved closer to me and looked at the orange going across my chest, "She's sick and I don't want to catch it."

A silence crept through the room, "Come on. You've never lied to someone you love to spare them pain bro?"

"Michel tell me the truth. Did they hurt my mom too?"

"No… they didn't Mædeleine. They didn't touch her."

"Michael… hey!" Johann snapped his fingers in front of my face.

"Get your fingers out of my face."

"You dozed off. Do we have a deal or not?"

"Fine. I suppose I don't have to say anything cliché here do I? Hurt her and I'll cut your throat in your sleep or something?"

He backed away and laughed like a nervous tick, "An art*eest* threatening *me?* It doesn't suit you."

"Get out."

His steps retreated out the door and it squeaked closed.

I opened the drawer where he was rummaging and moved some of the papers around. It was phone bills and bank balances. A statement from Minitar was folded in between two statements from Norges Bank authorizing a transfer in regard to a claim to an account in the International Liechtenstein Bank of Commodities and Trades.

Hild's face was whiter than usual, lit up by her tablet as she scrolled with her ailing finger some news web page.

"Who was it?" she looked up at me.

"Nobody."

"I've read the Odyssey Michelangelo," she rolled her eyes.

I chuckled, "What you are reading?"

"It's an article about a murder in the States."

"That's quite broad."

"A black teenager killed a university sophomore in San Francisco."

"Was the sophomore white?"

"Does it matter?"

"Always."

"It says it was his dream to attend Stanford Business School for his Masters. He was bright and affable."

"And the murderer?"

"He was some drug dealer. A cocaine dealer on the outskirts of town."

"Where'd the murder take place?"

She scrolled up, "In the kid's home."

"Whose?"

"The dealer's."

"So the question is, what was an *affable* white kid bound for the American *Dream* doing in the house of a cocaine dealer?"

She coughed, "I don't know," her voice was sultry.

"It talks about how bright the victim was, a picture of him graduating from high school wearing a suit probably appears on the front page."

She turned the tablet towards me and I saw a picture of him in his graduation cap with a pretty brunette standing beside him on the campus green holding his diploma.

"How laughably boring."

"Michelangelo! That's insensitive."

"They don't tell us, do they, those idealists, that he was just some junkie and some idiot white boy who was trying to buy cocaine and probably refused to pay? He was such an idealist, to bring the American Dream back for the rest of us, but he was too stupid to know you shouldn't try and rob a drug dealer."

"It must be painful to be you... so disillusioned," she coughed.

My response was staring at the silent wind knocking on the window above the arch of her bed.

"Well they should lock him up anyway."

"Do you know why there are so many people, not just blacks, in prisons in the States?"

"Because they have a huge population so the percentage of their criminals is higher."

"Yes but that's not the whole picture is it? I lived in Missouri when my uncle was working there as a cop. There is always racial tension there. You can't even talk about race. People will react negatively if you bring it up. How are we going to close the racial gap if we can't talk about it? Because there are high levels of institutional racism and there's a huge tension between the cops and the poor people in ghettos like Baltimore and Ferguson. My uncle would arrest a black kid holding someone at knifepoint and there'd be a news story about a cop killing or screwing with a black kid's rights once a week."

"So they oppress them and people have something to say about it."

"Since when has the news been interested in what the people think Contessina?" I walked over to the window to make sure it was closed and no wind could get through. Outside, snow landed against the glass and melted and its droplets streamed down to the pavement below, "The root of it all is the drug war, Nixon's great contribution to the world. This is not to rid the country of drugs... ghetto communities rely on the sale of cannabis."

"So they shouldn't sell weed."

I knew it hurt her to talk but her resolve was beautiful and she glowed every time her eyebrows furrowed in disagreement.

"There aren't many ways to have a decent income for these communities. It's not like they don't already work hard; they're forced by the cogs of the machine that oppressed them to trade in weed unless they can escape from their hell and go somewhere else. But this oppression comes at a price. Young black kids are therefore easy targets for arrests. Police officers like my uncle have arrest quotas so they too are borderline handcuffed and have to screw over impoverished citizens of the ghettos to get their bosses off their backs. On top of that, these strict drug laws are in place because the prison system is an industry of profit. They lobby for stricter drug laws and more arrests because they can extract more and more taxpayer money when their prisons are full. It's all about money Contessina, masked as it is by clever lobbyists and think tanks as a race issue meant to divide us across the color spectrum. Blacks, whites, Asians, Africans, greens, and purples suffer an uncontrollable tension and a horrific agony while corporations living in shades of grey make a killing."

She coughed, "Damn it. ... I do hate you Michelangelo."

"I love you too."

She sat up underneath the blanket, "What?"

"Let me make you some tea and warm up some soup. I think we have some left," I walked out of the room.

"Wait!" she tried to fumble out of bed.

"Lay back down Contessina. I'll take care of you."

She put her head down and closed her eyes and I felt her fever break.

II

THE HIGHWAYMAN

I couldn't stop thinking about that bank statement. *What are you up to Johann?*

Hild was still coming off the flu so I didn't want to bring it up in case her illness could be brought on by stress.

She moped around the apartment and we sat around and watched movies and read articles and poems all day. I seldom painted because it pained me to see her like this. She gets headaches too, coupled with the flu it's a damning combination.

I was reading her an excerpt from *Art as Experience* by John Dewey when I realized that moments in life have backgrounds. Sometimes something happens while other things are happening. Usually we abstract the foreground and forget the background. Sometimes the real essence of a moment is in the background, that silent chatter among tall tales of the sycophantic or the merging of colors over a lake as the sun sets in hopes that it'd be permitted to rise again.

The defining moments of a life are often mistaken as foreground moments, moments that are marked by heavy and intense melodrama that we believe have shaped us. Often, when we reflect on these moments we realize that it's in fact the background of a moment that marks defining moments of a life: a glance towards the sea long after the light has reflected the blue from your muse's eyes and in fact *not* the moment you looked at her, or years after seeing a painting with someone and seeing it again printed in the page of a book and realizing how that painting was the background to holding your beloved's hand in the foreground of looking at it. Now, upon reflection, the painting has acquired new meaning. A meaning that doesn't shape you until you come to that realization. Sometimes the realization comes moments after in the foreground but sometimes it takes years and many seasons pass before you realize what you've missed if you'd only been paying attention to the background.

"Michelangelo?" she walked out of her room and into the main room after her nap.

"What is it Contessina?" I put the book down and looked up at her.

She wheezed and coughed, "Don't call me that."

"You *are* a countess Hild. You should embrace it."

"It's not that. I make everyone call me countess. People only respect rank and wealth. With you... it's the way you say it."

"How do I say it?"

"Never mind. I'm too tired to have this discussion," she sniffled and rubbed her thighs with her hand.

"Are you cold?"

"My legs. ... Would you like to watch a movie?"

"Sure. Come sit down on the couch," I got her a blanket and a throw and cuddled her in, "You want me to boil some chicken or make you lemon tea?"

She looked at me in silence, "I do [a word I didn't hear] him. I do, I [another word I didn't hear] do," she seemed to whisper.

"Hild?"

"Sorry. It's the fever talking. I was thinking about Johann. I haven't heard from him."

"He sent me a uMessage," he hadn't, "He asked me how you were before he left and asked me when we'd join them," I think he actually preferred it this way. To trade off her name in these fancy hotels and bars and no Hild there to explain the booze on his breath or the whores in his bed.

"How does he have your number?" she looked at my forehead.

"He probably got it from Clo or Wolfe. You want me to show you?"

There was a moment where she contemplated it and I panicked but then she said, "No," and pressed her hand on her cheek. "Wait. You know how to use a cell phone? You can send uMessages?"

"Everyone's a comedian."

She laughed then coughed.

The kettle came to a boil and I sat down next to her and the Kumquat TV loaded up the list of films available.

"It's hot!" I handed her the mug.

She put it on her legs and her white, thin fingers pressed the buttons on the remote and scrolled through the movies. "What do you want to watch?"

"Lady's choice."

"*Casablanca*."

"No."

"You said lady's choice."

"I changed my mind," there was no way I was going to watch a movie where the guy lets the girl go with someone else. I will not play to the genre of a life lived through a lie because someone somewhere is dictating the terms and moments of my life.

"How about Hæven?"

"No. I've had enough of Danes to last me a lifetime."

"We'll call you the flumedian. You can open at the Apollo."

She laughed and wheezed again, "Stop making me laugh. It hurts my throat."

"How about..." I scrolled down, "Gladiator?"

She looked at me.

"So that's a no on Gladiator."

270

"Let's watch *La Notte,*" she took the remote out of my hands and highlighted it under *Foreign.*

Why did she keep highlighting movies with one theme?

I saw *el Secreto de sus Ojos* a couple of choices down, "No. Let's watch *the Secret in their Eyes.* I've heard only good things."

"What's it about?"

"A murder I think."

"Fine," she sipped her tea.

"You don't want to watch it?"

"I wanted something like *Eternal Sunshine of the Spotless Mind* or something by Godard."

"Don't be a cliché," I looked at the charcoal clouds blocking the sky behind her; snowflakes were no longer falling like in an impressionist painting: slowly and with divine purpose of being beautiful but now it was storming frozen icicles like the final circle of Dante's Inferno.

"It's not up to me," she sniffled.

"What?"

"Whether or not I'm a cliché."

"Who's it up to?" I condescended.

She pointed up.

"You look like that philosopher from the Raphael painting."

"Who?"

"Plato."

"That makes you Aristotle," she took my hand and stretched it palm down like the painting, "The contrast."

"They're not contrasting. Aristotle was a Platonist."

"Really?"

"Yes."

"I thought he was against Plato."

"No. They're in cohesion with one another."

"I heard differently."

I wasn't in the mood to dismantle some pseudo-liberal argument on why her education at Cambridge or Oxford or wherever told her differently, "Let's watch the film."

"How does a Dane end up with a name like Michelangelo? You'd pronounce it Mihellanyelo in Denmark right?"

"Yes."

"So why the shhh sound? Even in Italian it's Meekellanjelo. Did you add that?"

"No."

"Someone else?"

"Yes," the black hole of my soul permeated through my pores.

"A girl."

"Is that a question or a statement?"

"A statement."

"Okay," I looked at her hair, tied back and beautiful starting where her illuminating forehead ended.

"So how'd you get the name?"

"My mom had a PhD in Italian Renaissance Art. It was either Michelangelo or Raphael."

"Raphael... Raphael..." she muttered to herself and breathed it through her mouth, "No. Doesn't really suit you."

"And Mihellanyelo does?"

"Yes."

"Why?"

"He..." she inhaled as if she was about to sneeze, "He lived in..." she inhaled and passed it, "He lived in a sort of agony. The same kind of melancholy Clo was talking about; I see it in the corner of your eyes."

"So when you think of melancholy, agony, and loneliness you think of me. How nice."

"Yeah! Like that song *See the Funny Little Clown*."

"Or that Peza poem."

"Which?"

"We talked about it didn't we? Reír Llorando. It's a great poem."

"What's it about?" she was finally about to sneeze and she reached over the side table for a napkin and missed. When the sneeze finally came as she was reaching for the napkin it knocked the table over. Its drawer flew open and papers slid across the parquet.

"You've got to be kidding me," her cute nasal voice returned.

"I'll get it," I walked towards the papers and put the table back up. Handing her the papers she glanced at each one and nodded. I saw the one hidden behind the Norges statements and took it out. Was it divine intervention or just blind luck? I handed it to her and immediately her eyes widened in near perfect complement to the darting hail trying to pierce the awnings and glass windows of bank walls.

"You okay Hild?"

"What is this Michelangelo?"

I took the paper, "It's a statement for a deposit at a bank in Liechtenstein."

"I can see that," it was impatience in her voice that made me wonder whether she *really* knew what was going on. "What is it for?"

"It's a deposit for..." I took it and read the second page, "A cheque. In return for a claim filed at Minitar Equity and Insurance."

"For what?"

"There's a claim number here," I showed her the form.

"Michelangelo. Those are the numbers from the paintings we bought at Kaashibys."

"So?"

"Michelangelo those paintings are safe in my house up in Bergen."

"Can you check?"

A thought flashed across her eyes, "Never mind."

"Hild?" I took the paper and put it in the drawer.

"I think something's going on."

"What Hild? What's going on?"

"Johann. I had him deliver the paintings to my place in Bergen. He also insured them with Minitar. But if something happened and they went missing, why wouldn't he tell me? Why would he file the claim and deposit the cheque into an account that I don't know about?"

"I don't think he's the type Hild," I was becoming a regular politician in this lying thing. I could see why they do it. It's oddly satisfying and incredibly easy.

"You have to go to that detective Michelangelo. On my behalf. *This* is what he was asking about. Exactly this. Kara was killed. I think they had something going on. What if they planned something together? What if this got her killed? What if—"

"He didn't kill her Hild. Remove the thought from your head." He didn't have the balls to take another life.

"You still have to find out what happened. You're the only one I trust."

"When?" I asked and immediately berated myself. *When*, a tense only in existence when relative to time, and there is no such thing as time.

"Now. I'll call ahead and have them fuel the plane for you."

"I can't go now Hild. There's a storm and you need someone to take care of you."

"No. You have to go and find out what happened. Don't let them know you're there. Do it quietly. You know... the way you do things. You have to help me. I can't be associated with this. This is how you can take care of me."

I knew I'd do it for her. The second I saw him back here and saw the paper after he'd left I knew it'd eventually come to this. But I couldn't say anything. It had to be her. She had to come to this conclusion herself.

"Of course Hild. You know I'd do anything for you," I shouldn't have said that last part but I did, and now dear reader, we come to the point you've been waiting for, the moment I asked myself:

Did I just become a private eye?

III
THE BLESSED DAMOZEL

Back in Carthage I arrived. The land of the corrupt and the desolate. The sun wouldn't dare shine here. Afraid to turn the black into purple into orange into blue. I looked up and saw the stars behind the clouds. Stars that saw the truth. No matter how much they shine, they'll find the darkness hoping to overwhelm it at first opportunity. That's what a supernova is: stars attempting to burst the darkness away once and for all. Little do they know, once the light of their existence has faded long after they're gone, the darkness remains and spreads everywhere they've ever shined.

She set me up in one of her father's penthouses near Central Park. Despite being a hack appraisal for only a little while as soon as I walked into that aspect of her life: her rank and family and general being, I knew none of me could be worth even a small bit of her.

I was supposed to meet Britten at the station but he said it wasn't safe. He thought someone was watching him so we decided he'd pick me up and we'd drive somewhere.

The sky had whitened and the snowflakes falling in Barcelona were icicles thrashing the pang of shame permeating from my soul. Why was I ashamed and what was I ashamed of? I think I'd shamed myself in my ignorance. How easy it is to forget what you believe when confronted with comfort. *There is no such thing as love,* how immediate and seemingly unjustified this idea was the moment I saw Hild, and then doubly so when I saw Clo.

I stood in front of a CosmicLoots, one of the three on this half block waiting for Britten. My matches wouldn't hold in the wind and I felt myself freezing in time as if this is what it was to be remembered. My cigar was so cold when I put it on my lips that I spit it out and looked back into the café. The crowd was like every other crowd you'd ever see in a CosmicLoots. People who in their likeness to each other thought they were each unlike one another.

Couples danced with each other's legs under small circular tables and the lonely stared with wrinkled brows at NovelFaces profiles and dating apps hoping to have someone to play footsy with.

"Get in," Britten stopped in front of me.

"Detective," I walked around and crawled into the passenger seat.

"Now I know why Hell is ice and not fire."

"What?"

"The Inferno detective. Dante's. The bottom and final circle of hell is a frozen lake covered all around with ice where the devil is submerged from the waist down."

"Why?"

"Because he is the furthest from the warmth of the divine."

"Join the club," he drove towards Brooklyn.

Everything was frozen, from the pavement to the trees to women's hearts to my disbelief in time. There was scarcely a person on the street; people scattered like glittering stars over a clear night sky and yet some were consumed by the darkness of their souls.

"MOTHERF—" Britten slammed on the brakes and we slid two or three meters and cars honked behind us. He got out and kicked and knocked down a sign in front of four trees. He brought the sign back into the car and threw it into the back seat. Snow kicked up and landed on the leather.

It was an ad for Daskapeetal. A childish and innocent font ran over a blue background, *"Don't mind us. These were in our way but we're working hard to bring you a better future."*

We drove by the four remaining trees and Britten looked at the snow falling flat on the ground in its line.

"There were a lot of trees here," I said.

"Now there's only four."

"The Holy Square."

"Isn't it a trinity?" he asked.

"It used to be but we've evolved."

We went over the bridge in silence for a few minutes before he asked, "Okay Eycsüp, the father, the son, and the holy spirit. What's the last one?"

"Greed."

"That's a cardinal sin."

"Not even slightly. We value money more than any other creature and we'd do anything to get it. Think about how much we're sold the American Dream, think about how many times we've been told we're special and we have what's coming to us. How many times have we been told to be honest and caring and empathetic? None of those ideas caught on. But the love of money did. Why? Because it was already in our nature as the love of the physical and the unnecessary."

I could tell he was thinking about it all the way through and I dozed off and remembered riding my old Harley here with Clo when we drove through the old neighborhood. How long ago that seemed. In fact, I found it eerie that he doubled back near the canvas factory and went towards the river where we'd watched the water spit against the concrete. He stopped almost exactly where Clo had thrown the cigarillo out into the trashcan.

He stepped out and walked over to the river. Fluffy snow packed and flattened under my boots, the air was so thick and cold lungs hurt with every breath. Blood flooded too quickly in and out of my head every couple of minutes and with it, an unknown feeling in my veins. He breathed out and steamed up the air and took a few steps to the left,

"It must've been right here," he turned around and I noticed he was holding his gun.

"Detective?"

"Was it here?"

"Was what here?"

"It must've been here," he scraped and beat some snow back with his feet like a bull pawing the sand before charging, "Right here. You know what I couldn't figure out?"

I didn't respond and it wasn't the temperature freezing my hand into that unshaking feeling of inevitability.

"I couldn't figure out how you got him here. You, with that malnourished and wiry body sensitive to everything and him with that burly size and that vicious temper. But then I remembered, he drinks and he's hobbling everywhere. And then the kicker: they told me you used to be a soldier. The doctor-pawn, how oxymoronic. Did he call Mædeleine to come pick him from somewhere?"

I started listening the second he hollered her name; sleet danced on top of his hair when he turned to face me with the gun.

"That was the last straw. You were probably with her. Were you talking to her about your deployment? Cuddling in bed? You seem like a spooner to me," he pointed the gun into the air. "This is probably where you shoved him to the ground right? Was it a warm night? Or was it cool? Could you feel the breeze in those pretty blonde curls or was it cold? Was your hair frozen above your forehead?" he pointed the gun with both hands like a gunslinger stance, "He was probably drunk so he stayed down when you pushed him. Did he know what was going on? Did you permit him last words? No. You're methodical. No patience for sentiment. You looked him in the eye though, like the Bull, you looked him right in the eye; you know no fear. How did it feel when you squeezed the trigger?"

"Detective, I—"

"Don't..." he lowered the gun and took a step towards me, "Lie to me Eycsüp. Tell me about Ingolf. Is justice about putting people where they belong or simply about serving the interests of the law? Closing a cold case like this and freeing an *innocent* man from prison... they'll give me a medal. They'll give me a commendation. But that won't be justice. Ingolf was an abuser was he not? His friend, a rapist. He's in prison. Rapists belong in prison. Does it matter that he's there for a crime he *didn't* commit? And the person who committed the crime he's in prison for, he walks around *free* though he hasn't committed another crime?

Where do we stop then? Can we just kill all the rapists? All the criminals? Why have prisons at all?"

The snow burned my face. I took a step back and turned around to walk away.

"Don't walk away from me."

I had better things to do; I kicked some snow to the side and kept walking.

"It's your fault she's dead. She killed herself because you weren't there for her. You left her. You didn't save her."

That was when I stopped. I watched a piece of snow land on the back of my hand and melt. My fingertips were red with the cold. I turned around and made my way towards him.

He pulled the gun up again, let the clip slide out and bounce on the snow, and unloaded the last bullet from the chamber.

The second it flung out and rolled around in the snow I made a beeline for him.

My punches landed clean but he got a lot of good ones in; it was bloody and painful and the cold made it worse. It's a lie that the cold numbs the pain. Everything hurt three-fold. When we threw each other against the car and dented the driver's door we stopped. Exhaling in exhaustion and steaming up the air.

"Damn you Benjamin," I felt to see if any of my ribs were broken, "Arrest me now. ..." I had to catch my breath, "For assaulting a police officer. You win," I showed him my wrists.

He threw his badge where his gun had by now been submerged in the snow, "I'm not a cop. I just wanted the truth."

"You could've..." I breathed in the snow and my chest hurt, "Just asked."

"Let's go," he struggled to his feet and wiped some blood from his lips with his knuckles, "Get in," he picked up his gun and the clip and the stray bullet. There was a moment of silence where he picked up his badge and looked at it before slowly shifting his gaze to the frozen river.

I opened the passenger door, "Let's go *Detective*," I could tell he wanted to throw it in. He was a good detective and there aren't enough of those. I spit some blood into the snow and an intriguing red formed and became a shape.

The door stuck when he tried to open it, "One second," he closed it and opened the backseat door and chucked the Daskapeetal sign onto the frozen river. The door squealed open and he got in and turned the engine.

"Let's get the heat all the way up," he turned on the radio and Roy Rogers's *the Gambler* played. We laid our heads back and listened while waiting for the car to heat up.

"How'd you frame him? I looked at the file. There was nothing to suggest that Mædeleine's mom and Krazimox had a thing going on. In fact I'm almost certain her mom would've hated his friends."

"The police have *instincts* they always follow. If it's not the husband there's an affair going on, but with whom? The husband's best friend? You guys have go-to theories. I didn't push them any one way. They did all the work for me."

"Are we that stupid?"

"No. You're not. They were. Besides, they were happy with the result. I didn't know about the..." it was agonizing to say it, "Rape at the time. So I was going to let them know they had the wrong guy but then she told me and I thought he was where he belonged."

"Brilliance in simplicity."

"The best cases are the ones that are solved detective. It's never the master criminal who brilliantly evades capture; those guys become your Moby Dick and haunt the investigators for the rest of their lives. The facts and theories of the case simmer in your minds until one day, you figure something out. You can't hedge your bets that the investigator, regardless of his intelligence, won't have a moment of inspiration and reopen the case out of some *misguided* sense of justice," I looked at him, "The ones where the killer got away. Those are agonizing... you always wonder whether you're going to be caught. Everybody you see is an undercover officer looking specifically for you. But if the cops have got their man, you can march right into a cop bar and buy a round of drinks."

"I can't tell if this persona is Eycsüp, the persona of the brilliant artist and genius who gave up a doctorate in astrophysics, or this is what you want to show me."

"Neither can I. I pursue only beauty," I thought of Hild back in Barcelona, sick and cuddled under the bed watching some Follywood trash about the misunderstood woman who meets her prince charming at some bar. And though he's the perfect gentleman, he's also a prominent banker and has enough money to take care of her. And Clo, probably practicing in some dank room with a cello she doesn't really like and her hair weaving down near her legs with sound emanating through still and vibrating walls of the ideals of humanity and its pains.

"Damn fine job you're doing too. Artists..." he scoffed.

"Hmmm?"

"The countess and the cellist."

"Don't change the subject. I've seen the way you and your partner look at each other."

"I don't even know her middle name," he looked behind him and put the car in reverse.

IV
THE FIRE THAT BURNS UNSEEN

His phone rang, "Britten."

As he talked I looked outside towards the hot flashes of white snow trying to tear the ground apart.

"He's with me right now…"

I looked at him.

He kept talking while his gaze was fixed in my direction.

An ominous silence drifted through the car before he said, "Eycsüp."

"If anything's happened to either of them," my eyes filled with a rage like a snake crawling through my arteries and eating my venomous heart before bursting forth.

"No. Baldure and Lysettensen are fine. It's your friend Elroy Wolfe."

"What happened to him?"

"He was killed outside a bar following an altercation inside."

"Was he with anyone?"

"Witnesses said he was with two other men. Things got heated and another witness reported he tried to leave when one of them said something. Then both of them followed him outside where he was attacked by some others."

"Who were the others?"

"We don't know yet. But one of them was older," he knew more than he let on.

"Someone said something about a cello."

My ears perked up, "A *cello*? We have to get to Clo."

"Lysettensen is safe. We have bigger things to worry about," he peeled out and we got stuck in the snow for a second.

"What bigger things?"

"There's some civil unrest going on near Times Square on Fifth."

"Over what? Did you guys batter another minority or black man again?"

"No. They ran out of uPhones too quickly."

"You've got to be kidding me."

"I wish."

He turned the radio on where the breaking news talked about exactly what I would consider sacrilege not against God but against humanity. Only the first 350 people out of the 4000 camped out in front of the Kumquat store for days had gotten the new uPhone X. The rest, frustrated that they won't be among the first to QuickPic its sealed boxes and tell their friends about being the first to spend $1000 on a phone, had started trashing everything and breaking storefronts and fighting those in front of them in line. *Tear it all down,* they screamed in their All-Stars and beanies, these postmodern foot soldiers. *Tear everything down except the uStore and save the CosmicLoots low-fat latte.*

I thought about Elroy on our way back to the scene. Uniform officers in ski jackets shook and shivered holding hot chocolate and frozen coffee cups. Alicia kneeled before a body covered by a white sheet camouflaged in the snow writing something on the clipboard.

Everyone stared at us when we approached and she said, "Why isn't he in handcuffs?"

"Wait in the car," Britten turned to me.

I got into the backseat and watched them argue before Alicia kicked up snow as she blew towards the car.

"You should be in handcuffs," she slammed the door and muttered to herself, "Lucky son of a bitch."

"I didn't ask for it. If you think I manipulated him."

"I know. You're a lucky son of a bitch."

The idea of being lucky made me snicker in agony, "Why?"

"I don't know what's going on with him," she held the antifreeze button and the wipers cleared the windshield enough for us to see Britten transfixed over the body and its surroundings. He looked like an angel because a weird light hit him through the white cloudy skies. All the other cops watched him in awe and forgot to take sips of their coffees that would have surely been cold by now. "He's going through some weird phase. I've never seen him like this. I don't know what's changed."

"He's in love with you," if Hild and Clo were right, I knew the look in his eye.

"He's in love with the badge," she scoffed.

"If that were true Madame, as you so rightly pointed out, I would be in handcuffs right now."

She hit the wipers again and we saw Britten laying beside the body looking to the sky.

"Murder is murder. I think you should be in jail."

"Why don't *you* arrest me then?"

"He said *trust me.* He's never said that to me before."

"He sees things deeper than just trust and arrest quotas and convictions rates. If murder is murder; I'm a serial killer."

She unbuttoned the safety latch of her holster near her seatbelt.

"I don't mean it literally. At the behest of your president, I aided and abetted the murder of villagers in Iraq."

"What?"

"Public sentiment had gone from supportive to questionable to hostile. Our unit was told to do something. When we asked what they told us to be *proactive.* 'Splash,' Bump had said. Bump was this weird guy who'd been kicked out of the Air Force; he was the perfect amount of crazy to be a pawn. We called him Bump because he always looked down. He never looked ahead of him so he always bumped into anyone that was close to him. So Bump finds this village relatively close to us and convinces the rest of the crew to go and make the country proud."

"Oh Jesus. Do I want to hear this?"

"No. ... Anyway we gear up and head out in this scorching heat. I mean it was so hot the leather of our boots was melting onto our socks and legs. I'm the field surgeon so when I bring my stuff all the guys laugh that they won't need me. There's one tree there. Right in the middle of the desert. This green and full tree. It's beautiful. I stop by it for a second before they call me back into formation.

Finally the sight of tents in the horizon breaks the infinite hot sands. The unit sang so we didn't get bored. Now there is no Taliban in Iraq, but this was a 'Taliban village' Bump says—he didn't even know who or what we were fighting—and he just walks in and starts shooting..."

She didn't take her eyes off of Britten talking to a uniform officer and jotted something in his notebook.

"... So these people still lunging at us with forks and spoons and..." I swallowed, "Kids with cap guns firing caps at us. I turn around and face the desert behind me and they're all laughing. I search for that little black line in the distance that breaks the sand; the tree I'd walked past. Finally I hear Bump scream in agony because some guy had thrown a piece of metal, we don't know where he'd gotten it but the metal landed on his shoulder and tore his tendon where his arm met his neck. We weren't wearing our vests because we knew they weren't armed. It was so hot.... The guys pull me back and point me to Bump just bleeding on the sand with this sheet of metal in his shoulder blade. He's shaking and praying to me to save him and asking me if he's going to die, and I watch his blood trickle down from his neck onto the yellow sand where a weird orange formed. The sun sizzled through my helmet and shined on the specks of sand in that desert and it seemed to highlight Bump's blood. One of the other guys grabbed the guy that had the metal and brought him over to us. He's screaming at Bump that we got him and forces him to his knees. The guy starts praying and whispering Allah Akbar or whatever they say and kissing our melting boots and saying 'America Good,' 'America save us. Saddam bad,' and closing the eyes of a dead boy three feet from me," I didn't even realize it as I was talking but I was crying harder than I ever have before in my life.

"What happened?"

I wiped my eyes, "They executed him. Then Bump chuckled and spit some blood towards him," I sniffled, "He kept saying 'Doc save me.

Save me Doc!' And the other guys are yelling that I'm the Surgeon and that I'll save him."

"Were you able to?" she was staring at me through the rearview.

"I didn't want to. For some reason I hesitated for a second. I didn't want to save him. That was when I blurred the assumptions on the nature of right and wrong."

"You let him die."

"No. I realized that if I didn't save him I'd be like him. The empathy is important. It's what differentiates us."

"The guilty deserve death then?"

"We all deserve death. Everyone but the beautiful. The real Beautiful. I'm trying to tell you it's small time and frankly *unjust* to try to get me on the murder of a raping, alcoholic ogre. I'd confess to 18 counts of conspiracy to murder and aiding and abetting murderers."

"What happened after?"

"The massacre had to be covered up. They called it in the next day that we had on reliable intelligence that an Al-Qaeda operative was spotted in the village."

"You're joking."

I covered my face and cried into my palms for a moment before I hiccupped, "I wish... you're beautiful to him so I hate myself for telling you this but I want you to be liberated from the rage you carry with you before it poisons your beauty."

"Tell me that's the end."

"Surgical strikes leveled that village the next day, burying the bodies under the dry sand and snatching the souls that had survived. No one was left by the end of it. They gave me a medal for valiance and Bump a medal for bravery. They discharged me but sometimes I wonder if I ever left that desert. I wonder if I'm still looking for that line. I look down horizons sometimes, wanting to see that lone tree whistling back and forth among those burning sands."

She exhaled through her mouth.

"What's your middle name?" I asked her.

"Huh?" she answered after a while.

"Your middle name. What is it?"

"Nuala."

"That is a beautiful name."

"I get the impression that word doesn't mean the same thing for you as it does for the rest of us."

"Which?"

"Beautiful."

"It does. It is a beautiful name. It's an old Irish myth right? About the swans?"

She turned her shoulder and looked back at me, "How do you know that?"

"I like names."

Britten gestured with his hands to the uniform officers and ordered Alicia's assistant to load the body into the car to be taken to the morgue. Alicia got out to help them, "I'll be back," and walked through the cold to guide them.

"What was it you said? As cold as hell?" Britten sat back down and breathed into his hands.

"Her middle name. Would you like to know it?"

He rubbed his hair and the snow flew across the air, "Yes."

"It's Nuala. An old Irish myth. One of the children of Lir. They were swans."

"She *is* a swan," he let his hands fall to the steering wheel.

"Let us hope… you never hear her sing."

She walked back towards us once Wolfe was loaded into the other car.

"Shhh," Britten looked at me.

"Of course."

The door opened, "They have a location on Ventoni."

"About time. Get in," Britten put the car in gear.

"Shouldn't we drop him off?" Alicia fastened her seatbelt.

"No. He's coming with us," we peeled out into the road lit up by street lamps and the glinting diamonds of falling snow.

V
THE HUNTSMAN'S EVENING SONG

The storm had knocked out power to some regions and the mobs had descended upon certain parts of the city.

Had I missed a lesson somewhere? Was someone supposed to have told me something at some point in time but never did? How do I even begin to analyze this solitude? A solitude different from loneliness. Meditation? Contemplation? Was it something less divine than I liked to believe or was it simply… loneliness again? Was I alone even though I no longer wanted to be? Even though I detested other people and wanted little to do with them, I detested standing under the moonlight alone more? Even further, of the people I disliked, could a few of them be like me? Could they be enough like me such that I could accept them and they could accept me?

How many of my generation laid in their beds in the darkness of a room with their laptops on their thighs and cried themselves to sleep from loneliness? How many of my generation had been lost in the ocean of profit and greed? How many are alone simply because they are afraid of trusting anyone ever again? More than the hypocritical beliefs and paradoxical lives others led, all I really wanted was to hold a woman's hand under the pattering rain and look into her eyes. No… not *a* woman, but *the* woman. Then, and only then, would I belong.

"We'll have no backup," Britten turned to Nuala.

"Why the hell not?" she asked.

"The riots. People are breaking storefront windows. The captain wanted us on call and in gear too but I told him we had a break in the case and we thought Ventoni was going to flee."

"Is he?" I leaned forward.

"He's a lawyer. He'll either think he can talk his way out of or he's already slithered into a hole where no one but high-end escorts and cocaine dealers can find him."

I chuckled, "I wonder how they feel about dying."

"They don't."

"I dreamt I was dead once," I looked through the window and reached into my pocket for the cigarillo that wasn't there.

Alicia shrugged her shoulders like I was insane and looked at Britten.

"Have you ever had such dreams detective?"

He looked at me through the rearview. I wondered how a detective dreamt of death. Does he die a hero? Chasing after a kidnapper in order to save a little girl and as he busts through the door the kidnapper fires into his chest? Or does he dream of cases left unsolved as he watches the water spiral down the shower drain until his body finally gives out in old age?

"No I haven't."

"We're undermanned, they reported him playing cards in some dive. Illegal gambling hall I think," Alicia read the map in Britten's glove box.

"That shouldn't be a problem. We won't go in hot. We'll let them all go except Ventoni."

"Illegal gambling hall?" I asked, "What's his poison?"

"We don't know. The Fraud Unit has been trying to locate him for taking money from his clients."

"Since when is a lawyer stealing from his clients a crime?" I was bitter.

"He bit off more than he could chew when he ran for mayor," Alicia looked back, "Some people didn't want him to run; he's better in the shadows. We didn't even know he existed until he started campaigning."

Someone wearing a ski mask and black army pants threw a beer bottle at the windshield. Britten wanted to stop and get out but Alicia held his shoulder and didn't let him get out, "Let it go," she said. He abided.

"We've come too far to fall so deep."

He turned at the next cross street where a car had been turned over and set on fire in front of the library.

"The hospital of the soul," I said to myself.

"What was that?" Alicia asked.

"There's a car on fire in front of the library."

"So?" Britten chimed in.

"Libraries are hospitals of the soul. It's painful to see it contrasted with this… depiction of shattered souls right in front of me."

I dozed off into thought until Britten stopped somewhere in the night on a quiet street with the snow falling in haste and the sound of sirens competing with the howling wind for tearing out our ear drums. He pointed to a seedy bar a couple of doors down, "They'll be in the back."

Snow crunched and the wind laughed at us when Britten walked through the doors like a gunslinger from the old west. Townes van Zandt's *Mr. Mudd and Mr. Gold* played in low volume in the empty dive lit up in dark red and purple. The bar was empty with all the chairs up on the tables and a man mopping under one of them.

"We're closed," he looked at the TV above him flashing a news alert for a drone strike that leveled an Afghan hospital and killed everyone. Doctors and kids and women and men were pancaked with blood and fraying and trembling and dismembered. Then a shot of the president standing tall talking to the media flashed on the screen with a smile on his face and the words "We're winning. Democracy is inevitable now; the Afghan people can finally be free," rolled from right to left at the bottom of the screen.

Britten flashed his badge.

"We're still closed. I don't want no trouble. Get out," he turned the TV off.

"I want a coke," I walked past Britten and walked around the counter. Cops have rules. I wasn't a cop.

"HEY!" he dropped the mop and walked towards me, "I'm exercising my right to refuse service to anyone I want."

"Get him a coke, with ice?" Britten turned to me.

"Yes. Of course. Lots of ice," I stared at him like bullets that tear the flesh and burn through your body.

I turned off the music from under the counter and dimmed the lights. Britten used the silence to walk around the bar. I understood why they watched him at the crime scene.

"What are you looking for? We're closed damn it! I should've locked up," he muttered to himself.

The wood creaked and lamented under Britten's boots until a crackling shadow of a log that rises and falls stared at him through a glimmer of light behind one of the doors near the back. OUT OF ORDER was taped up on the door but an orange light came and went from behind it.

"You know what I read?" Britten asked.

"What?" the man picked up the mop again and went to mop the floor on the opposite end of the bar from the door.

"I read that if you don't want somebody to go into a place, put an 'Out of Order' sign on it. People will naturally think it's a restroom and will never enter. The thought of a broken restroom... is too frightening for us to see," he unlatched his holster and drew his standard issue Glock 19.

"There's no need for that officer," he increased his voice a little bit and I knew he was about to give them the signal that trouble was coming so I hopped over the counter and popped him once in the throat.

"Jesus!" Alicia ran over, "BEN! This is ridiculous," and helped him by guiding him to a chair near one of the other tables.

Britten whispered "Police" so low that only I heard it and then kicked the door down and pointed his Glock at the easily 7-foot monster standing closest to the door, "Don't anyone think about it. I'm a cop."

I approached from behind as quickly as I could and walked in with my hand in my coat pocket so they thought I had a gun.

A round table with clowns from all classes idled with loosened ties and rings and watches and keys were thrown in the center of the table or stacked in front of them. Four guys held everyone else in check and had them surrounded around the room.

Britten disarmed the doorman and walked in and stood in the corner, "You four, stand together there where I can see you."

Alicia walked in holding her revolver.

"Which one is he?" he asked Alicia.

"There was a picture of him in the paper but he doesn't look like any of them."

"You don't even know who you're looking for?" one of the guys in the corner said and laughed.

"Let me see badge again," another said.

"This is my badge," Britten put his gun on his eyeball, "Read my name. G-L-O-C-K. Badge number 19."

"You are all dead. Especially the pretty girl. We will do to her what you see in your nightmares," the first one said again.

I saw Britten's finger twitching on the trigger, "Everyone. IDs on the table RIGHT NOW!"

"Slowly. No sudden movements."

Cards flopped onto the table.

"Ladies first," I reached over and came out with my empty hand and grabbed her revolver as she walked over to the table and picked up the cards.

One of the guys at the table wolf-whistled when Alicia bent down to pick up the cards. I unloaded the revolver without them seeing and walked over to him, pointed it at his knee, and pulled the trigger.

The gun clicked.

"WHAT IN THE HELL? Are you insane?" he screamed.

"Apparently. Because it's not loaded," I took a bullet out of my pocket and loaded it into the chamber. When I pointed it at his leg again he put up his hands and starting babbling something.

"What? I can't understand you."

"What are you doing? Put the gun down. You're crazy!"

"Apologize."

"Okay okay I'm sorry!"

"Not to me. To the lady."

Britten's eyes widened. I think there he became the second person in my life who ever understood me, and neither of the two truly did understand me.

"I'm sorry! I'm sorry! Jesus put the gun down."

Alicia muttered the names and I heard her mumble something then "Zeetoe."

"Wait. That last one. Read it again," I'd heard this name before.

"Maximus Epochézētō," she read out.

"Let me see the picture," she handed me the card.

It was the guy with the light-green loosened tie and his pinky finger tanned except for a thin line where I assumed his alumni ring usually sat. Now it was sitting in the pot in the middle of the table.

"This is not Max."

"That's what the ID says. That's who I am," he lit a cigarette.

"This is the guy," I nodded to Britten.

He backed away from everyone but kept his gun on the doorman who was staring at Alicia like he wanted to consume her. I stepped in front of his eyes.

"He's ex-ARBiH," I said to Britten as he looked at me.

"SIT DOWN!" Alicia screamed at the guy with the green tie who was trying to leave.

"How can you tell?" Britten asked.

"Someone told me the soul seeps through the eyes," I kept his stare and watched him torture innocents and shoot to kill and watched him watching his friends die in regions unknown and his eventual rise to a doorman in some seedy front.

The world would've been a better place if I shot him right there; I wouldn't have even minded the jail time. What is so morally wrong about killing the wicked? Is it out of a misguided sense of respect for *human* life? A life that cruises through existence never caring for anybody or anything except the full charge of their dumbphones and the perpetually blinking thumbs-up button on their QuickPic account? Why is it so respected? Liars and thieves and politicians and lawyers all kill for profit and we never bat an eye and in fact applaud them for it; our enemies aren't human after all, but had I shot or maimed or even murdered the evil and the wicked and the exploitative, I would be made an enemy and punished with haste and a gradual hatred that manifests through the public eye in the murder of a murderer. It would be justified to kill *me* but it's not justified for me to kill. What a system.

"This is not Max."

"How do you know?" Britten pushed the guard out at last.

"It says so on his ID," Alicia showed Britten the ID while *Max* lit up a cigarette.

I chuckled, "I've met Maximus Epochézētō; he's an art history professor from Amsterdam. His wife committed suicide and he was visiting Barcelona and New York as part of his grieving process and reading this philosophically pessimistic hoopla."

Britten looked at the ID more carefully, "European IDs look different than ours," and eventually peeled the laminate where Max's true face was revealed underneath. "A clever mask but you are Ventoni."

"Ich möchte meinen Anwalt sprechen," were the first words out of his mouth.

"I don't have time for this," I was too frustrated and too in love and too angry at having to leave the ailing Hild back in Barcelona and being unable to hear Clo play at the Symphony Orchestra to abide by some outdated moral code set by the United Nations or the Geneva convention or whoever. Codes that they themselves don't follow. *No moral blueprint could ever be drawn up that covers every scenario beforehand, in a way that we can be certain to match the scenario with the ethical code of the blueprint. It's hubris to even consider this as a possibility for humanity. This incompleteness flows into uncertainty and people use this uncertainty as a rationalization to discard *all* moral rules. How especially true this is for the higher classes. Lawyers, judges, doctors, politicians, and bankers are the first to believe in nothing but the physicality of cash, for the physicality brings them a tangible (albeit empty) happiness they grasp, whereas the blueprint brings them an incomplete melancholy. They cannot be blamed for choosing the easy way out; humanity is after all, addicted to luxury and comfort.

I looked around and... oh delicious. A katana sat against the wall in the corner, no doubt loot from the five-card stud. I unsheathed it and flicked the cigarette out of his mouth, "I'll *cut* to the chase," testing it on my forearm first; it cut through as easily as a woman through a heart. Blood trickled onto the table when I slammed his hand on the table and outlined the tan line on his pinky finger.

"Whoa whoa whoa. This is getting out of hand now," he tried to jerk his hand away.

My laugh frightened the *brilliant* lawyer, "Getting out of *hand*! It's about to."

"You speak English now," Britten moved around me to stand beside him.

"We all speak English ja? We just don't like the way it sounds on our tongues. I admit that was stupid of me. Come on I had to try," he shrugged his shoulder, "You've done this before too ja?" he was every lawyer you've ever met, trying to talk his way out of anything, even out of death when face-to-face with the Grim Reaper. What is it with the ignorant and the mundane being the happiest?

I slid the katana away from the table and swiped it off the wood and it made that *shing* noise, "Answer every question concisely, precisely, and with complete truth and conviction. That is borderline impossible for your vocation but if I hear any lawyer talk or legalese or if your mask

289

of clarity slips into the slithery spineless snake that you are; you will lose a finger. That's the price of dishonesty in the mob culture where this sword comes from."

"I'm in the hole 200 grand. This was my last chance to get out. Vielen Dank."

"Five card. You would've gone further in. The King of Clubs plotted to make you pay but the outlaw Jack of Diamonds rescued your enemy because the Queen of Diamonds prayed for her son."

"Hä?"

I flipped over the hole card opposite his chair: the Ace of Diamonds with the other three aces and the Jack of Diamonds showing before I flipped his hole card over, the King of Clubs with the other kings and his Queen showing.

He looked up at me, "How'd you know?"

"Wickedness has its dues."

"Focus. ... You were saying; get out from under who?"

"You know the guy bigger than God you just pissed off? His *boss*. If you thought that guy was scary you don't want to know about his boss. He killed his chef for overcooking his eggs once."

I put the sword back on the table and moved towards his finger.

"HEY HEY HEY! I'm talking here come on man!"

"I said no circles."

"That's enough! MEN!" Alicia finally had enough.

Britten walked around and whispered something in her ear and while he walked away I stared at Ventoni, looking into his eyes for his soul; I couldn't find it.

"Verdammte Scheiße! You're the guy! *The guy*."

"Which guy?" Alicia walked over.

"He's the guy. *The guy*. He's the one who knocked out the Bull!"

"Tell me about paintings. Fake but expensive ones," the sword creaked along the wood and this time I went near his tie, "I don't really like green."

"Okay he really *is* crazy. Get him away from me. Bitte."

"Where'd you hear he was crazy?" Britten sat down in the chair next to him, forcing me to lower the sword off the table.

"You'll arrest me. I've already lost my license. I can't go to jail," whoever said lawyers were sharks grossly overestimated their fear of death; they'd sell their soul to occupy some meaningless space for a minute longer.

"Do we look like we're in the arresting the little pathetic fish business?" I laughed at him.

"We can't arrest you anyway," Britten tucked his badge into his jacket pocket, "This isn't by the book. Just tell us what you know."

"That's what I'm trying to tell you. There are no names. It protects the business when there's no names."

"Where do the checks go? Someone has to write these checks and sign for them and someone has to deposit them," Alicia circled the table.

"That's the thing. It's all done through subsidiaries and shell companies. It's the name of companies. The names of the companies are numbers, and each of them have their own bank accounts and insurance claim forms. Even if I was working with you to shave time off or for a deal I couldn't tell you what you wanted to know."

"Minitar."

He looked up.

"You know something," I put my leg on a chair and the sword on my knee.

"Ja. It's the company that insures our paintings. Someone buys the paintings. We insure them. Then we file a claim for them. Saying they're stolen or water damage or something. Since the appraiser is on our side nothing can go wrong... the insurance company pays out then declares bankruptcy and applies for federal bailout funding."

"How clever," Alicia touched her badge.

"What went wrong this time?" Britten asked.

"The woman. The woman usually lets her boyfriend do the buying and she hangs up the paintings somewhere in estates in her houses where no one sees them so we can do what we do and no one is the wiser. But then she hired someone new to buy her paintings for her and he was following up with the paintings and asking about the prices so we had to clean house. The boyfriend is the one who set it all up. I don't know his name. Always wears a...how do you say? ... Um... *Schal*.... English, what a barbaric language... SCARF! Scarf. He always wears a scarf. It's just his style. He's an alcoholic gigolo but the dumb bitch had no idea..." he laughed.

I snarled towards him with the sword and Britten stood in between us, "What's her name?"

"Haven't you been listening? There are no names!"

"Things got so out of hand. I got into debt, then they wanted some fancy cello as payment for my debt and I couldn't deliver on the deal. Now with this painting stuff going sideways who knows if I'll make it out alive."

"If anything happens to either of them. You won't. I'd insure that."

"Hey!" Alicia tapped me on the shoulder, "Go cool off."

I walked outside into the main bar to relax myself. Simon and Garfunkel's *the Sound of Silence* played and the bartender was coming to in the corner.

Britten and Alicia came out with Ventoni in handcuffs, "The paintings are in a silver Chevy Tahoe outside."

"We've got them. Checks have been deposited. I have the slips back in Barcelona. I can't believe how easy it was. They reported them stolen. If we find them and link them to Minitar and its parent companies and subsidiaries we've got them."

"My murder cases are still open. Who killed all these people?"

"Those'll probably remain open and go cold detective. It's probably those same mob guys. Anyone who knew too much or got too close was taken out."

"I don't know anything about any murders. You believe me don't you sweetheart?" he brought up both his hands and tried to slick back his hair.

"Shut up!" Alicia pushed him forward.

I punched the bartender once more and knocked him out again on our way out.

"So much brutality. So much rage."

"Usually I paint. I haven't been able to since all *this* started. Not really."

The sun had set but it was still snowing. Glittering flakes weaved through the forest of antennas. It had by now claimed the territory it fights for each day. Winter nights rule the immensity of the sky. In some way this immensity of space rules everything but since that's a darkness only emulated in the night, darkness has no choice but to claim it as its own.

"You know what the real problem with not talking or asking questions is?" Britten asked, "The problem with closing your mouth is that it becomes far too easy to open whereas the problem with opening your mind is that it'll become impossible to close."

We walked through the street where we saw the parked Tahoe five or six cars up. If only we had this information before. I wondered whether Clo had played any of her own original compositions tonight.

"That's funny detective. You ever think about a career in law instead of law enforcement?"

The darkness was lit up by a bomb under the Tahoe, turning the snowflakes into pieces of burning ember. An Ivory Tower of flames lifted the remains of the Chevy into the air. Britten had pushed Alicia and Ventoni down into the snow and was looking up at me standing front and center, watching the fire reflected on the trunk of a blue Lexus LX. The man riding in the backseat was the doorman back in the bar.

Britten called it in as sirens behind us howled from the Kumquat store blocks away. I listened to my breathing and the Tahoe sizzling the specks of snow landing anywhere close to the fire. The wind tore at my face like sharp iced knives tingling under my face and knees.

Ventoni tried to wrestle to his knees and coughed, "I broke my arm! Take me to a hospital!" he got up holding his arm.

I walked up to him and punched him in the stomach, he groaned with pain. "Where are they going?"

"Probably to tie up loose ends. The only one left is—yechh," he spit, "The Dutch guy with the scarf."

"Where's he going to be?"

"He's staying with the cellist at her brownstone. How lucky for them huh?" he laughed and sat up in the snow, "Two birds with one stone," he spit up blood onto the snow and it dissolved and the orange from the fire lightened it to a milky brown like blood droplets on hot sand.

"Not as long as the outlaw Jack of Diamonds hears her call," and I sprinted towards Madison.

"Michelangelo! Wait!" Alicia yelled after me.

I slid back and turned, "No. I can't. You guys have to wait for the cops. Who knows how long that'll take tonight. I have to finish this now."

"Take this!" Britten ran to the car and threw me a gun from under his seat.

It was a Ruger Old Army converted to shoot .45 colt cartridges. It had a sleek mahogany leather holster. I measured the barrel at 7.5' and it was fitted with a gold eagle polymer gunfighter grip. It looked like it was used in shooting competitions back in the day.

From war in the desert to war in the concrete jungle. We displace ourselves in space but nothing changes.

VI

THE LADY OF THE LAKE:
SECOND CANTOS: PART II

I guess we were destined to be together, if universes aligned and black holes merged elsewhere. I didn't want to be destined for anything; I wanted them both all to myself. I envied the universe for having both of them in it. The concept was absurd; it was impossible to love at all let alone love two people at the same time. Absurdity was everywhere; like the way we tolerate the Arab countries despite all their backwards "laws" and injustices because they have oil. It was a law like that; a universal one but one that also made no sense to us, not because of its incomprehensibility, but because of the way we're taught to think about things. You can't be in love with two people at the same time because everyone is supposed to have a soul mate and a soul mate is *one* other person you match up with perfectly, never two. What if space cut up my soul in three? Is there a limit? Isn't three the divine number anyway? What if the three of us were supposed to be together? How grand that I even entertained this idea without believing in marriage or justice or even love, and how dangerously close I threaded the needle between what was deemed rational while being as oppressive as those same laws in the blackened-by-the-darkness-of-oil Arab lands. Chloé would never marry. She was in love with her craft. She could take her cello as her husband and live on a diet of beats and rhythms. Hild was in love with the idea of marriage. The princess marrying like a Disney princess should, giving as much money as possible to the inflated prices of caterers, planners, venues, and everyone in between, and kissing an undeserving chump like Johann as the winter sun set in the afternoon of the Plaza Hotel in a city like New York or Florence. Neither of them would even have me so even if I fooled myself into accepting the concept of love, and then furthering the concept into accepting the notion of marriage, both of them would say no, and the black hole of my soul would spread like a disease to my body. Besides, marrying either of them would be unfair because I'd always be thinking about the other.

Sliding on the hood of a 2004 BMW 635, some teenager yelled "Destroy the establishment man." Another screamed "YEAHH!" and threw a homemade Molotov cocktail made with a bottle of Smirnoff he'd bought on Fifth Avenue earlier that day stuffed with a ShamWow knockoff at a café window that immediately fragmented like the pervading moments of my life.

"Bring it all down," a slightly older one said to everyone around him, "We're taking it all back. This is ours now! Damn these politicians. We'll be better!" he vowed as he smashed the windshield of a 1999 Toyota Camry.

How simple the American narrative. Suppose you have two hands. The American political system will cut off both hands. You'll then hear that those with one hand will be along the upper class and those with two will be part of the elite few. Then politicians will come along and tell you their plan for giving each American two hands. The people will buy into this and fight the disillusioned in favor of the politician. They are never for themselves and the politicians are *only* for themselves so no one is for the people.

The snow was red with blood and orange with flames and green with envy; the night grumbled with the ice. The streetlights on Chloé's street flickered on and off anxiously and settled on the latter. I walked around back and broke in like a prowler in the night. I grabbed a shoe near the back door. Something clattered in the main room and someone shuffled on the sofa. The low volume of the news reporting a Muslim terrorist attack on a Chevy Tahoe near Times Square talked about Islam conquering the western lands and compared the number of mosques to the number of synagogues and churches.

"City's gone to shit," a voice murmured to no one in particular and I saw the light of the TV extend out into the hallway where I was crouched.

My eyes adjusted to the dark and I threw the shoe towards the opposite end of the hallway. Johann's outline walked towards the sound and what I assume was searing pain of a cutting bullet opened up his left shin and he kneeled before the abyss. I appeared out of the darkness,

"Where is she?" the light outside flickered back on and the snow was virginal and white before it flickered off again and the darkness consumed it with its gravity.

"Johann?" a figure in white descended the steps, "Michelangelo! What are you doing here? What the hell are you doing?"

Johann screamed in pain and cried and moaned like the bitch he was.

"Where's your cello Clo? The Stradivarius."

"It's in the main room in its case."

"This prick told them where it is, he set you and Hild up. He's been extorting money from her for as long he's been with her I can imagine."

"Please. Bro. I need a hospital," he just looked and clutched his leg around the wound, "I'm going to die."

I laughed, "You're not going to die you pagliaccio. You're young. With enough hard work and physio you'll walk again," I pointed the gun at his other shin.

"WHOA WHOA WHOA. Please! NO!"

"Michelangelo!" Clo walked ahead of me and stood in between us.

"He could've gotten you guys killed. He's been stealing from her! They're coming for your cello because he told them."

"I don't know what—"

"Deny it again," I pressed the gun into his shin and he burst into tears.

She shoved me back, "Give me the gun Michelangelo! Give it to me!"

I decocked the hammer and handed it to her and when I did, our hands touched and the pink of her hands lit up the maroon dark red of my blood.

"Are you in love with me?" Mædeleine had asked. How direct. How wonderful. How ethereal.

I'd never been permitted the gift of love but the question slithered through my brain and down to my torso and into my heart and demanded an answer from my soul,

"What *is* love?" I'd asked her seriously because I was too stupid to know what it was.

When Clo's hand touched mine there, and the moment of looking into Hild's eyes when we were under the blanket... that moment in time... if the waves of the sea could thrash the sands and not wash away their purity I would still be there for them. If the stars didn't shine in the night sky and instead hid behind the clouds they'd still be my light. If the trees danced during windy storms and their lips shivered in the cold I'd still want to kiss them. If a deluge of slush and sleet froze me in place in the long arctic winters of the north, I'd look to them to thaw my heart. If a flower would blossom out of the earth through despair and the bleak agony of unknowing, I would cry until they'd reach into my soul and breathe light into it until our hands no longer touched and their lips were forever cold as I stood over their graves and in the hopeless agony that would become my life. It would be something like that I think. That is what love would be.

"Thank you."

A shadow danced under the flickering light outside but no one knocked. The handle of the old Victorian door turned and a lock pick started jingling just outside the door.

"Clo. Is there somewhere you can hide?" I looked and saw a shadow zoom at the back door at the end of the hallway where I'd entered.

She nodded.

"Go there. Hide. Don't come out whatever you hear. Don't come out until either Detective Britten or his partner gets here. For anyone else use the gun."

"What about me?" Johann groaned. The light from the TV flashed the pretty handsome boy toy as the winner of *Too Pretty to Work*.

"Shut up."

The door clicked while she ascended the stairs and her white gown flapped through the misty air.

"Oh God I'm young. I don't want to die," Johann wept again.

The monster from the bar came through.

"Get out," I screamed.

He nodded to the guy standing beside him and the smoke from his gun hazed the space around his fingers. The thin line surrounding the universe pulled me towards it and the gravity kept me frozen.

My fingertips turned Tuscan red when I touched my chest and the line of orange from Barcelona melted slowly and deliberately into my chest. The blank canvas depicting *love* would remain forever blank and that was the way it ought to be. I fell to my knees to the sound of Johann thanking God that they'd arrived followed by begging for his life like a dog.

Floating up and looking at the city below I saw Britten's car pull up to the house and park behind the Lexus. Through the pale clouds under me I saw the land of screaming ghosts, steaming manholes, and ascending sirens; where the green of avarice, the blue of melancholy, and the red of blood saturating its soul became the echoed notes of a Stradivarius, and I tasted the bitterness of THIS UNIVERSE'S MOST BELOVED DELUSION: LIFE.

All' alta fantasia qui mancò possa;
ma già volgeva il mio desiro e il *velle*,
sì come ruota ch' igualmente è mossa,
l' Amor che muove il sole e l' altre stelle.

My deep power of imagination failed me here
but my desire and *will*
were turned like a smooth wheel by
the Love that moves the sun and the other stars.

CLOSING LINES OF DANTE'S COMEDY;
PARADISO;
CANTO XXXIII;
LINES 142-145

www.ingramcontent.com/pod-product-compliance
Lightning Source LLC
Chambersburg PA
CBHW021206250626
47155CB00008B/2697